ANTIBODY

CHRIS WILLIAMS

Edited by Angela Brown

Cover design by Nuno Moreira

ISBN: 978-1-0879-7348-7

Ebook ISBN: 978-1-0879-7349-4

For Richard

Beware that, when fighting monsters, you yourself
do not become a monster.

- FRIEDRICH NIETZSCHE

THE SMELL of coffee infused the apartment.

Rubbing the sleep from his eyes, Peter looked around to see if she was still here. Her clothes from last night were gone, along with her purse and coat. Dianne must have brewed a pot before leaving. That was nice of her.

The coffeepot was still warm, so he made a cup and returned to bed, sitting upright against the wall in his New York City efficiency. The cup in one hand, he reached over and retrieved his phone with the other and opened the messaging app.

8:12 a.m., Peter: Thanks for the visit. Sorry I missed you.

He gave it a thought and sent another.

8:12 a.m., Peter: And the coffee! <3

Next he opened his sleep app. Peter had gotten five and half hours of sleep last night. *Not great*, he thought. A couple of drinks will do that, though. It messes with the ability to get a full night's rest. His heart rate was higher than normal too, according to the app. Peter wondered if tracking his sleep after he'd been drinking was even worth it. He took off his watch, which in addition to telling the time, monitored his heart rate, and set it on its charger. He was already over wearing his watch all the time. He bought it at the start of the year as a kind of New Year's resolution to be more fit. Now it only seemed to serve to nag him into putting in his steps and washing his hands for twenty seconds, reminding him of his high heart rate, and, thanks to its connectivity to the sleep app, haranguing him to get more sleep. Those were all good things to want to improve, Peter knew, but the constant need to always do the right thing had grown tiresome while he largely confined himself to his apartment. If he wanted to know what time it was, he could just use his phone like he did before he'd bought the damn thing.

8:14 a.m., Dianne: Sorry about the coffee.

8:14 a.m., Peter: It tastes like shit! ;-)

Peter hadn't even begun drinking it. After one hearty sip, he grimaced and put the mug on the nightstand.

8:14 a.m., Peter: Ducking hell, that's gross lol

He made a mental note to figure out how to get his phone to stop autocorrecting "fucking." Who the hell ever writes "ducking"? It was a fleeting thought as his attention was immediately diverted to checking social media. He scrolled through the Internet and his feeds mindlessly, seeing celebrities behaving badly, political memes, shared memories of happier times, and new updates about Allen's death.

"Shit," he muttered.

Allen's own website had posted the news. Under the photo of Allen smiling with his wife on a recent ski trip was the following statement:

Last night, at the New York-Presbyterian Hospital, Allen Jennings passed away due to virus-related complications. While we were hopeful that the treatment he had been receiving would turn his health around, we are saddened that he could not make it. His wife and child want to thank you for being such good friends and keeping him in good spirits the whole time. Read more...

But Peter couldn't read more. He scrolled through the new comments, not really reading them.

Peter and Allen hadn't been very close; they'd overlapped in their circle of friends. The most time they'd spent together was at a Yankees game. They both worked in the same field, programming, but never the same company. This was the fourteenth person he personally knew who had died of the virus. The closest was his grandmother, Mema. As the nursing home where she'd lived didn't have any way for her to stay isolated, the virus wiped out everyone in the home in a matter of weeks.

8:21 a.m., Dianne: If you're going out, F and A are both down. FML

Dianne must be trying to get home to Brooklyn.

8:22 a.m., Peter: Thanks for the heads-up.

Initially he wasn't planning on going out. It was Saturday. He had nowhere to be, and his weekly routine of playing online games, ordering pizza, and binge watching shows (or porn, if the mood struck) was something he enjoyed. It didn't require leaving the apartment, and it scratched his antisocial need to avoid people. His coffee, however, tasted putrid and coppery, and his apartment somehow felt more cramped and stuffy, as though he couldn't breathe.

He sent a text to Miles Ahmadu, his coworker who lived three blocks over.

8:24, Peter: Come get coffee with me. Khave has outdoor seating. I'll buy.

Peter used the time between texts to ready himself for the journey. He walked to the bathroom, where he rinsed his face and fixed his hair. No need to shower, he figured, and why bother brushing his teeth if he was about to drink coffee anyway?

He stepped into a pair of briefs and his black jeans. He didn't pay attention to which shirts he wore, just that he needed two. A black scarf went with his coat with the faux-fur hood.

His phone buzzed.

8:29 a.m., Miles: It's too fucking freezing to sit outside.

8:30 a.m., Peter: We can walk around then. I need the air.

In the kitchenette, Peter took out his daily vitamin pack and immune booster pack from their tiny cardboard boxes next to the coffee mugs in the cupboard. He looked for the red mug he habitually used for his vitamins, but it was gone. *Did Dianne take it with her when she made coffee?* he thought. That annoyed him initially. But he realized he now had another reason to go to her place. He poured the remaining coffee into the sink and put a scoop of creatine powder in with some water; no sense dirtying another mug. The water tasted acrid from whatever coffee remained in the mug, and his daily vitamin pills and powder didn't go down easily, as though he had swallowed them sideways.

8:33 a.m., Miles: KK, meet you in 10

It would take ten minutes to get to the coffee shop. Just getting out of the building would take five. Peter threw on his coat, attached a black facemask to one ear, and stuffed his pockets with his wallet, keys, and phone. Then he stepped out of his apartment for the first time in a week.

He didn't encounter anyone on his way out of the building. It was a clean getaway. No awkward exchanges, no uncomfortable elevator rides—or, if he forgot his face mask, nasty stares and comments. Next to the apartment building's front doors was some hand sanitizer, which he applied before pushing against the door rails. He ignored the thermal scan device next to the hand sanitizer when it beeped its alarm at him; those things were always wrong anyway. He quickly attached his facemask and stepped into the quiet cold air.

New York City had been in lockdown since the beginning of autumn, when people started getting sick and dying. The hospitals were immediately overrun with patients experiencing mild to severe fever symptoms. The fever symptoms weren't the problem.; it was what came after that forced hospitals to triage. Anyone with respiratory issues, nausea, a high temperature, or difficulty breathing were prioritized. The ones who started bleeding out were moved to holding areas to die. Once a patient's skin leaked blood, that meant the body was falling apart and liquefying. There was nothing the hospitals could do but isolate them. No one knew how to treat the virus or how to keep patients alive. The city—the entire world—had gone into lockdown almost immediately. Airports closed and grounded all planes. Roads were barricaded, and bridges were blocked. Unless you were military, you weren't traveling anywhere.

Eventually, collected and calm, the US government created guidelines for getting around. The facemasks stayed on, no matter what. Businesses had to meet safety guidelines, including thermal checks, contact tracing, and proper ventilation; the list went on forever. All Peter knew was he was working from home for the near future, which suited him just fine.

The street outside his building was empty; no one was on the sidewalks. Peter looked up and down his block to check if the police were blocking the intersection as always. Chain link fences surrounded cop cars at both intersections. It looked like the cops and their vehicles were being fenced in, rather than their preventing cars from getting in.

As Peter walked by an intersection, an officer turned to him for inspection. Wearing masks was enforced. If the cop was wearing a mask, Peter couldn't tell; their protective gear and armor covered them up completely. They were more armed than the army. Peter kept his head down and moved along, doing his best not to be conspicuous.

In truth, he was more annoyed than nervous. Intimidated? Yes. Cops these days were showing their true colors as authoritarian thugs. But Peter was outside, in the fresh air, where people were saying the virus couldn't thrive. It was airborne, but you'd have to be in a stagnant room to catch it. He heard people compare it to being near someone farting: "You wouldn't want to be in a crowded room when someone farted, would you?"

The downtown skyline poked out above the rooftops of the buildings on the street. Peter could see the building where he worked. Even though many of the lights stayed on, the building was empty. Zenith Pharm had just leased several floors when they'd consolidated their American offices. Then the lockdown happened just as he was setting up his new office. His desk plant had to be long dead.

As much as Peter had been looking forward to his new office, working from home wasn't so bad. He didn't have anyone interrupting his analysis all the time by coming to his desk and asking inane questions he had no interest in. He could work on his chemical simulations in peace. It was almost absurd to have an office at all. All the servers were networked with labs around the world. If he needed more servers, he could just create some virtually.

The downside to being remote was how his work life and home life blurred into one constant work life but with a bed. He was used to the crunch of long hours. But before all this, he could at least unwind with a walk or a stop by Hartley's pub. That didn't happen anymore. His superiors leaned on him even more. There were more deliverables, tighter deadlines, less time to sleep.

In the end, it paid off when he made a major breakthrough on his project. He successfully created a virtual simulator to test antigen candidates. Zenith Pharm's use of recently acquired machine learning drove the software to production. News of the breakthrough made the firm's stock tick up a few points, and for his efforts, Peter was rewarded with some much-needed time off.

He used his brief vacation to think about his job. A recruiter from a competitor, GenNTech, had been trying to reach him for a month. When they finally got a chance to talk, they gave Peter an offer he couldn't refuse: better pay. Peter knew the code; he could do it in his sleep. After he gave GenNTech a guided tour of the code he wrote, they practically begged him to come on board.

On the opposite sidewalk on the next block, a woman and her daughter walked in the opposite direction. The child, maybe nine or ten years old, was bundled in the poofiest coat and hat. She looked like a tiny Michelin Man drinking a hot beverage. Peter got misty eyed seeing other people out in public again.

Just the night before, he somehow had managed to convince Dianne to come over to his apartment. It was the most direct human contact he'd had in months. They stayed up all night. It was the most intimate he'd felt with someone. They'd make love, order takeout, watch a movie, nod off, then fooled around some more. Being with another person reminded him how important it was to be around others. Now he wanted more. Seeing Miles again, even six feet away with a mask on, would be worth it.

The coffee shop had a small line of eight people starting from the cafe's door. The entrance had a makeshift Dutch door with the bottom half in place. An employee in a coat and mask and face shield took orders while customers stood to the side as they waited for their coffee to be made. The door sign read, NO CASH. CREDIT/DEBIT ONLY and had a card reader next to it. All the coffee shop's windows were boarded up. A bleak scene, but a welcome one.

"Here you go." Miles was there, waiting for him with two paper cups of coffee, one in each gloved hand. "I went ahead and got us two lattes. They were keeping my hands warm."

"Thanks for coming," Peter said, accepting the cup at arm's length. It was almost too hot to hold. He blew on it, forgetting he still was wearing a mask.

"The park is finally open. Want to check it out? I was going to take Toby, but he and his mom are at her parents," Miles said.

"As long as it's not crowded. You didn't go with them?" The park was always five degrees colder to him. Peter wished he had dressed warmer; he felt a bit underdressed, looking at Miles and the others in line.

"Stuck with work. The enrollment program went viral for some reason. I've got every twenty-something celeb, influencer, DJ, and rich kid applying. Okay, their agents and parents are applying, and calling and attempting to go above my head, trying to get their guy in. I have a chat with Davis after this afternoon to go over costs. He's got some questions about quarterly expenses."

Peter nodded as though he understood what exactly Miles was talking about. "How do quarterly expenses work in a plague?"

"The exact same way they did before."

They headed up the empty avenue toward Central Park, only a few blocks away. Peter walked in the street to stay with Miles while still keeping an acceptable distance, while Miles, on the sidewalk, sipped from his cup. Peter was barely interested in his coffee anymore. The cold air on his face was enough to wake him up, and the walk was warming him up now; hot coffee would just make it worse. With a free hand he clumsily stuffed his scarf into his coat pocket.

They had to walk around two ambulances and bright red-and-black plastic tape that marked off the entrance to a bodega. Inside the shop, through the remaining windows that weren't boarded up, Peter saw a white opaque wall of plastic sealing off an area in the back and several power cables that led from the ambulance vans past the plastic barrier. One of the trucks was from the FDNY. The other was privately owned, with the unmistakable Zenith Pharm logo on the sides, front, and back.

"One of ours?" Peter asked.

"The medical division finished construction on their own hospital last month," Miles replied. "They've been offsetting the burden on the hospitals for a while. The City doesn't have the means to dispatch as many contamination units as needed." He gestured to the white plastic walls inside the bodega. "And we've got access to our own drugs, so a patient can opt in for trial vaccines or therapies if they want."

"I had no idea," Peter said.

Miles shook his head, "They never tell us this stuff in our all-hands meetings. It's covered in the quarterly meeting notes, but no one goes to those except investors and the media. I only knew about it because someone was discussing it during the executive training program." Miles took a sip of his coffee. "I haven't seen you at the last few meetings. They're virtual now."

"I've been meaning to go; I've just been enjoying my time off. You know?"

The bodega was a scene that didn't invite lingering. They left the store and ambulances and resumed their walk toward the park. After about a block of mutual silence, Peter broke the ice. "So you'll probably hear about this at work anyway, but I, um, I'm giving my notice on Monday." Peter looked at Miles for his reaction.

"Mm-hmm?" hummed Miles while drinking from his cup.

Peter expected more of a surprise...or a protest. He went on. "Yeah, I've been at this for...what? Four years now? I'm pretty much old school compared to everyone else on my team. I thought it was time to try out new things."

Miles finished the last of his coffee and looked for a nearby trash can. "I get it. It sucks to lose you, but also, congrats on the new gig! Where are you going exactly?"

Peter hesitated. He glanced around as if anyone near them would be interested. Of course hardly anyone was near them—two kids walking with grocery bags with their heads down and a man talking on his phone while walking briskly. "I'm not actually supposed to say. I've signed an NDA. Like, I can't even talk about it with Dianne. I haven't even told her yet. You're the first person I've talked to about this. Officially I'm taking a sabbatical to recover from burnout."

"Dude. You're going to work for a competitor! Which one?" Miles asked excitedly.

"I can't tell you, Miles. I technically can't work for a competing company for a year and a half after quitting." This was true. If Zenith Pharm learned that he would do the same work for a competing company, he'd go bankrupt in litigation. Possibly jail. Everything he had written was their intellectual property. Even though he had written every line of code to make it happen. "Look, the pay is huge, and it's a step up to directing my own team."

Peter and Miles made it to a crosswalk at an intersection that surprisingly had traffic. They were mostly taxis, but some cop cars and large military trucks also slowly paraded down the avenue. Peter finally pulled down his facemask and took a drink from his coffee now that it had cooled down. "Jesus, fuck!" Peter spat out the coffee and tossed the whole cup into a nearby trash can. "That's so gross. Did the world's coffee suddenly turn to shit?"

"Do you think the skating rink is open now that everything is frozen?" Mile said, trying to change the subject.

Peter pulled off his coat and stuffed it under his arm. "You want to skate?" he snapped. "Hey, was your coffee shit too? What did you order?" Peter tried shrugged off his anger. Bad coffee wasn't worth getting worked up over, but it just set a whole mood. Now he was too warm. He realized Miles knew a secret. He wished he didn't tell him about the job. And who the hell wants to go ice-skating?

"No, it was pretty good actually. I usually just get Folgers and save my money," Miles said. "You all right?"

"Sorry. I shouldn't have brought up the job thing. I know that puts you in a bad spot."

"Oh, don't worry about me," said Miles. "Just make sure your story is airtight both in and out of work."

"What do you mean?" asked Peter. They got a walk signal and crossed the street onto West 57th. The street had actual traffic, so the two shared the sidewalk as they walked.

Miles paused in front of another ambulance idling on the sidewalk—another one from Zenith Pharm. "Like I said, you need to make sure your story for leaving is airtight. Think about insider trading. Before we went public at our old start-up, we couldn't say shit about an IPO. Remember? All the work we do for Zenith Pharm is super secret for the same reasons, right? Well, you see this ambulance?" Miles pointed at the logo on the side. "We had plans for half a year before the plague even dropped to start this service. We initially wanted to be in poorer communities that needed help in hospitals that lacked resources. Then the lockdown happened, and we had to pivot. If news got out that we weren't prepared for this, it could have played out differently in the markets. Our competitors would have seized the opportunity to beat us to the punch. This was years in the making, and everyone has to be careful, Peter." Miles paused to let that sink in.

"I'm not telling anybody, even Dianne. I figured I could tell you because we're friends, but—"

Miles interrupted. "I get that, but you still talked about it, didn't you?" He took a cautionary step; conversations still needed to be socially distanced, after all. "The recruiter to whatever place you're going? You talked to them, right? What about your future bosses? You ever talk up a big game? Maybe try to impress them with your technical skills by showing them your past work?"

Peter realized this was no longer a friendly chat. His face flushed and was wet from sweat. He wanted to change the subject and move on. "Look, it's fine. Your mega-corporate multibillion dollar company isn't going to miss me," he retorted. "Can we get some caffeine? I'm already getting a headache." He swiped his forehead, wiped his hand on his pants, and rested against a brick window ledge.

"A word of advice, Peter: the next time you talk to GenNTech's recruiters, use a personal laptop or do it in person. Well, as much as one can do anything in person." Miles said.

"Jesus, you think they know?" Peter said, out of breath. He looked down in dismay. He might already be on his way to jail. Zenith Pharm was probably all set to serve him papers as soon as he signed in on Monday.

Peter noticed his pants were filthy for some reason. His lap had a gross dark streak across his right thigh. He curiously touched it, trying to recall how it had gotten like that. They were clean when he put them on this morning. He turned his hand over, and it was red. A small red drop landed on his palm. He jerked his head up to the clouds to see where it had come from. Maybe paint had spilled from a window above. The sky was bright gray, and the building against his back was a silent monolith.

Mile's frowned as he leaned against the ambulance truck. "Rancid taste, Peter? It's a common symptom. High body temperature. You're walking around without a coat in thirty-degree weather. That's hematoma you're experiencing, by the way."

Peter looked back at the hand he'd used to wipe his brow. He touched his face and examined his hand again; it was covered in his blood. He stood up fast in a panic and lost his balance as his knees buckled. He fell on his hands and elbows on the sidewalk, all the while touching his face to check for more blood. He wiped it off, but there was more on his hand. He wiped some more—still more blood on his hand. His eyes were blurry with red, which he couldn't blink it out of his vision.

Miles knocked on the side of the ambulance. The back door opened; two people in white hazmat suits emerged with a portable gurney and hoisted Peter onto it. He felt a hard prick in his right arm.

"Miles!" Peter yelled. "Jesus, Miles! Fucking help me." A sloppy wet cough escaped his mouth. He tried to break free from the two figures' hold on him, but he was trapped in place. Miles was now in front of the ambulance, talking with another figure in a hazmat suit. The figure handed him a clipboard and pen, and he wrote short marks on it and handed it back.

Panting wildly, Peter was fully restrained. "Miles! Help!"

Miles followed Peter as he was loaded into the back of

the ambulance. He gripped Peter's foot in comfort and assuredness. "It's going to be fine, Peter. You're not getting fired. But this is really serious. I've got to quarantine for the rest of the week! I was supposed to join my wife at the in-laws. Snowy mountains. Skiing. All on hold now."

Peter coughed violently. His lungs no longer stung with the biting cold air of winter; rather, they were sticky and warm. Hard plastic was pushed onto his mouth and nose as he began to feel very tired. The last thing he heard was Miles saying, "We're going to take good care of you, Peter. Just as you took good care of us."

ALICE WHITMORE WOULD ALWAYS REMEMBER where she was and what she was doing during the two most important events in her life: when the plague was unleashed in America and when she escaped with her life in Europe. The first event occurred while she was working at a crowded bar in California and all the TV screens switched to breaking news. Everyone stopped and watched footage of the town of Mountain Home, Arkansas, burning in the night. Roads in and out were blockaded with military vehicles. When Alice dropped her tray of drinks, shards of glass nicked her shins, but no one noticed.

The second event would happen three months later, after the plague had spread globally.

Alice was back in Virginia, living with her former classmate in a one-bedroom apartment, when she learned she was flying to Europe. She stared at her phone for a long time, replaying the conversation in her mind. Her phone, wrapped in a hard red plastic case that held the cracked screen in place, rested face up, reflecting the ceiling back at her. She had just gotten off the line with a person representing Zenith Pharm to accept her application for their study in Europe.

Alice was going to leave tomorrow.

She didn't have much time. She should be stressed, but the relief of being accepted was so great that everything else seemed minor. "The Study" had garnered a lot of media attention over the past few months. While other drug manufacturers and pharmaceutical giants were pushing their own vaccine studies, Zenith Pharm touted a revolutionary system of developing a safe, effective cure without the need for thousands of human participants.

More importantly, she'd get paid.

Alice would earn ten thousand dollars to participate in a two-month study with seventy-nine other college-age participants. All to help Zenith Pharm's scientists find a cure for the arenavirus, commonly known as the Ozark virus. Some local cave plunderers had taken to a newly discovered cave system and thought it would be a great idea to pet all the animals they met along the way. A few days later, the entire world demonstrated their inability to follow safety measures, and Alice found herself in a pandemic with nowhere to go.

With this money, she could continue to pay for her education and housing when college eventually resumed. Before the pandemic had closed everything down, Alice had worked part-time at an off-campus bar in Los Angeles, bringing drinks and bar food to her classmates, none of whom suspected a fellow USC student was working evenings for tips. They didn't put much thought into tipping at all.

The sudden shutdown of schools across the country might have solved her problem of paying tuition, but it was the closure of restaurants and massive unemployment that left her with looming rent and bills. Eventually she was forced to return home to rural Virginia. Her parents, Wyatt and Beth Whitmore, lived twenty minutes outside Harrisonburg.

Her return was fine enough for her parents, but they had their own money problems. They couldn't financially support her education, and quite honestly, her going to college was more her idea than theirs. A trade school—something cheaper, more local, less *liberal*—was what they had in mind. A trade school would have given Alice a more immediate career in their opinion. "Something to help pay back all the raising we did." Her father kept this financial guilt over her head when it came to anything Alice wanted to do with her life. But Alice wasn't keen on sticking around. She had no interest learning how to repair motors or cut hair. She wanted to be as far away as she could get from Virginia.

She was dispirited when she returned home. All her classmates and friends were sheltering in place, and she couldn't say goodbye. However, they wished her luck, and to stay safe, via text. Traveling by airplane meant subjecting herself to the constant monitoring of thermal cameras, waiting in isolated spaces walled by clear plastic dividers as she was shuffled through security, and spending several hours on an airplane with half its seats removed to keep passengers apart. It was all for the safety of her and others, but it didn't make her feel safe. She felt like a thing to be afraid of around other things to fear as well.

* * *

Alice spotted her dad as she stepped out of the baggage claim area of Reagan National Airport. He drove a twenty-year-old red Ford truck with enough bumper stickers on the tailgate and rear panel to remind her that her father was a racist. He waved at her when she came through the automatic glass doors of the baggage claim area. He had shaved his beard since she'd last seen him; it made him look younger, even though his smile betrayed the wrinkles around his eyes. Though she wore a face-mask, she hoped he knew she was smiling back. She slung her luggage into the back of the truck, ignoring the new stickers tacked to the rear panel, and climbed into the passenger seat. Her father slipped his own mask on when she wasn't looking.

"Keep wearing that," he told her. "And keep the window down a bit."

So much for the warm reception. By the time Alice had left for California, she and her father had been jousting in arguments and meanspirited replies. As a child, she had taken everything her parents said with obedient submission. It didn't please her father to endure her rebuttals, counter-points, passive insults, and challenges to his authority, and Alice had those in spades. She hoped, naïvely, that during her time away, tempers would have cooled and this home-coming would mend their troubled relationship. They couldn't change each other, but they could at least try to respect and love each other again.

Maybe he would ask about her life: *How was college? Did you make a lot of friends? How are your grades? Have you gained weight?*

"Took you long enough," he said, pulling back onto the airport road. "I had to circle six times. That mall cop wouldn't let me park."

"Gee, Dad, if I knew it was going to be such a hassle, I would've found my own ride."

"We live hours from the airport, Al. What are you going to do? Book an Uber? This isn't the metropolitan utopia you're used to."

Alice felt her old combative self slip over her skin like an unwashed hoodie. "I'm happy to see you too, Dad."

She heard her father's measured sigh over the roar of the truck. He patted her knee. That would be his way of apologizing; he was too proud to say it out loud. They spent the rest of the drive listening to talk radio, arguing with each other in total silence.

Instead of going directly home, Alice's father took a different route. They wound up taking a side highway that led to a remote location where the Bull Run Woodsmen gathered every Sunday after church. She had attended with her parents until she'd grown old enough to decline participating.

Noticing the change, Alice looked to her father for answers. When he didn't react, and kept his eyes forward, she said, "I thought we were going home."

Her father cleared his throat. "Your mom and I are setting you up at the ol' mill for the week. You've been out around other people, and, well, we just need to make sure you're safe."

"Are you serious? Dad! I've been living for months in safety. Everyone on the plane got temperature checked before boarding. I'm not sick."

Her father didn't reply.

"Look, I can isolate in my room for the four days. I can even camp outside in a tent if I have to."

"It's too risky having you in the house, and a tent would expose you to ticks."

Fuming, Alice sank into her seat. This wasn't about her parents' safety. This was punishment and pettiness. This had her mother's fingerprints all over it.

The Bull Run Woodsmen were a militia group. The property where they convened had an old log mill that had been retrofitted as a cabin on the property. The mill was the only thing historic about the place. The interior had the trappings of furniture and long tree blades from a bygone era, with modern amenities. The cabin sat next to the giant steel multiport garage that was large enough to house a gun range, a training center where members showed off their latest guns and gun-part accessories, and a mini kitchen for coffee and catering.

When they pulled up to the old mill, Alice's mother was waiting beside her Honda Civic. She was pulling on a cigarette when she saw them and put it out before applying her facemask. She waved to Alice when she stepped from the truck and slammed the door.

"Look who's back. Welcome to Virginia, Al!" her mother called to her as Alice dragged her luggage to the mill.

Her mother followed her inside. "You can use my car if it's an emergency, but please don't make contact with anyone." She set the keys by the door. "I went ahead and brought some leftovers for you and stocked the pantry. I don't think Sly's Pizza delivers this far out, but maybe they can meet you halfway." Her mother's country charm gave her words a singsong voice.

Alice flung her suitcase onto the bed and checked her phone. At least there was a signal she could use. She needed to find her friends and figure something out. This living arrangement was already going south.

"Sounds great, Mom."

"It's only until Sunday. Then you can have your old room back. Nothing's changed; it even has all your posters."

"Let's hope I live till then."

"Perhaps if you'd chosen a closer school, we wouldn't be in this situation."

Alice pocketed her phone and turned to face her mother. "Yes, how shortsighted of me not to factor in a global virus outbreak in my college selection. I'm surprised they even admitted me for such carelessness." Alice had her mother's eyes; she recognized how they narrowed into cold stares without her eyebrows moving.

Her mother's eyes softened. "We'll see you on Sunday. I've told all the Woodsmen to expect you. Even Reed's boy."

Alice stood still inside the cabin as her mother and father drove off. The sound of the truck faded away; only the birds and insects and the tussle of windswept tree branches remained.

"Shit."

In truth, Alice didn't mind the isolation. It had been a long time since she'd known the peaceful quiet of the country. Staying here would also give her time to continue her studies without the distraction of her family's politics pecking at her every decision. Come Sunday, however, the full force of a militia would be upon her, every member a cloned version of her mother and father.

No doubt they'd tease her for moving to California. She'd gone soft, they'd say. She now smokes pot and hates God and guns, they'd say, even though she knew at least twenty of the boys in the militia were either smoking pot or dealing it, along with stronger substances. Sunday would be a strong reminder to get back to California, or anywhere else, as soon as possible.

Over the next four days, when Alice wasn't studying, or

texting with her old high-school friends, she was checking her apps. That was when Zenith Pharm came across her feeds. At first she'd see an ad to enlist in a study, and she'd scroll past it without another thought. But the ads persisted, propagated across multiple social networks. Popular influencers on social media posted videos about Zenith Pharm and their interest in this study. Zenith Pharm had gone from a blip of a mention to an unending trend from which she couldn't escape.

By day four, the phone calls started. Alice tried to ignore them. She pushed the "decline" button, just like she ignored every other spam call. By midday she finally took a chance; they'd probably stop if she talked to them and told them to put her on their "do not call" list.

Before she could speak, a young-sounding man cut to the chase. "Hey, Alice! I know you're incredibly busy and probably have a million other priorities, what with everything that's going on and all, so I'll get right to it." He paused briefly. "I'm a recruiter for Zenith Pharm. We're developing a vaccine for the Ozark virus, and we need participants for our study."

"Yeah, I know all this."

"You do?"

Alice laughed. "Whatever algorithm I fell into, I've been inundated with ads and videos about it."

"Great! So you know, this would be an all-expense-paid trip to our European labs. You'll get a base pay of ten thousand dollars for your time there. I'll leave it to payroll to sort out the details. Listen, unless you're already working with GenNTech or Pfizer or whatever, we'd love to have you apply to join us."

"I really don't think so. I only answered to ask that you stop calling." She was already tired from this conversation; this guy's perky tone had sucked the energy from her.

"Ha! Okay, no problem. I know how you feel. I've got family priorities and immediate needs, and those things gotta come first. I get it. I'll take care of opting you out. But feel free to contact me if you change your mind. Have a great day." The phone call ended.

* * *

It was Sunday, after church. Alice had just emerged from the cabin, wearing her favorite USC sweatshirt, which she'd bought at Goodwill. It was in great condition and would remain that way thanks to her incredible ability to make clothes last forever. She was pulling her brown hair back into a ponytail with a scrunchy when she spotted a familiar face.

"Alice? What are you doing here?" Sam Reed, her old classmate, wore a silicone half-mask respirator and clear plastic goggles. He and Alice had graduated together in a class of eighty seniors and had practically grown up together. His father had driven her home from their club meetings and martial arts practices more times than she could remember. He'd also cover her school lunch when she couldn't afford it. In return, she kept people from teasing him about his abundant freckles.

Sam stepped out of his pickup truck dressed to go hunting, from his rugged jacket, to his gun holster, to his thick black boots. He came toward her with open arms then thought better about hugging and just waved.

Aside from the respirator and goggles, he looked the same, maybe a little bigger in the waist. She couldn't help smile and waved back, secretly wishing for a hug instead.

Seeing Sam again was the part of coming back home she didn't mind.

"Seriously. I heard this morning you were in town. I couldn't believe it." Sam scratched the back of his head where the visor's straps pulled at his curly red hair. "I can't believe your parents made you stay out here of all places. Did you sleep here?"

"It's comfier than you think," she lied.

"I wish I knew sooner; you could have stayed at my place. I have a futon. Have you reached out to anyone from class?"

"Mandy Hofstetter and I stay in touch. She's good. She offered to let me room with her in town instead of being so far out."

"Rooming with your childhood best friend sounds like a better arrangement than staying with your parents. She, uh, seeing anyone?"

"We have social media, you know. You could look her up and find out. Or call her," Alice said. She already had looked up everyone from their graduating class: *Where Are They Now? Harrisonburg High Edition.*

Sam was still scratching at his hair. "I tried Facebook and Instagram, but it's not really me. It's all my parents' friends sharing jokes and posting food pics."

About ten to fifteen other men and women roamed from their vehicles toward the open bay garage. Everyone wore some sort of face covering. In Los Angeles a few anti-mask protests were featured in the media; Alice thought they were a national embarrassment. She cringed at the idea that her more liberal friends back in LA thought this was how the other side thought of the virus. It was true, for the most part. The Bull Run Woodsmen, however, treated it as another military exercise in preparation. And as with their handguns, shotguns, and semi-automatic rifles, everyone had to show off. Only the best top military-grade facemasks and impact-resistant headgear were allowed here.

Sam fumbled in his jacket pockets and handed her a plastic-wrapped facemask. "Before you start getting stares. The Woodsmen take this stuff very seriously. They think the government created the virus, and they're not taking any chances."

"Right! You got an extra handgun too in case I need to shoot the virus? I want to make sure I really fit in." Alice put on the white mask with a casual movement from muscle memory. "Everything is shut down in California—no schools or anything—so I'm staying here for a while until things reopen."

"*If* they reopen. The Woodsmen are already planning some kind of commune where we can be self-sustaining. The Harpers and Atwoods pooled their resources and made a bubble. Co-op farm, shared vehicles, like one of those hippy communes."

"Becky Harper and her family? They've been hoarding food for years. I'm surprised they haven't moved into their bunker."

When Sam laughed, his bright eyes showed signs of laugh wrinkles Alice didn't notice before. They were both older, she realized. Growing up around the same kids, they all looked the same all the time. It wasn't just from attending the same schools from kindergarten through high school; it was also 4-H Club, jujitsu, band practice, shooting club, sports, and sleepovers. Now, after just a couple of semesters being away, Alice saw how much things had changed. She knew several of her former classmates were married now. She wondered if Sam was married.

There was a lull in conversation as Sam aimlessly

nodded. "Oh, hey," he finally said. "My dad just bought new Kalashnikov shotgun. The MP-155 Ultima. We're gonna do a few rounds. Interested in joining us?"

"I've never heard of it." Maybe it was the old feelings of these gatherings, but she liked the idea of doing some target practice. She was a better aim than her father; at least she used to be. Maybe a little reminder would help let him know she was still part of the family.

"Oh, you're going to like it. Come on!" Sam led her away from his truck with kidlike enthusiasm.

Under the unnaturally blue fluorescent lights in the garage, Alice spotted her mother and father chatting with the other militia members. They stood by the far wall, which was decorated with patriotic slogans, group photos, and posters provided by gun manufacturers. Sam noticed them as well and stopped to look back. His expression was hard to read, but hers was not.

"Hey, uh...my dad's setting up by the range. Meet you there?" Sam said.

Alice wondered how long her parents had already been at the militia ranch. It was their idea to isolate her after all. Maybe they didn't realize they hadn't checked in on her over the past week and would exclaim in joy as they hugged her and folded her into their conversation with their fellow militia friends. Or maybe she could follow Sam, who was genuinely eager for her company.

The range had a makeshift sound-dampening wall that divided it and the rest of the garage. It was carpeted with sound-absorbing foam to help keep the rest of the structure from sounding like a warzone during use. Alice and Sam found his dad, surrounded by fellow members, commenting on his new gun—the latest in military-enthusiast-lifestyle weaponry.

When Sam had said it was a shotgun, Alice had imagined the kind she used during skeet shoots, with a shiny marbled-wood stock and a double-barrel end. What Sam's father showcased, however, was matte black with a white ceramic shell set at hard angles as though it had been 3D printed or a prop used in a science fiction movie.

"Well, if it isn't Alice Whitmore? Come here!" Sam's father's eyes lit up over his mask and tactical helmet when he noticed her standing behind his son.

"Hey, Mr. Reed." Alice smiled through another hug. This was certainly a warmer reception than she'd received from her own father. She suspected he was more excited for his son. She squeezed him back.

"Ow, okay, not too tight." Mr. Reed said with a rasp.

"Sorry! I didn't realize."

"I'm only kidding." He cleared his throat as he stepped back and rubbed the left side of his chest. "All that fresh air from the California beach must be good for ya." He leaned in a bit. "Maybe you can take Sam with you when you go back. Get him out of here for once."

Sam blushed through his face shield and headed away.

"That's your new toy?" Alice said, changing the subject.

With an air of pride, Mr. Reed patted the side of the shotgun. "Kalashnikov MP-155 Ultima!" He picked it up to show off its design and set it back down with a heavy thud. "We're going to test it out. Douglas was able to bring down a Vector for us to try out too. Stick around! Excuse me. Just going to get some fresh air. Dang mask is on too tight." He chuckled as he stepped away.

Left alone, Alice looked around the idle crowd of facemasks and face shields and helmets, not recognizing anyone. Not really. By the end of high school, she all but had refused to attend these gatherings. The excuse she gave was she needed more time to study for her upcoming SAT exam, but in reality she was embarrassed by it all. This only added to the growing chasm that was the relationship with her and her parents.

She found Sam trying to look busy at a nearby bookshelf, reading the latest from Mrs. Ford's self-published spiral-bound cookbook. Everyone got a copy.

"Have you tried her potato chip chicken casserole yet?" Alice asked.

"Don't knock it. I suppose it doesn't compare to all the kale and avocado recipes back at college."

"First of all, kale is good for you. And they sell it in town, you know."

"Seriously?"

"Yup. Local organic kale. They sell it at the co-op by the post office."

"We have a co-op? And it's good?"

"Kale? No. I hate it," Alice said. That made Sam laugh. "Definitely do not recommend."

Sam sighed as he replaced the cookbook on the shelf. "Sorry about my dad. He never lets up with you, by the way. One homecoming dance, and he's already made up his mind for me."

"Sam!" A man behind another mask pushed his way between them. Before he could respond, the man was already pulling him away. "Your dad's got it. Hurry!"

"Got what? Wait!" Sam said as he was tugged back through the garage to the outside.

A circle had gathered around Mr. Reed. He was on his knees, struggling to take his helmet off while coughing violently.

"Keep the mask on, Paul." A woman stood nearby with her arms out, palms facing him.

"I'm fine! Just having a hard time breathing." He wheezed and staggered when he grabbed his ribs.

"Dad! Okay. Look at me. Look at me." Sam ran up to him and refastened his helmet and focused his father's gaze toward his. Alice came to the other side to help support Mr. Reed from falling over. Once he got a clear look at his dad's face, Sam's expression change from a panicked confusion to a focused stare. "Dad? Dad, listen to me. You're showing signs of hematidrosis. We're going to get you to the hospital. But you need to keep your helmet and mask on."

The words made everyone step away from Sam's father. That seemed to calm Sam's dad down for the moment. When he turned to Alice, she clearly saw the fear in his eyes as blood collected in the seal of his goggles. A part of Alice's mind thought about the hug he had given her earlier —she should be worried for her own safety and for Sam's as well. But she couldn't break her focus from this sweet old man who was now in the throws of the virus' effects. Sam's father tried to shake away from his son's grip, but he stumbled backward, pulling Alice with him as she tried to help keep his balance.

"The hospital can't help me. Only good thing they offer is housing the dead!"

"Mr. Reed," Alice said, "it's only a forty-minute drive if we hurry. I'm sure if—"

Through the coughs and lurching sounds, Sam's dad tightly gripped Alice's wrist. He uttered, "Take care of him." Then he pushed away from Alice, unholstered his gun, and shoved it under his jaw.

Growing up, Alice constantly had lobbied her parents to enroll her in programs and courses with her friends. Instead of ballet, she played baseball. Instead of horseback riding, she learned to throw axes and hunt deer. Instead of going to computer camp, she was taught military combat. Instead of doing an internship for biology at the wetland preserves, she learned about all about guns and self-defense.

Sam's father pulled back the slide of his gun and started to squeeze the trigger. Alice saw herself move on its own, as if watching from above. Her hand moved with automatic muscle memory. It was a motion she had performed over and over from her training. Alice firmly gripped her hand around the gun barrel; the grip needed to be tight. She pushed the gun away as it fired. Her head rang from the bang, but it didn't register to her. Her arm shook from the discharge as the grasped the barrel in place. The gun couldn't fire again without manually reloading it. She couldn't let Mr. Reed get the chance. She twisted the gun in his grip backward, and his hand relented from the unnatural bending. She popped the cartridge and tossed it away from his reach.

Mr. Reed fell onto his back.

Sam, yelling, ran up to his dad, but Alice couldn't hear him over the ringing in her ears.

A pair of hands pulled at her shoulders, trying to coax her back, but Alice had to see. Did she stop Mr. Reed in time? She saw Sam's on top of his dad, calling to him. Mr. Reed's chest moved up and down. Alice caught a glimpse of his helmet as everyone came toward him and blocked her view. The helmet's visor had a bright white scuffmark. He was alive; now they could get him to a hospital where he would have a chance.

"You did good, Alice." She realized it was her father pulling her back. His eyes smiled warmly at her. "Not even Hollywood could soften you." He hugged her tightly.

Alice pulled away. "Not even Hollywood could soften me? Jesus." The curse hurt his eyebrows. "I know we had a deal to isolate before I came home, but I'm going to stay with Mandy Hofstetter. She's got a place in town."

They both watched Sam help his father to his feet and lead him toward a car parked next to the garage.

"Is that what you want?" her father asked.

"Well, Mandy and I have been talking. And I could run errands for you too. And..."

Sam, in the distance, shouted at his dad. Alice looked up to see his dad break free and run into the garage. Sam and some others ran in after him. Alice's heart sank.

"No..." she whimpered.

A sudden flash and bang erupted from garage.

* * *

Ever since Alice had moved in with Mandy, she didn't reach out to anyone else. Not since her family's militia had gathered and Mr. Reed had killed himself a month ago. There was an online only memorial service, but Alice couldn't bring herself to watch it. Sam hadn't contacted her, not that she could blame him. Her parents didn't contact her either.

The last interaction she had with her parents was her mother freaking out that Alice had stopped a gun with her bare hand. It didn't matter that Alice had tried to justify it by explaining how a close-range gunshot of an infected person would have released blood droplets everywhere. It didn't matter that she simply didn't want Mr. Reed to die.

For Alice, it didn't matter that her mother was right to be upset. It had been years since Alice had been taught how to disarm someone like that. She'd never even used that move outside of class, and she'd put herself in danger. No amount of winning arguments with her mom in her mind had changed that. What her mom didn't know was that she liked it. She liked the violence of it and she hated herself for that. She felt good disarming Mr. Reed. She liked how her racist, gun-loving dad approved of it. She knew how easily she could fit in with her family and her classmates. She could join a gun club, hang out at smoky bars, and get picked up by former high-school football players. Update her profile photo with the latest fish she'd caught while drinking on a boat. She just needed a Confederate flag to hang in her window to complete the look.

Alice needed to leave town. Zenith Pharm wanted to take her to another continent.

Mandy lived in an apartment complex just off the college campus in Harrisonburg. It was a one-bedroom, but the couch was comfortable, and both Alice and Mandy enjoyed each other's company. Maybe it was the lockdown, how it kept people isolated and alone. For Alice, the constant company of a dear friend was exactly what she needed. Their combined unemployment checks took care of food, rent, and utilities. When they weren't binging on their favorite movies, Mandy helped Alice with her application to Zenith Pharm.

In addition to the many forms, and their numerous questions, Alice was expected to provide Zenith Pharm proof of a negative Ozark virus test, her medical history, her family medical and mental history, blood type, history of drug use, height, weight, ethnicity, gender and pronouns, passport, social security number, permission for a background check, and information regarding her social media profiles. Alice also needed to produce a video essay about herself describing why she wanted to participate in the study. Mandy often made videos for social media and did the heavy lifting by putting the piece together.

The entire process lasted about a week. Alice chatted online with program managers and product directors, though she couldn't tell the difference between them. They were interested in getting to know her and following up on some of the answers she'd provided. They were, however, less than forthcoming about providing answers to her questions. What were her expected duties? Why was this happening in Europe, when she was American? How far along were they in finding a cure? It was well enough, she supposed. After all, she was still in the application phase of the process. Until she was accepted and signed the appropriate NDA forms, she wasn't going to get much information.

Then, after a couple weeks of not hearing anything from them, she got the phone call.

Alice and Mandy were downing beers on the small patio at Mandy's apartment overlooking the parking lot, listening to Mandy's favorite streaming station, when the phone rang.

"It's them!" Alice ran inside and closed the sliding glass door so the music wouldn't drown out the phone's volume.

"Alice? It's Miles Ahmadu. Hope your day's been going well. If it hasn't, I've got some good news that might turn that around."

"That sounds promising." Out of habit, Alice curled her hair around her finger.

"Sure does. The selection committee has approved you for our program. I know you had to wait a long time for our response, and I'm sorry for that. We've had some last-minute changes, though, and need to address them before moving forward."

"Oh...okay." Alice tripped on her words. She had gotten

in! She looked back to Mandy, who was watching through the doorway in earnest.

"I'm sending you a series of documents to digitally sign, as well as some much-needed FAQs and program information. When you get a chance, please download and sign into our app."

"Uh-huh."

"I know we discussed the short turn-around time for you. Are you still able to travel tomorrow?"

"Yes."

"That's great to hear. I'm booking you a driver now. He'll call you to confirm the pickup time. Unless you have any questions, you should be all set."

"Okay. I mean, thank you." Alice ended the call and turned to Mandy.

Mandy picked up Alice's unfinished bottle of beer and joined her inside.

"Hey. Sorry, hun. Here, this'll help." Mandy handed Alice the beer, which Alice took without thinking. She was still processing her thoughts and didn't even hear what Mandy had said. "You know," Mandy continued, "we still got unemployment. You can stay here as long as you want¬ —you know that. Classes will pick up again any time now, and you'll be back in LA before you know it."

"I got it," Alice said.

"Okay," Mandy replied, as though Alice meant she understood.

"No. I got it! I got accepted!"

"Alice, that's so great! Cheers!" Mandy and Alice clinked their bottles and took a drink. Mandy did a little celebratory dance. "You looked so calm and still I thought it was bad news. This means you'll be able to afford going back to school."

"I was in shock." Alice didn't know when classes would start officially. However, Mandy was right. Student loans and scholarships only went so far. A few extra thousand toward tuition would be a huge help.

She saw the email notification on her phone and opened it. It started with a general run-of-the-mill "welcome aboard" statement, followed by a bullet-list itinerary and what to expect.

Then another email came in. Then several more, needing her attention. Zenith Pharm needed her to digitally sign a deluge of agreements, regulations, NDA contracts, and waivers.

Mandy performed another tiny dance of joy. "Well? What's next? Tell me everything."

"Here's what I know." Alice pulled on her beer while scrolling through her inbox. "Mmm, I should go over the docs soon. I was in one of the last groups selected. The program is already underway. Because of a 'timing issue' on their end, they want me to join the last leg of participants and need me right away. That means tomorrow morning."

"Tomorrow? Shit. We have to get you to the airport. Norfolk and Reagan are hours away." Mandy looked for her keys. "You've got to get home and pack! Do you have a ticket? Where are you flying?"

Alice swallowed the last swig from her bottle and set it beside her phone. "It's all taken care of. They're picking me up here. The flight's already booked. And I'm pretty much already packed. I've been living out of my suitcase since I got here."

Mandy grabbed two more beers from the fridge, popped the lids off both, and handed one to Alice. "Picking you up! Talk about money. Then what? You just go to some building and hang out for two months?"

Alice shook her head. "It's a castle, actually. In Romania. They've got this retrofitted castle where they've built a testing facility. It's on the up and up, but I'm basically going to Frankenstein's castle."

"You mean Dracula's castle."

"What?"

"*Frankenstein* takes place in Switzerland. Dracula is from Romania."

Alice eyed her. "Drink your juice. Anyway, it's a converted castle, full of guestrooms and modern facilities you'd find in a nice hotel that happens to have a drug lab attached."

"Just like that abandoned school bus next to the elementary school turned out to be a meth lab."

Alice nodded. "It's exactly like that. Want me to bring you some rocks from Europe?"

"More candy for Mandy."

Alice took a cold swig of her beer with a somber expression. "Maybe I shouldn't explain all this actually. I have NDAs and contracts to sign to keep this all secret."

"I promise I won't tell the other dealers," Mandy replied. "We should celebrate. Seriously. I'll order a pizza while you pack. You wanna call anyone? We can social-distance party."

Alice thought about it briefly. *Hi! I know I just got back, but we're having a goodbye party. Wanna come?* Maybe she could let her parents know the good news. *I decided living in California wasn't enough to hate America, so I'm going to Europe.*

She let out an exasperated laugh. "God, no. Just us girls." The beer was crisp, cold, and washed down all her worries.

* * *

Norfolk International Airport was a ghost town compared to the last time Alice was there. It was only a few weeks ago that she had come home. People were scared, stressed, and didn't want to be anywhere near each other, much less breathe the same air for several hours in flight. But now, even in the early afternoon, the airport had minimal staff to hand out boarding passes. Alice could count the number of passengers at the airport on her fingers. All the food courts and mini shops were shuttered. Security, however, was as present as ever.

Her driver, who picked her up at 6:00 a.m. and didn't say much of a word to her during the trip, dropped her off at the terminal, wished her luck, and peeled away. He wasn't rude, just distant. Perhaps she was feeling anxious being in a closed space with someone, even if they both wore masks. She knew the feeling of being in closed spaces. She didn't much care for being near strangers either. And she was about to do it again for several hours.

The boarding process from check-in to takeoff remained the same as before. The airport was busy enough to make checking in through the various cattle-sorting lanes' unending voice announcements to let passengers know to keep a safe distance of six feet, and facemasks were required at all times. People caught not wearing facemasks would be stopped and possibly removed. Alice kept a whole pack of masks in her carry-on.

When she walked up to the gate for Lufthansa Air, the attendant immediately responded with smiling eyes. "Alice Whitmore?"

Surprised, Alice replied, "Yes? Am I late?"

The attendant stood out from behind her counter and

reached for her luggage, "Oh, no, we're not boarding for another twenty minutes. You're the only woman listed on our gate manifest. I can check this in for you." She attached an adhesive ribbon to the luggage handle. "We'll just put it up front. I don't think we're limited on space!" She laughed.

Alice was impressed. Zenith Pharm had booked a whole plane just for her. Or was it because she was the only woman on the plane, so everyone else had to be men? She sat in a row of seats that faced out to the gate. From there, she saw the giant white plane hugged into the gate's jet bridge. She checked her phone briefly: no messages. Workers outside, wearing yellow safety vests and facemasks, moved between the planes and structures in some trade-secret fashion that made the airport capable of receiving hundreds of planes a day. Even in a mostly abandoned airport, they still worked to make it all happen.

Twenty minutes hadn't fully passed when the attendant called to her: "You can go ahead and board now."

A flight attendant was waiting for Alice at the door to the plane; she welcomed her and let her know she could sit anywhere she'd like in the first-class cabin. Alice had never flown in first-class, much less on an international flight. The cabin was huge; it had the largest airplane seats she'd ever seen and were spaced far enough apart for her to lie down. Each row had two seats, one window seat, and one aisle on either side of the plane. Alice headed to the back of the cabin and looked around, thinking of which seat she'd want to spend the next sixteen hours in. She decided on seat 2-D.

Excited to try out her first-class seat for the first time, she quickly stowed her backpack and purse in the overhead bin and climbed into the seat.

"This is nice," she said to no one in particular.

Zenith Pharm was really rolling out the red carpet for

her. When she stretched her legs, she could barely reach the small storage chest placed against the back of the chair in front of her. The display above played a looped video: Lufthansa welcomed her on behalf of everyone at Zenith Pharm, a Monostori Company®.

"Can I bring you a beverage, maybe some champagne?" The same flight attendant came up to her with folded hands. Alice looked at her name tag: Heidi.

"Oh, thank you, Heidi. I, uh, I'll take a Coke if you have it. I didn't bring much cash with me." Alice already had planned on not spending US cash once she was out of the country—not that her debit card was stocked with dough for champagne either.

Heidi gave an understanding smile, or at least her eyes seemed to. "Meals, drinks, and entertainment are all complimentary for our guests. You sure about that Coke?"

"In that case...how about a rum and Coke?"

"*Genau!*" Heidi said something in cheery German and walked away.

Alice continued her inspection of her seat and its features. The sidearm lifted to reveal illuminated buttons with icons that hinted at various ways to adjust her seat. One button moved the storage bin in front of her; she pressed it and got an instant footrest. Another made the seat transform into a bed, something she definitely was going to try later. Over her shoulder, snaking over the seat, was an adjustable reading light.

She got up and was reaching into her carry-on for her current mystery-thriller selection when she was startled by a boisterous sounding male voice behind her.

"Is this seat taken?"

Alice turned and looked up to see a blond man in a blue

facemask and a matching sport coat that barely fit around his chest. He gestured to the seat across from her.

"Sorry. Stupid joke. We're the only ones here." He reached out his elbow, the new international sign for a non-handshake. His arms comically strained against his sleeves. "Hi. Spence Dixon. Ready to save the world?"

THE FLIGHT to Norfolk was behind schedule, and Darren Montoya was going to be late. As far as he was concerned, there was no reason any flight should be late at this point. It wasn't as if airports were fighting traffic jams anymore. Yet, as it was, Darren's plane was late taking off due to a mechanical issue, setting him behind a whole hour. That completely erased his layover at Philadelphia and then some. Sure, the pilot made up time by increasing speed, but his connecting flight to Norfolk had its own issues.

Some belligerent passenger loudly argued that she didn't need a mask because the plane was so empty. This wasn't true, of course. There were people on board, all wearing masks...*because we're not assholes, Karen*, he thought. Darren had three facemasks with him, all black from the same online site. He already had changed one out on the first flight and thrown it in the garbage. The plane was at 25 percent capacity per new restrictions, but Darren would have been more comfortable with the percentage being even lower. To him, being around any number of people was asking for infection.

Darren's flight to Norfolk put him in the back of the plane by window seat 26-A. He continually checked his watch, hoping he wouldn't miss his connecting flight. Occasionally he reached for his pocket, feeling for the nondescript black thumb drive. By all rights, he shouldn't be here. If he had any sense for safety, he'd be as far away from Zenith Pharm as possible. He should be at home, keeping his parents safe, and just ride this whole thing out. That was the original plan.

Although the plane was late to land in Norfolk, the final plane was waiting for him. Sure as the airport ground crew would transfer his luggage, he moved as quickly as possible through the airport to reach the gate at the second concourse. The gate was empty, but he could see the plane from the window, and the woman at the gate was waiting for him.

He handed her his ticket. "I have a piece of luggage from the other plane."

"No worries," she replied. "It's being loaded now. You're all set. Enjoy your flight!" She handed him back his ticket, letting him pass into the jetway.

The flight attendant welcomed him on board and let him pick his choice of first-class seats. In first-class sat a man and a woman in the second row, 2-C and 2-D. They looked up at him as though he had interrupted a conversation. The woman was clearly a student, judging from her USC sweatshirt. She reminded him of his classmates who were more focused on their classes than themselves. As long as their clothes passed the smell test and they caught the bus to get to class in time—sometimes from someone else's home from the night before. Darren had been guilty of that as well. The man, in his crisp jacket, was dressed like he was selling a car. Or maybe, judging by the size of the man's torso, he could be attending a sports press conference.

Darren chose 1-A and stowed his duffle in the overhead, sat in his seat, and immediately buckled in. He double-checked to make sure he had his thumb drive. His phone buzzed in his other pocket, and he pulled it out to see what wanted his attention. The latest notification was a group chat app's direct message. The older notification from this morning was a text from his dad: *"COME HOME!" A little late for that, Dad*, he thought. Of course, it might not be too late. His father could call the police. With the influence his dad had, he might find out which flight Darren was on and report his missing son. He might even have someone waiting for him when Darren stepped off the plane and drag his ass back home. But he was nineteen now. He was an adult, and that wouldn't work. Right?

Darren spotted a female flight attendant move to close the door to the plane. This was it. He looked over his shoulder at the two people, who had resumed their conversation. Was it just the three of them? Maybe there were others in general seating. A voice on the intercom spoke in German briefly. Still worried that his dad had the power to stop him, he wondered if the voice translated to "Get that guy off the plane!"

The flight attendant came up to him. She wore a crisp navy-blue uniform with a gold color stripe on each cuff and a matching gold-colored facemask. "We're about to take off. Would you like some champagne once we're in the air?" she asked in a bright German accent.

Darren took that to mean this was really happening. "Yes, thank you." He smiled as much as he could with his eyes. At best, he would look more tired than happy. He could feel the bags under his eyes against his facemask.

He wasn't sure how to pull off having champagne with his mask on. With a straw perhaps. If the manifest only had three passengers, there might be enough space not to worry about masks. This was in such contrast with his past several hours stuck in a confined space with total strangers, not knowing who was a carrier. When Darren had spent the past few months alone with his parents, he didn't have to worry about masks or other people. Suddenly, overwhelmed with claustrophobia, he was surrounded by them in tightly confined spaces.

The plane made its way on the tarmac, and the screens in front of all the seats started a welcome video. It was in German with English subtitles. A man in a similar navy-blue uniform suit with its golden-yellow tie explained how and when to use the seat belts, where the emergency exits were located, what to do in the event of a water landing, and something else, but Darren was already looking at his phone, checking his messages from his group chat.

Anon28D36: You're doing the right thing. Also very brave, kid. Either way I'm roofing for you.

Anon28D36: *rooting

Anon9G32A: Thanks. Just made the final flight. If you hear from me, you'll know it worked. Deleting app.

Darren hit "send" and closed the chat app, then deleted it from his phone. He set his phone to airplane mode before a flight attendant could complain. He checked his other apps to see if any of them needed to be deleted. One was an end-to-end encryption chat app. Deleted. Two other group chat apps. Also deleted. An authenticator app required by one of the apps he'd just deleted. Not deleted; that one had been a pain to set up, and he wasn't going to go through all that again. Two dating apps, four video apps, email—those were fine. Zenith Pharm's official testing program app. The rest were first-party apps. He switched to the music app.

In a cabinet embedded in his seat, Darren found a complimentary pair of headphones. He put them on, connected them to the phone, tapped "play," and closed his eyes. He'd done it; there was no going back. Relief washed over him. His shoulders lowered, his neck cracked as he twisted his head and relaxed his jaw. He sank back into the deep cushions.

Through the headphones, electronic music beating away, the roar of the engines picked up. Darren felt the inertia of acceleration; this was always his favorite part of a plane trip. His body was pulled down farther into the seat as the plane lifted into the sky. For several minutes it kept going up and up. He turned to look out the window to see the world shrink below him and float away until there was just the ocean and clouds.

A chime rang out just loud enough to make its way to his ears. The same flight attendant and a male attendant, in the same outfit as who'd appeared in the safety video, stood at each aisle of the cabin.

"Lady *und* gentlemen," the first attendant said. Darren pulled off his headphones to listen. "We are now at cruising altitude. Our air filters are running at full capacity. You may now take off your masks." Both attendants reached up and removed their golden-yellow masks to reveal bright, impressive smiles.

Darren looked back at the only two other people on the plane. Both were as wide-eyed as he must have been.

"The same filter systems used in highly sensitive facilities and hospitals are installed on this plane," the attendant continued. "It's quite safe. I am Heidi. This is Michael. We will be bringing your drinks out shortly." Heidi turned toward the drink bar next to her and set out glassware. Michael, the other attendant, walked to the back and disappeared through the exit to the other part of the plane.

Hesitantly Darren pulled off his mask and stowed it in the storage cabinet in front of him. The bridge of his nose was slightly red from the friction. *Clean filtered air*, he thought. *Virus free.* He couldn't tell the difference; it still smelled the same.

"Excuse me." The voice was soft and polite. Darren turned back toward the two passengers behind him. The woman continued, "Maybe you could help us settle a bet?"

Darren suddenly felt a little foolish remaining so far apart from the two other people he'd be spending the entire flight with. Here they were already getting to know each other, and he was avoiding them out of habit of social distancing. Darren came over to the seat in front of the woman. She was pale with clean skin and long brown hair, pulled into a ponytail that hung over her gray school sweatshirt with red letters that spelled "USC Trojans" and her fitted distressed jeans. By her appearance and the way she sat, she looked like the most relaxed person on this flight.

The man, even sitting down, looked taller than Darren. He had a law line only slightly sharper than his sport jacket. He dressed as though he belonged at a sports press meeting. His eyes were blue, and they looked directly at Darren, making him avert his own eyes to avoid getting lost in them.

Darren almost reached out his hand but stopped at the last second to make a raised-hand gesture. For a moment, he forgot they needed to keep some distance. He had just come from a flying petri dish, after all. "Hi, I'm Darren Montoya."

"Alice Whitmore!" she replied. Her voice was delicate but possessed enthusiasm. Like she just started sharing a great story. She boldly held out her hand. "Nice to meet you. Don't worry; I've got plenty of hand sanitizer."

The man also raised his hand with a half grin that betrayed a laugh line and tiny creases next to his blue eyes and blonde lashes. "Spence Dixon," he said confidently. He could have said his name was Clark Kent, and Darren would have believed him. "I guess this is it, huh? Just the three of us?"

"On the whole plane?" Darren asked as he looked toward the general-seating cabin. "This is it?"

Michael reemerged with warmed towels for each of the three passengers. Each took one and freshened their faces, then resumed introductions.

"I arrived first and the plane was empty. Only you two came on board after," Alice said. "Spence was telling me his previous flight was empty as well."

"Where from?" Darren asked

"Oregon. I mean, from Oregon. I'm at school in Massachusetts," Spence clarified. "I was part of the bubble program at Harvard for prelaw, but even that got shut down when one of the faculty got sick. I ended up living in a dorm with nineteen other students." Spence just had to drop in his Harvard credentials, Darren noticed; he also picked up on how he'd paused after "prelaw" for effect.

As they talked and gave their introductions, Heidi arrived with drinks, along with three small dishes of macadamia nuts, and served the three passengers beverages on their corresponding trays. Darren took his champagne, sans straw.

"What about you?" Alice asked.

"SF State," Darren said. "Undeclared."

"Oh, is that where you were staying?" Alice asked. "I was at USC, but I came home after the school shut down. I couldn't afford to stay there with rent and no work and all."

"No, no," Darren clarified, "Sorry. I mean I was attending SFS. But I've been living with my folks. Helping them out. Mom mostly. She can't afford to get sick. My dad works from home, running his software company. And I've been living at their home twenty-four seven. But my flights here were insanely crowded. Maybe I should keep my mask on just in case, you know, I picked up something."

"Come on. You're not that ugly. Right?" Spence laughed at his own joke. Darren couldn't tell if that was an insult or a compliment. "These filters?" Spence pointed up at nothing in particular, "They're Dixon/Meyers. They're the only ones FDA approved as being a hundred percent effective in killing the Ozark virus," Spence was more than happy to assure his cabin mates. "It's more effective than being outdoors."

"Dixon? As in Spence Dixon?" Darren asked.

Alice mouthed "wow" before taking a drink from her glass.

"It's my dad's company," Spence admitted. "Honestly I didn't know they were being used on planes. It wasn't until the stewardess—I mean, flight attendant! Sorry—mentioned it."

"So you're the heir to the filter empire?" Darren asked.

"Father"—he said the word with a deliberate aristocratic accent—"was in the lamp business, specializing in ultraviolet lamps and tents, like for plants. When the outbreak started, he came up with a way to use the lamps as a way to 'nuke' the virus. It's not good on people, but UV light kills it. He partnered with the guy, Meyers, who did ventilations. Got some capital funding, hired some engineers, and made it happen. The next thing we know, it gets fast-tracked through the FDA, and hospitals in New York begin using it. They don't even bother field testing or doing whatever trials you have to do—the urgency was so high."

Alice made an approving nod. "Could you imagine if they could get this into every school? Every bar and restaurant even? Are they expensive to make?"

"Expensive enough," Spence said with a shrug. "We can't make them in China yet. The US government is blocking it from happening. Which is stupid, this isn't groundbreaking tech. It's just nuked air!" Darren read Spence's resentment about not expanding to China as more of a reflection on how his father must feel about it.

"How about this?" Alice was looking at her seat's video display playing its animation, with "Zenith Pharm, a Monostori Company®" constantly reminding the passengers who was paying for their meal. "New York hospitals are at the moment now managed by Zenith, right? They clearly liked your dad's product so much they put it on this airline. They're probably using the filtration system at the place we're staying too." She gave a wry smile. "Daddy pull some strings to get you here?"

Darren wouldn't have told someone he'd only just met that their "daddy" was pulling strings. Alice was clearly much more familiar with Spence than Darren. To Darren's relief, Spence laughed and gave her the finger.

Darren couldn't help wear a perpetual grin. This was the first time in months he'd been around people his own age, in close proximity. It was an odd moment, he realized. IRL! In sixteen hours, there would be more of them. Talking to each other, sharing dumb jokes, arguing over movie franchises.

Alice held up her rum and Coke. "Fellas, here's to a safe

flight and good friends."

"And a cure," Spence added.

"Yes!" Alice affirmed, and took a satisfyingly slow sip from her rocks glass. She held it for a few seconds before swallowing.

Darren didn't know much about champagne. He knew that it knocked him on his butt, so he counted on it this time in hope of some rest after an anxiety-filled day. For a moment, among hopefully new friends, everything felt a bit more promising and bubbly.

Dinner was served later that evening. Despite the flight compromising just three passengers in their late teens and early twenties, with the palettes of Taco Bell enthusiasts, the crew still ran their flight as though it served rich jet setters, world leaders, and millionaires. For an appetizer, Darren took a look at the menu when it was handed to him. Lacking confidence in ordering the correct thing, he went with what was the simplest.

"Simple," however, was a relative term. His dinner began with Jerusalem artichoke with beluga lentils and goat cheese and pumpernickel. Spence wanted to try the "weirder route" of pan-fried slices of oxtail filled with porcini mushrooms. Alice chose caviar and garnishes.

Spence grimaced at Darren's plate. Darren paused and glanced up at Spence's reaction. "What?"

It turned out Spence never had had artichoke. "I don't eat strange plants. I had okra once, and it was awful."

"You chose oxtail, but artichoke is too weird?"

Spence shrugged. "This is meat and mushrooms."

"It's really good. Here, try this." Darren pulled a fleshy leaf from his plate. "Here comes the artichoke plane." He made propeller plane noises while guiding the roasted piece of vegetable to "the hangar" of Spence's face. Darren briefly feared this might not be the kind of interaction Mr. Yale machismo would appreciate, but Spence didn't flinch or react. He dead face watched as Darren's hand inched closer and closer, as though they were in a standoff, until it was too close and Spence's mouth pinched and muttered, "uh-uh" in disapproval.

Alice covered her mouth to laugh while chewing. "You can't have one piece of artichoke? Something you never tried?"

Darren set the artichoke leaf on Spence's plate. Spence, caving to peer pressure, took the piece by the fork and put it in his mouth. He chewed a couple times and said with a full mouth, "This is disgusting." He forced himself to choke down the offending fleshy leaf.

"You ate a vegetable! Good job" Alice slowly clapped.

"Honestly," Darren said, wiping his fingers clean with a napkin, "some of that was probably hand sanitizer."

For the main course, Darren chose beef tenderloin with peppercorn sauce, and smoked mashed potatoes. Spencer ordered creamy veal goulash with mini savoy cabbage and spätzle, a German breaded noodle dish. "When in Deutsch-land," he said. Alice opted for the dish as well. For dessert they all agreed on cardamom crème brûlée.

Food and chatter settled into quiet observation once the plates were taken away. By the time the sun had set, only the cabin lights lit their surroundings. The inflight movie was a computer-generated action flick staring Bill Forge, or his likeness at least. Darren turned off his screen. Heidi came back with a small stack of folded brown clothes, offering each of them pajamas to change into. Alice took her up on it. She got up and accepted the top pajama set and went to change in the lavatory.

Darren glanced at his phone; it was past six on the East Coast. It must be a few hours later in whatever time zone they were flying over. He took a set of pajamas from Heidi and retrieved his toothbrush and paste from his duffle bag. While he waited for Alice's return, Spence stood up to remove his jacket. Darren noticed he was tall enough that he risked grazing the ceiling. As he pulled the jacket off his shoulders, he asked. "You think they have a coat hanger?"

"I doubt it," Darren replied. "They have caviar, champagne, hot towels, and sleeping clothes, but no hangers."

Spence gave him a slight glare as he left to find a closet for his jacket.

Alice came back donning the brown PJs, carrying her clothes in her arms. She looked at Darren, who was holding a pair of his own pajamas. "Bathroom's all yours."

The bathroom was spacious, large enough to lie down, with room to spare. Darren changed into the pajamas and pulled out the USB drive from his pants pocket. He couldn't risk it falling out and getting lost. He caught himself in the mirror holding the drive. His eyes were heavyset and weary from travel. "You are *so* in deep, man," he whispered.

For the past several hours, he hadn't given any thought to the real reason he'd signed up for this two-month study. Now it was foremost on his mind. The tasks he was set to accomplish played in his mind once again. Attach the drive to the first server he could find, expose it to an outside Internet connection, and report its IP address to the application waiting at the other end. Three easy steps, ones Darren practiced doing several times before leaving. But he began to doubt himself. He didn't know what he was walking into;

for all he knew, all the students would be stuck in their rooms, and he'd never get access to any servers. He'd never obtain the secrets he promised to deliver to GenNTech, Zenith Pharm's top competitor.

As he opened the door to the lavatory leave, he suddenly stopped when he nearly collided with a wall. No, not a wall. Darren looked up along a white broad undershirt to find Spence waiting for his turn to change.

"They've got lockers for us to use if you need one." Spence leaned in a bit and tapped Darren's shoulder. "They come with hangers, by the way."

"Ah! Mystery solved."

Darren got the full sense of just how tall Spence was. Darren wasn't short; he considered himself average height. Even though he towered over his folks, he found himself eye to eye with most of his friends. Spence, however, was a good half foot taller. The lavatory might have been roomy, but the hallway was barely wide enough for them to pass. Darren stepped aside as Spence moved to enter. As they passed, Darren's body recoiled at their awkward proximity. It wasn't the kind of closeness he knew from a packed bar or a party where people freely crowd around one another without much thought. It wasn't from being around someone without a mask either. It was the towering presence of the giant in front of him that made him uneasy—and the rich jock kind as well. He knew all too well how guys like Spence acted when it came to protecting their hypermasculinity. He'd had more than one experience in school when a jock had shoved him against the locker wall for the crime of a lingering look or, less, merely existing.

Spence smelled of fresh deodorant; no, this was too close.

But then Spence blurted, "See you later" and hurriedly closed the door.

Darren immediately returned to his seat and stowed his clothes and thumb drive into his duffle bag. A soft black blanket waited, neatly folded on his seat. He sat down with the blanket pulled over his lap and tried to figure out which part of the seat he needed to activate to recline. He looked over his seat with its numerous pockets, hideaway tables, and over-the-chair snake light, but got lost trying to figure out how to transform it into a bed. Finally he turned to Alice and asked, "Hey, which buttons do that?"

Alice already had figured out how to adjust the seat into a bed and was getting settled in with her phone and earbuds. When she lifted the arm cover of her seat, green LED buttons glowed, showing all the various ways the chair could adjust. "Just use this one here." She pointed to a button with an icon resembling a bed.

Darren found his chair buttons and positioned his chair to lean back further, but not all the way. He pulled out his phone and opened to his notes app to review the instructions GenNTech had given him. He used the storage container in front of him as a footrest, pulled the blanket up to his shoulder, and immediately fell asleep.

* * *

When the pandemic hit, Darren was living with his parents in their Mountain View, California, home while he attended state college. His mother was already immuno-compromised after a bout with breast cancer, so his family didn't take any risks when it came to exposure. They paid for the best commercial filters. No one left the house. Every surface was sanitized regularly. Every purchased item was delivered and dropped off outside, then cleaned before use.

For Darren's parents, the inconvenience of lockdown only extended to no longer being able to dine out at restaurants and go shopping. For Darren, he might as well have been grounded. Living at home wasn't his idea to begin with. But he didn't do well on his college entrance exams, and San Francisco State University became his only option after his dad pulled some strings.

By his parents' logic, living at home made perfect sense. The cost of living in San Francisco was too high for a student. Being at home would keep Darren from being distracted from his studies. Being in lockdown might as well have been their idea.

His parents were already on his case for his grades and drug use, and they just about burned the house to the ground when they saw his arm tattoo sleeve. Darren hated that they were such hypocrites about how he lived his life. His dad, as recently as a few years ago, had gotten his own tattoo of a two-headed goat on his chest. Both were college dropouts. They often reminisced over their early years: the parties, the concerts, the drugs. Based on the photo albums they kept, they were right. Back then, they were young, attractive adults with the energy to frequently party with friends. His father, a proud second-generation American, for all his indiscretions during his youth, was now a strict father locked arm in arm with a protective mother.

When Darren tried to assert himself, or point out their double standards, they'd say the same thing: Darren was too irresponsible, or too young, or the world was too different and dangerous now, or the classic "As long as you're living in this house, *chino*..." An ironclad defense Darren lost to every time.

It wasn't all bad. He and his dad had set up a home gym in the garage together. Getting the parts turned out harder than they'd realized. Any gym equipment worth having was out of stock. So Darren's dad showed him how to set up software to monitor websites for changes. Once a product page switched from "Out of stock" to "Add to cart," the software would notify him.

His dad spent most of the day in the spare bedroom/office on conference meetings. No longer the breakout software engineer who'd written a small artificial intelligence program, Darren's dad moved on to becoming a CEO who pushed his tiny program into a publicly traded company, DynaImaging. When it wasn't sucking up other small software companies into its behemoth enterprise software, it was performing data modeling that powered everything from autonomous video game characters, to cutting-edge computer graphic realism in movies, to genetic research for Zenith Pharm, which owned a major portion of his dad's company. Darren remembered the moment when Zenith Pharm started working with DynaImaging. His dad was so happy, almost giddy. His business took off, sure. More important to Darren's dad, the software got better—astronomically better. The resulting improvements trickled throughout DynaImaging's various software suites, and the results were staggering. What was thought to take years for artificial intelligence to achieve, his dad was boasting results of in days.

Darren's mother had set up a small workstation at the kitchen table to work with the other board members of her fundraising scholarship event for the academy he had attended as a kid. She got involved in helping as soon as Darren started attending classes there. It wasn't much work, as far as he could tell. But he could tell she really enjoyed the work, and it kept her mind off what was happening just beyond their house's walls.

Meanwhile, Darren spent all day in messaging in chat rooms and playing games with his friends. Paranoid that his dad would check the firewall logs, or whatever it was that tech dads did when they wanted to snoop, Darren made sure he used a VPN at all times. When he'd eventually lose interest in the same chat rooms and online games—or binging on streaming channels or even porn—boredom nudged him toward darker areas of the web.

The algorithms used by various sites to keep users engaged had pulled him toward political video essays and long blog articles. What followed was more and more fringe and conspiratorial. The articles were interesting at first, like the ones about inside jobs and Deep State politics. Conspiracy videos were in abundance and became gateways for far-right ideologies and anti-Semitic rants that garnered millions of views.

Darren wondered how much of the recommendation software was a part of his dad's company.

The rabbit hole of machine-curated content eventually found him watching reaction videos to a documentary called, *Zenith Pharm Controls the World*. This caught Darren's interest: Zenith Pharm had a controlling interest in DynaImaging.

All the "video reactions" were nearly identical in tone and structure, but none of them had a link to the original documentary. "Hey, everyone," one such video began. "I'm sure you've seen the video that's going around that's caused quite a bit of discussion." *No, I haven't*, Darren thought. "So I wanted to weigh in and offer some thoughts about what it all implies. However, I want to be clear in that I do not agree with the allegations made in the video. This is pure speculation. Also, at the risk of my channel shutting down over copyright issues or whatever, I won't be showing any of the footage from the video. This is a bit of a spoiler discussion, so if you haven't seen the video for yourself, well, you were warned."

Darren tried to search for the video itself with no luck. Maybe it had been taken offline. Did Zenith Pharm purge it from existence? That only made Darren more interested in finding it. He reached out to the people who made the reaction videos to see if they knew where the video might be accessible. Eventually someone messaged him back with a link he could use.

The forty-five-minute film was less of a video than a glorified slideshow with audio. The narrator had augmented his or her voice and laid out the theory that Zenith Pharm was interconnected to hundreds of powerful companies and politicians. Through their network, they were a secret government that controlled anyone and everyone. Phone companies used cellular data to track people's movements. That data was used by machine learning to model the behavior of the population to create "sickness forecasting" to manipulate stocks by providing well-timed vaccines.

The video slideshow flipped animated diagrams of various well-known companies with thick red lines that strung them together, decorated with newspaper clippings as evidence. A recent South African Ebola outbreak was resolved thanks to emergency vaccine manufacturing just after Zenith Pharm had filed a patent for a new antibiotic they'd developed.

The video went on to explain that Zenith Pharm used

analytic data on social media to influence people to stop taking vaccines for smallpox. They manufactured a debate about the current vaccine's efficacy and safety so they could have huge sales when they introduced a new smallpox competitor.

The video finished with its final theory that the Chinese government owned a stake in Zenith Pharm. By manipulating people into getting sick, or avoiding vaccinations, China was tricking Americans to be weaker. The final slides faded into images of Chinese Olympic athletes holding up their numerous gold medals.

Darren felt a bit let down. He wanted an exposé, something investigative and concrete. Instead he'd seen paper-thin scraps made out of common truths. Companies bought other companies all the time; they even bought stocks in other companies. It must have been last week when Dyna-Imaging started negotiations to acquire yet another business. Darren's father was excited about the news. They'd use machine learning to plot evolution paths of bacteria. But that's not a conspiracy; that's preparing for when certain antibiotics stop working because the bacteria become too resistant.

Incensed that this video was taken seriously, Darren tried to debunk it. He left comments that pointed out the obvious bits that didn't make sense. Surely, that would deflate its credibility. Instead he got angry comments. When he suggested the conspiratorial aspects of the video were as ludicrous as other theories, like a flat earth or a fake moon landing, he was called naïve. When he accused the video of being racist and anti-Semitic, he received a string of racial epithets.

Not all the responses were bad. Some users engaged

with him and posited their own "evidence." One user noted that Zenith had taken over New York's hospital system. Now people were disappearing for experiments under the pretense they'd died of the Ozark virus. Another user suggested Zenith had manufactured the virus and falsified the reports that it occurred in nature. And another user accused Zenith of buying television studios to promote their products through new TV shows. An example was a new reality show, *Mommy Issues*, about a group of bipolar women in Los Angeles. Another was a young adult vampire drama, *Multi-Bitamin*, where the main characters had to take supplements in order to endure sunlight.

Another user claimed to have proof that CEOs and politicians were connected because they belonged to a cult:

I worked at a law firm and won a settlement on a class-action suit against Zenith Pharm. The firm frequently represented Zenith in legal matters. While I didn't make partner or anything, my colleague and I were invited to join an executive training course called Path of The Shepherds. I'd never heard of it; they have no website. I couldn't find anything about them online. But I went to a few of classes. The first Collection of Learning—that's what they called their classes—was the same generic motivation mumbo jumbo. I did, however, make some introductions in what I thought would be good business connections. From what I could ascertain, these were people who worked for companies already in "the network."

The next Collection of Learning was different. It focused on keeping pacts, keeping what's between us just between us, because being outside of the pact is "corruption of achieving success." Their exact words!

Even the discussions in our meetings were to be kept between us. In other words, no snitching. Later classes were about the human mind and the hidden power we haven't tapped into. And for every point they made, they had symbols they drew on the whiteboard, almost like hieroglyphs. By the end of the meeting, the whiteboard looked like another language had been scrawled across it. No, I didn't take a picture.

By then I knew it was nonsensical, but, again, great for my career. That is, until they started the class with a ceremony. Lights out, red candles in front of a video screen. Someone I didn't recognize spoke through teleconference. At first I thought it was like a fraternity hazing thing. But I learned the Shepherds believe in the "exchange of power": what is behind you is how to get to what is in front you. To get what is behind you and in front of you, you must see both with two heads. I saw the symbol for the exchange of power on the screen and recognized it immediately.

Now, I've been to the office gym with my bosses and noticed their tattoos before. I thought it was from a band in the sixties. These guys were old and probably got them at Woodstock or whatever. But in the darkness, on the screen decorated by those fucking red candles, was their tattoo: a goat with two heads.

That was too much for me. I dipped, as they say. My leaving the program didn't go well. I had several urgent meetings with my bosses, who explained the importance of know what's right and said I should take a hard look at my future. I ended up quitting and moving to another city. Now I work in immigration law. Point is, I've seen that tattoo afterward in the news. Recognize this guy?

Attached was a screenshot from a tabloid site. Some paparazzi had managed to capture Bill Forge at his private beach, sporting the same goat tattoo on his back. He was starring in a movie that was supposed to be entirely AI generated. An entire blockbuster movie without the need for a studio or crew—just his likeness and voice acting. Darren's dad was quite excited about it.

> This other picture is from an autopsy of Senator Kent Dashert in 1952 (way before Woodstock). He was assassinated after being accused of being a communist. Notice the same goat tattoo on his back. His head wound wasn't included in the report as his entire head was removed. Reasons unknown.

The next image was a black-and-white photo of a half-naked old man with a fat back with the same tattoo next and a large opening in his flesh, likely a gunshot wound.

> Look, it's possible this isn't a cult. Maybe it's a really stupid club that takes itself too seriously, like the Masons. The point is, if there were ever an Illuminati that secretly ran the world, it's not some drug company; it's the Shepherds.

Darren felt cold, his arms prickling with goose bumps. DynaImaging meddled in other industries and grew larger with each acquisition. In Darren's world, it only meant his family got richer. His dad's company was based in the most affluent part of the tech industry. In Darren's mind, it made sense that AI software would be highly sought after. Could his dad have gotten those acquisitions and deals through a network of cult members instead? *Now who's the crazy one?* he thought.

More comments continued after the post. Users flipped back and forth between the Shepherds being a secret cabal of billionaires or a religious cult that trafficked children to drink their blood; others said they sold their souls for immortality or spouted on about whatever favorite conspiracy theory they could.

Whoever made the original post didn't reply to any of them. *Maybe that's all he knows about the Shepherds.* Darren decided to add to the chatter and created an account for himself using an anonymous email; he was assigned the handle "Anon9G32A."

> *I know for a fact that the CEO of DynaImaging has a goat tattoo. I recognize him from my gym. It's clearly visible on his back. This must be how DynaImaging is connected to Zenith Pharm.*

He submitted the comment and immediately thought he should delete it. He was narcing on his own dad after all. He refreshed the page, and there was a comment on his comment.

> *Bullshit. As if some millionaire goes to a public gym. The only way you'd see the tattoo was if you were fucking him. It's a secret mark, remember? Not exactly something to show off. Nice try.*

Darren wrote back.

What's more realistic? That I go to the same gym with a rich person I saw in the locker room or that they're all trafficking children and drinking blood? Whatever.

There was a new email in the fake account he'd set up.

From: Anon22ffe2

Subject: Can you prove any of it?

Juan Montoya doesn't belong to a gym or sports club. He used to jog the park paths, but no longer. So how could you see a tattoo?

"What the fuck?" Darren's stomach dropped. Was this all public knowledge? His dad had been featured in popular magazines and done several interviews over the years, so it was likely his dad's personal life would be available to anyone searching for these kinds of details.

This was a mistake, Darren realized, and deleted his original comment and signed out. He disconnected the VPN connection and closed the laptop. He'd had enough of the dark web staring back at him.

His mom and dad were in the kitchen preparing lunch and asked him if he wanted some when he walked in to get some milk. Mom was wearing a pink-and-yellow apron while slicing cheese, and Dad was putting mayonnaise and lunchmeat on bread. They laughed at each other's dumb jokes, gossiped about their jobs. They made their son take a sandwich with him before he returned to his room. Typical cultists.

That night, feeling bored while lying in bed, Darren pulled out his laptop and signed back into the VPN to browse his usual porn sites. Out of habit he glanced at his email. There was a second email from the same user:

From: Anon22ffe2

Subject: Hi, Darren

Darren threw his laptop off him like it was a spider. They'd found him. They knew about his dad. They knew he had made that comment. He went to the window and looked out onto the street, expecting a blacked-out van to be parked in front of his house. The street was empty and dark with no traffic. He shook his head. *No. This was a lucky guess from a troll.* The dark web was full of stupid jerks with too much time on their hands. Darren was over it; he wasn't going to participate in their "red pill" group conspiracies any longer.

He picked up the laptop from where it had landed on the mattress; the email looked back at him, unread. He signed out, closed his connection, and closed the browser tab. His usual account had a new email waiting for him.

From: ian.jennings@GenNTech.com

Subject: Sorry for the scare. Let's discuss an opportunity.

Hi Darren,

 Making connections is what I do for a living, and I'm very good at what I do. It's why GenNTech hired me. We believe Zenith Pharm is performing clandestine operations that have unwittingly involved other companies. This includes your father's company,

DynaImaging Enterprise Systems. I would like to discuss this with you further.

The attached doc contains instructions for connecting to our VPN for a conference call.

—Ian Jennings

1 attachment

Darren read the email several times, trying to wrap his head around how he had come to an invitation to online chat with someone working for a direct competitor to Zenith Pharm. They must have been desperate to find some edge over their rival. *That's it,* he thought. *They'll use anything to make Zenith Pharm look bad, and they'll drag my dad down to do so.* Why they'd go so far as to make a whole string of stories and fake documents to look like his dad's stupid fucking tattoo was part of a master conspiracy to psych Darren out. *Oh, God, that's clever.*

But that meant they had to know Darren was hitting these sites. Was his VPN not secure? They would have been tracking him for who knew how long. They knew of his pervy search queries. Shit! All this to get at his dad too.

Darren realized he was starting to think just like posters on those conspiracy sites, but it didn't matter. This "Ian" from GenNTech had his number; he was persistent and would continue to reach out. Darren just wanted it all to go away.

The attachment in the email was a text file with a new VPN service and a video chat address. Darren plugged his earbuds into his laptop and added the new VPN to his network connection settings, then clicked the "connect" button. Once the connection was established, he launched the conference app. It was a live video of a bald man in his fifties with a gray goatee and glasses that reflected the screen back at the camera, his face lit in unflattering blue computer light. The city skyline behind him was San Francisco; he was close.

"Darren? I'm glad you called! I'm Ian Jennings. I work in security for GenNTech. I evaluate and assess threats to our IP and prevent theft."

Darren took a deep breath. "I don't know what you think this is, but I'm not a part of it. Whatever you've cooked up to blackmail my dad isn't going to work."

"Son," Ian Jennings said with a wry grin, "a bit of advice: next time you use a VPN service, check to see who owns it."

Darren's stomach dropped. It wasn't his dad they were blackmailing; it was him. "I haven't done anything illegal—"

Ian Jennings interrupted. "I'm sure you're not very pleased I found you. I suggest you cover your tracks better. Even anonymous browsing can be traced with the bread-crumbs you left behind." Darren's cheeks flushed. This guy had seen everything he'd done online. "Darren, that's not what we're here to discuss. We at GenNTech are concerned that Zenith Pharm's vaccine research violates established laws set by the FDA using your father's company technology in machine learning to shortcut the process."

They lost him. "How?" Darren asked. "My dad sells his software to everyone. It was because of machine learning that they predicted a meningitis outbreak a couple of years ago in Africa. It was all over the news."

"We suspect the opposite actually." Ian Jennings adjusted his posture to lean forward. "There's good evidence someone at his company used an algorithm in finding likely targets to get meningitis. They then caused a much larger outbreak by targeting people to congregate in large gatherings through social-media engineering.

"We've got the same software more or less, and we're not anywhere near the level of research they are. Zenith Pharm developed a breakthrough antibacterial drug to treat meningitis just prior to the outbreak. By engineering the outbreak in Africa, they were able to sell vast quantities and enjoy the uptick in their stocks. In fact, in the past eight years that we could analyze, their best-selling drugs came on the market around the same time people became highly sick and in need of those very drugs.

"If Zenith Pharm acquired one of the world's biggest machine-learning pieces of software, it would have been a red flag with the Justice Department. But if they're secretly working together—that's an acquisition with the serial numbers filed off."

Daren sat up straighter in bed. "Hold up. What does this have to do with the Ozark virus or the Shepherds? Do you actually believe all those theories on that site?" Darren couldn't imagine that was the case, but here he was, on a video chat with a security expert and a federal agent, implying otherwise. "You really drank the Kool-Aid, didn't you?"

"We can't identify the virus, Darren," Ian Jennings said, "It's not an arenavirus, despite what the CDC and WHO have told the populace. At least, it's not of a class we've seen before. If I thought Zenith Pharm had innovated a new way of developing a vaccine for it, and it would save billions of lives, I'd let it go. As for the Shepherds, there isn't much to go on other than it being a clubhouse with no paper trails.

"Right now the only method we have for this virus is isolation. You catch it, you die. Now we have Zenith and

DynaImaging performing dubious miracles for profits. They've done it before; they're doing it again."

"You think this virus was planned?" Darren asked.

"In the past ten years, every time we faced an emergency outbreak—be it meningitis in Africa, the recent swine flu, even measles outbreaks among children—Zenith Pharm and DynaImaging have their fingerprints all over it. Now we have a virus no one has ever heard of, and their response matches the patterns we've seen from them time and time again. We think there's ample concern they're working together in a terrible plot. We're facing an extinction-level event. We need to know what they know."

There was a long silence. Darren finally spoke. "Okay, good luck with that."

"Fortunately my luck came around when I found you." Ian Jennings's face twisted into a smirk. "Here I was trying to answer my bosses' questions as to how the competition was performing dubious miracles without having any inside information, when you came along."

"Dude." Darren held up his hands. "I don't know anything. All this stuff you're talking about? Crowd manipulation and conspiracy stuff? I can't help you."

"Sure you can! You can help keep your father out of jail. I think that'd be a big help, don't you?" Ian Jennings's smirk turned into a wide smile. "I've gathered enough dirt on DynaImaging and Zenith Pharm to hand over to the DOJ. And our lobbyists will ensure an immediate investigation. That would really suck for your family. The kind of stress it would put on your mother would be awful. She's already gone through so much."

"Hey, go fuck yourself!" Darren wanted to end the call right then, but he didn't dare.

"It's all good, Darren. We just want to know what they

know. That's it! Normally we'd hire someone to get us that information, but Zenith Pharm has become impenetrable. They moved all their research overseas. A Romanian castle they purchased for their executive retreats has been retro-fitted to house a large-scale research center. They're taking volunteers to participate in human trials."

"The Study. I've heard of it. Everyone has. I thought it was just a marketing gimmick."

Ian Jennings ignored him. "You're going with them. I can ensure that you're selected. You certainly have a back-ground that fits who they're looking for, but first you need to access your father's computer."

SPENCE WOKE UP IN A PANIC; he didn't know where he was. It was loud and his bed was unfamiliar. He sat up to get his bearings and look for clues, only to finally realize he was on a plane.

Amber lights from the aisle glowed dimly. He saw Darren's seat had a divider pulled up for privacy; Alice's seat was empty.

Spence pushed the rubble from his eyes. Alice stood at the service bar at the front of the cabin. She drank from a teacup while talking to Heidi on the other side of the bar in hushed tones.

Spence made groggy steps toward them. Heidi smiled brightly when she noticed his approach. "Would you like some warm milk to help you sleep?" she asked. Alice turned to demonstrate the cup of warm milk in her hands.

Spence shook his head. "What time is it?"

Checking her watch, Heidi responded, "It's two a.m. Eastern."

Spence tried not to yawn but failed as he spoke. "That

makes it eight a.m. in Germany, right? How long until we land?"

"About four hours from now. You've got plenty of time if you want to try to rest," Heidi said.

"I think I'll get a head start on the jet-lag thing. Can I get a coffee? And maybe a water, please?" Spence asked.

Heidi smiled again. "You got it. I just made a pot for the captain. Be right back." She turned and went to the galley behind the drawn curtains.

Alice was still nursing her cup of milk. "I got maybe an hour sleep. I'm not used to sleeping on planes, it turns out."

"Me neither. I woke up not knowing where I was," Spence recalled.

"Did you know none of the crew have left the plane in three weeks?"

"Really? Huh. So they just stay here? Where do they sleep?"

Heidi returned with a mug of fresh coffee. "We stay in a hotel. Not on a plane! Could you imagine? That would be real cabin fever." She handed him a large blue cup with steam pouring over the brim. It was too hot for Spence to sip from, but he held it and let it warm his hands until it got too hot. Heidi set a chilled bottle of water on the counter and continued. "Alice is right in that we've been doing the same flight for almost a month. There is no other work right now. International travel *ist nicht*, except for us because of the circumstances. Almost all my coworkers are furloughed. So, like you, we're part of the program too."

Spence dared a sip from his mug. "Don't you miss your family?"

Heidi shrugged. "Of course. But with me working, they can stay home and stay safe with each other. We send constant texts to make sure we're all safe."

"How many more trips are there? Is this an ongoing thing?" asked Alice.

Heidi counted the flights on the fingers of her hand. "First, it was just the employees. Then it was you, students, always in waves of eight. And a couple of single-passenger flights in between, which I don't think is very efficient."

"Seems like a waste of fuel. And then you have to take everyone back too," Spence said.

"There have been no return flights yet," Heidi clarified. "I think maybe a different airline."

Spence imagined that once The Study was done, they could pack everyone on normal planes. Everyone heading back would be confirmed having tested negative, and there would be no need for his father's air filters. Hopefully they'd come back home with a vaccine in tow.

Alice chimed in, "Heidi was telling me our layover in Frankfurt is only to get the rest of the passengers." Heidi nodded.

"How many?" Spence asked.

"Five more," Alice answered.

"A full eight, huh?" Spence gave a yawn and reached for a water bottle. "Welp, I'm going to try and wake up and get ahead of this jet lag." He turned and headed back to his seat. Alice and Heidi resumed their chat.

Spence casually peeked around Darren's seat divider. Darren was curled up on his side. Only his curly black hair could be seen through the airline-branded blanket. He reminded Spence of his dog back home, hiding in his bed. Spence resisted the urge to scratch the top of Darren's head and call him a good boy.

Spence sat back down and reached for a book he'd stowed in his messenger bag. It was a small travel guide of Romania. He'd hoped for a book that covered Monostori

Castle and its history, but he found Romania was sorely lacking in English-language books on the subject. Most online resources were only focused on the infamous castle that housed Vlad Țepeș, known today by "Dracula." Perhaps the history behind the man, the myth, the blood-sucking legend would have been an interesting read, but Spence thought it'd be "so American" to visit a country, and the only book on hand was about a fairy tale story. He imagined what it must be like for a Romanian to encounter a tourist, and all they cared about was visiting the vampire castle. For all Spence knew, they might be proud of it.

Spence adjusted his seat upright and secured his coffee cup and bottle of water. He flicked on the reading light behind him and thumbed through the pages of his book. It began with several full-color pages of photos, painted monasteries, small villages, connecting roads, mountains, and landscapes. He hoped this vaccine program allowed for enough downtime to make excursions to see the sites; maybe he could get a small group together to see some of the other castles.

Or maybe he'd just go by himself, now that he thought about it. Darren and Alice were nice enough, and they seemed to enjoy his company to a point. But he couldn't be too careful. He didn't want to be in a position where he'd slip up. When he'd passed Darren on the way to the lavatory, it was like Darren could tell Spence was all wrong; he saw it in Darren's face. The other students at Harvard couldn't; he was lucky in that sense. The dorm mates he'd stayed with during their "bubble" were more concerned about themselves and how others perceived them. As far as they were concerned, he was just a rich hick, or a dumb jock, whose dad had gotten him into school.

And they were right. Compared to them, he was dumb

and a jock. Back at his rural high school, he'd played all the sports. He'd said all the right things. He'd made all the right friends. He'd stayed away from the band nerds and theater kids. He'd acted just like his teammates. He had been religious around his parents. He was what everyone wanted him to be.

No one at school even questioned why he had disappeared for a month. After his parents caught him with the farmhand's son in his room, he went away to a church therapy camp. His family was scared for his soul and wanted him to be safe. He came back good as new, and he was going to stay that way.

And now they were sending Spence to another "camp" to be made safe. Only this camp had Darren: dark shiny hair, skin of a deep shade, that melting grin, slight body odor. Spence closed his eyes to pray.

A loud *bing* rang out, and a male voice with a thick German accent announced their approach to Frankfurt. With a jolt, Spence opened his eyes and realized he had fallen back asleep. Daylight flooded in from the windows on his right; his travel book sat closed in his lap. Alice was busy putting her hair up in a tail. She was back in her college sweatshirt and pants. He watched Darren slowly rise from the moving incline of his seat like a vampire rising from its coffin. He already had changed out of his PJs as well. Darren looked around, caught Spence's eyes, and gave a sleepy grin. Spence averted his eyes.

Michael, the flight attendant, appeared from behind the curtain at the rear of the cabin. He asked the three of them to bring their chairs upright and to fasten their seat belts. Michael reached across Spence to remove the cold coffee cup from its holder. "I'll get you a fresh cup once we land," he said, smelling like fresh aftershave.

"Hey, do I have time to get dressed?" Spence asked, already leaning forward to get up.

Michael had an air of "busyness" to him. "Yes. Please hurry, though."

Spence went to his locker for his clothes then entered the lavatory. He quickly changed, fixed his hair, splashed some cold water his face, and gave a quick smell inspection before returning to his seat and fastening his seat belt.

The plane touched down on the tarmac at Frankfurt Airport with ease and slowed into a nice mosey speed toward their designated gate.

Heidi appeared before the three of them wearing her golden-yellow mask again, her hands clasped. "We are only here to pick up the remaining passengers. Because we are taking on outside air from the airport, I must ask you to put on your facemasks for now." Spence still had his mask in his coat pocket and pulled its straps over his ears. Heidi waited for Darren and Alice to comply, then gave a short nod and headed toward the door.

Spence could just barely see her standing by the door, ready to greet the new passengers. It was a minute until the first new passenger appeared, then another, then the rest. The first two, a man and a woman in matching tracksuits, took the seats in front of him, 1-B and 1-C. They also had matching features: blond, pale, distinct eyes. Maybe Russian? Eastern European perhaps.

A woman sat next to him in 2-B. It was her perfume that he noticed first; then it was the money. He could see it in her perfectly styled shiny, wavy red hair; her tight-fitting black leather jacket with white racing stripes down the arms; and a standard blue hospital mask (something disposable after getting makeup on it, he was sure). She held up her phone in a way to take her photo straight on, then at an angle, then to the side, which brought Spence into the frame.

"Say cheese!" she directed with an affectatious French accent.

Caught off guard, Spence reactively squeaked a smiling "Cheese!" through his mask, just in time for the snapshot.

She returned to her phone, looking through the images she had taken. "Which one do you like?" she asked.

Spence craned his neck to look at her screen, "Oh. Um. I'm sure they're all good."

"Hmm," she murmured with an unaffected tone.

"I mean, the one with me in it is obviously the best one. I thought it'd be pretty obvious."

The woman gave him a side-eye glance. "I'll think about it." She set her phone in her red purse and stowed it in the storage compartment in front of her. "Can't post anyway. I'm out of minutes." She pointed her elbow toward Spence. "Hey, I'm Hannah Bell."

Spence extended his elbow and gently bumped it to hers. "Spence Dixon."

"Spence Dixon. How American," she said coolly.

"It is?" Spence didn't regard his name as ever sounding American. Western, sure. When he thought of American-sounding names, it was Mack or Buck or Dale, something bland, like Wonder Bread. "Everyone boarding is from Europe, I take it?"

Hannah nodded. "If I remember right, the two in front are brother and sister Alex and Yuri Petrov. They are Ukrainian." She gestured to the man with brown hair tied into a man bun with a well groomed beard in seat 1-A. "That's Scott Wilson, and that's..." She pointed to the last man next to her in seat 2-A. "Harry Brown. Cutest British accent ever."

Harry heard his name and looked up. "Hmm?"

Spence pointed out Darren and Alice to Hannah. Hannah recited their names to commit them to memory. She had been in Monte Carlo at the time of the outbreak, was stranded with her parents at a hotel, and hadn't been back home in Toulouse for weeks.

The plane and its crew began its ritual of flight: the captain spoke over the intercom; the plane maneuvered its way on the tarmac; and the welcome video played once again in front of everyone's seat in unison. Eight passengers from different parts of the world sat together exchanging greetings and pleasantries through their masks until finally the plane reached cruising altitude and the filters had completed a full cycle. Heidi and Michael once again came out and told the passengers it was safe to remove their masks. Spence didn't hesitate; neither did Darren or Alice. He had just gotten used to talking in close proximity without a mask and was eager to get to that stage of the flight again.

"It's fine," Spence assured Hannah, who shrugged before taking hers off.

The others eventually followed with suspicion, but soon all eight finally saw one another's faces for the first time. It was like before; Spence could see Hannah and Harry both had the same expressions of doubt. Scott, in front of Harry, looked relieved.

The flight attendants repeated their in-flight services with flutes of champagne and macadamia nuts for the new guests. Everyone enjoyed warm face towels. Michael brought Spence a fresh cup of coffee.

Scott Wilson, in 1-A, had just taken a sip of his champagne when he asked in a bright Irish accent, "So this plane has the ability to kill the Ozark virus by circulating the air? Why isn't this used everywhere?"

"I imagine they're quite expensive at the moment, don't you think?" Hannah offered. She was right. The price was too high for most people to afford. Despite efforts to mass-produce them, Spence's father had to raise a lot of initial investment capital, not only to get his filter unit through FDA—which meant paying lobbyists to lean on officials to fast-track the process—but also to spin up factories overnight just for a handful of hospitals. Even then, there was a waiting list. He was surprised to learn they were able to install them on an airplane.

Spence was about to contribute to the discussion, but he remembered how he'd sounded earlier while talking about his dad's invention. He hadn't intended to, but he'd come off like some bragging rich kid. This time he didn't volunteer that information.

The flight attendants went to each seat to unfold the table stands hidden on the side and put down tablecloths for each of the passengers. To each row, they wheeled out breakfast carts containing options of pastries, fresh fruits, meats and cheeses, creme fraiche, eggs, and bacon. Spence chose eggs and bacon and a croissant with butter and jam. His new neighbor selected blueberries, yogurt, and water.

Spence found himself surrounded by other people's conversations; there was about an hour and a half left of flight time. He thumbed his travel book to the maps and found the city of Bucharest, their flight destination. He tried to find the castle they were staying. It wasn't under "M," for Monostori. Under "C," he found a listing of castles, but Monostori wasn't included. Maybe it was under "H" for hotels or "L" for lodging, but there was no listing.

In the chapter about castles was a colorful photo of Bran

Castle, the most famous in Romania, for belonging to Dracula. As Spence scanned through the chapter, he didn't see any mention of Monostori.

Spence leaned to Hannah, who was enjoying her yogurt. "Where in Romania are we going, exactly?"

"Lupeni," she said flatly.

Spence shook his head. "That's right. I remembered the castle Monostori, not the town it was next to."

"Are you looking it up?" she asked.

"Trying to, but the castle isn't listed." He flipped back to the maps to find the town of Lupeni. It wasn't near Bucharest; it was closer toward the middle of the country near a small mountain range. Lupeni was relatively small, with a single main road. On the map, Spence traced his finger along the road markings, hiking trails, and points of interest, but nothing indicated any sort of castle.

Hannah leaned in slightly to see what he was looking at. "It's probably won't be listed as a castle on that map. It technically is a castle, but not a historical landmark or anything now that it's a bizarre research center."

Two hours later, the plane touched down at Bucharest Henri Coandă International Airport and parked just beyond the gates. The eight passengers and the crew had replaced their facemasks by the time the filter units turned off. Waiting outside the door was a staircase that led to the tarmac.

Cold wind and bright clouds hit Spence as he stepped down the boarding stairs, making his first steps in another country. Another continent, in fact. From the photos in his book, Spence expected rolling hills and snow-peaked mountains looking over the horizon. Instead, all he saw was flat land. The back of the airport runway just kept going to a vast field dotted with small apartment buildings, along with tiny cars that traveled along a road. Someone could have told him they'd landed in Kansas, and he'd believe it.

Waiting a few yards away from the end of the steps, Spence and the other passengers were greeted by a woman wearing a deep-purple blazer and black skirt. A small silver goat pin was attached to her lapel. Her hair was pulled back tightly, and she wore a black facemask with the official Zenith Pharm logo in white on its cheek. Behind her were two men in black military fatigues loading—more like tossing—luggage into the back of two black vans with tinted windows.

"Welcome to Romania!" the woman greeted the eight passengers as they walked toward her. She had a standard smile and followed it with formal nod to move business along its schedule. "I'm Ms. Ellen Birch, director of Program Enrollment for the Arenavirus Vaccine Initiative. Some of you have spoken to me personally, or folks on my team. I'm here to invite you all to Monostori Castle!"

Alice pulled out her passport to show Ms. Birch. "Are we going directly to your testing place? Don't we have to check in with customs?"

Ms. Birch briefly closed her eyes and inhaled before answering her often-prepared corporate copy. "We want to ensure your exposure to the public will be as limited as absolutely possible. To do this, you will be forgoing entering the public airport or public spaces for the duration of your stay." With a confirming smile, she gestured toward the big black vans.

"Is that legal?" Spence asked himself.

"Do you care? I don't." Scott Wilson lugged past him with a giant green satchel over his shoulder and onto the first van.

* * *

Spence spent most of the four-hour drive to the facility staring out the window to a view of fields and forests, sparse with small towns and old cars. He occasionally referred to his map to check their progress. Each town that passed was another moment closer to yet another step just to get to end this journey. It wasn't until they got past the city of Pitești, the halfway point, that Darren tried to get Spence to participate in the conversations with the rest of the van.

From behind Spence, Darren gave Spence's shoulder a firm grip. "You okay, bud?" Darren, Scott, and Harry were in his van; Ms. Birch, Alice, Hannah, Alex, and Yuri were in the other. Spence turned to Darren. He couldn't see his smile anymore but felt it anyway.

Spence shifted in his seat to face Darren, making sure his shoulder was free from Darren's warm hand. "Yeah, I'm good. I'm just tired from the flight." Spence held up his book showing the map. "We're about halfway to Lupeni, by the way."

"We were just telling each other which schools we're all from and our majors and such." Darren leaned back to his seat, pointing to Harry. "He's from the UK, studying epidermis?"

"Epidemiology," Harry clarified while fixing his overgrown bangs. "This is right in my field actually. I'm eager to learn just how Zenith thinks it can take—what?—less than a hundred people and come up with a vaccine."

"Isn't that how it happens?" Spence asked.

"No, mate. Most vaccines take years just in the first phase of exploration before ever getting around to be tested on people. Maybe they have a new process that makes testing and exploration a parallel process." Harry looked at their blank faces. "The big three phases for vaccine development boil down to research, testing, then approval. And then, after, there's the matter of getting it distributed. Each step along the way requires a ton of red tape from the EAM, the FDA, and other regulators. I think they're far more along in developing a vaccine than what they're telling the public. It's all very exciting."

"Well, sure," Scott replied from the front of the van. "They're competing with all the other drug companies in the world. If they have an upper hand, they're not going to risk some other company get an edge."

"You think they're holding back data that could help other scientists from finding a cure? Why would they do that? People are dying left and right. We're literally melting into blood," Spence said.

Scott made a fingers-rubbing-for-money gesture, "It's about the money, dude. This isn't some small team of scientists. It's a mega corp. Biggest drug company on earth. They own unfathomable resources to cure the world ten times over. They get this drug made, they'll be even richer. Think about it. ImmunoWorks, Total Health Research, GenNTech spend their days coming up with new drugs to treat the same diseases. As soon as a patent expires...*boom*! New drug to earn billions of dollars to replace the old drug."

Harry offered a counterpoint. "When it comes to antiviral and antibacterial drugs, scientists and doctors are addressing better ways to stop infections. Not all drugs made to fix a virus work the same way. Some are found to have long-term effects that newer drugs can address," he said, fixing his bangs again. "Take AZT, for example. It was fast-tracked back in the eighties to stop HIV from spreading. But it didn't really work the way they thought it did. Over time, people still got sick; the virus mutated to resist the drug; and bone marrow was being depleted. Nasty stuff. Now we have ARV and PrEP working together not to get rid of the virus but to stop its spread. And we're not stopping there either. I read there's even research trying to expose the hiding HIV-infected cells in concert with the use of the ARV."

Scott shook his head. "That'll never happen."

"It's possible." Harry corrected. "By activating T cells where HIV is hiding, it can flush them into the open, and the current drugs can reach it."

"No, I mean, there's no incentive to make HIV curable," Scott said stroking his beard to a point. "Take the common cold. Why don't we have a cure for that?"

Spence and Darren were now watching a tennis match in some great debate.

"Well, the cold is made up of several base viruses," Harry said. "And then there are all the sub viruses from those. So having one vaccine for all of them would be impossible. We haven't come up with a broad-spectrum antiviral solution like we have with antibiotics."

"No, it's because they'd lose sales. All those cold syrups and throat lozenges and pills people take for the cold," Scott said. "That's billions of revenue every year. They don't even work! They just make you boozy while your body does all the heavy lifting. Everybody in the world gets the cold a few times a year; we're customers for life. No way there would ever be a vaccine for that."

"So it's a conspiracy." Darren jumped in with intrigue. "They could find a cure, but the money is too good, huh?"

"No, it's that research takes a lot of funding." Harry wasn't having it. "And there are programs looking to find common RNA among the cold viruses that help the body identify them during an infection."

"But who funds that research?" asked Darren.

"Are you taking his side? Did you even sign up for the same vaccine program as me?" Harry really working on keep his bangs in place now.

"I mean, nobody dies from a cold," Spence added.

"Unbelievable! Anyway..." Eager to move on, Harry continued. "It's my hope at least that this 'vaccine initiative'"—he was making air quotes—"can contribute to my thesis on pandemic-response methodologies and optimizations."

Spence was impressed. "You're already writing a thesis?"

"Well, no. Not yet, actually. I'm still in my second year. But it's never too early to get a head start." He paused for a second and added. "That sounds a lot more pathetic saying it out loud."

"When you find the cold cure, you can say you told me so!" Scott laughed, deflecting from coming off so negatively regarding Harry's career path.

"Epidemiologist." Spence pointed to Harry, then to Darren. "Undeclared." Darren nodded. He pointed to himself, "Prelaw." And then he pointed to Scott.

"Poli sci, Boston," Scott answered.

"Oh, we're practically neighbors then. I'm at Harvard." Spence worried mentioning Harvard would be like namedropping. He'd gotten mixed reactions from people when it came up, as though he were bragging.

If Scott thought that was bragging, he didn't acknowledge it. "We're certainly neighbors for the next two months at least." He moved to an empty chair next to Harry to continue their debate.

Darren sat closer in his seat to Spence and spoke more

quietly, with a raised eyebrow. "Can I tell you something if you don't get mad?"

"Sure?" *This isn't good. Was I staring?* Spence thought. *Oh, God. He must have noticed me staring. So fucking stupid.*

"You don't strike me as the Harvard lawyer type," Darren said. "Not to be an asshole, but I get more of a jock vibe. Sports. Or, I dunno, a lumberjack?"

Spence scrunched his face, "Seriously? I get enough of that in school." It was true and it annoyed the hell out of him. Darren looked at the floor. "It's all good, I promise. Although I've never gotten accused of being a lumberjack."

"What else is there in Oregon?"

"Truth be told, I'm not really the Harvard type. Just ask my classmates. The sooner I finish, the better." *Why the fuck are you sharing this?* he thought.

"You don't want to be in college or Harvard?"

"I heard it was pretty easy to get a law degree at Harvard. I've met people who boast about their Harvard degree who are complete idiots. A lot of them work for my dad."

"So you're just going because it's not hard?"

Spence could feel Darren's disappointment. "I didn't have any plans for school, but my dad insisted I at least take community college classes," he explained. "But then, the pandemic happens. Dad gets rich. Suddenly he's all about his family having the life he couldn't have. Next thing I know, he's all over me to get enrolled somewhere legitimate. Most schools were already closed, but Harvard was one of the few trying the bubble thing. And it made my dad real happy to have a Harvard son so..." Spence trailed off. "Plus Harvard is a long way from Oregon."

"Lucky for you, Romania is ever farther."

* * *

It was just after noon local time. The two black vans passed through Lupeni and continued several miles on the road until they made a right turn on an unmarked dirt road heading uphill toward a large mountain range. They continued uphill until they reached what must have been the boundary of the property. Tall chain link fences with coiled razor wire ran into the woods on both sides and disappeared in the distance.

They stopped at the chain link gates long enough for a security guard to manually open them to let them pass. Spence noted the guard's holstered pistol and some kind of automatic that was slung over his shoulder.

The trees seemed smaller, less dense than he imagined. Oregon forests were deep and thick and tall. Trees covered entire hills and mountains, leaving only their rocky peaks for the snow. Here, the woods had room for giant patches of tall grass and wildflowers among flat gray rocks.

They reached the top of the hill to see more and more rolling hills that worked up to a mountain in the distance. They made another right turn onto another road that was more of a path than a road. They were no longer going uphill but still deeper into the woods, until finally they reached their destination. The driver shut off the engine, turned to his passengers, and spoke to them for the first time. "*Vino afară*," he said, making the international hand gesture for "Come here."

They all piled out while the drivers tossed the luggage from the back of the vans. Spence looked around, but there wasn't a castle in sight. Behind Ms. Birch, he saw a small white structure constructed from cinder blocks, concrete, and metal. It had a single metal gray door for an entrance; above it, a yellow light buzzed.

Ms. Birch looked among the eight guests, drawing in their confused expression. With a polite smile and clasped hands, she announced, "We're here!"

ALICE WAS IN DISBELIEF. She and the other guests stood staring at not a castle but an oversize painted brick building. Something had gone very wrong. Where were the other guests? Was this a trap? Were they being kidnapped?

Ms. Birch stared back at them as though she'd already given them a cue to do something but they'd all missed it.

Spence was the first to speak. "Is the castle underground?"

Ms. Birch's face changed from confusion to surprise. "Oh, my goodness, no! No, no, no. This isn't the castle. Monostori is a kilometer up still." She rubbed her forehead with her delicate fingers and sharp red nails. "In my haste to get all of you here, I completely neglected to mention that we must first verify there is no infection of the virus. This is our isolation facility." She waved at the white slab of a building. "This is where we must quarantine and get test-ed." Ms. Birch turned and headed for the gray door.

"Hold up! We've already tested negative. I tested nega-tive in the application, and then on the car ride to the airport." Alice pointed to the other travelers. "We've all been in close proximity to each other. For hours. Are you saying we've been exposed somehow?"

Ms. Birch held the door open to a dark unlit interior. She paused with a measured breath of patience. "This is a required step for everyone before going any farther on the property, including myself. Every time I leave the grounds to fetch our guests, I must also isolate. The good news is that isolation lasts less than a day, thanks to our better understanding of how to test for infection. If we start now"—Ms. Birch checked her watch—"well, it's just past noon now. We can have the tests administered as soon as six thirty in the morning." She observed their disappointment. "The sooner we get started, the sooner we can get to the castle and unpack." She held the door open and waited for the eight test subjects to begrudgingly enter.

Alice grabbed her luggage and followed the others inside the bunker. It was a long hallway with evenly spaced doors along the walls, each with wire-enforced windows. The end of the hall was an elevator door with an emergency exit door beside it. Alice wondered how far the elevator went down.

Ms. Birch closed the door behind her with a heavy thud that got everyone's attention. "If you could choose a room and get settled in, we can begin. We're having lunch delivered in thirty. It's a box lunch. Harry, I understand you're vegetarian?" she announced down the hall.

Harry yelled back from the other end. "No, I'm gluten intolerant, I'm afraid. No bread."

"Ah, well. To each their own, I suppose. Just eat around the bread," Ms. Birch said. "Everyone, trust me. This is the least-fun portion of the trip. Let's all make the best of it. It'll be over before you know it."

Alice found herself in a small cell with brick walls

painted white, a metal floor, and a small window. In the corner was a tiny bed next to a metal toilet next to a built-in sink. There was no way she was going to use that. "I'm in a jail cell," she muttered. "I just walked into a jail cell."

She checked the door to make sure she wasn't locked in. It opened. The door only locked from the inside. She went to the entrance of the building, and it opened to the outside too. She could leave if she wanted; she wasn't locked up. Ms. Birch was correct: this was just an isolation facility to make sure she and everyone else were cleared. A shitty isolation facility but one nonetheless.

Alice returned to her cell and lay on the bed. As the ceiling light glared back at her, she took a long breath and exhaled. It was...nice? No. Quiet. After a day of flying and driving nonstop, she was on the quiet ground. So quiet. She wondered if the others were settling into their jail time or if they were having a negative reaction to all this uncertainty. She wished Ms. Birch had mentioned this sooner. It wasn't even mentioned when she was interviewing for the program. But everyone was supposed to go through this, including everyone else already at the castle, living a vacation away from all the world's troubles.

Her thoughts turned to her friends and family. She pulled her phone from her back pants pocket; she hadn't bothered looking at it since she'd boarded the plane. There was one notification waiting for her. It was a message from Mandy sent twelve hours ago: *Thinking of you. Big hugs and have fun!*

She opened the app to reply, but it was stuck in a perpetual loading state. She had no signal and didn't think to get a SIM card for the trip.

Lunch came after a sufficient bout with boredom. A man in a white lab coat with a medical facemask and face shield handed her a brown paper bag. He then took out a thermal scanner and checked her temperature before word-lessly leaving the room. She heard the door from the next cell over open and close, then another. That would be her listening entertainment while she dug into her lunch, which consisted of a large pretzel with poppy seeds, sausage slices, cheese slices, an apple, a bottle of water, and a napkin. The pretzel was salty and oily and chewy, and she wondered if Harry wouldn't mind giving her his.

Alice only brought one book with her, a text book but not useful to pass the time with any enjoyment. Instead she opted for a nap. She turned off the light to complete dark-ness and lay on the bed, thinking about all the things described to her about the castle. She'd get to take a tour of the original structures, walk the trails, and be around people her age without the fear of bleeding to death in horrible agony.

The child of man will come to your field. Take them to your breast. Feed them to your fire that their blood runs true. Let them witness the kingdom you have built and tremble to their own small ends.

Let them fail in their path and fall before you. Remove the strong from the weak and raise them to become your right hand. For the strong are the ram, rare and worthy, vessels for my army.

Your revenge is my gift and my wrath.

* * *

The door closed loud enough to wake Alice from her nap. Another paper bag was waiting for her on the floor. How long had she slept? Her phone said it was 5:00 p.m. It was still early morning back home. If she were back in Virginia, she and Mandy would have started the day with a drive for coffee and bagels with the money they got from unemployment. They would set up on the couch to watch the morning news and maybe one of the morning talk shows before Alice went to the dining table with her course books for remote classwork.

Alice examined the contents of the bag. It was more of the same as she'd had for lunch. She wasn't very hungry but agreed to help herself to the pretzel. She retrieved one of her schoolbooks from her luggage, an anthology of philosophy essays for "Phil 200: Ancient and Medieval Philosophies." It was the only book she'd made herself bring. Alice wasn't sure how much free time she'd have or if she'd run out of things to do at a castle in a foreign land. She also felt a book on philosophy would be a good tool to help her navigate the state of the world. Here she was, practically fleeing a worldwide plague to live with a bunch of college students in an isolated castle. It was all a part of saving the world. Was it noble? Was it selfish? Why her and not someone else? At the very least, it was a book she had a hard time getting through, and it was an easy way to fall asleep to if she wasn't sufficiently caffeinated.

* * *

She lay down and drifted off. In her dream, the server was only gone a short time. He must have made the cocktail himself and immediately returned. "One hard lemonade," he said as he set the glass on the table next to her and moved onto his next station.

Alice eagerly took a long-awaited sip from the tall cool glass. Ice clinked as she pulled from the straw. Sweet and sugary, sour and crisp, the cool liquid traveled down her throat.

In front of her, a pool was filled with happy splashing and laughing men in trunks and Speedos and women in bathing suits and bikinis who batted giant inflatables about. Except for one person. Darren pulled himself out from the water and onto the deck, letting the water fall away. His black curls shook themselves loose as he walked over and lay on the deck chair next to her. His tawny beige torso sparkled from the water.

"Don't you want a towel?" Alice asked.

He laughed and turned on his side to face her. "I'll let the sun take care of drying me off." The sun beat down, and a warm breeze flowed over her bikini-clad body as they observed the pool at play. Darren took giant gulps of water from his glass until trickles dripped down his dark neck. "Isn't this great?" he said with a satisfying sigh. "We've only been here a week, and thanks to our blood tests, they found a cure! Now the rest of the trip is just us."

Alice heard someone cough nearby. Usually that would be a cause for panic. Coughs meant sickness. Not here, though. It was probably someone getting pool water down the wrong pipe. Not worrying about that cough meant not worrying about being around strangers. Not having to wear masks. No more people dying from an unstoppable illness.

"It's such a relief, to be honest. And to have met every-one. Including you." Alice's gaze flowed down Darren's torso and felt her suit tighten. This wasn't the place for getting physical, but she let herself reach out and touch Darren's hand.

Darren made a sympathetic face. "Maybe you should focus on getting better, don't you think?" He glanced at something next to her.

Alice looked over to the IV pole and tube inserted in her arm. Someone was still coughing, but no one around the pool looked to be struggling at clearing their lungs. Darren's look of sympathy turned to worry.

"I'm fine, though," Alice protested. "I tested negative."

"You're coughing so much," Darren said. But Alice wasn't coughing! Her breathing was fine; someone else was coughing. Darren rose from the deck chair and took a step back. "Maybe I shouldn't be near you. It looks like you're sick."

"I'm not coughing! I feel fine." Alice protested. Everyone in the pool turned their attention to her. Alice looked for whoever was coughing but couldn't see anyone. She reached for the tube in her arm to remove it and recoiled at the sight of her skin. Beads of red sweat had collected on her arm. She tried to wipe it away, but the warm sticky red substance kept seeping through like a rag being wrung out.

Blood dripped from Alice's bare stomach and thighs onto the deck. People screamed. She tried to stand, but the deck chair held her in place; she couldn't escape its slippery cushions. Now Darren was gone, and everyone was scrambling out of the pool in a panic.

Two figures in hazmat suits rushed to her and grabbed her by the arms. Pinned by the rubber gloves, she was pushed downward. They pushed her through the chair. The pool deck below her gave way. She fell into the ground, ever downward, until the IV pole caught her by the arm and suspended her over a deep black hole.

She tried to grip the IV tube with her other hand but couldn't reach it.

"You." Alice looked into the blackness. A voice. A gaze. A presence unseen. "Come. I will fill you. Feed you. Or destroy you." The IV tube slipped out of her arm, and she fell, flying quickly into a sea of utter darkness until she threw herself awake with as much of a violent jerk she could muster.

Alice was back in her cell. She frantically checked her body for blood. Her hands were shaky, and she was sweaty, but there wasn't any blood. And there was no puncture mark in her arm where an IV drip had been. Her hair and clothes felt damp from sweat. She could smell herself and realized she desperately needed a shower.

"Fucking hell," she muttered through deep breaths. She'd had a long day of traveling, sleeping in strange and unfamiliar places. It must have taken a bigger toll on her than she realized, and quite frankly she didn't appreciate what her dream world had come up with. She reached for her phone, which rested under the overturned philosophy book. It was 2:35 a.m.

Alice reached into the paper bag provided for dinner and pulled out the bottle of water, which she drank in almost one go. After replacing the bottle cap, she heard coughing. It was coming from the other side of the wall. There were other sounds too. A door opened nearby, and several sets of footsteps and chatter competed with the coughs. She went for the door to find out what was happening, but the door was locked.

She checked her lock on the doorknob, but it wasn't in position. *The door must be magnetically locked*, she thought.

She banged on the door. "What's going on? Is everything all right? What's happening?" she shouted, and listened for a response. She heard other knocks too from farther away.

She knocked again. "Hey! Open up!"

The door made a clunk sound before opening to a figure in a white hazmat suit holding a white plastic container shaped like a lunch box. Alice felt a tinge of panic in her chest, and she remembered the dream of two figures in hazmat suits pushing her into the earth. She tried to look out into the hallway, but the figure stepped in front of her.

"We need to test you now," the woman said urgently. She stepped into the room, and the door closed behind her. Her tone was curt. "Have a seat on the bed. We'll start the test now."

Alice was about to comply, but the coughing sounded worse.

"Who was coughing next door? Are they okay?" she asked the woman in the suit. When she didn't respond, Alice took a step toward her, and the woman flinched. Alice asked once more, "What's going on here?"

The woman adopted a less stern tone. "Scott Wilson is in the next room. He began showing signs of infection. He has a high temperature and is having difficulty breathing. The coughing you heard..." She held up her container. "We're moving him to an on-site medical-care facility. If you and the rest of your unit have been exposed, the virus has been in your system long enough for us to detect it. We were going to wait until morning, but the test is sufficiently accurate enough." The woman held out a free hand to gesture toward the bed.

She followed Alice to the bed, sat next to her, and opened the container. Alice watched with interest as she pulled out a large sterile tube that held a long plastic swab, a white credit card-size two-layer piece of cardboard, a digital timer, and a small white fluid-solution container that reminded Alice of what her dad used to clean his contact lenses.

"You've probably seen something like this on the news," the woman said. She opened the tube and pulled out a swab.

Alice set herself in position. She was familiar with this; in fact she had taken the swab test a couple of times already. Just like the first time, the woman had Alice lean her head back so she could insert the swab into her nose. Alice felt the pointy pressure of the swab move into her nose, pushing what felt like the front of her brain; then it was rotated to get a sample around the entire swab. And just like that, the swab was removed. It was only for a second, but Alice felt every millisecond of it.

The woman opened the card, placed the swab against a strip of paper inside, and applied the contact lens solution on it to activate the strip of paper and pick up the gathered material from the swab.

"This will only take a couple of minutes," said the woman.

Alice looked at the folded cardboard; the entry hole had a drawn line inside it. "When I had the swab test, they had to send it away to a lab, and it took seven days to get results," Alice recalled.

"This isn't anything new. We can test for antigens of any virus this way," explained the woman. "Just like with a pregnancy test, we're looking for specific genetic markers that tell us if the virus is present. If it is, there will be a second line. Normally a test like this isn't effective in testing asymptomatic people. But this is one special virus." They watched the card in silence.

Alice's thoughts went to Scott, and the sound of his coughing playing over in her mind, invading her dream. "Is Scott going to be okay?" she asked.

The woman, who remained focused on the card, answered, "You're aware of the mortality rate? It's not looking good for him. We have an aggressive antiviral therapy regimen we can perform on him here. You and the other participants signed a waiver for it already, should anything happen. But even then, the long-term outlook for his health is grim." The woman paused and gingerly rotated the card to make sure the solution inside was completely covering the strip. "Did you know Mr. Wilson?"

Alice shook her head. "Not really. We hadn't had a chance to meet yet."

More noise came from Scott's cell. The woman said, "His room is being sanitized. Wiping down the handles, washing the bed, things like that."

A digital timer sounded three short beeps. The card had only one line; Alice wasn't infected. Relief washed over her. Every time she'd had a test result come back negative, it had always relieved her stress, but this one felt more consequential.

"You're clear," the woman said clinically. She then placed the tube, swab, and card into a plastic red contamination bag, sealed it, and packed it into the white container. Before leaving the room, she said, "It's very late, but we've got a ride to take you to the castle now. I don't imagine you'd care to stay in this tiny room any longer than you have to." She closed the door behind her.

Alice agreed with that. She immediately reapplied deodorant and changed her shirt. There was no mirror to help in fixing her appearance, but it was dark out, and she didn't care if she had a case of bed head.

Outside in the night, Alice saw Ms. Birch waiting next to a white van. She stood just outside the range of the building's outdoor lamp. Only the moon, which hung bright and full, gave any light to the ground and trees. Alice pulled her luggage up to stand alongside Ms. Birch and waited for whoever else might be arriving. The air was cold and crisp, and Alice saw her exhalations from her mask-less mouth. The clear black sky shone with bright stars shimmering slightly out of place, from her point of view in another part of the world.

"This is certainly an unfortunate turn, Ms. Whitmore." Ms. Birch broke the cold silence. "However, I'm relieved you're okay. I assure you, Mr. Wilson is getting the very best care."

"Mr. Wilson... Scott was the only one infected?" Alice asked.

"Fortunately, yes! Everyone else's tests came back negative."

One by one, Alice saw the other guests sleepily step out of the quarantine jailhouse. Darren, Alex and Yuri, Hannah, Harry, and Spence emerged in various states of dress and with expressions of stress and worry.

Ms. Birch opened the van doors, and without being instructed, everyone automatically filed in. Alice took the farthest seat in the back. She and the others might have just tested negative for the final time, but that didn't dissuade her from habitually avoiding people in closed spaces—something she'd been doing for months. She felt guilty, even a bit foolish. At one moment, they were all together in a plane with state-of-the-art air filters, feeling carefree. Next, they were down one person who might die at any moment. It could have been Alice. Or one the plane crew, who undoubtedly needed to be tested as well.

Alice wanted to go home. The dream played over in her mind like a guilt trip. Lying in the sun by the pool, enjoying drinks and selfishness. She'd be lying to herself if she believed this whole trip was to help find a cure. Everyone who'd come here as part of The Study, including herself, just wanted to be on vacation.

THE SOUND of dirt and rocks crunching under footsteps outside the van grabbed Darren's focus. He'd gotten very little sleep and couldn't pay attention to much of anything. Maybe jet lag had played a factor. He wasn't sure why he was holding a folder stuffed with papers. Ms. Birch had handed it to him, along with everyone else who'd gotten into the van. In the dark of the van, he couldn't see the bright imagery on the front of the folder, welcoming him to the "Arenavirus Vaccine Initiative."

Darren sat in the front passenger seat. He only caught parts of Ms. Birch's instructions to review the contents of the folder and to orientate themselves to the castle with maps and activities, prioritize meeting their testing schedule, and under no circumstances were they to leave the grounds during the research trial.

Behind him, Darren noted that Alex, Yuri, and Spence wore tired, blank faces. Behind them, Hannah stared out the window next to Harry and Alice, who seemed to be the only ones paying attention.

"Mr. Montoya?" Darren's attention came back into

focus. Ms. Birch was looking at him. "Would you mind buckling in? The road is a bit bumpy, and I'm not the best at handling a large vehicle in the middle of the night."

Darren silently sat forward, pulled the seat belt over his shoulder, and snapped it into place. The van started up, and the headlights lit the dirt and grass road ahead of them. Ms. Birch drove on. They drove away from Scott Wilson, somewhere coughing, possibly dying, alone.

Everyone sat in silence as they rode up and down the dirt road. The darkness around them was broken by the stars from the treeline and the van's weak headlights. At some point the trees would give way to open skies. *Are we near cliffs or lakes or large fields?* Darren wondered. The road would level out and continue through a windy path before going up again, straining the van's engine, and flatten out again and repeat more than Darren bothered to keep track.

Low lights on red roofs peaked into view. Golden lights from tiny windows gave structure to the castle, which finally was coming into view, its walls lit up by ground lights. Castle Monostori stood against the black sky as though it were holding back the darkness. Darren and the others leaned forward in their seats to take it all in. The van pulled up alongside the castle, which stood impossibly high above them. A wide red carpet led to double sliding-glass doors under a well-lit red awning.

Ms. Birch put the van in park and turned off the engine and headlights. "I'll meet you at the reception in a couple minutes. I'll have your keys programmed for you when I return." She paused for a moment, as if waiting for a response, then simply exited the van and walked through the castle's entrance.

Darren and the others exited the van as a man in black

slacks and a black polo shirt stepped out from the entrance with a luggage cart and proceeded to load the bags from the van onto it. Darren stepped through the automatic doors and into what looked like the reception area of a hotel. To the left stood Ms. Birch at the concierge desk, a phone tucked under her chin while she typed at the computer behind the counter. In front of him stood a wide column of dark stone with etchings carved into its face and painted in gold. The etchings were three large circles that connected vertically. The first had male and female sheep and a man holding a shepherd's crook. Below it, the middle circle held the castle. Below it, the last circle held a collection of village houses, with the words *"În oraș, El ne cheamă"* captioned beneath. The entire wall was illuminated by recessed floor lamps.

Darren walked around the large wall that separated the reception area from the rest of the castle; it opened to the lobby area. The room was spacious, with several options for sitting: in groups along plush red couches, or more intimate pairings of matching chairs next to side tables set on marbled flooring, all cast against a glass-and-steel-framed wall that looked out into the darkness. At the far side was a dining area along with a bar with stools. The bar came with two mounted TV screens turned off and a stocked wall of liquor. On his left, toward the front of the castle, sat two elevator doors with hallways on either side. Darren imagined those hallways led to conference rooms and offices.

Four floors of walkways held up with narrow stone columns surrounded the lobby. Each floor was identical: narrow walkways with ribbed stone arcs wrapping along the entirety of each floor. Darren saw someone on the third floor smoking against the delicate stone railing. Above him, a door opened, and music he didn't recognize played from beyond the sounds of conversation and laughter.

The ceiling was a glass and white-painted-steel dome that let the moon poke through to the lobby below.

Darren noticed Alex and Yuri Petrov muttered to each other in Ukrainian. Yuri caught Darren looking at them. "I was saying shame they turned such an old castle into a Hilton. We would never do that to our castles."

Darren looked back out to the empty lobby. He didn't think "Hilton" when he examined the room. "You don't have castles that are hotels in Ukraine?"

"We do. They are all over the place, but they're original. Everything is the same as before. This. This is like American Medieval Times castle," Alex scoffed.

"Then I hope the food is better," Darren said.

Hard clacking footsteps approached. Ms. Birch came up and gave Darren a white keycard with "405" on it. "Here are your keys." She handed Alex and Yuri theirs as well. "You were supposed to have your first blood screening in the morning at nine, in Hall A." Ms. Birch gestured at the nearest hallway. "Given the circumstances, I've moved it to eleven. The test is explained in your packets. If you can fast beforehand, that would be best. However, if you must consume something, please do not have any caffeine. Your luggage should be waiting for you on the fourth floor." Ms. Birch turned to see the man still outside loading luggage onto the cart. "Once the bellhop actually finishes getting your luggage, that is." The man outside picked the last item and closed the van doors.

Alice held the elevator door for the bellhop. He meagerly said thanks as Darren and the others made room for him and the cart. Up close, the bellhop looked their age, somewhere in his early twenties. His pale face had seemed paler than it probably was due to the contrast against his black hair, styled intentionally messy.

Their rooms were all on the fourth floor, next to one another. One by one, they found their door and keyed themselves through, took their luggage, and closed the door behind them. Darren tried a couple of times to get his door lock to flash green, but it just beeped in error. From the neighboring door, room 406, Spence called to him. "You okay?"

Spence already had his door open and was about to enter. Darren was about to say, "I'm fine." It was an auto response for most questions like that. "How're you doing?" "How's it going?" But one of the people in his group was infected. It was the middle of the night, and he was so tired that he was fumbling his stupid key to let him in.

"No," Darren shook his head. "I'm not okay. You?"

Spence shrugged. "Not really. Also not a fan of being this high up. More of a ground-floor guy. I could use a drink."

"I don't think that'd be a good idea if we're going to be giving blood in the morning."

Behind him from room 404, Hannah stepped out and lit a cigarette. She took a long drag and exhaled. "Nicotine is on the list of *non-non*," she said. "They've got a stocked minibar."

Spence and Darren looked at each other. "Fuck it," said Darren. "Come on. I'll split one with you." Spence smiled, and at that moment, Darren felt like he had a partner in crime. Darren finally got his door lock to turn green and open for him. He let his luggage keep the door open as he looked around the room.

It was much smaller than he'd realized it would be.

Taking up most of the room was a single bed with dark wood posters and a canopy with red draping and a matching bedspread. Two nightstands stood on either side, with digital alarm clocks that read, "03:30." The walls were stony brick and lit with sconces meant to look like torches, including the bulbs, which lit like amber flames. The bathroom also took up much of the space. Upon inspection, it was very modern, with metal walls, glass shower doors, an aluminum toilet, and sleek mirror lighting over a wide ceramic sink bowl. It felt surprisingly narrow inside given how it appeared from the outside.

Darren found the mini bar sat inside the bed-matching dark brown dresser. He placed his luggage on top of the dresser, next to the small television, and opened up the tiny fridge.

"Anything good?" Spence asked, as he stepped in.

There was a bottle of water, a bag of nuts, and a small glass bottle of clear liquid labeled, "Țuică." "What do you think this is?" When he twisted the lid open, with the snapping of the plastic seal, and put his nose to it, his eyelids shut out the vapor.

"Vodka!" he exclaimed. Darren grabbed a glass from the bathroom, poured two heavy shots, and gave it a taste.

"How is it?" Spence asked.

Darren swallowed and waited. He didn't necessarily have a clean palate for taste tests, but the vodka felt crisp with no aftertaste, and it would do the job. He took a stronger sip, handed the glass to Spence, and said, "Not bad."

Spence took up the glass as though he were being offered a gift. Darren sat on the bed with a hearty sigh. His stomach felt warm, but his mouth burned a little.

"Okay. That's pretty good, right? Or am I just tired?"

said Spence, who sat next to him on the bed, the only place in the room to sit.

"Yes to both, I guess. It could use ice." He took another sip and held the glass between them. There was maybe enough for one more drink, so he'd let Spence finish it.

Spence took the hint and finished the glass before handing it back to Darren. "Looks like the worst is behind us, right?"

Darren poured a two more estimated shots and took another sip. "How do you figure?"

"Just everything. Think about it. Between the pandemic, the virus, and the trip up here, things can only get better."

"Better for Scott Wilson?" Darren said.

"I didn't mean it like that."

"Here." He handed Spence the glass after another sip.

"Thanks." Spence sipped and winced a bit as he swallowed. "Look. All I'm saying is, people are going to continue to get sick. That's just a fact. Even with masks and staying safe, it's going to happen. Even after a vaccine is found, it'll take a long time to treat everyone. I'm not trying to sound insensitive. If everyone could come here and be safe, I'd be all for it. But they chose us. And I, for one, plan on making the most of it."

Darren nodded, not saying anything. But the truth was, Spence did sound insensitive. Darren wanted to point out how in the course of a few hours, they'd met a young man they were supposed to live with and maybe befriend. They'd share the same space, share this vaccine program experience, and hopefully come out of it changed. Just like Spence, or Alice, or any of them. Scott Wilson likely would die. It could have been him. Or Spence.

This had started out as a conversation for unwinding

after a really bad day. But Spence's remark really annoyed him more than it should have. Darren felt a brief moment of his equilibrium shifting and realized the vodka was having its effect on him, making him aggressive.

Instead of confronting Spence regarding his vodka-infused morals, he forced himself to let it slide. Spence had a point; he should be looking forward, rather than remain fixated on the past. "Let's hope for the best. Right?"

"Mm-hmm," Spence muttered through another sip.

A voice of reason floated in the distance of Darren's mind. It told him, *One drink turns to two drinks turns to a hangover. It's time for bed.*

He pushed the thought aside, as he always did. "I have to confess something."

Spence handed him the glass. "I didn't mean to come off like that." His words ran together too slightly for Darren to notice. "Oh. Sorry. What is it?"

Darren let a regretful swig of vodka down the hatch and looked at Spence. His focus strained. "Don't tell anyone," he said.

"What?" Spence asked.

I'm secretly here to hack servers in a bit of light corporate espionage for a drug competitor, and I want to be crushed under your weight while we make out.

"I'm really afraid of needles," he admitted instead.

Spence belted out a laugh that must have carried over to the neighboring rooms. "Boy, did you sign up for the wrong program." He took the glass back and finished the last swig of warm vodka. "What are you going to do tomorrow? They're going to draw blood. You can't exactly fake that."

It was true: he hated needles. It wasn't the pain they caused; it was the how they pushed into his skin. Growing up watching scary movies, he cringed whenever characters were stabbed or tortured, having their skin torn and punctured. That's what needles did.

Darren shrugged. "I'll suffer through it. Not like I have choice now."

"I thought they asked about that in the interview."

"I lied."

"Dude." Spence laughed. "Am I going to have to hold your hand?"

I wouldn't object to that. "I'll be fine. I had to get allergy shots as a kid. It sucks, but now you know in case you see me crying or something."

Spence finished the last of the glass, and for a moment, they sat silently in an imbibed moment. The air vents quietly hissed cool air. Somewhere down the hall, a door closed ungracefully.

Spence's breathing was slow and heavy. He slowly stood, holding on to one of the bed posters. "If I have any more, I'll need a cab. Catch you tomorrow?"

"You bet," Darren said, watching Spence leave.

Moments later, he heard Spence's door open and close. He was supposed to get up and brush his teeth and change into his boxers. Instead he pushed himself onto the bed and lay down. He reached into his pants pocket and felt the thumb drive against his fingers.

DESPITE FINALLY GETTING to sleep sometime between three and four in the morning, Spence still managed to wake up before dawn. Not even jet lag could break that habit. Given the circumstances, he wanted to force himself to get some rest. By his calculations, it was worse not to be fully rested for the day than it was to keep a strict morning schedule. But as it turned out, his mind was already wide-awake with the various morning routines he planned on performing. It was like he and his mind were of two entities, and there was no convincing his mind to change itself. He could always take a nap later.

It was still dark when he found the gym on the first floor. It was small and mostly consisted of free weights and treadmills. All of which were occupied. Spence returned to his room and counted through several sets of push-ups and sit-ups. While he stretched, he studied the additional materials in the orientation folder.

The front of the folder was black, with "Castle Mono-stori" in white in the center. Spence opened it and examined each paper inside. First was a welcome letter from the

CEO of Zenith Pharm. Next a map of the entire castle and property. It laid out the accessible trails, vantage points, mountains, cemetery, staff lodging, and the isolation facility.

The next paper was a map of the castle itself. The front half of the castle was originally built centuries ago. Self-guided tours were available from ten to four. The back half of the castle was built on top of structures that were destroyed. This newer part of the castle included a swimming area and hot tub, three conference halls, a gym, and a convenience store across from the reception desk.

After the maps came the menu. Breakfast was served from seven to nine in the morning: pastries, cheeses, sausage and eggs, cereal, and coffee. Lunch was available from noon to one in the afternoon: a buffet of potatoes, cabbage rolls, polenta, minced meat rolls, lamb haggis, and pork greaves. Three of those Spence didn't recognize. And dinner was from five to seven and listed as "seasonal."

Events and activities. Hiking tours, a forest obstacle course, karaoke night, poker night, wine tasting, and a cooking class were scheduled throughout their two-month stay.

The next document was his itinerary. He was part of group four with twenty people. Eighty people in all. It was seventy-nine now. Group four had their blood tests on Monday morning at 9:00 a.m.; groups one, two, and three had theirs on the Fridays, Saturdays, and Sundays before. It occurred to Spence that fasting the night before would put a damper on any weekend plans the guests might have. On the other hand, it was two months of nothing to do, so did weekends even apply?

Behind his itinerary was a collection of stapled papers. It was his contract. He recognized it from when he had signed it online. His dad had his lawyers go over it beforehand. It contained standard clauses for a nondisclosure agreement, along with information regarding basic responsibilities. The attorney explained this was a common agreement in programs such as this. It didn't list the rules—like not leaving the grounds—but it explained the consequences of forfeiture of involvement, the repayment of expenses, et cetera.

Spence gathered all the documents and placed them back in the black folder. It was just half past nine. He reached over to the nightstand. His phone was charging from a cable plugged into the lamp next to the bed, the only outlet in the room that supported US plugs. The only other outlet was in the bathroom, with two tiny circular holes. His phone had no cellular signal, but he did find an open network for guests among the other locked Wi-Fi networks. Even though it was free, download speeds were painfully slow. Either everyone was using it at the same time, or that was just how the Internet worked in this part of Europe. There was a notification waiting for him: Zenith Pharm app reminding him of his upcoming blood work.

Some of his phone apps worked but loaded slowly, while others didn't work at all. The Zenith Pharm app he had to install worked just fine. He pulled up one of the social-network apps and waited for it to slowly update. Image posts timed out, so he scrolled through text posts to get his news. Hospitalization rates continued to climb as more people continued to catch the virus. Riots had continued uninterrupted in the states of Missouri, Arkansas, and Oklahoma, where the Ozark Mountains were located. An estimated 890,0000 people had died in the US over the past three months, with one million expected by the end of summer.

Spence switched to his world clock app. It was ten in

the evening in Oregon. His dad would already be asleep by now. He was like his father in that they both turned in early and woke up before the sun came up.

He was curious if anyone else at the castle was using any dating apps. He kept his dating app icon buried in a subfolder folder and behind several others, and he always made sure it was no longer running when he was done using it. Notifications were always turned off. As with most of the profiles on the app, his photo was just his torso.

However, it wasn't loading. Either the Internet was too slow, or perhaps the app was blocked in this country. It was well enough, he supposed. In a group of eighty people, he might have been recognized.

Spence hopped out of bed, left his phone in his room, and headed down to the lobby. Morning light revealed the other side of the far glass wall. A large blue pool rested silently against the rolling mountains. The lobby was alive with about a dozen people gathered around the chairs and couches. The guests were making introductions and small talk. Spence overheard a few of them griping about coffee and hunger. He supposed if there wasn't any television worth watching or news to discuss (and who would want to?), there was always the topic of food.

Spence noticed everyone was around his age. He stood out as the only person in jeans and a T-shirt. He noticed women in designer shoes and men in jackets like the one he'd worn on the plane. Was he at the wrong event? This was a clinical trial, but they were dressed like they were already here vacationing in this luxury castle when the program had just sprung up around them.

Harry Brown and Hannah Bell stepped out of the elevator. Now those two were dressed as the latter. Hannah wore a pink top with wide sleeves, her hair resting in perfected scarlet waves on her shoulders. Harry sported a buttoned-up blue shirt with white cuffs, tan pants, and no socks. They looked like a couple he'd expect on a fashion runway. Harry spotted Spence and gave a short upward nod as they walked over. They were in the middle of a discussion when they came up. Hannah ended with, "They seem to arrive just days of each other."

Harry brought Spence in the loop. "Hannah thinks almost everyone here arrived at the same time. A day apart from one another."

Spence looked among the other guests and their nice clothes. "It's like a damn church meet and greet." Harry and Hannah gave him blank stares. "You know, when everyone in the pews stands up and says, 'Hello. How're ya doing?' and everyone shakes hands before the sermon starts?"

Hannah squinted. "That's not a thing, is it?"

"Definitely not where I'm from. It must be American. Church service in my town consisted of sitting quietly, singing a couple of hymns, and listening to the vicar telling us to live a more pious life," Harry said. Spence felt a tinge of embarrassment. Harry continued, "Anyway, I'm never shaking hands with anyone again. For better or worse, this pandemic has taught me that I hate shaking hands. Never did like it. Especially with other guys."

"Why not with guys?" Hannah asked. "Is it gay to shake hands now?"

"First, gay guys don't shake hands. They hug. All my gay friends do, at least. I swear, it's unavoidable. Another form of greeting I want to avoid. Am I right?" Harry glanced at Spence, the only other guy in the conversation, for acknowledgment, who quietly nodded. Harry went on to explain, "It's straight guys who have to shake hands like they're gripping on for dear life. They want to see who can give the tightest grip. All I want to do is wash my hands afterward. Such macho shite."

"Hi, I'm Spence, and I want you to know how balmy and firm my grip is. And I definitely didn't wash my hands earlier." He held his hand out to demonstrate.

Harry reached out and gripped his back despite admitting he hated it. "Hi, Spence. I'm Harry. My fingers are unusually cold, and you're not going to enjoy touching them."

The elevator opened again, and Darren Montoya and Alice Whitmore appeared, followed by Alex and Yuri Petrov. To Spence's relief, Alice and Darren dressed casually. He didn't want to be the only one in just a T-shirt and jeans. Alex and Yuri were in another set of tracksuits.

Hannah noticed the siblings' attire and commented, "Did you two already work out?"

"No, this is for afterward," Alex said.

"You're going to work out after giving blood?" Harry asked.

Yuri shrugged. "It's not like we're donating a liter. Instructions said that along with fasting, no exercise either. Which sucks, but afterward, we're both running one of the trails that goes up the mountain path. You should come."

"I don't think I could keep up with Team Ukraine," Hannah said. "Is there any snow nearby?" Yuri shook her head. "Pity."

"Team Ukraine?" Spence asked.

Hannah lit up, as though she had a revealed secret. "Alex and Yuri Petrov were in the winter Olympics last year! Alex was cross-country, and Yuri was snowboarding. I did an online search on everyone the moment I learned your names." She turned to Alex. "You're a big deal."

"We're really not," protested Yuri. "Olympics are

canceled for the time being. All the parks and recreation facilities are closed too. Ukraine and other countries, not just ours, can't afford to keep them open."

Alex added, "We thought about going to Canada to continue training, or maybe the Alps, but travel is restricted. The only way we could even get inside the EU was through this program. This is literally all we can do right now: give blood, go running. Then maybe skip to Switzerland afterward."

"You probably could skip out if you wanted," Alice said. "No one checked our passports. That's probably due to travel restrictions. How else would we all get here otherwise?"

The crowd's attention turned to a large wood-and-iron door that began to open. A man in a white lab coat with a digital pad stepped through, along with Ms. Birch. "Good morning!" Ms. Birch called the group to attention. "I trust everyone slept well."

Spence heard Hannah slip to Harry, "I didn't sleep well at all."

Ms. Birch continued, "We're running very late this morning, so let's be quick to get through this. The sooner we finish here, the more time you'll have to enjoy this sunny day. Shall we?"

The man, Dr. Hensen, stood at the door guiding the nineteen guests into the hall. "Find a seat anywhere and we can begin. Please."

Unlike the hallways above with replicated castle architecture, the hallways on the first floor were modern and stale. The crowd stepped through the last door into Hall A. The room's plain white walls were lined with mounted video screens above medical workstations and rack servers that were occupied by lab technicians dressed similarly to

Dr. Hensen. Power cords and data cables veined across the red carpet, between the stations, and a grid of twenty aquamarine mechanical chairs and metal lab tables full of medical equipment.

Spence sat down in the first free chair he could find. Dr. Hensen stood by the doors and waited patiently until he saw everyone was sitting in place. The room lights turned off. From his lab coat pocket, he pulled out a small black device and thumbed a button on it. The screens on the right and left sides of the large room flashed to life, playing the same video in unison.

Dr. Henson waited until he had everyone's attention. "I want to begin by formally welcoming you to the Arenavirus Vaccine Initiative. For some of you, this is your first day here, so you haven't yet had the opportunity to explore the castle and the scenic forest like the others. I won't take too much of your time."

He pressed the clicker in his hand, and the screens played a new video. It was something Spence had seen before in the news, a computer-rendered visual of the Ozark virus. It was a grotesque multi-sided ball, like a role-playing die floating in place with giant spikes covering its surface. It reminded him of an ocean mine, waiting in the water for a ship to bump into it.

"This is the Ozark virus," Dr. Hensen said, "a kind of arenavirus that doesn't fit within the known classifications of the arenavirus species. It's transmissible from person to person and travels via water droplets and on surfaces. The Ozark virus is incredibly lethal. To date, three million people have died worldwide, and four million others are dying." He emphasized "–ing." "Worse, the recovery rate is around three percent and only achievable through intense medical therapy. The long-term effects of those who have recovered are devastating. Organ failure, aplastic anemia, stroke, intracranial hemorrhage, psychosis...the list goes on. While some patients are able to produce antibodies, we don't know why."

Spence had heard all this before. He suspected this was to remind everyone this wasn't merely a vacation.

The screen switched to a new video. It was scientists in lab coats and protective eyewear busily moving vials into centrifuges, injecting fluids into trays of tiny vials, and working in airtight rooms behind thick glass doors. "In normal vaccine research," Dr. Hensen continued, "we explore multiple methods of finding an effective vaccine. We might clone a white blood cell, use the partial RNA of the virus, use a weakened version of the virus, or whatever has the most effective response. From there, we test these options on animals until we determine the best option. Then phased trials begin in people—starting in small groups of a few to thousands of people from a diverse collection before we even get FDA approval.

"Normally this process takes years. In rare cases, less than a year. Our goal is to have a vaccine we can begin shipping in six months." Dr. Hensen pressed the clicker again. Once more the screens changed to a server room. Racks and racks of server units, each flickering cool blue lights in a coordinated matrix of data processing.

"Just below us, farther below the parking garage, the utilities and storage, and backup generators, we have built a dedicated server farm using breaking software technology. RAMS: Rapid Antiviral Machine learning Software from DynaImaging. This software vastly increases research speed." Dr. Hensen's voice was a little more animated now. "A few years ago, we devised this method against an outbreak of meningitis to create a broad-spectrum antibiotic. It was truly groundbreaking. We simulated the human response through DNA sampling across a group of people and engineered an antibiotic with stunning accuracy. That was just a few years ago, keep in mind. Since then, our software has improved, and our servers are faster. This time we're using the same strategy to predict which antiviral methods will work best.

"This process takes about a week. Our server can run millions of simulations per sample an hour. By next week we'll have a candidate to live test you with." Dr. Hensen paused when people in the room gasped and muttered. "This is not the vaccine. This is a baseline for the servers. How your body responds to the candidate will be measured the following week by testing your immune response. This gets measured by our servers for accuracy."

Spence had seen machine learning in action. One of his college dorm mates had to program a virtual robot to teach itself how to walk. The program took its errors and successes and reiterated the task thousands of times until it passed. The outcome was comical. The stick-figure robot waved its arms around to keep balance and ran sideways. Not very efficient, but it got the job done. Spence couldn't imagine the kind of brainpower needed to simulate an entire bodily infection.

Dr. Hensen flicked the lights back on, and the other lab tech people began the process of collecting blood. After a while, it was his turn. A woman in a lab coat came up to him and opened a small box; she didn't look at him. She applied a printed label to the glass tube and another to a card and handed it to him with a pen. "This is your test ID. Please fill your name in on the line." Spence wrote his name and handed it back to her. She set it in the small box and attached the tube to a needled syringe. "Roll up your sleeve, please." He complied, and she tied a rubber tourniquet above his elbow. Spence turned his head away for the next part.

He wasn't afraid of needles. He always got his annual flu shot. As a child he had gotten several allergy shots to combat his hay fever. He just couldn't stand watching it happen. He imagined that just like Darren, whenever a TV show had a scene that involved needles, he'd turn his head and wait for the moment to pass. Spence looked around the room and spotted Darren anxiously exiting the hall after the technician had finished up. And just like the scenes he shied away from, it was over. The tech placed a bandage on his arm and tossed the tourniquet.

"All done. See you next week." She walked to the next person.

Spence was one of the first few to finish. He looked around the room. There were still several guests left for these lab techs to get to or finish. Harry was in one of the chairs with a needle and tube still attached to his arm. He was trying to engage the lab tech in what looked like a lot of follow-up questions that only seemed to annoy the one drawing blood.

In the hallway outside, Spence found a cart and tray with assorted cookies and cups of orange juice. He grabbed a snickerdoodle and chewed a piece while making his way back to the lobby. There he found Alice and Darren talking with Ms. Birch and a man in hospital scrubs who stood with his back to them, only speaking with Ms. Birch. Spence made his way to the catered breakfast options arranged neatly, along with chairs and tablecloth-covered tables.

He poured himself a grateful mug of hot coffee. Then he poured a second. Keeping his snickerdoodle in his mouth, he walked over and handed the mug to Darren.

Darren thankfully took the cup and patted Spence's shoulder. He and Alice wore grieved expressions. "It's Scott," Darren said.

Spence pulled the cookie from his mouth. "Scott? The guy who came with us here? How is he?" Darren gripped his shoulder.

Ms. Birch approached him and looked at him coldly. "Around five this morning, our doctors declared Scott Wilson dead from acute respiratory distress as a result of the Ozark virus."

ALICE FOUND HER SELF OUTSIDE, having the sudden need for air. The sound of Scott Wilson's cough echoed in her mind and wouldn't leave—but she didn't want it to leave. She imagined his last moments, alone, in some unknown medical area. Was he coughing until the end? Did they intubate him? Was he comfortable? Was he frightened? She recalled footage of the hospitals with overrun ICU beds holding patients with blood flowing onto the floor. News channels had played it up for the macabre spectacle. She could see Scott's face in the footage: his proud beard and curly mustache clotted with blood, each cough emitting flecks of blood spittle. His eyes bulged in pain as he struggled to keep the blood from pooling in his lungs.

It was her first time outside since her arrival. Beyond the automatic sliding doors, out from the red awning that covered the gravel road, a collection of park benches sat occupied by Hannah and a few other guests. They were smoking.

Hannah's brow furrowed when she noticed Alice

approaching. "There you are, *mon ami*! Hey, what's wrong?"

"What's wrong? Scott. He's gone!" She waited for Hannah to respond but got only a blank expression. "Scott. He traveled with us here. Ms. Birch just told us he died this morning. Jesus."

"I heard. Did you two know each other very well?" Hannah said, then took a drag from her cigarette.

"Well, no. But it just brought this whole trip into perspective. I think coming here was a mistake."

A man standing next to Hannah put out his cigarette in a small stand with discarded butts. He was black, average height, and wore clear acrylic glasses. "I'm really sorry to hear that." He held up a pack of cigarettes to offer one to Alice.

She shook her head.

"This is Peter Behrend, aka LaterGan. Tech-review guy," Hannah said. "This is Alice Whitmore."

He shook her hand. "You shouldn't leave. It's a lot worse out there than it is in here. I think this is the safest place to be right now."

"Is it? We were on a plane with Scott for hours, then in a van with him for hours. Even after all the steps they took to keep us safe, what's to say it won't happen again?"

"People die, Alice." Hannah said. "Lots of people are dying all over the world. Scott got exposed to the virus. We did not. He might have been reckless and, in turn, put us at risk too. I don't know. At this point, if you're dumb enough to get sick, you get what happens."

"You think Scott deserved to die because he got the virus?"

Hannah exhaled a long stream of smoke. "Honestly I'm

starting to think people who aren't taking steps to be safe might as well be playing with a loaded gun."

Alice slumped on one of the benches. "I don't think getting sick should be a capital offense."

"If we hadn't been tested that second time back at that fucking bunker, we'd be dead too. Everyone in this whole theme-park hotel could be too."

"Is...this the first person you know who died from the Ozark virus?" Peter asked.

Alice shook her head. "Back in Virginia, some people I knew died of it. My grandparents and their retirement home were wiped out in the first few weeks. A couple of friends from high school. One guy...I knew his father; he ended up taking his own life."

"I heard him coughing in the night," Hannah said. "Scott. I knew that cough from my dad's cough when he got it. We were staying at a hotel in France when everything broke out and we couldn't leave. Dad started showing signs, and they put him in the room next to ours, and we'd talk to each other on the phone while they attached tubes and monitors to him. I was with him until the end."

Alice squeezed Hannah's hand. She couldn't fathom losing one of her parents like that. She'd watched the stories on the news about people forced to die apart from their loved ones. She'd heard people refer to hospitals as "video-chat hospices." "I'm really sorry," Alice said.

Hannah stood up and composed herself before any tears escaped. "That is why we are here. Right?"

Alice nodded. "To find a cure."

"And," Hannah said, "to save ourselves from having a complete fucking mental breakdown! We weren't brought here just to be a bunch of lab rats. We can enjoy ourselves.

Take a break from the world. Make friends." Hannah gestured to Peter, who smiled in response.

Alice knew Hannah was right. She thought if she enjoyed herself, she was somehow guilty of ignoring the world around her. But the opportunity to enjoy herself was there whether she took it or not.

Alice stood up too. "Okay. What should we do then?"

"Your call. It's not warm enough to go to the pool yet, but rumor has it a pool party is in the works for this evening."

Alice scratched the back of head and looked around. She could see the scale of the castle; it dominated her view. Its pale-gray walls were capped by angled vermillion roofs that stood against the clear-blue sky and warm sun. "This might sound lame, but I thought a tour of the original castle would be nice."

Alice had expected Hannah to scoff at the suggestion, but instead she looked enthusiastic. "Sounds great," Hannah said. "Should we see if Spence wants to come? He was trying to learn about this place in his guidebook, but nothing came up. How about you?" She turned to Peter.

"I've got a draft due to my editor." Peter pulled a phone from his pocket. "This phone won't come to market until next quarter, but they're eager to see how this works, and me being here of all places has a lot of attention."

"Take it to the castle with us. You can test out the camera's low lighting or whatever," Hannah said while texting to someone Alice assumed was Spence. "They're on their way."

They followed a cobblestone path toward the front side of the castle. Alice noticed the original castle walls were less uniform in their smoothness. Cracks decorated the rough features. Path-work fillings were painted over in spots along the wall; they hadn't had time to age with discoloration.

As they passed a large round tower, they came upon the main entrance. Two very tall wooden doors stood ajar from the white stone archway that led into the castle's courtyard. Alice gave a shiver as they passed through the gates into the courtyard. The castle walls kept the sun from warming the courtyard and made the area look dark and foreboding. Although the courtyard was flat and empty, the walls and building were adorned with walkways and windows and steps that went in directions Alice couldn't follow.

Spence, Darren, and Harry found them gawking at the surroundings.

They made their way to the great hall at the other end of the courtyard facing the gate. The windows reached up high enough for the sun to send dusty beams of light down to the lacquered wood flooring. A couple of other guests were walking in the hall, taking photos of the pillars that reached up to the vaulted ceilings.

Alice walked along the back wall. There, several photographs, paintings, and lithographs were mounted with informative guide boards. The first exhibit was a picturesque oil painting of the castle in its original state. The back of the castle, now a four-story hotel, was once a large obelisk-shaped tower more than twice the castle's current height. Instead of a bright-red tiled roof like the smaller towers and battlements, the giant tower served a massive bonfire that made the clouds glow red and orange. The painting was titled, *Turnul de Foc* (*Tower of Fire*).

She and the others toured the hall, viewing the various diagrams and photos, taking in the notes from each one at their own pace. Eventually Alice wandered alone out to the courtyard and aimlessly explored through the seemingly random doors and passageways. She made her way up to the second story of the castle wall, which led to an entrance to one of the towers. Once inside, she followed the tower's staircase to the top, where she found a man in a gray suit gazing out the embrasure.

The sound of her approach made him turn. He wasn't anyone she had seen from the staff or any of the lab coats that had taken her blood that morning. He was older, maybe forty something. Gray hair marked their boundary at his temples. "This is my favorite view. Come. See," he said.

Alice stepped closer and looked out toward the unending trees that blanketed up to the bare mountains. Tufts of fog grasped for purchase of the forests. They were truly away from the rest of the world. "It just goes on forever. I didn't realize how remote we were."

"I try to take in the view while the weather is nice," the man said. "Well, even when the weather is bad, it's spectacular to look at. I find that I need to come up for air every now and then, less I completely bury myself in my work. It reminds me what we're here for."

"You work here?"

He extended his hand to Alice. "Robert Davis."

"Alice Whitmore," she said, shaking his hand.

"Yes, I spotted you coming up the path earlier. You arrived last night along with poor Scott Wilson. Rest his soul. I learned this morning. His family was notified, and we're returning his body for their funeral arrangements."

Alice assumed this man worked at the castle and had enough knowledge of the program to identify the guests on sight. *At least Scott will get to come home*, she thought. She wondered if she died here if her family could even afford to bring her back. It was more likely they would ask she be cremated here so as to avoid any risk of exposure.

"I take it you work here?" Alice asked.

"You could say that. I'm the VP of accounting. I was about to visit the armory; I like to count the swords. Care to join me? It's not accessible to visitors, but I have the key."

"So you're pretty familiar with this place?" asked Alice.

Robert nodded. "I like to think so. I come here often enough, and I do like a bit of history."

They went back down the stairs and exited the tower.

Robert led the way across the high wall toward the second tower. "Monostori Castle was built in the fourteenth century by Templar Master Jacques Monostori, a wealthy aristocrat who moved here from France. The Monostori family was a financier during the Anti-Ottoman Wars, and Jacques's grandson Florin Monostori was granted lordship over the land.

"The initial part of the castle was originally a fortress to guard against Mongol invaders, but after Florin was granted lordship, he rebuilt it to appear more in line with the gothic architecture seen in other castles around Europe."

Robert walked up to the locked door of their destination and worked the lock until he could open the door. He held the door for Alice, and they walked into the room. Just like in the previous tower, the steps along the wall also led upward, but the walls were adorned with antique guns and swords. Glass cases housed even older swords. A large cannon on wheels sat next to a small pyramid of cannon-balls and assorted stick tools.

Robert walked over to a mounted pistol, pulled it from its hooks, and inspected it in his hand. "Then, during World War II, Nazis occupied the area. They took over the castle as a military and medical outpost. The original tower, before its destruction, was their medical ward for experimenting on captured Jews, gypsies, and Allied soldiers. The king at the time, King Michael, managed a nice little coup d'état that drove the Nazis out, but not before the Tower of Fire was destroyed."

Alice's knowledge of history didn't extend much past the United States. And of that, she often had learned two sides of it—one was what she picked up from literature and documentaries; the other was public school curriculum. She leaned over the glass case, which displayed an old-looking sword. It was long with a small red cross at the end of the handle. A yellowed paper placard by it read, SWORD OF SHEPHERD JACQUES.

Robert noticed Alice's interest. "The sword of the last-known fallen Knights Templar."

"Fallen?"

Robert pulled at his coat as he and Alice stood over the case. "After the Crusades ended, there wasn't much need for Knights Templar. They were supposed to protect travelers on their way to Jerusalem, but they became a bit redundant—and very wealthy. That was something the king of France was quite envious of after squandering his country's wealth on petty wars. So the king did what any good monarch does: he assassinated the pope and replaced him with another who would let him kill the knights and take their money.

"On Friday the thirteenth, 1307, King Philip IV rounded up the Knights Templar for the crimes of practicing heresy, worshiping Satan, engaging in homosexuality — anything really—and had them tortured into confessing. In the end, he burned three at the stake, including the last grand master, Jacques de Molay." Robert gestured back toward the sword.

"Those who evaded capture either joined other holy orders or fled. Jacques Monostori was said to speak with

Jacques de Molay on his final day; he agreed to flee here with twelve other knights. Unfortunately he died, and they recovered his sword and his ashes and took all the money they could find to live here."

"So was it true?" Alice asked. "Were they an army of gay devil-worshiping heretics?"

Robert placed the gun back on the rack and gave the room a final look to remember his visit. "I can't say if there were any gay knights; what happens in the order stays in the order. However, in his journals, Monostori felt betrayed by the Church. The pope had turned his back on the order. Without the protection of the church, they could no longer be shepherds tasked with protecting the Lord's sheep. Monostori wrote that he would become a shepherd for Satan—which, in retrospect, would be heresy. Shall we?" He opened the door for them to leave then locked it close.

Alice had a million questions. How did a bunch of Catholic knights simply switch teams? Were they in cahoots with Nazis? And how did this place go from Satanists to Nazis to a multinational drug corporation? Or was all of European history this fucked up?

More guests had arrived inside the old castle walls. Alice spotted Harry and Hannah meandering in the main courtyard with the sun finally touching the cobbled grounds. They hadn't noticed her and Robert Davis above them. Hannah was dialing in obvious body language that said, "I'm available," while Harry was eagerly chatting about a subject only he was interested in.

Alice turned to Robert. "You're telling me the accusations were actually true?"

"Only after the fact. You see, Jacques de Molay's final words while on fire were his pleading to be avenged. Some say it was a prayer, but Jacques Monostori believed it was a curse only the Devil himself could fulfill. And it worked. The pope died shortly after, and the king's family line dried up."

"Okay, that didn't happen."

"Oh, it very much did," Robert said. "Pope Clement V died of an illness not long after. The church where he lay in state caught fire from a lightning storm, and the fire pretty much destroyed his body. King Philip died of a stroke while hunting; his last surviving heir never had children."

"Are you sure you're not a historian?"

Robert shook his head. "Anyone who works here long enough learns this castle's story."

"Oh. So you're staying at the castle too? Where are the labs and your office? Is there another building near here?" Alice couldn't see over the walls anymore, but she didn't recall seeing any other buildings. Maybe they were just over the hills, like that isolation bunker.

"Aside from a few service buildings and a barracks for staff, there are no additional buildings on the land. Everything is underground. The labs, server rooms, medical, offices, even a boardroom. We're way underground where the castle was rebuilt."

Robert left Alice in a surprised expression as he headed down the steps away from the wall and its battlements. She followed him through a doorway into a low-ceilinged hallway that led to a large room with iron bars and shackles chained to the walls. A prison cell perhaps? "It's all underground?" Alice asked.

"It's a shame we donated the torture devices to museums." He seemed to ignore her. "The rack, pillory, that chair with all the spikes. They were always attractions for visitors." He pointed to an empty corner of the room.

"What do you think this place is? A castle? A hotel? A secretive underground science lab?"

It was a rhetorical question, but Alice answered anyway. "Depends on who you ask."

Robert raised an eyebrow.

Alice stepped around the room, lit only by the sun that traveled from the hallway. If there had been evil committed in this room, it had long faded. It was just another part of the old castle. Were it not for the chains, it could have been mistaken for a storage closet.

"For me and the others, it's a resort," she said. "Maybe it serves as a corporate retreat. The land is certainly set up for recreation. But underground research? Why hide it? For aesthetics?"

"It's certainly not aesthetics. Culturally the people of Romania carry deep emotional scars from their country's alliance with the Nazis. Hitler was obsessed with the occult. The rumors of occult-based mutilation and experiments tainted the castle's prestige. So, when it was purchased from the Monostori family, a castle restoration, sans Tower of Fire, it became. And, yes, it does make an excellent corporate retreat for our numerous subsidiaries.

"People wouldn't appreciate seeing this land become home to another medical experiment site. And Zenith doesn't want that image. Even if the experiments are done on virtual DNA."

"Do you and the other employees stay in the castle? Or is that underground as well?"

"Staff quarters," Robert replied. "As much as I enjoy staying in one of the suites, I need just a bit of separation from the 'resort life' you and the other guests enjoy. Got to keep focused on fixing what's happening outside these walls."

Alice scoffed, "Less you meet the fate of Prince Pros-
pero?" Robert's face looked genuinely surprised. "I had to
read the collection of Poe's work in college. Honestly I just
read the *CliffsNotes*."

"Ah, *The Masque of the Red Death*. Is that what you
think of this place?" Robert asked.

Alice shrugged. "I little bit, yeah. High fences, armed
guards wielding, what are I assume, illegal Vectors. Meanwhile, we hide away from the world and plan on hikes and
parties."

"Ms. Whitmore, you have my guarantee that we are
very much not hiding. Very soon the world will finally see
what we have done here."

The next morning, Alice took up Yuri and Alex's offer to
join them for a morning jog. They'd found a trail the day
before that they liked and were going to test it out before
dawn. Alice didn't sleep well the night before. She kept
dreaming about the castle collapsing on top of her, the
massive server rooms, and the testing labs under the weight
of the castle exploding into pieces as she and the other
guests were crushed under the rubble.

At 5:31 a.m., when she was already awake, her phone
buzzed. It was Yuri in their group chat, waiting for her
outside.

She found the siblings in another set of matching tracksuits. The Olympic symbol rested proudly on their shoulders. There was no blood work today so no fasting was
needed. They'd helped themselves to coffee before staff
services could make it.

Alice accepted a cup from Alex. "Thanks. I need this."

"Still tired?" Alex asked.

Alice shrugged and nursed her cup. "I'll get there. I kept waking up from bad dreams. Yesterday I learned about the history of this place. It's pretty gruesome."

"Welcome to the rest of Europe." Yuri was crunching on a granola bar.

The sun wasn't out yet, but they could see well enough during the predawn hours. The combo of chill air and coffee gave Alice plenty of energy to run the trail with Alex and Yuri. When she started the last stretch of mile two, however, the siblings were well ahead of her.

By the time she reached them back at the castle's side entrance, their breathing had returned to normal, and they were drinking bottled water. They both gave her a high five.

Yuri chuckled. "Again?"

Alice's hands were already on her knees, and she was shaking her head. "You two go ahead. Coffee isn't sitting right. That's plenty for me, I think."

"Okay. Same time tomorrow?" Alex patted her back and ran off with Yuri before Alice could confirm.

Alice walked into the entrance and noticed the artwork on the dividing wall between the entrance and the courtyard: three circles connected by a line. The first circle had a triangle inside. In the top corner was a human figure holding a shepherd's staff. The bottom two corners had a sheep and a ram. The middle circle contained an image of the castle based on its outline, including the missing Tower of Fire with its bonfire on top. And in the circle on the bottom, there was a depiction of houses and buildings that surrounded a large pillar looming tall. Nothing satanic about that. If there were a fourth circle, Alice thought, it would depict little demons with pitchforks.

"It's from an etching." A small voice to her right spoke.

She recognized him as the bellhop from her first night at the castle. He was pulling out a plastic bag of trash from a can by the wall. He was skinny and pale, with a sharp mouth.

"Excuse me?" Alice asked.

"That diagram." He rested his garbage sack against the can and came over. "So this guy who built this place? The original castle, that is."

"Monostori?"

He snapped his singers. "That's the one. He was this guy who—"

"Oh, I got the whole tour on him from Robert Davis. Fallen knight. Satanist. Might be gay."

"You met Mr. Davis? I'm surprised he said any of that." His voice wavered. "I was only going to say when Monostori left the church, he wanted to make a new one. He had a lot of ideas, but he also made art like this. It's from a book he wrote in his final days, *New Exegesis*."

"You give tours as well?" Alice said, thinking she'd made a lighthearted joke, but his face grew worrisome.

"I'm not assigned any tours actually. I could, but I'd have to get permission from Ms. Birch if you wanted to go—"

"I was kidding! It's all good. I'm Alice, by the way."

"Vlad Alecsandri." He smiled and scratched at the back of his head.

Alice regarded his awkward posture and pale skin. She didn't know anyone so pale. Maybe he had a touch of albinism that kept him that way. Or maybe he was a freaking vampire; he would come to her room and drain her blood as a new perk for the satanic castle.

"Can I ask you something?" Alice asked.

"Sure."

"How do you know so much about the place? Was that part of your employee training?"

Vlad shook his head. "I'm from here actually. I live down in the City. This is usually my summer job when school's out."

"Oh. I'm surprised you're not part of the program. Seems like you'd have a foot in the door."

"Making friends, everyone?" A short, pointed voice came from around the corner. Ms. Birch approached them carrying a sealed manila envelope. At her appearance, Vlad visibly shrank.

"Here." Ms. Birch handed Alice the envelope. "It's from Robert Davis. It seems you're getting to know everyone here at the castle." Alice could hear Ms. Birch's annoyance through her smile. She didn't understand why, perhaps Ms. Birch would prefer that everyone to stay in their rooms for the duration of the program.

"What can I say? Everyone here is so friendly." Alice smiled at Vlad. She accepted the envelope, unpinned its flap, and pulled out a stack that was pinned together with three brass binding pins. The top page read in large type, "*The Masque of the Red Death* by Edgar Allen Poe." She held it up to Ms. Birch, whose eyes widened in confusion. "I think it's a reading assignment," Alice said.

* * *

The sun was setting when Alice replied to Hannah's group-chat text to join her at the pool. She had hoped to run into Vlad again, at least to apologize, though she wasn't sure what for. She could apologize for Ms. Birch's attitude, and she wondered if he had gotten into some sort of trouble for interacting with a guest. But there was something about his coyness, his kindness that made her want to interact with him more.

The back of the castle was in the golden warmth of the sun, and the sounds of laughter, music, and splashing echoed into the lobby as Alice exited into the back patio area. She had attended a few parties in high school and a couple of campus parties at the urging of her classmates, but she'd always left shortly after arriving. She thought they brought out the worst in people. They weren't so much parties as they were messy competitions to get as drunk as possible.

By that standard, this crowd might as well have been those students' parents. The pool deck wasn't rambunctious at all. Most people were actually sitting on the sides, having conversations with a cocktail or beer bottle in hand. Bar tables scattered around the deck kept the standing guests busy with their own chatter.

Alice found Hannah with Alex and Darren floating at the far end of the pool. Spence and Harry sat dangling their feet. Hannah gave a squeal when she saw Alice. "Aaaliiice! There you are! This pool is sooooo warm!"

"I'll take your word for it." Alice was only wearing a pair of shorts and a T-shirt. It was obvious Hannah was already lit, but seeing her cool posh exterior give way to joyous effervescence made Alice smile.

Hannah gave Harry her glass of mostly ice. "Can you hand me my phone? I want a picture of you guys!" Alice wondered how many drinks Hannah needed to get there. Then she wondered how she could get one herself.

Hannah made them all squeeze together for a group photo. Alice had to admit it was a nice moment. She hadn't really let herself have "fun" since arriving. Maybe she would feel guilty later, but for now she let herself enjoy it.

Harry stood up with his glass and Hannah's. "I'm getting a refill. BRB." He took a few steps and turned to Alice. "House margs? That scary-looking bartender makes a mean cocktail."

"I never turn down a margarita," Alice said. Harry stepped away, giving a wink so corny, if his hands weren't holding glasses, he would have given her finger guns.

Hannah was working with the photo she took and asked, "I need your handles so I can tag you. I only have Harry's."

"You have his handle? Sounds serious," Alice said.

"You could say we're at the 'friend request sent' stage."

"Right on."

Hannah gave a devilish grin. "What about you and the professor?"

The question grabbed the attention of the others, who looked at Alice with mixed expressions. She didn't realize Hannah noticed her talking to the VP of accounting. Alice flushed for a second but came back with, "Oh, it's super serious. We're thinking of naming our first kid 'Ozark.'" She thought that was simple enough of a joke that they could move on, but Hannah continued to look back at Alice, waiting.

"He works here, for Zenith Pharm. He's part of the whole underground lab thing. He had access to parts of the castle that aren't open to the public. I got a tour. Learned a bit of history. That's all."

It was Darren's turn to tease Alice. "I bet you got a tour." Alice kicked water in his face.

Harry returned with a tray of three drinks in rocks glasses and handed one to Alice. With a strong sip, Alice took in the moment of her and her new friends enjoying nice weather. Dipping her feet into the pool, she wished she had changed into her swimsuit and suddenly experienced a bad sense of déjà vu. It was of her dream only a couple nights before. That terrible vision of infection symptoms making her bleed from her skin and the ground sucking her into a pit to be swallowed up by an unseen monster.

Feeling a cold hand on her knee, Alice jumped. "Alice? Sorry. Didn't mean to startle you." Darren's hand pulled back. "It's your turn."

They were all looking at her.

Alex, sitting next to her, asked, "Where do you want to go after the vaccine cures everyone? I said Olympics, naturally. Probably Yuri's as well." Yuri wasn't around to give his answer. He was over by some people poring over a laptop and speaker equipment. He looked as though he were part of the sound crew helping with their playlist. Alex's eyes always had tracked back to him, making sure he was okay, wasn't getting lost, or wasn't running around with a knife. "First time he's been happy since the plague began. Maybe he can stay here then."

"I guess I'd be happy to go back to college, just to have life return to normal," Alice said. She hadn't given much thought about life after all this. She first had to figure out how to survive this current crisis. She was treading water, not realizing she should think about reaching for the edge of the metaphorical pool.

Harry confessed to never having visited Africa, or much anyplace else, and would make that his first priority. Spence would take a road trip with his friend back home. Darren would move to Hawaii and never come back.

"I like Darren's idea," Hannah said while guarding her drink from getting splashed.

"You can come with me!" Darren exclaimed.

Hannah's eyes widened. "Oh, yes! I was in a freediving

club in Oahu last year. So much fun, though I think any beach would work for me."

"Freediving. Like, no scuba gear?" Darren asked.

"If you haven't done it, it's totally worth it. You basically have to learn to hold your breath, all while swimming with a giant tail fin."

"That doesn't sound fun at all. How long can you hold your breath?" Alice asked.

"The longest I went was four and half minutes without swimming. Though it's more of a party favor now." Hannah took a sip.

"Hey. This is a party! Can you do it now?" Alice said.

"Oh, no. Not with all this tequila on the brain. When I first started, I could only hold my breath for a minute. Some people go for eleven minutes. But they show me techniques and how to work through the urge to breathe when your body freaks out." She took another sip and went on; the real party favor was explaining it. "So we have the same genes as seals and otters, and our bodies actually are more efficient at holding our breath underwater. It's called the mammalian diving reflex. It took practice, and I had to keep telling myself that my body spasming was normal and I actually had a lot more time than my body was telling me."

"I think I just developed a new phobia," Alice said.

Alex made a kicking motion with her dangling legs. "This is as far as I get in the water."

Darren took a healthy drink from his glass and managed to get a piece of ice to chew on. "Count me in. Being able to hold my breath that long would improve my love life."

Spence almost spat in his drink.

"What? We all got to go down from time to time," Darren said, proud of his dirty joke. Alice almost felt

Darren was looking at her when he said that. But he was looking at everyone for a reaction.

The bar ran out of house margarita mix shortly after the music began. The sun had set, and a chill covered the back patio. The seven of them managed to get one last round in before the bar switched to only beer and water. Despite the patio being filled with like-minded college-age fellow testing participants, Alice and the others were perfectly content forming their own clique. This was their group chat in dance form.

Yuri made sure to point out every time one of his songs came up on the playlist. Turned out he had an affinity for nineties boy bands and had fought hard to make sure they were a part of tonight's line-up. When one of his songs came up, everyone danced and sang along to the words.

By the tenth round of boy-band cameos, Alice was struggling against a strong buzz and starting to think bad ideas. Bad ideas were the behaviors of other partygoers, whom she always held judgments against. She never drank too much, always kept her wits, and always knew when someone had bad intentions. That was how she was raised; she couldn't deny that no matter how much she resented it. For reasons she couldn't explain, or didn't want to examine, among the six strangers she felt safe. Drunk and safe.

She already had danced between Darren and Spence. Sober Alice would have suspected Darren was trying to get closer than just being dance partners; Margarita Alice hoped so. She professed to Hannah they were "best bitch-es." She was about to switch to beer when, finally Sober Alice shouted, *Oh, God! Don't switch to beer. Switch to bed!*

Hannah grabbed her arm. "Come smoke with me, would you?" Alice was glad to have an excuse to duck out; her normal tactic was to merely ghost. She turned to Darren to say good night, but he was hanging on Spence's shoulder, laughing with Yuri and Harry over what was no doubt a crude story she had no interest in hearing.

Hannah's and Alice's rooms were next to each other on the fourth floor. Hannah pulled out a cigarette when they reached the doors, and Alice ducked into her room to get some water bottles from the mini fridge. Hannah was leaning against the railing, watching people mingle in the courtyard. As she pointed to one of the people, she sighed. "I thought that was them."

"You thought that was who?" Alice handed her a water bottle.

"Charley Suits," Hannah said. "They're a famous makeup artist celebrity. They have over five million followers, their own line of makeup too. I never saw them without their face on. But yeah, that's Charley all right."

Alice squinted at the person in the lobby. Charley Suits was sitting with three other people telling a story.

"That over there is Paul Stone." Hannah pointed her cigarette to a man entering the lobby from the pool deck. He was shirtless, and his arm was locked with a woman equally as tan. Alice recognized him from television; he was a drummer who had gained notoriety from a televised wedding that quickly dissolved. Now he hosted a reality show where contestants ate only Zenith Pharm brand foods to lose weight.

"Looks like he's found a date," Alice remarked.

Hannah peered over the rail at the woman. "That's his fourth one so far."

"We haven't been here a week! Is he here to help fight the virus or spread infection?"

Hannah coughed, trying to suppress a laugh. "Good thing we're in with Big Pharma. Besides, what else is there to do? People get lonely. Isolation will do that. Plenty of hooking up is afoot."

"Like you and Harry?"

Hannah winked as she sucked on her cigarette.

Alice leaned against the rail, her equilibrium struggling under the influence of alcohol. "Man, why am I even here?"

"What do you mean?"

"Darren's dad is some super-programmer billionaire. Spence's dad invented life-saving air filters. We've got a famous makeup celeb. A reality star. Alex and Yuri are Olympians. That Peter guy is a famous tech influencer. For all I know, Harry lives in his own castle..."

"His mother has a Nobel in chemistry, and he's following her steps in epidemiology." Hannah held in her breath from dragging on the cigarette.

"Of course."

Alice looked at Hannah: the look of "And?" Hannah finally exhaled her smoke. "I'm a competitive gamer, number-one streamer in Europe. Won three international events. South Korea hates me. Just signed a six-figure endorsement deal for a clothing line." As the last bit of smoke left her lungs, she seemed to see Alice's face drop a little. "I started noticing people immediately. I recognized a few people I follow online, but the more guests I met, the more of them I looked up online, it's very clear that this is a 'who's who' event, not just a vaccine research effort."

"Is that why you agreed to this? Why leave France and your job to do this?" Alice asked.

"At first my agent pushed me. She thought it was a brand-enforcing opportunity." Hannah put out her used cigarette into the sand pile on the ashtray stand. "But I really do want to be here! Losing my dad like that...I'd do anything to help find a vaccine. I left my stream, my revenue, canceled tournament events. It didn't matter. I couldn't justify not coming. Of course my agent thought it would become a cause célèbre. So what about you? What's your claim to fame?"

"I'm nobody," Alice said.

AFTER THE FIRST FEW DAYS, Darren felt settled in at the castle. By the end of the first week, he was bored. He established right away that there was no access to any servers. Hall A was only opened when the guests were getting tested; afterward the doors closed. When Darren ascertained whether he could possibly sneak in, he learned its doors were magnetically sealed; a keycard was needed to unlock it, but a power outage could do the job too. *Which would be easier?* he wondered.

The bartender, security guards, the lab coats, housekeeping, and Ms. Birch all had noticeable access cards, either attached to other keys or to a lanyard around their neck. Security all kept theirs at their waist. They also carried large weapons; Darren noted that. The bartender frequently kept his keycard attached to an elastic strap around his arm, along with physical keys. He also looked like a hit man. Ms. Birch captured everyone in her vision; Darren couldn't even look in her general direction without her noticing. And the likelihood of her forgetting her keys was as high as a strand of hair escaping her top bun.

The kitchen staff had keycards. Maybe one of them would leave one in their apron by accident. To check, he'd just need to go inside the kitchen after hours—the doors to which also required a keycard.

Alice was friends with Vlad from housekeeping. Maybe more than friends; Darren had seen them laughing in the hallway. He'd be doing his rounds and she'd just happen to bump into him. They'd stand there laughing about the happenstance of running into each other. Their body language was awkward and tooth-achingly adorable. Vlad might be a possibility.

Darren put a pin in his espionage plans. He didn't see a clear path to getting access to a server. Not only that, but he also didn't know if his patch was on the servers. Zenith Pharm might not get software updates for months. Instead, he focused on other opportunities. He and his initial group of friends had mostly gotten to know the other guests. It didn't take long to notice cliques and circles take shape. Wealth and fame played a central role in the new bonds that formed around the castle. Social media influencers flocked together immediately, while stock investors and technology enthusiasts joined in frequent debate and speculation.

Darren often found himself chatting with them. Mads Porter, who live-streamed stock trades in online currency, was a stocky ginger whose energy level ran at one hundred. He had dozens of questions about DynaImaging. How did decentralizing neural networks actually work? What was the commonality between photo rendering and DNA imaging? Could he somehow build a model prediction for blockchain trade prices? Darren tried to speak to it, but he wasn't an expert. Luckily, Peter Behrend was more up to date with what Mads was referring to.

"You're trying to get in with Darren's dad, Mads?" Peter asked. They were seated in the lobby, enjoying a breakfast of sausages and eggs. The castle had updated its menu to be more appealing to American tastes and added dry cereal with milk that was room temp.

Mads was having a beer and a bagel. "We're here, right? Why not network while we're at it."

"If there's a product that can be made from machine learning, my dad will want to make it. Honestly. You can ask him when we get back," Darren said. Nowadays, his father focused more on buying than creating. He was so interested in cornering the market, he'd bought the entire block; if someone else came up with the block-chain predictor thingamajig, he'd buy that too.

"Maybe the next time you call him?" Mads's enthusiasm was relentless.

"Dude, you're kidding me," Peter said.

Darren swilled down his sausage with some coffee. "I'll have him come on your show." Darren glanced at his phone: a notification from the Zenith Pharm app. It was already 9:00 a.m. "Guys, I'm up for the baseline shot."

"Got mine two days ago," Mads said. "It didn't hurt, but I had the worst fever that night. I got super weak, dehydrated, all that stuff."

Mads was in group B. The other guests shared the same story about their baseline shots. They'd suffered a sudden fever that lasted several hours, but they were completely okay the next day.

"Mine went fine," Peter added. "I had some rough nightmares, but that's been happening already lately. Be sure to take some aspirin before bed."

The nineteen guests of Group D gathered in Hall A,

now unlocked, in the same chairs they'd first sat in when they arrived. Dr. Hensen stood by the door until he saw everyone was in attendance.

"How was everyone's first week?" he asked. A few murmurs rose from the group. "That good, huh? Our week went very well. A reminder: today you'll receive a baseline shot we'll use to stimulate your immune system. After a week of your body having time to produce sufficient antibodies, we'll take another blood sample for analysis.

"I'm sure you've heard from the other guests that you'll feel some mild fever-like symptoms from the shot. This is a normal response and should only last a short time. Usually it will occur later in the evening. I recommend you stay hydrated. Aspirin is available at the little bodega in the lobby."

It was the moment Darren hated. The needle. A male lab tech approached him with a tray of prepared syringes set perpendicular, each with a name on it. He glanced and recognized the name "Yuri Petrov" of one of the syringes.

"Stay here for fifteen minutes after your shot, okay?" the tech said, looking down at his clipboard. "Name?"

"Darren Montoya."

There was a pause. "Okay, you're good to go. Your results were corrupted during last night's server update, so we're running it again. We should have a baseline for you in a few days. Your Zenith Pharm app will notify you when it's time." The tech stood up and moved on to the next person, his keycard flopping around his neck.

As Darren went to leave, he passed by Spence, who whispered, "You dodged a bullet."

"I guess I did. I'll see you outside later?" Darren asked.

"Oh. Sure. Whenever. Let me know."

Darren thought they had plans for a hike with the siblings. Maybe it had slipped Spence's mind. Over the past week, Darren felt he had made a real connection with Spence. Out of everyone he'd gotten to know, Spence was someone who really liked his company. But Darren noticed it never happened around others. It wasn't perceptible initially. The subtle shift in Spence's demeanor from one situation to the next was common for everyone. People act differently depending on their circumstances; it could be based on other people's moods—for example, while sitting with a friend at a nice restaurant or talking to a police officer.

At some point, as the guests got to know each other, and those cliques started to appear, Darren noticed Spence making his own friends too. They'd be at the bar watching a sports program; Spence had relaxed charm, while chatting with the boys. Darren knew it well. When Darren joined them, Spence became just a degree more distant.

He wasn't cruel or cold; in fact he was pleasant. And Darren got to know his sports-watching friends as well. It was fine; Darren was just projecting. That's what I always do, he thought. Project and internalize. Think of the worst. *They'll call you a fag as soon as you leave. You're just embarrassing Spence. It's so obvious to everyone.*

Darren changed into cooler clothes for the hike. In the group chat with Alex, Yuri, and Spence, Alex said, "The southern trail is closed. But we can take one of the east trails." Alex and Yuri had become his adventure buddies. Together they'd explored half of the trails on the property. They maintained a log of which spots had the best views and also kept an album of selfies at each spot.

"Heading down now," Darren typed.

The room door next to him closed with a thud. That

was Spence's room. Darren stepped out and spotted him in gym clothes.

"How'd the shot go?" Daren asked.

"Oh! It kind of hurt." Spence rubbed the Band-Aid on his shoulder. "Usually shots are nothing. Like a tiny scratch of pain. But this one sucked."

"I'm sure the hike will take your mind off it. Yuri and Alex are already downstairs."

Spence sucked in through his teeth. "Shit. I made plans with the guys to play touch football. I screwed up."

Darren did his best "fuggedaboutit." "What? Not at all. You should go have fun. I can't play football for shit."

"Half of them never played American football before. Trust me, you'd do great. We still on for the treetop obstacle course tomorrow?"

"I thought you said you were afraid of heights."

"Yeah, but like, roller-coaster-ride heights."

"Okay. Well, we'd better get going."

They both rode the elevator down to the lobby in silence. Darren was even quieter on the hike.

* * *

Darren ate dinner alone. Everyone in his group complained of fatigue and went to bed early. Mads and Peter were at tables with their own groups. He could have joined them, and they would have gladly had his company. Instead he dined on his plate of roast chicken and arugula salad with pine nuts, and two glasses of Malbec alone.

"Excuse me." Darren looked up to see Vlad, the bellhop, standing before him.

"Hey," said Darren.

Vlad placed a small aspirin packet by his plate. "Could

you deliver this to Alice? I'd go but..." Vlad looked over to the front desk; it was empty. "Ms. Birch doesn't want me going up there when I'm not on duty." Darren knew that meant Ms. Birch didn't approve of staff fraternizing with the guests.

"Sure, sure. I'm about to head up there anyway. I'll make sure she gets this." Darren smiled sympathetically and pocketed the tiny envelope.

Vlad looked up at the fourth-floor room where Alice slept. His narrow face was contorted with concern and fear. "Thanks," he finally said, and left.

It was still a little early. The kitchen closed after seven. guests' plates were removed, and the pool deck began filling up on cue. This was usually when some of the guests deviated from their groups and cliques and into romantic pairings. It started pretty early from Darren's arrival, but it wasn't surprising. A bunch of college age grown-ups no longer living in isolation eventually would get horny and find like-minded horny people. And stupid, stupid Darren found himself horny for the unreciprocated. *That's what's happening, you dolt. You're climbing the wrong tree. A hot tree. Ugh. Go to horny jail!*

Darren made his way to the bar, and ordered an Old Fashioned from the angry bartender. Darren watched as the bartender grunted and worked the various liquids over a rocks glass. His keycard slapped against his thick arms as set the bottles back in place on the wall behind him. If Darren tried to take the card now, this man would surely break his hands. The bartender set the glass down unceremoniously on the counter, gave Darren a solid glare and moved onto the next guest.

He made his way to the fourth floor to lie down. But first he needed to drop off Vlad's aspirin. Alice was wrapped in a white bathrobe, covered in sweat and hair in completely disarray.

"Here, compliments of the house." Darren handed her the packet of aspirin.

"I'd rather have that." Alice said pointing to his cocktail.

"Vlad seemed pretty worried. And I think he got in trouble with Ms. Birch."

Alice moaned. "I can't with her. I got to lie down." And closed the door.

* * *

Darren's phone chimed. It chimed a few more times before Darren woke up. He had fallen asleep while nursing his drink and scrolling news now that the internet had finally improved. The rocks glass sat next to his phone in a tiny puddle of condensation.

It was the group chat app that sent multiple notifications.

> 11:14 p.m., *Spence: I'm really burning up. Should I call for help?*

> 11:22 p.m., *Spence: This really hurts. Anyone else in this much pain?*

> 11:42 p.m., *Spence: I think I'm dying.*

Darren willed himself up. He was still dressed. He didn't even kick off his shoes before settling in for his pity party of one. He didn't think Spence was actually dying. Spence knew the Zenith Pharm app had emergency services. He could also phone the front desk for help.

Spence had his own pity party and wanted others to know it.

Spence came to the door in boxers and a thoroughly soaked shirt, its neck stretched and curled from abuse. He looked five inches shorter and fragile. He was a top-heavy figure that would topple over at the slightest breeze. This was how Darren was going to look when it was his turn. Would Spence be there for him when it came time?

Darren stepped into Spence's room and guided him to his bed. "Here. Have a seat."

Spence collapsed on the mattress. Darren put his hand to Spence's forehead; it was warm, but he wasn't on fire.

"How do you feel?"

"Everything hurts. I'm too hot. I can't get warm enough either." A sotto voce description.

"There isn't anything to do about it but rest. Maybe football wore you out more than you realized?"

Spence curled into a ball, pulling the covers over him. "I didn't know it'd be like this."

Darren sighed. "I'm going to get you some ice and an aspirin. Would you like that?"

Spence nodded.

Darren grabbed the ice bucket from the bathroom and set the door hook to keep Spence's door from closing. A couple of minutes later, he returned with ice and aspirin. Spence was lightly shaking.

"Okay, take this." Darren helped Spence sit upright to take the aspirin and glass of ice-cold water. Spence managed half a glass before he felt too weak to continue and lay back down.

Darren stood up to leave. He was tired and not in a mood to nurse the guy who had ditched him earlier.

"Just. Stay for a little bit?" Spence whispered.

"I'm right next door."

"Please..."

Darren sat in the chair next to the dresser. "You got it. I'll wait until you fall asleep."

Spence shuffled the pillow under his head and yanked the blankets into place, trying to get comfortable. He was like a dog trying to find that one perfect restful position before finally settling down.

Darren watched with heavy eyes as he eventually stopped stirring and his face relaxed under his matted blond hair.

* * *

Darren was awake, flat on his back, and couldn't move. His eyes were without expression; his face held no emotion; he was paralyzed. Below him was Spence, who slept peacefully in his bed, flat on his back. Darren wasn't looking up; he was looking down from the ceiling of Spence's room.

Spence was surrounded by three figures in black robes with tattered hems. They stood to the left, right, and foot of the bed. They muttered words Darren couldn't understand. Their spindly hands with fat knuckles waved various items over Spence's body in prayer: bone antlers, a string of teeth, a curved blade.

At the head of the bed stood another man. His hair was white, sparse, and wispy. It fell to his shoulders, and he wore a black rubber butcher's apron. He held out a digital tablet and thumbed at the contents. Darren realized it was Spence's profile from the RAMS program. An animated DNA strain played on a loop in a window next to a grid of metrics. The loop was the same and brief, and Darren could see the DNA catch little black flecks, like dust, onto its proteins. New protein strains grew along the lattice until it formed a triple helix.

"Very promising, Spence Dixon," the old man said in a gravelly singsong voice. From his apron's front pocket, he pulled out a collection of tiny bones and let them float into the air. The bones tumbled over in place as the man fidgeted with their placement. He scrutinized their positions briefly and noted his observation on the tablet.

Darren heard footsteps out of view. Small and quick. A two-headed goat hoofed around the side of the bed, occasionally sniffing at Spence's body. It clopped between the figures and the old man, who paid it no attention as he continued his prayers and notetaking.

"Oh, yes. Put him on the list," the old man said excitedly.

The goat made tiny bleats from each of its mouths.

The old man snatched the bones from the air and returned them to his pocket. He looked up. "Such a good friend you must be. Keeping an eye on things? Keeping him safe?" He chuckled then raised a finger and shook it once. Darren felt a lash on his cheek. His instincts told him to cover his face with his hand, but he still couldn't move. The old man shook his finger again. Another lash on this other cheek. They both burned on his face. A tiny drop of blood fell from Darren's face onto Spence's blanket. Spence remained asleep.

"Such," *scratch*, "a," *scratch*, "good," *scratch*, "friend!" Darren felt more lashes with each word. The old man's finger pointed at each spot as he mocked him. Drops of blood fell faster with each tear in his skin. "Such a good friend! Such a good friend!"

Darren couldn't move. He couldn't scream in pain. He couldn't even close his eyes. Trickles of blood poured onto

Spence's bed. It pooled in the blanket's folds; it crawled over Spence's sleeping face and flowed to his clavicle.

The old man's laughter continued with his arm waving like that of a symphony conductor. The goat bleated as it hopped around.

THE SYDNEY OPERA house has twelve stories of underground parking, the largest underground parking facility in the world at thirty-seven meters. For the winter Olympics, Norway built the world's largest underground auditorium buried fifty meters inside a mountain in Gjøvik, Norway. Jinping, China, runs a large Hadron collider 2.4 kilometers deep, making it ideal for blocking background radiation.

Robert Davis's office resided underneath two garage floors, another floor for power generators, one for water systems, one more for storage and supplies, and then an entire level for running server farms. He woke up on his couch wearing the same clothes he had the day before and noticed the ceiling lights were still on. There was no knowing what time of day it was, save for the clock on his desk, which indicated he'd managed to get four hours of sleep.

Being this far underground unnerved him. Years ago he'd mounted the schematic drawing of the Jinping lab by his office door. He hoped it would help put things in perspective. The diagram showed the structure constructed under a mountain as deep as seven Empire State Buildings. It didn't shake his fears. Instead, Robert saw an immovable mountain while he was under a once-already-collapsed six-thousand-year-old castle.

As a child, he had no problem being this far underground. He and the other children had explored forbidden depths of cave systems at the risk of earning their parents' wrath. Now, however, even with years of experience and wisdom that make one more rational over fears, Robert always felt the constant presence of being surrounded. Surrounded by the earth, by his job, by the consequences if he should fail. The world above him could come down on him at any moment.

On a normal trip to Castle Monostori, he would have his pick of the suites in the castle above. He enjoyed those trips. He'd even find time to visit old friends still living in the City. Trips from New York to Romania only happened when projects from the labs in the castle exceeded the scope of their parameters. The most common reason was equipment upgrades. He'd audit the facilities, make the right requests, and see the accepted solution was executed within budget and on time.

Zenith Pharm might have spent decades since its inception preparing for this moment, but its founders, the fallen knights, had spent centuries. When would the world end and how would it be carried out? Plagues were already part of their history. The Black Plague waxed and waned needlessly well after its most devastating time period. When the Great Plague of London arrived in the seventeenth century, it was clear just how easy illness could obliterate the fragile limbs that held society together. Medicine, they realized, was the key. Medicine was power.

Robert took his bathroom kit to the men's room in the

hallway to freshen up. The "office floor" hadn't been updated since the early eighties. Its hallways wore beige cloth paneled walls, while the floors donned a faded maroon carpet. They were lit by discolored fluorescent tubes that passed through plastic gold grates.

Robert washed his face and used a wet cloth on his pits and groin. He fixed his hair and decided to forgo shaving. Tomorrow he'd take a proper shower in the employees' lodging. He looked presentable enough in the mirror. He still considered himself attractive, if not more mature. The silver flecks in his hair were becoming more pronounced, and now they were in his stubble too. White chest hair grew over this stark-black two-headed goat tattoo. He felt the inked skin over his pecs and kneaded them against his unkempt chest hair. He was practically petting it. His pact. His seal.

Robert never gave age much thought. It wasn't something he'd have to worry about if he played his cards right. But the presence of an entire castle, filled with youthful college-age guests, made him more aware of his maturity.

He thought of Alice Whitmore. It had been nearly a week since they'd met. When he learned of her arrival, he had tracked her movements and made sure to be there to meet her at the castle. He wanted to see her in person, to get a sense of who she was and how much she knew about this place. She didn't know any of it, of course, but he had hoped.

She was attractive. Her strong European features she inherited from her ancestors shone through. She was smart too and would make any husband proud. He could definitely...no, no. He was old enough to be her father. A very young father of course. It was no matter. He had his role to play; she would have hers in time.

Robert returned to his office to find a woman sitting in

his desk chair with a steaming mug resting on his desk; the aroma of the coffee greeted his approach. Dr. Rachel McCormick was in her lab coat, with her short blond hair and black-rimmed glasses, waiting for him as though he were late for an appointment. "Good morning, Mr. Davis."

"Doctor." He opened up a wall closet with a series of identical jackets and shirts and pants on hangers. He unbuttoned his rumpled shirt. "Are you here for something specific or just to watch me change clothes?"

"I brought you coffee. Also, some good news from our lab results," she said, holding a tablet.

Robert pulled on a fresh undershirt and buttoned up a new white shirt over it before changing out of his pants and underwear. He didn't particularly care if Dr. McCormick saw him naked. She already had a habit of going past boundaries. She often helped herself to his office without knocking. She made inappropriate jokes. And she was flirty to the point of frustration. In his mind, if she wasn't going to land the plane, she might as well see what she was missing out on.

Dr. McCormick cleared her throat. "Anyway, you mentioned something about last night's patch update from DynaImaging?"

Robert removed the packaging from a fresh pair of white briefs and tossed his old ones in the basket at the bottom of the closet. "All the servers and terminals got the update and brought upgrades across the board. RAMS is practically a whole new version. Guests now have a new real-time response with PCE, which should reduce Internet bandwidth complaints significantly."

Dr. McCormick kept her eyes on her tablet as she spoke. "I'm sure that'll make the board very happy."

PCE, or Predictive Content Engine, was originally built

for real-world social-media manipulation. The right algorithm could convince an entire demographic to change their health style and choice of drugs. Targeting just one group in a remote area of the world, they could tailor everyone's online experiences without having any actual contact with the real world. The guests' phones were already hacked to point to PCE instead of the Internet without their notice. When one of the guests saw the news while at the airport, he insisted on returning home out of concern for his family's health. After a PCE video chat with his "mom," he was convinced his family was perfectly fine. Now the guests would get even more affirmation that everything would be okay as long as they stuck with the program.

Robert zipped up his pants and took the coffee. "There's more. The patch notes indicate that DNA imaging and simulation cycles have decreased by more than two-thirds! What was going to take six days is already completed. We've got our first group of Ram candidates ready for second-phase analysis."

Dr. McCormick raised an eyebrow. "You're kidding." She scrolled over the charts in his report on her tablet. The deltas between this patch and the previous patch were as he had said. Across the board, their subsidiary, DynaImaging Enterprise Systems, had made its software significantly faster. "No doubt this'll make their animation studio very happy. I'm sure their next blockbuster movies will make a mint," she said.

Robert scrunched his brow. This was a big deal. How did she not see it? "This was our bottleneck! It's been removed, so we don't have to take an entire week per batch of blood samples to find a compatible donor. We can run tests in just a couple of days!"

Dr. McCormick got up and stepped toward the door. "I

understand you and everyone in the City are eager for more Ram candidates, but we have our own bottleneck. We have to follow medical protocols for their safety. There are anesthetization rules, and I'm the only one on staff who can perform it. Some of the candidates need to be coma induced. Do you want any of them to be awake in the hands of that...butcher?"

The coffee had lost its heat, and Robert finished the cup in one gulp. He caught a tiny dribble on his cheek before it could reach his new white shirt. "Thanks." He handed her the cup. "Care to show me the Ram candidates we have so far?"

His card activated the elevator panel and he tapped B-6. "I understand your position, Doctor. However, the safety of our candidates can only go so far. Once they pass through your ward, it's out of your hands. The truth is we're behind schedule already. I'm getting pressure from below regarding the delays. This means you can expect more candidates very soon."

Dr. McCormick didn't respond. Good. He knew she was already putting in long hours. They all were. But she'd been doting over the Ram candidates like they were her patients. They weren't; they were just cattle. The sooner she realized this, the easier her job would become.

The elevator doors opened to part of a long hospital hallway network, with white plastic tiles and yellow walls and strewn with gurneys and medical equipment. The end of the hall was closed to solid secure doors with large biohazard symbols. Behind them, blood samples sat in giant glass refrigerators and automated digitizing stations, along with live samples of the Ozark virus. Robert and Dr. McCormick walked past the nurses' station and looked in the first hospital room.

Dr. McCormick tapped her tablet and pulled up a profile of the sedated patient, "Harry Brown. Over there is Trent Posman, Ali Stewart, and Lilah Yu. Both Steve Hansen and Tanner Phillips have gone downstairs."

"How many did the City request?"

"They haven't asked yet, but we can keep these ones sedated until they're ready."

Robert looked over the tablet profile of Harry Brown. Twenty-two years old, attending Oxford, on track for a promising career in epidemiology. Should the next few steps fail, it would be a shame. He would have made a great fit at Zenith Pharm. Robert tapped the tablet to pull up the pending test results. "Alice Whitmore. Her test is still in the queue?"

"We got a false negative on twenty-two guests, including hers. That doesn't prevent a baseline shot. But it means we'll have to rerun them. Twelve other tests became corrupted after the server update. Labs didn't store the blood properly after they ran the samples through the DNA sequencer, and they all got hemolysis. Ms. Birch is convinced the guests aren't fasting properly before drawing blood. Either way, I think we should adjust the schedule for new tests."

"I'll leave that to you and Ms. Birch to coordinate. Just try not to cut off their fun. We want our little lambs to enjoy themselves while they're here, right?" Harry shared a room with three other patients. Everything mimicked a normal hospital room, from the wall-mounted televisions, to the small restroom in the corner, to the faux window and drawn curtains. Robert stepped closer to examine Harry Brown's state. He was still in the pajamas he'd worn when he was abducted. He looked peaceful even with an IV drip running from his arm, which kept him sedated.

"You could be the one, Mr. Brown. You could also be just another sacrifice against the wall. Let's hope it's the former." Robert moved a fallen lock of hair from Harry's face. "I'll ask the City to do what they can to take more Ram candidates, Dr. McCormick. They'll need their strength and can't afford to lose much weight." He leaned in close to Harry's ear and whispered, "Save us, dear boy."

DARREN WOKE up unable to move. He was incredibly warm and sweaty and pinned, but somehow he felt comfortable. The problem was he didn't know where he was. From his limited vantage, it looked like his room but different. He looked down to what held him in place, and it was Spence's arm. Spence lay on top of him, breathing in a low snore.

How did I get there? he wondered. He remembered sitting in the chair, mildly annoyed, waiting for Spence to fall asleep. At some point, he must have moved to the bed and dozed off, but he had no memory of that.

He slowly peeled out from under Spence and quietly moved toward the door when Spence woke up.

"Hey, you're still here. You stayed all night?" Spence asked.

"Guess I did."

"I hope you don't mind. Around three a.m., you were snoring so loud, sitting in the chair. I couldn't wake you up. Shook you and everything. I pulled you to the bed just so you'd breathe normally."

"I don't snore!"

"Well, you do when you sleep vertically."

Darren's shirt was damp and cold. Spence was soaking wet with sweat. His sheets and blanket looked like they'd been taken out of the dryer too soon. "How are you feeling? You look exhausted."

Spence sat up and stretched. "I feel great actually. I'm a little tired, but I feel great otherwise." He reached for the ice bucket, but there was only water in it. "I'm also thirsty as hell."

"Here." Darren reached for the bucket. "I'm dressed. I can get some ice for you."

Spence stood and handed it to him. "Are we still on for the obstacle course?"

Darren was a little taken aback. Just last night, Spence had bemoaned his near-death experience. Now he wanted to climb trees and traverse ropes? "Sure you're up for it?"

A familiar bright smile climbed to life on Spence's face. "I feel fine. Really."

"Okay then. I'll be right back with your ice."

The shower was running when Darren returned. He saw Spence in the reflection of the shower. He tried not to let his eyes linger while Spence stood under the showerhead. "I'll meet you at ten?" Darren called.

"Sounds good," Spence called back.

Darren returned to his room in an odd giddy state. At first he thought he had crawled into bed with a guy in the throws of a fever only to find out Spence had pulled him in. Even if Spence was only trying to keep him from snoring, Darren woke up in bed with the guy he was truly crushing over. He heart skipped and his arms prickled. He really did have a crush. That hadn't happened in a long time.

He felt a little bad for waking Spence up last night. Poor Spence, having to haul him out of the chair and into bed.

And then onto the ceiling.

Such a good friend.

Darren ran into his bathroom and vomited. Tears erupted from his eyes, and he choked out bile from his stomach. His eyes were bloodshot from the pressure, and snot hung from his nose. He tried to be quiet. The walls weren't thin, but he couldn't stand for someone to hear his wailing. He turned on the shower and crawled in before he could pull off his clothes. He didn't understand why he was being so emotional. Shaking, he cried uncontrollably until he was exhausted and the water had lost its warmth.

Darren's arms ached from gripping his sides. He turned off the water, dried himself off, and took a long look in the mirror as he regained his breathing. He focused on his heartbeat and breathed through it. He envisioned his day ahead. That's all there was to think about.

"Think about the day ahead," he told himself as he stood in the mirror. "Think how much fun you'll have. How much fun your friends will have."

Such a good friend.

When Darren made his way down to the lobby, Hannah was sitting at the table surrounded by Alice and Alex, with Spence and Yuri standing behind her. Hannah held her head in her hand, and Alice held her other hand.

Darren caught the tail end of Hannah, saying, "This is fucked up. Is just leaving even an option?"

"There has to be a good reason. It must be an emergency," Alice said.

Spence leaned to Darren. "Harry took off in the middle of the night. He and Hannah were hanging out earlier, and he went back to his room, and that was it."

"Hanging out when? You all went to bed super early," Darren said.

"We fucked. Okay?" Hannah could hear them chatting. "It was before the fever hit. We were there, together, afterward. He noticed his symptoms picking up." Her voice shook. "He gave me a kiss and said, 'See you at breakfast, love,' Then grabbed his clothes and went. I guess he went all the way back to fucking England." Hannah began to cry.

Alice turned to Darren and Spence. "I think I'm going to stay here and spend time with Hannah. You should go ahead without me."

Hannah protested, "No. No, you don't have to do that. I'm fine. I'm just upset." She wiped a tear from her left eye. "Seriously, it's just a man. I keep falling for them all the time."

Alice persisted. "I know you're fine. But this is a fucked-up situation. You guys go ahead. Seriously." She squeezed Hannah's hand with both of hers. Hannah reached over and gave her a hug.

"Well, I'm not staying behind." Alex stood up from the table. "We'll be back in a few hours, yes?"

Yuri was behind them, chewing a sausage skewered on his fork. "All right, let's go finally!" Alex punched his arm. "Sorry, Hannah."

* * *

Darren followed a staggered process of other guests making their way into the forest along a path that led over a hill and into a park area designated with a sign in Romanian he assumed meant, WELCOME TO THE OBSTACLE COURSE. When they arrived, he estimated there were around thirty people at the first part of the course. Looking around, he didn't see much of a challenging course. He'd expected walls to climb, tires to jump over, rope swings. Instead, everyone was handed harnesses, gloves, and helmets from a man and woman geared up with a matching shirts that read, "Monostori."

The two people pulled the equipment from a large plastic trunk. Behind them stood a tree with a ladder attached. That's when Darren realized the course was high up in the trees. This was a tree rope course. The entire course was four parts: a rope bridge, a climbing net between trees, a series of log swings, and finally a zip line.

"Oh, shit," Spence said, looking up at the rope work above him. His face went a shade of pale.

"Right? Isn't this awesome?" Yuri was already in his harness, putting on his helmet. Both he and his sister had the energy of two cats reacting to the sound of a tuna can opening.

Spence's face had gone slack. Darren stepped into his harness, "You okay?"

"That's really high up. I don't think it's safe."

Darren pointed at the long black cable that ran along the course. "See that wire? It can hold a ton of weight. We'll be attached at all times." That didn't seem to assuage the fears of Spence, who stood frozen in place. "And..." Darren pointed to the trees between each course. "Every part of the course has a ladder. See? If you can't go any farther, there's always an out."

On his way to the head of the line, Yuri blurted loudly, "Spence, you can't be afraid of heights. You're so tall!" Spence glared back at him.

Darren was trying to fit into his harness when the female instructor came over and offered to help him step into the straps correctly. It was a bit too snug in the crotch and made his shorts bunch up and look funny. But pretty much everyone looked just as ridiculous. She helped

Spence into his as well, having to adjust the straps to accommodate his height.

Everyone received the same guidelines from the other instructor at the first tree. "Only one person at a time. The tree platforms at each stop can only support two people, so if there are two people ahead of you, wait until you can go. Make sure your zip-line trolley is secure before each course. Use both hands and feet at all times. Do not use your phones. Be encouraging to others."

When Darren's turn came up, he began to climb. The ladder was new and sturdy, not budging from the shifting of his weight. At sixty feet, he climbed to the first platform, a slab of wooden planks attached to the first course: a rope bridge. He looked down to Spence below him and waved. Alex was behind Spence, scratching his back for support. Spence grimaced a smile.

The bridge was three ropes in an inverted triangle. Two to hold on to, one to step with. Darren could see only one other person across the bridge starting their way to the next course. He fastened himself to the zip line and pulled down against it to test the weight to make sure he was secure, then stepped out. With both hands gripping the outer ropes for balance, he struggled his way onto the bridge. The ropes were strong against his grip and footing. He looked down and experienced a wave of vertigo. He shut his eyes for a moment, instead focusing on the end of the bridge and making sure not to look down. One scoot after the next, he was across the expanse before he realized it.

Darren stepped onto the next platform and looked back for Spence, who was already taking in the fullness of the first rope challenge with a stark white expression.

"Spence, I'll wait here for you. It's really a very short bridge. You can totally do it!" Darren shouted. Claps and shouts of encouragement resounded from below. He heard Alex's accent among the voices.

Spence, for all his panic, fell into the mechanics of the task at hand. He was fastened to the zip. He gripped the rails and stepped onto the bridge. Darren watched him, scrutinized every facial expression and eye movement to read his mind. Spence was looking down at his shaking feet.

"Look at me! Don't look down!" Darren yelled.

Alex was already at the top when Spence reached the halfway point. Darren heard Spence's breath quicken. He spoke calmly. "You're halfway done? That's great. Come here. I'll help you up, big guy."

Through his trembles, Spence managed to say, "This was a bad idea."

"Nah. You're doing great. If you make it across, I'll let you punch me in the face."

"I'm so going to punch you in the face." Spence kept scooting along. He was close enough to Darren to reach him. Darren grabbed Spence's harness and pulled him to the platform. Spence immediately grabbed on to the tree.

Alex cheered from the other side. The claps from below went unnoticed to Spence. He unhooked his zip line. "I think I'm done."

"Sure!" Darren helped Spence to the ladder; Spence couldn't figure out how to climb down without letting go of the tree for dear life. "Will you wait for me? At the end of the course?" Spence just nodded and moved down the steps with clear intent.

Spence made it all the way down before moving on to the next challenge, the net. It was a vertical wall of roped netting that went across to the next tree. It looked about the same distance as the first challenge, but when Darren climbed onto the wall, it immediately leaned against him, making him lose his center of gravity. He couldn't imagine Spence doing well on this one.

Alex was already behind him by the time he climbed across the next challenge. "You are so slow! You are like sloth!"

Darren laughed through his tired breathing. "Have you ever seen a sloth?"

"We have zoos, you know."

"Is that where you live?"

He heard Yuri laughing below. "My sister is a monkey!" Alex shouted something in Ukrainian at her brother, which only elicited more laughter.

The next challenge was another bridge, but instead of a single rope, square wooden steps swung independently from their own suspension. *Once more into the breach*, Darren thought as he found his footing on the first step. Immediately his back seized up as he tried to keep balance. He pulled himself with the rails and made his next step more prepared.

One step after the next, and he was at the final part of the course, the zip line. Spence was on the ground at the end of the course with Yuri waiting for him and Alex. Spence looked at his feet, hands in his pockets. Darren held on to the zip trolly and pushed himself off, allowing gravity to do the rest of the work. The zip line was a guided descent to the final touchdown with a scattering of people clapping for his big finish.

Darren unclamped his trolley from the zip line and stepped out of the way for Alex, who immediately came up behind him. The female staffer helped him out of his harness and helmet.

He found Spence off to the side, trying to look invisible

despite being an entire head taller than anyone else. "Please don't punch me in the face," Darren said.

That got a smile out of Spence. "It's all good. I should have known better. I can't even do Ferris wheels."

Yuri and Alex came up to them, congratulating everyone, including Spence. He took it graciously enough. Alex said she was going to head back to the castle to check in on Hannah and maybe find out what happened to Harry. Yuri was still in his harness and helmet; he still had a couple more rounds in him. They both took off, leaving Darren alone with Spence, who probably wanted to be anywhere except the scene of his own embarrassment.

Darren asked Spence, "How about you? You headed back?"

"No. I think I'll go for a walk actually. I could use the air."

"Do you want some company? There's a cemetery at the top of that trail. I heard it's got a great view. Not too high up." That was a dumb suggestion; Spence was more than capable of doing what he wanted, and Darren had pestered him enough today. But Darren couldn't help his enthusiasm. There weren't any macho cliques around. And Spence seemed genuinely excited to hang out this morning.

"I'd like that," Spence said.

"Great! It should be farther up this trail. I didn't bring a map with me."

"We'll figure it out. I don't have anywhere to be. Do you?"

They found the cemetery grounds located in a clearing in the forest. A stone fence surrounded the plot of land, its iron gate left open with one of its hinges broken free.

From the cemetery, they could see the entirety of the land, the other hiking trails, the very tiny castle with its tiny pool, the hills that surrounded it, and the mountains behind them.

Spence let out a low whistle. Darren was breathing heavily from the long hike. "Not too high up?"

Spence scoffed. "Let's not talk about that."

They took in a self-guided tour of the old headstones along a path toward a white tomb in the center. The headstones were either unmarked, or too old and weathered to show their names. Most appeared to be several hundred years old. Tall grass and small bushes slowly reclaimed parts of the cemetery. Only the tomb looked like it had any upkeep.

Darren listened to Spence remark on what he'd learned in his guidebook. "There were some cemeteries worth visiting just for their notoriety. This one cemetery has each headstone hand carved and painted with a depiction of the cause of death, captioned with an epitaph. There were thousands of them. The pictures had a very Romanian Catholic vibe. They were full of crosses with above-ground burial plots like sarcophaguses. These don't look anything like that. These look really plain. Like the ones back home."

"Disappointed?" Darren asked.

Spence shook his head. "Just surprised. No crosses, no visible plots, just big rock slabs and grass."

They approached the large white tomb in the center of the cemetery. The tomb's iron gate door was closed. its mounted metal plate read, ÎN ORAŞ, EL NE CHEAMĂ.

Darren gave a useless attempt to open the door. He could see through the gate to a stairway that went underground to total blackness. He was glad the door wouldn't open.

Spence grabbed a handle on the gate and lifted it. To

Darren's embarrassment, the gate swung open. "Let's check it out!"

Darren pulled out his phone and worked to flick on the light.

The tomb was cool and quiet as they descended. Even with the flashlight, Darren and Spence needed time for their eyes to adjust to the dark. They led themselves down a set of stairs into an underground room. The room was so long the flashlight couldn't reach the end. The wall had shelves cut into its sides. Each shelf housed skeletal remains covered in deteriorating cloth. Some of the skeletons lay with a sword and shield, brandishing a red cross across their chests and a knight's helmet on their skulls. They looked so delicate, as if touching them would turn them to dust. Darren and Spence walked along the wall in silent reverence, taking in every set of bones, with their mismatched armor and occasional sword.

When they reached the end of the room, they found another caged gate with another set of stairs behind it. The same plate was attached to the gate: ÎN ORAȘ, EL NE CHEAMĂ.

Spence stood directly behind Darren. "Just how deep does this place go?" he said quietly.

"What if it goes on forever?"

"I've had dreams like that recently."

"Like what?" The talk of dreams unsettled Darren for some reason.

"It's the same one too. I'm trying to get somewhere, and I keep going down. Down paths, stairs, elevators, ladders. It never ends. I never reach the bottom. Meanwhile something is coming for me. Whatever it is I'm trying to get away from never stops chasing me."

Darren stared at the gate. What if the tomb did keep

going down? What was down there? What would he find at the bottom?

He turned to Spence with a shiver and slightly bumped into him. "I think I just creeped myself out."

"Is it your turn to be scared?" Spence hadn't moved.

"I didn't want you to feel left out."

"Did you want to keep looking around or head back?"

It was almost a dare. *I dare you to keep going.*

"You'd go all the way down to the bottom?" Darren asked.

"Well, I wouldn't go alone."

How long have we been standing like this?

Darren felt Spence touch his waist. He froze. His heart leapt into his throat when the slight touch became a pull. The dirt under Darren's feet crunched as he stepped in close. Spence's body odor was fresh and acidic, like cedar. A sudden inhalation of air entered Darren's lungs as their lips met.

Quietly in the dark and cool of the tomb, gentle, unsure, timid kisses grew. Spence's arms wrapped and pulled Darren into his chest. His lips were salty and minty. Spence pushed against him with his stubbled chin, shifting his weight. Darren felt their groins slowly grind. Spence's heavy breathing matched his. Their mouths were hungry. They were starving. They had waited too long for this.

Darren felt the tinge of his betrayal. He'd doubted himself all this time. It took a dark forbidden underground tomb to bring them together. He wished it would have happened sooner. Either way, it didn't matter. They were here now.

As suddenly as Darren had fallen into his arms, Spence jumped as a distant clang echoed in the tomb. He pushed Darren back and looked to the source of the sound. Another flashlight shone through from the steps above. Voices filtered through. People were coming down. Spence took a giant step away from Darren.

A guy and girl stepped through, shining their phones at the bodily remains in the walls. One of the lights flashed on Darren and Spence, which caused a startled scream.

Spence spoke loudly. "It's just us!"

There was male laughter. "Holy shit, you scared the shit out of me!"

"Sorry," Spence said.

"Not you. Her!" the guy said. They giggled in frightful recovery as they continued their exploration. "Whoa, check these people out," he said, pointing to one of the skeletons in the wall.

Darren reached for Spence's hand, but he was already heading toward the steps. Darren moved with him back outside, leaving the two visitors to their own underground tour.

"Sorry!" Spence immediately responded while rubbing the back of his head. "I didn't mean to do that."

Darren's stomach fell. Spence didn't mean to kiss him. "Oh." Darren looked down at his feet.

Spence took Darren's hand in soft apology. "I didn't mean to freak out. I..." Noticing more people making their way around the cemetery, he let go of Darren's hand.

Darren followed his line of sight. Some of the other guests were walking around headstones, taking selfies, not paying attention to anyone.

"Nobody cares, Spence. Even if they did, who cares what other people think? It's not like you're at risk of getting gay bashed."

Spence was pacing, trying to come up with the words. "I know. It's fucked up. I know who I am, but it's not that..."

"It's fine. I get it."

"No. It's not fine." Spence slumped against the tomb wall. "How I was raised, how I was taught. I had to go to a camp for fuck's sake. It's not fine at all. And I like you. I really fucked it up." He pulled at a blade of grass.

Darren sat next to him. "You were sent to a camp? For being gay?" he asked. Spence nodded. He'd never known someone who'd been put in a camp. "Conversion camps" was what they called them. A place for Christians to torture children into being straight. That would fuck anyone up.

"I guess you're out, right?" Spence asked.

Darren nodded. "I came out as bi in high school. It wasn't a big deal. Everyone was mostly cool with it. Sometimes my friends would get confused when I was dating a girl. Other than that, I'm glad I came out. I've been much happier."

Darren snuck his hand into Spence's when he noticed no one was around. "You don't have to do anything you're not comfortable with. I was in the closet for a long time. It's not easy, and the last thing you need is someone pressuring you before you're ready."

"Yeah, well, maybe I need someone to pressure me." Spence squeezed Darren's fingers.

"I can pressure your butt."

Spence laughed. "Baby steps, please."

Darren stood up. "Tell you what. Let's hang out at the pool while it's still nice out. We can spend some time together. Just you and me."

The man and woman stepped out of the tomb, squinting at the light. "So fucking creepy," said the guy as they left the cemetery, not even noticing Darren and Spence.

"Or we can go back in the tomb and close the gate behind us," Spence said.

Their walk back had a calm silence. The sounds of birds and bugs filled the conversation for them. Darren was no longer sure how to make small talk. Spence had just admitted his feelings for him then collapsed into his own shame for that very reason. Darren never knew the guilt of liking men. He never considered it to be a bad thing any more than liking women. His parents had always been supportive. His friends in school didn't care about each other's sexuality or gender. He didn't grow up in a rural conservative religious home.

"So how was camp? Like, what happened?" Darren finally asked.

"Well, lots of prayer. And lectures. And writing. Also, I was molested."

"What the fuck?"

Spence kicked at a rock on the path, "Took me a while to come to terms with that. The church sponsored my trip. They made sure I was well aware of the consequences for being gay. Even when I came back, everyone treated me differently. Like an ex-con. I've was reformed, but now I have a record.

"So I put myself into the role they wanted. Do the part they wanted me to play, and I could be accepted. I played that part; I played it like I was going for the Oscar. I've been doing this role so long, I'm not even sure if I'm the real me sometimes."

Darren didn't know what he could say to that. Instead he risked a one-arm hug around Spence's shoulders. Spence one-arm hugged him back.

By the time they returned to the castle, the pool deck was already busy, and most of the chairs were occupied.

"I'm going to see if I can find a couple of chairs," Darren said. "Do you want a drink?"

Spence pulled at his shirt. "Yeah. I'll meet you out there. I'm going to change. I'm starting to reek."

"I'm not complaining," said Darren as he went to look for a place to sit. The weather was warm, the sun beaming down a constant force of heat against everyone's bodies. The patio was packed with sunbathers; chatty conversations flowed around every table; and floating pool chairs bumped together amid the splashing.

Darren returned to the lobby and planted himself at the table closest to the pool to keep an eye out for a table to free itself. He could also see Spence from the elevator to find him here instead of trying to spot him from the crowd.

Several minutes passed, and restless boredom eventually set in. He could see up to the fourth floor, but saw no sign of Spence emerging from his room. Maybe he was showering. Darren remembered his brief glimpse of Spence in the shower that morning.

Out of boredom, he checked the apps on his phone. He scrolled through the photos and videos he'd taken. There was the castle, the room, more of the castle, the hills and mountains, selfies of him in the castle, pictures of the trail and the other people he'd hiked with: Spence, Alice, Harry, Hannah, Alex, and Yuri.

A video of the cemetery tomb was last. He didn't realize it, but he must have accidentally hit "record" when he'd turned on the flashlight. He pressed "play" and watched the shaky footage of the walls and ground as the camera panned around then moved to the back of the tomb with skeletons resting in its walls. Even in the safety of the castle, Darren found the footage unsettling. There was the gate. He paused on the gate and looked at the words written on the metal plate: ÎN ORAȘ, EL NE CHEAMĂ.

He switched to the browser app and searched for "Romanian to English" and found a result. He entered "in oras, el ne cheama," hoping he didn't need to use special characters. It came back with "In the city, He calls." The cemetery didn't have any religious markings except for the crosses on the armor in the tomb. "In the city, He calls" must have been some kind of message for the armored dead. Maybe a religious or local saying.

Darren played more of the video. "How deep does this go?" That was Spence. Now he almost wished they'd gone down farther. Maybe then they wouldn't have been interrupted. "Did you want to keep looking around or head back?" After a moment, he heard them kiss. It happened much faster than he remembered. The video became unintelligible as the camera jostled against Spence. The kiss was much shorter too. Back then, it felt like an eternity. "It's just us!" Spence called out to whoever had interrupted them. The camera steadied as Darren turned off the recording; the final frame rested on a figure in a black cloak looking back from the other side of the gate.

Darren visibly jumped in his chair as he dropped the phone on the table. The screen froze on reflective eyes glowing on a pale face, captioned by the sign ÎN ORAȘ, EL NE CHEAMĂ.

ALICE STAYED with Hannah while her friends went to do the ropes course. She didn't realize her friends could just leave Hannah in a state like that. It was obvious from Hannah's distress over Harry's departure that the two had become close. They already were spending time together since she'd spotted them at the old part of the castle. She remembered the way Harry stayed by Hannah's side at the first pool party, and Hannah would ask for little favors like getting her another drink or accompanying her for a smoke.

Hannah dried the tears from her face. "Why am I so upset? Jesus. I mean, it wasn't anything serious. We had some fun. We talked a lot. I thought there was something there. Next thing I know, he's gone completely and checked out."

"Have you asked Ms. Birch when he left?" Alice asked.

Hannah kept checking her phone for notifications, not hearing the question or ignoring it. "He's getting my texts, but I can't call him with whatever phone plan he's got. Ugh. Am I the only one here with spare SIM cards that work?"

Alice spotted Ms. Birch working at the computer

behind the front desk. She left Hannah and Alex and beelined for her. Ms. Birch's brown hair was again pulled back in a tight bun, and she wore a matching brown suit jacket and skirt with a silver pendant of a baby goat attached to her lapel.

Alice saw Ms. Birch spot her approaching and tightened her posture, readying herself for the interruption. "Good morning, Ms. Birch. I was wondering if you could find some information about our friend Harry Brown? We can't find him anywhere."

Ms. Birch didn't stop typing at the computer. "Monostori is a very large place, Ms. Whitmore. Should I form a search party?"

Alice crossed her arms. "His room is empty."

"Sounds pretty obvious to me that he checked out. This isn't Hotel California. Eventually people can and do leave here to return to their homes."

Ms. Birch must have only one mode of talking, Alice thought, finding her dismissive condescension infuriating. "Are you serious? People don't just leave without saying goodbye. I'm talking about someone's safety, and your answer is 'It's a big place'?"

Ms. Birch looked up at Alice with a raised eyebrow and extra-loud keyboard tap. "Here it is." She looked back at the computer screen. "Checkout time: two forty-five a.m. Mr. Brown was taken to the airport in Bucharest. A return flight to England has been arranged for six a.m."

"He really checked out?"

"Quite. It seems he and two others have canceled their plans with us. I've been on the phone all morning with legal to resolve their contractual obligations. I suspect I'll be working like this for the remainder of the program, giving trends." Ms.

Birch pulled papers from the printer below the desk as they arrived. "People are dying, Ms. Whitmore. It's not unreasonable to ask to leave in order to bury your loved ones."

"No, I suppose not. It's just so sudden," Alice said.

Ms. Birch paused her computer activity, folded her hands on the desk, and looked directly at her. Alice braced for another snarky dismissive. Instead Ms Birch spoke like she was offering friendly advice. "Take it from me. The time will come when you have to leave. It will be sudden and terrible. The last thing on your mind won't be about the friends you made here but instead getting to where you need to go as soon as possible."

She was right. If Alice got word that her dad or mom caught the virus or suffered any serious injury, she'd return to them immediately. Goodbyes could wait. She wondered if Hannah would understand.

"Thanks for your time, Ms. Birch." Alice left a little embarrassed for jumping to the wrong conclusion, and she was a little put off by the unusual softness in Ms. Birch's tone. Maybe she had been making other wrong assumptions.

Alice's update helped Hannah feel a bit better. "You know, it is what it is," Hannah agreed. "I'm not doing this pity party over a guy I just met. When he gets back to merry flipping England, he can call me."

"Until then, you still interested in going to that ropes course?"

"No, it's too warm now. I want to have mimosas and talk shit about people."

Alice smiled. "Great. You can introduce me to all the famous people I don't know here."

"Hey, I'm famous," objected Hannah.

"I know you are. I just think it's time I started seeing other famous people."

Hannah went to order a round of drinks and returned a couple of minutes later with two other women Alice had seen several times around the castle. "I have no idea who these are, so we're all going to make new friends."

They spent rest of the morning and midafternoon chatting with the other guests over more mimosas and charcuterie. Hannah stayed by Alice's side to keep her in the conversations. "Don't be a wallflower, Alice," she said. "You're the most interesting person here." Hannah gave her arm a light pinch. "Just be yourself. It's so much easier."

"Easier for who exactly?" Alice replied.

"Claire Montag!" A cheery woman with curly hair and a round rosy face hopped into the chair next to Alice and extended her hand.

"Alice Whitmore." She shook her hand.

"I've seen you around. You're on the fourth floor, right? I'm not tracking you or anything. I'm just a people watcher. I'm on the second floor. Group two."

"So you got a head start on the program, so to speak," Alice said.

Claire nodded. "Oh, yes. I already had the shot and resulting fever. I was fine by the next morning. My friend Zach took two days to get back to normal."

Alice picked up a garlic-stuffed olive from the cheese board. "So what were you doing before you came here?"

"Well, I was working for this law firm just after graduating and studying for the bar before all this happened." Claire made a sweeping gesture and laughed. "You wouldn't believe how tedious it can be remote working with a boss who can't figure out how to operate a videoconference app."

"Ah, I dodged that bullet. I was on unemployment after they shut the bars down," Alice said.

"See? I was on track to getting furloughed as well when these people reached out to me. I guess I traded one set of bloodsuckers for another!" Claire gave a nervous chuckle before taking a sip of her drink.

"So you're a recent graduate? Not a social media influencer or an Olympian?" Alice asked.

"I know, right? My group, also group one, we were just some college students or recently graduated. Now there are musicians, athletes, actresses, and the occasional oligarch relative." Claire pointed her chin to a slender man chatting up Hannah. However she was feeling after learning Harry had left, Hannah was soaking up the attention.

"What do you mean 'we were'?"

Claire shrugged. "I mean, when you're done, you're done. Half my group ended up leaving last night or early this morning. I'm one of four people still here from my group."

"How did you find out?"

"Housekeeping was already cleaning their rooms when I got up. They were all empty."

"Just like that? You didn't get any farewells from anyone in your group? Notes or texts?"

Claire shook her head. "At first I was kind of upset. Just leaving without saying goodbye? I thought we were all becoming friends. I guess that's just me. I even called my mom like I was homesick. But she reminded me, 'You're going to save the world' and all that. So I'm sticking it out."

"Someone from our group left as well. I wonder how many from the other groups are gone."

Claire hummed an "I don't know" as she continued

with her drink. "Maybe we'll get more celebrities in their place."

This didn't sit right with Alice. Both Claire and Hannah had people leave with no notice. She wondered how many others also had left. She looked up to the fourth floor and noticed Vlad pushing a housekeeping cart down the walkway. He stopped at room 402 and entered. Harry's room.

Alice stood to leave. She leaned toward Hannah and said quietly enough just for her to hear, "I'll be back in a bit. I'm gonna take a nap."

Hannah pouted. "You can't go. I'm too emotionally fragile, remember?"

Alice patted her shoulder and made way to room 402. The cart was just outside the room, and the door was propped open. Vlad's back was to the door as he tucked a new fitted sheet onto the mattress.

"Thanks for the aspirin last night."

"Ah!" Vlad jump and turned, clutching his chest. He face was even whiter somehow. He relaxed when he saw Alice and sat on the unfinished bed. Vlad's eyes were heavy with exhaustion; he had the look of college student who had stayed up all night to cram for an exam. "Oh, my gosh."

"I didn't mean to startle you." Alice sat next to him. "Do you do everything in this place? Bellhop, sanitation, housekeeping..."

"Feels like it. We have other staff too. The kitchen staff and the bartender, security, and Ms. Birch. Normally housekeeping is outsourced, but safety restrictions make that impossible."

"I didn't realize."

"No one else from the City wants to do labor in this

place either. We're really short-staffed. At least we can still outsource laundry service."

"Wait. Are you the one who turns down my bed?"

Vlad blushed. "I mean, I turn down all the beds."

"This whole time I didn't know there's been cute boy in my room." Alice gave him a smirk. She did find him cute. Politeness might have been part of his job description, but his shy demeanor was refreshing in comparison to the rowdy garishness she saw in other men her age. "Every time I see you, you're always working. Days and nights. You must not get much down time."

"If I'm here, I'm working." Vlad got up and gathered the old sheets from the floor.

"So you must have been here last night when Harry Brown checked out," Alice said. Vlad's arms were full of dirty linens; he looked as though he had forgotten what to do with them. Alice continued, "I remembered you were here to take my luggage when I first arrived in the middle of the night. I assumed you work nights as well. You'd have seen Harry and the others check out last night."

Vlad stammered, "I...just try to keep my head down. I don't ask questions."

"What kind of questions? Questions about why these people checked out so suddenly?"

Vlad looked back at Alice; his eyes had become blood-shot. A tiny signal in her brain told her to prepare for bad news. The kind of signal that braced her for bad news when her parents had called out of the blue, just after the pandemic broke out and thousands of people began dying. It was her grandparents, on her father's side.

"I didn't know what this program was about. I really didn't," Vlad said.

Alice spoke slowly. "What is this program about?"

Vlad went to the cart and stuffed the old sheets into the laundry bin. He motioned to her. "Come with me. I have to show you something."

Alice got up, annoyed at not getting a direct answer, but equally worried that what he had to show her was worse. They rode the elevator to the lobby then headed down the far conference hallway to a door at the end. Vlad pressed his door key to a panel, and the door unlocked with a beep. He looked back to make sure no one could see them. Then he pulled Alice inside to a staircase going down.

"Where are you taking me?" she asked.

"Shh. Please be quiet. We can't get caught," he whispered.

Alice tracked the door exits on the staircase as they went farther down: G1, G2, B1, B2. Vlad stopped at B2 and very slowly turned the handle and peeked out. He pushed the door fully open and motioned for her to follow. It was dark on the other side, but she could see beyond Vlad's face. She went to exit with him and heard a distant door above her open. She froze. Vlad's eyes went wide, and he motioned faster.

"This is the last one?" A man's voice from above echoed in the stairway. Hard steps and the sound of something dragging came down toward them.

Alice stepped out, and Vlad, as quickly and quietly as he could, closed the door.

He pulled out his phone and turned on a light. "Quickly!" he whispered.

Alice stayed close to him as they hurried down a concrete floor. She could barely see the metal storage racks they walked past. "Where are you taking me?" she whispered.

"Here."

They came upon a shelf and turned left. Alice could see contents on the shelves as the walked on. There were boxes with bright labels she couldn't read, large jars of pickles and cherries, and giant quantities of canned food. She recognized the stacks of pool filters and water-treatment chemicals, cleaning supplies, and power tools; they were in the storage area of the castle.

Vlad stopped at the end and opened another door. "This room used to be empty. I found these..."

The lights came on. Alice's and Vlad's eyes met as distant heels clacked toward them. Vlad stepped into the room and Alice followed. Alice was too concerned about not making a sound to notice what was in the room with her. The sounds of footsteps were closer now. The sounds of two men in mid conversation rang throughout the basement. "It's like they packed their whole fucking house to come here."

"Get down," whispered Vlad. He was crouched behind a pile of assorted luggage. There must have been twenty individual pieces of luggage stacked haphazardly in the center of the room, which was no bigger than a closet. Before Alice could look at one of the tags, Vlad grabbed one of the larger suitcases and rested it on top of them.

Alice managed to pull herself into a fetal curl on the floor; she pulled herself in as close as she could. Vlad was on top of her with the luggage resting on his back. Alice tried to not breathe. She heard Vlad forcing very controlled, slow breaths. His face was mere inches from hers. His legs and arms pinned her in place. He was cold against her skin.

The footsteps stopped at the door.

Alice and Vlad became stone.

The door opened and the steps came inside. Something made a thin rumbling sound. Then hard metal clicks. *It must be luggage*, Alice realized. Someone had rolled another person's luggage down there with them.

"If this keeps up, we're going to need a bigger room for all this luggage," said one of the men.

"Why bother keeping them? Why not throw them away?" said the other.

"Sure. Nothing suspect about a bunch of packed luggage showing up in a landfill. Think! Besides, they're not staying here. It's just temporary until we sort everyone out." The first man grunted and hoisted the luggage up and set it on top of the pile. He grunted again, and Alice felt the pile shift next to her. "Nope. Nope. Nope!" he said as the luggage fell backward on top of Alice and Vlad. A silent puff of breath from Vlad brushed against Alice's ear.

One of the men let out a defeated sigh. "Oh, fuck it all. Give me that." Alice felt another shake of the luggage pile.

"We need to clean this up. It can't be all disorganized like this."

"Fuck that. We've got enough to do. We'll give it to the little prince to clean up."

The other man chuckled.

Alice, a statue of knots and cramps, listened to them stomp away for what felt like hours until the lights shut off and sound of a door closing echoed throughout the basement. They waited several more seconds before they finally moved.

Vlad pushed himself up, letting the luggage fall away from him. He turned his phone light back on.

Alice took her time standing, not knowing if she'd have to duck and hide again at a moment's notice. She saw Vlad sitting on the pile, watching her. If he was waiting for her, she didn't know what to say. She looked back at the pieces of luggage and examined some of the tags. Alice read them all in disbelief. "Parker Devereux, Los Angeles," "Tamaryn Ellis, Pensacola," and "Harry Brown, London."

"Alice, it isn't safe here. These people didn't leave." Vlad kept his voice to a whisper.

Alice grabbed a piece of luggage belonging to "Mads Porter" and opened it. Clothing was crumpled into place, toiletries shoved into any place that fit. She checked the pockets and pulled out a wallet and passport with a young man's face on it.

Alice held up the passport. "They didn't leave?"

"They were taken."

"Taken. Taken where?"

Vlad put his face in his hands.

"I have to get out of here." Alice shoved Mad's belongings back and replaced the luggage. She climbed over the pile and left the room. It wasn't elegant or quiet; she didn't care. She got to the door and found it locked. Vlad was right behind her. He used his keycard to unlock it.

Vlad followed Alice back up the stairs until he heard a door above them open again and grabbed her shoulder. Alice wanted to barrel forward, consequences be damned. Vlad opened the door to G1 and tugged at her to follow.

It was a garage. Alice could see the blue of daylight from the garage entrance. Multiple vans that resembled the one she had arrived in were parked near the entrance. If she could get the keys, she thought, she could probably barrel her way through the gate. They might come after her. They knew this country better. And she didn't know where "here" was.

"Technically guests are allowed to be here. We can walk back without trouble," said Vlad.

"Walk back where? To my room?" Alice snapped.

"I still have finish housekeeping." Vlad's voice was sheepish.

Alice's anger swelled inside her and swirled in her chest with fear. Vlad rocked on his heels and rubbed his hands together in a nervous tic. He looked as fearful as she felt. He never had told her where the other guests had been taken. If he knew, he was too scared to say it.

Her anger deflated like a sad balloon. Vlad would get in trouble if he didn't finish his job cleaning up after the body snatchers. And Alice didn't need to return to her room at all. She could sleep in the goddamn lobby.

"Let's go." Alice took Vlad's cold hands in hers and headed out of the garage. She imagined Hannah and the others still sitting around tables in plush seats completely unaware that their friends were gone, taken to some place she didn't know. She didn't know if they were even alive. Should she tell Hannah and the others? If she told them, it might cause a panic. Ms. Birch would no doubt try to spin it some way: "We're shipping their luggage separately," she'd say, or some other made-up story.

It would be pretty obvious that Alice had gained access to the storage area through Vlad. What if they dropped all pretenses and took everyone all at once? Could they pull it off? There were more guests than there were staff. But the guards were armed. They were strapped with submachine guns, which were considered illegal back home.

Alice was trapped at the castle, she realized. She didn't know why they'd put on so much pretense. She didn't know where the others had been taken. When she thought on a possible answer, it only brought up more questions. When she spotted the bartender at the back entrance to the castle smoking with a woman in a chef's uniform, her next question was who was going to make her a drink.

Look at them, she thought, *all part of the show. Just a couple of hospitality workers at an old satanic castle here to make your stay a pleasant one.*

They rested against the side of the building and eyed Alice and Vlad as they came up to the entrance. "Giving your girlfriend a nice tour, prince?" The bartender was too stacked for his own good; he probably opened beer bottles with his pecs. The cook laughed out smoke.

"Hi, Marius. Just a little walk. That's all." Vlad's didn't make eye contact with the bartender.

"So you just fraternizing or are you cleaning more than just her sheets?" Marius smirked and turned to Alice. His eyes had a permanent glare that started to look very punchable. "Enjoying our little program so far?"

Venom filled Alice's veins. She knew she had to play along, though, just not for her own safety but also Vlad's. "I think it's neat. As in whiskey neat, when you're done here."

That made the bartender laugh. "Shit. You got it."

She and Vlad were heading toward the entrance when the bartender grabbed Vlad's arm, making him flinch. "Ms. Birch has been asking about you. Might want to—"

Something in Alice snapped. She saw the fear in Vlad's eyes; he was terrified of this man. Alice moved in front of Vlad and removed the bartender's grip from Vlad's arm. "We're both going inside now." *This was a bad move*, she realized. *He's twice your size. This is it. This is how I disappear with the others.*

The bartender's face reddened, and he looked like he could spit. He grabbed Alice's wrist. "Don't you fucking touch me!" But Alice did touch him. She touched him just as she'd been taught in class. It was a common move (how to escape a wrist hold), but this time it felt incredibly satisfying. Alice raised her gripped arm behind the bartender's wrist so she could grab it with her other arm. Turn with your hips. She twisted her body, and the bartender was pulled off balance. She didn't need him to let go; she didn't want him to. She pulled hard enough that his momentum headed against the wall, where she joined him with her weight. He barked loudly as he was slammed face-first against the stone wall.

Vlad and the cook both stood back, mouths agape.

"The feeling is mutual." Alice was breathing heavily. "You need both wrists to make that drink?" She leaned on the bartender's wrist and heard him cry out. That was enough. Alice stepped away to let him recover. This was the first time she'd felt in control of anything since she'd arrived. It felt great. It felt dangerous too.

"Careful, Marius. If you take too much damage, they'll reclaim you," said Vlad, who looked at her with exhilaration.

Alice took Vlad by the hand and led them both inside. She didn't want to stick around in case the bartender wanted a second round.

"Holy shit! How did you do that?" Vlad asked as they quickly stepped away.

"I grew up taking a lot of silly classes: fighting, shooting. Daddy's little militant. I always resented being forced to learn that stuff."

"Sounds pretty useful to me."

The lobby was largely empty. Darren was sitting alone, on his phone. Almost everyone else was on the pool deck. None of them had any clue something was wrong, Alice thought. To them, this was just another day in paradise.

She felt a little jealous. If she wanted, she could join Darren and pretend nothing was wrong. They could talk about the fun activities they'd participated in. He'd talk about that ropes course, and she'd talk about hiding in the luggage storage area and beating up a bartender who had assaulted her. As friends do.

"I better get back to work," Vlad said. "Are you going to be okay? I can check on you later. If you want, of course." Kind to a fault.

"How much later?" asked Alice.

* * *

Fire from the torch threw dancing shadows onto the shiny rocks. Stalagmites only slowed Alice down as she went in deeper, down into an unending cave. The ceiling crept lower the farther she dared go.

The watery floor trickled against the centuries of mineral deposits, but her feet stayed dry. Sulfur and smoke hung in the air.

She willed herself onward to see where the tunnel... cave exited. The water had to flow out somewhere. The farther she went, the narrower the path became. She felt out with her free arm to keep from bumping against the sides. It was getting harder to breathe. Her lungs hurt from the acrid air as she pushed forward; her heart pumped harder too. Was it because of the lack of oxygen? Maybe it was the adrenaline her body had used to tell her to be afraid and turn back.

She should go back, but there was a sound she was ignoring. She didn't want to know what it was. It was soft. Wet. It could have been the normal way water moves against stone. Drips and splashes happen in caves. An animal, like a bat or salamander, using the cave for shelter. Or Scott Wilson's body coming to cough in her mouth.

No, keep going forward. That's the only way out. Got to

get out. It was the only way to answer His call. He reached for her, and His call had pulled her here. He'd said the truth was down here. Here for her, the worthy.

Alice wanted to be worthy. Worthy of something. Anything. Everyone was so far ahead of her. They had so much wealth and class and families that didn't constantly believe in radical conspiracy theories. They must have already made it through the cave for sure. She was so far behind.

A step in slick water behind her made her spin around. Her torch lit up the cave walls to show nothing, but in the shadows where the torchlight couldn't reach, a pair of glistening, flickering eyes floated in place low to the ground. Alice took a step back. The eyes moved forward, staying in the darkness. Alice stepped back again; the eyes followed.

She kept stepping backward, trying to keep herself from stumbling, but her legs wanted to collapse. Her free arm struggled to guide her; it was trembling so much. No matter how much she moved away from the eyes, they stayed with her, flickering with the torch.

Alice stepped back against a rock wall. It was the end of the cave. There was no exit, no opening to leave. The cave just ended. She was trapped. Cornered. Alone with that thing.

She wasn't worthy.

Alice slid down the wall, slumping to the ground. The water no longer trickled past her. It just stopped at a shallow puddle that barely covered her feet. Alice looked up at the eyes; they didn't move.

"Why are you doing this?" she cried. "Why am I here?"

The eyes moved forward again, the light slowly giving shape to the structure around them. Alice couldn't make out all the details right away. She saw protrusions and curves; it wasn't a person. A few more steps and she saw horns, long ears—an animal... a sheep! It was black, but the light was there to see it all. It had two sets of black horns jutting from its head, and smoke wafted off its wool. The musty smell of the cave grew thicker the closer it came.

The sheep came up to Alice close enough that she could pet it if she wanted. Or she could grab its horns and give it a good shake for scaring her. She looked into its eyes: no longer the stalker monster in the shadows, but a lonely sheep that was probably more scared of her than she was of it.

Alice was no longer shaking; she no longer felt alone. She might be behind everyone and in this dead-end cave, but she was okay now. She let out a deep sigh. "Hey there. You know a way out of this place?"

When she gently placed her hand to the sheep's nose, it lifted its head straight up and bleated as loud as it could. A fast cloud of flies escaped its mouth and swarmed Alice.

* * *

Alice could still hear the buzzing of the flies in her mind as she splashed her face with water from the bathroom sink. She stared into her hands as cold water flowed over her cupped fingers. Her breathing and heart rate slowed a little bit with each cooling splash. Her hands pushed into her face as though to shield herself from the lingering memory of buzzing flies emanating from the black sheep's mouth.

Beside her bed was a note.

I didn't want to wake you. I meant it when I said that was amazing. Be back later. :-)

—*Vlad*

She smiled at the memory of Vlad coming back to her room, even taking a nap with her after sex and a shower. He didn't mind that he was behind in his housekeeping duties. When she first saw him that day, he looked tired and upset. But by the time they both dried off, he seemed happy, even refreshed. His face wasn't even as pale as before.

From the hall just beyond her door, Alice heard muffled yelling and knocking. It sounded like Darren calling for Spence. His voice was short and assertive. Alice put her ear to the door to hear what they were saying but could only make out Darren's voice.

"Spence. Come on. Don't do this. I know you're in there." Darren knocked loudly on a door. "At least check your phone!" A couple of seconds later, Alice heard the loud slam of a door closing.

Alice opened her door and looked toward Darren's room. At the far end, two people were walking toward the elevator. Darren must have gone to his room. Alice turned and saw Hannah also looking out of her doorway.

"What the fuck was that?" Hannah asked. She was in the middle of attaching a pair of hoop earrings and wearing a flowy white dress with a gold belt and matching shoes. Her hair was freshly curled, pulled up with a white-and-gold hair clip.

Alice shook her head. "Hey! I—"

"Oh, my God. Girl, you cannot hold your mimosas." Hannah hugged Alice. She smelled of fresh hairspray and sweet perfume.

"I guess I ended up taking a longer nap than I realized," Alice said, remembering the lie from before about needing a nap. "Where are you heading?"

Hannah stepped back to show off the look she'd put together. "The only place to go around here: the pool. You joining?"

Alice shook her head. "You have fun."

Hannah shrugged and made her way toward the elevator. Alice could see the pool from where she stood. Just like the previous nights, the same people were chatting and laughing and drinking.

Alice waited until the elevator doors closed behind Hannah then went to room 405. She knocked gently, and within seconds, the door sprang open. Darren wore a look of panic then made a disappointed face upon realizing it was her.

"I guess you heard that, huh?"

"Just a little bit. Are you and Spence fighting or something?"

Darren's brow pinched. "Or something. I guess. Maybe I screwed up. That's not important right now."

"What happened?"

Darren looked at Alice for a few seconds as though he were deciding what to say. He pulled the door back. "Come on."

Alice followed him in; both sat on his bed. Darren stared at the floor and kneaded his hands. In a hushed tone, he said, leaning in, "You can't tell anyone. This place? This isn't what you think it is." As Darren said it, a volley of cold nails slammed into Alice's chest. "It's supposed to be Zenith Pharm's offshore testing lab, but it's so much worse than that." Darren bit his lip as he came up with what to say next. Alice braced herself. "The thing is, I came here thinking Zenith Pharm was pulling a scheme to manufacture the pandemic, just like they did in the past. But now I'm thinking they're a cult or something."

This wasn't the truth bomb Alice had hoped for. "A cult, huh? Can you expand on that?"

Darren shook his head. "I'd heard rumors. The Internet is full of theories about this company. Some sounded far-fetched, to be honest. But now I'm not so sure."

"Like what?"

Darren ran his fingers through his hair as he looked up at the ceiling. "Things like Zenith Pharm is part of a secret society. They have these 'Shepherds' planted in all sorts of businesses and governments; apparently they make the Illuminati look like a Boy Scout group. For example, my dad owns DynaImaging, which powers Zenith Pharm's DNA software. He's got this tattoo that's the same mark these Shepherd people have."

"You're not making any sense, Darren."

"I know it sounds crazy. This was all supposed to be a bit of light industrial espionage against Zenith Pharm. I was going to get their secrets and expose them for what they're doing." Alice looked shocked. "I was contacted by some people who'd been investigating them for years. They said what my dad was involved in could endanger our whole family. So I agreed to help them. I didn't really have a choice."

Darren reached into his pocket and showed Alice a tiny USB stick.

"What's that for?" she asked.

Darren pulled a laptop from the top drawer in his dresser. "The plan was to attach the USB drive to one of the computers on their network. They have their own network separate from guest Wi-Fi, which I can't see. The program on this drive is auto-executing, so I don't have to do anything. Just connect to their servers and download their data, information about the virus, and their testing methods and results, and bring it back for evidence."

"You can make a computer auto-run a program? Aren't there security measures, user permissions, and stuff to prevent that?"

"There are," Darren agreed. "That's why I put in a patch to their software to get around that from my dad's computer back home. His servers are constantly getting updates and bug fixes. It's all automatic. They should have the software updates by now."

Alice didn't know how to respond. She was just told her friend was basically on a secret mission to steal data about the vaccine to expose this drug company. "I don't think these are people you want to be messing with."

"What do you mean?" Darren's knees shook as he fidgeted with the USB drive.

Alice wasn't sure if she should warn him about Harry and the others. He already looked so stressed. If Darren provoked the wrong people, they could make him disappear as well. And if she told him, he might freak out even more. "Darren, you're trying to steal valuable data from one drug company. I can think of a lot of other drug manufacturers that might go a long way to get their hands on what Zenith Pharm is doing to get an edge on their own vaccine. If you really think dangerous people are running this operation, do you want to be on their bad side?"

Darren put his laptop back in the dresser and pulled out his phone. "I've been rolling this over in my head ever since I got on the plane. The thing is, I convinced myself to drop the whole thing. I'm not even sure I could get access to a server if I wanted to. Their operation seems locked down.

"Then I met you, Spence, Hannah, the Petrovs, and well, I changed my mind. Instead I wanted to just have fun and breathe, not be stressed about all this cloak-and-dagger stuff. But I can't shake these terrible dreams lately. Maybe I've read too many articles about these 'Shepherds,' and it all rolls around together with some really dark shit."

Alice thought back to the dreams she'd had after she arrived. They were faded, but there were moments she couldn't scrape out of her head if she wanted to. Did Darren have the same experience?

"I've been having some very scary dreams lately," Alice said. "At first I thought it was related to jet lag or stress from traveling or being in a new place. But they haven't gone away."

Darren's face became dark. "My first night here, when we were in that bunker, I dreamed I was holding my heart in my hands. I handed it to a robed man, and he ate it."

"I was pulled into the ground, where someone I couldn't see was waiting for me."

"I was pinned to the ceiling, where this old guy in a rubber apron made me bleed out."

"I was trying to get out of a cave, but this sheep filled with flies came at me."

"Okay, that's fucked up," Darren said.

"Do you think the other guests are having nightmares like us?" Alice asked.

"I don't know. Let's ask...oh, wait; he's avoiding me." Darren tossed his phone aside.

"Who? Spence?"

Darren opened his phone, pulled up a video, and scrubbed to the end. "This is someone from my dreams. Right here in real life."

"What is this?"

"I accidentally recorded this. I thought I'd just turned on the flashlight. Spence and I checked out the tomb at the cemetery. It goes down into this, well, a tomb. And then we kissed, and then we got interrupted by other people entering the tomb. Now he's locked himself in his room and won't answer the door or reply to me."

"Okay, talk about burying the lead! You two kissed?" Alice said, astonished.

Darren shook his head, "Yeah, yeah, yeah. The point is, I didn't see him when we were down there. But here he is on my phone. I'm having these fucked-up nightmares, and he's in it. And I'm really freaked out." Darren went back to the dresser and pulled out a bottle of vodka from the mini fridge. It was already partially empty. "I'm making sure my REM is getting suppressed."

Alice watched him pour a shot and down it. He poured another and offered it to her. She took it. "Here's the thing, Darren. You might be right." She didn't care for the taste of vodka by itself, but she endured it anyway. It burned her throat and she coughed. "I wonder if your dreams and my dreams are probably happening to the other guests."

"You think so?"

"Nobody likes to talk about their dreams. I sure don't, just because I can't stand to hear about other people's dreams. Everyone here is so determined to have a good time. I just passed Hannah, who was going off to party some more, right after finding out Harry's gone." She coughed through the rest of her shot before handing the glass back to Darren. "I don't know what's going on, but it's all too much."

"How so?" Darren asked.

"Everything about this place keeps getting shadier and shadier. Why does this property have heavily armed security guards?"

"Uh...to protect us from people coming in with the virus?"

"You know the history of this place? It was built by Satanists, given to the Nazis, and is now owned by a mega corp."

Darren nodded. "Capitalists."

"Everyone who works here is openly hostile. Ms. Birch, for example. She blatantly lied to me today. And the bartender—"

"That guy is scary."

"He grabbed my arm when I was with Vlad earlier. I gave him a wall to kiss."

"Are you serious?" Darren handed her a refill shot. "What about Vlad?"

Alice blushed a little. "I'd say he's the exception."

"But he works here, at the shady satanic Nazi medical castle."

"He showed me something earlier. The guests here aren't checking out. Their luggage is still here. In the basement."

Darren quickly picked up his phone and made a call. After a couple of seconds, Alice heard a ringtone chime in the room next to them. "Thank god for Wi-Fi calling. Hey, please just call me."

Rapid knocking came from down the hallway. Darren took a look outside. Alice heard Hannah from the hallway: "Is Alice with you?"

Darren nodded and opened up the door for Hannah. She looked as white as her dress. "Come outside! It's on the news. The virus. It's mutated."

IT HAD BEEN three days since Robert Davis had been able to pull away from his office long enough to take a much-needed shower. He was working two desks really. Romania might be seven hours ahead of his office back in New York, but that didn't alleviate him of the responsibility of being available for videoconferences in the middle of the night. By the time his last meeting ended at 6:30 p.m. Eastern, it was 1:30 a.m. for him. He had only a few hours of time to rest and reset for the next day, and for once, there wasn't anything that needed attention.

The City was making preparations for more Ram candidates. His worries about being stuck with a bottleneck weren't as much of a problem as he'd thought. Perhaps he shouldn't have overreacted to Dr. McCormick. She was only doing her job. She had just as much vested in the project's success as he did.

Still, if he was supposed to manage the entirety of this castle's logistics, that included everything below it. If something went wrong, if anything broke in the chain, from their

New York offices to here to the underground labs to the City, he bore responsibility.

Robert already had to answer for one of the guests dying from the virus. When and where did Scott Wilson get exposed? How many others had been in contact with him? What was his Ram candidacy compatibility? That last question was moot, but stakeholders wanted answers.

He made a note to have something delivered to Dr. McCormick and the lab staff as thanks for their hard work. Their workload would be pushed even more in the upcoming days. Since the discovery of the Ozark virus mutation, he had shortened the timetable. Still, morale needed to be maintained.

Everyone on staff needed to be retested for the new strain. The entire castle staff had to begin quarantining by morning, including Shepherds. That meant the guests would have to fend for themselves for the day. Ms. Birch was already preparing the facilities and coordinating the staff.

Robert took the elevator to floor B1: security, utilities, power generators, and the elevator hub to the rest of the castle. It was the only way to get to the ground floor from his office. The security office was closed, but the black-and-white monitors stayed on. He paused to observe the wall of displays rotate from view to view of the cameras located in various parts of the castle: the grounds of the property, the gates, the fences, and guest rooms. The fascination of peering into people's lives—be it sleeping or fucking in their rooms without their knowledge—no longer held him. It was like watching farm animals in their pens. He only cared that they were safe and fed.

G1 was the only floor with a hallway that ran along the same path of the rooms above. Along the path were elevators underneath every room. Twenty of them that led to the twenty rooms on every floor. An elevator chimed behind Robert. The doors for elevator six opened. Two men in black hotel uniforms carried an unconscious and rather bulky guest by the arms and legs. They weren't doing a very good job of it as they tried to lift him to a gurney by the doors.

Robert had made sure he'd committed every guest to memory. This was Spence Dixon, room 406. "You two sure you got that?" he called back at the two employees.

One of the men grunted. "Fucker's heavy."

Robert waited until they secured Mr. Dixon to the gurney. "We're going to start making more rounds like this in the coming days. Make sure you wear back-support braces. I don't want to see you injuring yourself bending to pick up the guests."

One of the men made a confused expression. "We can't get hurt, remember?" But he was already holding his back when he said it.

Robert held up a finger. "Oh, we can get hurt. We just won't die from it." He turned and walked away. "Seriously, fellas. Safety first."

He took the last elevator to the ground floor to the modern, clean-smelling hallway behind the castle's main lobby. The conference room that served as their station for blood work and vaccinations was closed. The access panel next to it was lit red for "secured." On the other side of the hallway, Robert swiped his card to exit into the reception entrance. The cool fresh air filled his lungs as he stepped outside.

The chorus of nighttime bugs and the dirt crunching under his feet carried him along his path to the staff barracks, a single-story compound kept hidden by the treeline. The full moon lit his way through the wild grass and shrubs to a small brick-and-clay cabin. The sign above the doorway read, STAFF ONLY.

The energy poured out of him once he was inside the tiny metal space. Next to the door, he pushed the "down" button and began his descent, his respite from the world above once again over. This was the quickest route to the City's main housing district. He had his own room—or closet space—with a bed waiting for him in a Khrushchyovka style building, a panel building popular in soviet-style public housing. His was one of the few that stood freely in the massive cave system. Other buildings had walls of the caves carved to make room. They disgusted him; the people who lived here. They were determined to cling to their secrets and control in shadows and holes. Whatever influence they had over the world, they were too cheap to pay for New York housing.

It was a relic of the past to cling here. Soon it would no longer be necessary. Robert Davis was part of a plan. A great plan. He should know; he had made a PowerPoint about it.

His room was dark, untouched, clean, and ready for his return. But he promised himself a shower to get the sheen of greasy filth off him. Fresh towels, washcloths, and toiletries were in place and waiting.

Robert stepped out of his clothes, letting them fall like dead skin onto the tile floor, and closed the shower curtain behind him. At some point, he was going to have to actually soap up, but the massage of increasingly warm water pressure shooting at the top of his head and down his back was all he could focus on.

Something, however, itched in the back of his mind. Had he forgotten something? He'd been so busy trying to get everything done on his agenda, maybe he had over-looked something. Something he was putting off...or ignor-ing...no, calling.

It bugged him like the fear of leaving the stove on. A meeting. He had missed a meeting! No, that couldn't be it... Shit!

Robert wiped the water out of his eyes but couldn't see. He was in total darkness as the shower poured down on him. His eyes struggled to adjust to the blackness. He reached for the shower handle, but it was only partially there. He was only partially in his shower. He was partially somewhere else too.

His vision adjusted, and he made out a robed figure sitting in front of him, barely lit by a candle on the dirt ground. The candle was surrounded by markings made in wax, blood, and bone dust. He recognized the man under the hood from his crooked nose and long black beard.

Robert let out a long sigh, spitting water from his mouth. He begrudgingly sat down before the man letting the dirt clump onto his wet skin. "It's well past midnight."

"I was up and so were you," the man said.

Robert fixed his posture. "How can I serve, Father Asdomus?"

"We've been getting a lot of selections, Brother Davis. I was surprised at the rate you've been able to deliver them. You must be feeling very confident."

"Uh, I feel confident in the selection so far. We've made significant progress in determining which of the guests are suitable Ram candidates." Robert didn't expect to be giving a midnight status report. Something was wrong; Father Asdomus wouldn't have called upon him unless there was a problem directly related to something he had done.

"Ram candidates?" Father Asdomus asked.

Robert Davis leaned closer and lowered his voice. "For the *Z'njm Sej'pal*."

"Oh, right. Rams. 'The Sheep, the Ram, and the Shepherd.' That makes sense. I've been so heads down in these rituals, I'm surprised I can still speak English." Father Asdomus rubbed his temples. "Here's the thing: *Z'njm Sej'pal* is a sacred ritual. It takes great care and great time to perform it correctly. Our temple of connection needs time to heal. But you're sending down these candidates in a state that can't wait for the temple to be prepared properly. To perform *Z'njm Sej'pal* at the rate needed would cause a rupture to His Dark Realm, and we don't need that attention."

Robert could tell where this was going. "I understand there's concern about the rate at which these candidates are chosen. I can assure you the selection process was very rigorous. Some are family members of Shepherds already and therefore have a strong likelihood of success. Others have demonic chart readings that line up perfectly for our program; a High Elder has visited each of them to confirm their viability. I understand there's a risk to the membrane between our world and His. Our Elder in residence has assured me the concern is unwarranted."

"'Let them fail in their path and fall before you. Remove the strong from the weak and raise them to become your right hand. For the strong are the rare and worthy vessels for my army.'" Father Asdomus let the words settle in the void of their presence. "Let it not be said that our ancestors didn't have a flair for the dramatic. Nonetheless the prophecy is being fulfilled. This is our test. We cannot fail it."

"I get what you're saying. There was a meeting last year on the rate of conversion and the membrane's viability—"

"You would burn a skyscraper to the ground if it meant hitting a deadline! Tell me, Brother Davis, what good is having a world to rule if all that is left is a scorched wasteland? Would you have us rule ash?" Father Asdomus's voice echoed in the air.

Robert blinked shower water out of his eyes; the water was still running down his body as he sat in the dirt. His eyes fully adjusted to the darkness now. Just behind Father Asdomus, an altar table made of wood and iron stood covered in worn-down candles dripping onto bones and horns and feathers. A robed figure he didn't recognize was working an incantation; he did, however, recognize its purpose. This was a ritual for him. He was going to be given over and undone–killed–if Father Asdomus wasn't satisfied with this conversation.

It wasn't fair. He had done everything to the letter —*more* than the letter. He had excelled at making all this happen perfectly. And for that, he was expendable? Did they think they could do better?

"Father, the people brought to you were selected from the very methods prescribed. We follow them exactly. The scrolls of Z'njm Sej'pal are very specific about this. You yourself have studied them for centuries. We aren't cutting any corners to rush this project."

"You did it for each and every candidate?"

This was a trap. He knew he was being baited to admit he hadn't followed the ritual of finding for every person. He needed to get out of this line of questioning. "The process obviously works. I can bring your concern to the other warrens. Perhaps one of them can take on the workload."

"Who is Alice Whitmore?" Father Asdomus asked.

The robed figure at the table snapped a tiny bone in half and placed the pieces in the center.

"Alice Whitmore is among the group of candidates we found to have a high success likelihood in the program."

"Rob, you've got three fucking seconds to stop lying to me and explain why she's here, having never gone through the ritual you claimed you so fervently followed." Father Asdomus help up a manila folder; they must have taken it from his office at some point. He was right; Alice would never be visited by the Elder or go through *Z'njm Sej'pal*. Her files only contained her NDA contracts and some administrative filings.

Robert took in a deep breath, careful not to breathe in water. "Alice Whitmore is the direct descendant of Jacques de Molay."

The words stunned Father Asdomus and the figure behind him. who froze in position. Father Asdomus's face was unmoving as he stared intensely across the single candle, reading Robert's face for any sign of deception. If he thought he was lying, Robert would be dead.

Father Asdomus finally said, "Grand Master Jacques de Molay did not have any family. He and his lover Geoffroi de Charney and other Templars suffered seven years of jail and torture only to be burned at the stake. There were no heirs. De Molay denounced his confession of sin. He rejected His Dark Offer."

"Did he? He certainly took back his confession, but he cursed the king and the pope. Before he died, he called upon his Master to prove their innocence by exacting revenge against his accusers. He used his own immolation to perform the curse. Shortly after, Pope Clement V died, as did King Philip; his bloodline dried up, ending the Capetian dynasty.

"But! De Molay had a mistress in the years prior to the arrests. As soon as she found out she was pregnant, she married an English merchant and fled the country. The father rejected her and her newborn son, but they kept the name, and he started his own family under the name Blake Whitmore. Alice Whitmore isn't here to be a Ram. She's here because she's family."

"'And you will find the false son, a bastard among men, cursed by His Dark Gift,'" Father Asdomus recited.

"'May his father's revenge never end,'" Robert recited back.

"You're absolutely certain of this?" Father Asdomus asked.

Robert nodded. "The lineage checks out. The only way to be certain is through our DNA imaging. The first test had a false negative; we're doing another one shortly. Someone screwed up and gave her the same fever shot as everyone else. If it's her, and Jacques De Molay really did accept His Dark Gift like I suspect, she might be the one from the prophecy."

Father Asdomus leaned in close, the shadows on his face dancing in the light of the candle. "Make this your first priority. I'll get the test results for myself. If she is the heir to Grand Master Jacques de Molay, she'll no longer be part of your program or concern. In the meantime, slow your roll with these candidates. If the portal ruptures before it has time to heal, I'll be your least problem to worry about." Father Asdomus sat back, extended his hand, and pinched the wick of the candle, snuffing it out.

Robert was back in the bathroom, sitting on the shower floor. Dirt was still stuck to his legs and buttocks. Nausea flowed through him as his mind shook off the sensation of being in two places at once.

He constantly felt the pressure of two ends pushing against him from above and below. Above was the rest of

Zenith Pharm, the other Shepherds with their own expectations about this program succeeding. Below was a scared old priest who knew only of ancient scribblings and dark whispers. Father Asdomus might be a threat to him, but it was no bigger than the light of his candle.

He rinsed off, dried, and went to his room to change into a fresh suit. No time to shave. It was time to get back to work.

SPENCE'S HEAD WAS THROBBING. It wasn't a hangover, but the ache was familiar enough to one. He felt stiff, cold, and his arm itched.

The fog of waking up hadn't yet lifted. He licked his dry lips as he lay on his back. He had no recollection of going to bed. Did he get so drunk he couldn't remember what happened? It must have been bad enough that he didn't even remember drinking. The only time he ever got that drunk was his first year in college at a friend's house party. The next morning he found himself on their couch, still drunk, curled up in a blanket with two cats sleeping on his legs.

This wasn't that. He didn't feel drunk. He felt pain. He winced at the intense light that shone in his face from above. He tried to sit up, but his arms pinned him down. Hard metal arm restraints held him in place. Spence looked down his body and saw the thick metal shackles bolted over his wrists and abdomen and feet into a metal table.

His neck cracked when he twisted his head to try to figure out where he was. He rolled against the metal table as he observed the IV drip connecting his forearm to a stand with a drip bag. Sticky pads on his exposed chest led wires to the heart-monitoring equipment next to him; it noted his rapidly increasing heart rate. An armband fed to a machine to monitor his blood pressure.

Was this a hospital room? But he was restrained from moving. Did he get arrested and put in some Romanian hospital room? Was this what they looked like?

The walls were metal and riveted into place with enforced steel beams setting the frame of the room. If he weren't bolted in place, he could have reached out and touched them. The door, just past his feet—a thick slab of grey-green painted metal with a small viewing window—closed shut. Behind it, he heard the distant sounds of screams and cries over the low rumble of air ventilation.

Spence was starting to panic. How did he get here? What was the last thing he remembered? He thought about being back in his room for something. He was looking for something. Something for Darren. *Oh, God, Darren.* He was supposed to meet him at the pool deck. But how he had ended up here was lost on him. Maybe he had gotten sick. Maybe he'd been infected with the virus somehow, and this was where they took the sick.

If he was infected, that meant he'd infected Darren; probably others were infected too. This must be where they took Scott Wilson when he got infected. They must have known they couldn't help him, so they put him in a room like this to bleed out and die. And now Spence was here and going to suffer the same fate. No wonder they used a metal table. Die alone in a cold room made of metal. It was easier to clean. There was probably a drain underneath him to make is easier to wash out the contaminated fluids when they disposed of his body.

Spence let out a feeble cry, a pathetic attempt to laugh at the ironic justice of it all. *Just add it to the sin of homosexuality*, he thought. If he didn't get AIDS or any of other diseases his dad, pastor, or camp counselor had warned him about, it had to be Ozark virus to serve God's justice. All over a guy he liked. Just one kiss. That was all it took to know God's punishment was real.

Maybe Darren was nearby in one of these cells, waiting for his lungs to fill up with fluid and his skin to sweat out blood like a milk bag.

Tears rolled from his eyes into his ears. His chin quivered uncontrollably. He coughed out, "Oh, God!" involuntarily as he replayed a single moment in his mind. Down, deep, alone with Darren in the dark. In his entire life, through prayer, penitence, he had pleaded for forgiveness and relief. All his efforts to push away this one sin had been completely undone in one moment. And never had he experienced a more vivid, exhilarating moment in his life.

It was Darren, this guy with dark shiny curly hair that fell perfectly on his forehead. His curiously deep-brown eyes cut through all of Spence's armor every time he looked at him. Someone Spence couldn't imagine would ever think of looking in his direction not only liked him but also had kissed him, held him, and pulled into him. Wanted him. And Spence had blown it. He had jerked away and acted like a coward.

Now it was time to die. He would carry his sin into hell. And burn alone.

As Spence lay lost in his thoughts, footsteps led up to his cell door. The whine of unoiled metal rubbing together resounded as the door swung open. In stepped an old man wearing a black rubber apron with a digital tablet in hand. His white hair was slicked back and matched the crisp white shirt underneath; his boots looked well worn as he stepped up alongside Spence.

The man gave a long, early, satisfying look up and down Spence's body, which made Spence stiffen. He watched the man pinch his brow and purse his lips, which held firmly as his watery eyes fluttered between him and the tablet. A few moments later in quiet evaluation, their eyes met. The man winked and said, "Well, now. Spence Dixon, looks like you're next! We normally move our candidates right after confirming our results. It saves time. But your friend was keeping an eye on you, and we didn't have time after clearing his mind." His voice was fragile yet intense. Each sounded word raked against Spence nerves. The old man gave a well-practiced kind face. "He must be such a good friend to keep an eye on you. Speaking of eye—"

"What's happening?" Spence asked in a gravelly voice.

The man rolled up his white sleeves and brought over a rolling tray. He pulled out a pair of green rubber gloves and worked them over his hands. "What's happening is your blood work is finished. Turns out you're a compatible match. Ninety-eight point four percent success rate! That's one of the highest we've had."

"Success rate?" Spence realized he wasn't sick with the Ozark virus after all. "You mean you have a vaccine?"

The man donned a pair of safety glasses while inputting into his tablet. "Ah! You know, I've been down here so long I forget who knows what. Personally I like to go with the truth. After all, to have knowledge is to be free. No, no, no. You're the vaccine. Or rather, soon you will be." The man crossed his arms over his rubber apron and put on his serious face. "You're about to undergo a very important procedure. There are two possible outcomes. One, you come out of it being reborn. A Ram of the herd. A hybrid of man and truth. Blessed by the beings beyond the realm of earth! Or two, you come out of it...well, not dead but not good."

"I don't understand. Am I sick or something?" Spence said quickly.

The man tapped the "sleep" button on the table and set it on Spence's stomach making him shiver at the touch. "I'm sure you have lots of questions. Why are you here? What happens next? I get these all the time." He sighed and rubbed at his paper-thin temple. "Let me help. My bedside manner isn't great, but it's much better than it used to be." The man chuckled lightly. Even his laugh had an irksome effect.

"Please," Spence cried. Tears welled up even more in his eyes. "Why am I here?"

"It's called the *Z'njm Sej'pal*. It's much like *Bli'lg Caep'nej*, but without all the sacrifice, acts of sin, all that effort. It dates back centuries from our sacred texts. They're old names, I know." He pulled up a chair and sat close to Spence's face; his breath was putrid. "Down here, we become Shepherds, caring for the flock. We join our souls with a demon. Then, for the next hundred or so years, an inner battle plays out." He tapped Spence's chest, making him flinch. "A fight for dominance of the soul. If a Shepherd manages to last long enough, without getting badly injured or dying, they become immortal. If they fail, the demon reclaims their soul and their host. 'Reclamation.' Did you know one of guests here was actually already a Shepherd? It's a good thing we caught it! *Tsch.*

"It's a tedious, grueling ritual—much too complicated to perform it for anyone who wants it. No. Instead we're putting you and the others through a much more stream-lined version. Less fuss and muss on everyone's part." The old man held up a scalpel and twisted it in his hand to let the glints of light run along its sharp edges. "This is more of an exchange. You give a part of yourself, and a demon in return gives you the gift of unholy life. Literally, their blood joins with yours, and with it, all the genetic knowledge to fight any virus they are immune from, including the Ozark virus."

Blood pounded in Spence's in his ears. When he tried to speak, it wasn't his voice any longer, it was weak and shaky despite his effort to be calm, slow, and controlled. "Why would a demon be immune to the virus?"

"Where do you think it came from? Did you know there are over two hundred species of demons capable of surviving in our realm? There are the tiny little monsters that slip through the cracks between our worlds that create myths and legends we use to scare little children. The occasional pests that leech on our souls and need exorcising. They bring with them diseases that we as humans aren't ready for. Diseases that can transform us, other us, or simply kill us, just like what's happening now. They've been around forever. Incredibly hard to transmit. Usually person-to-person bites, maybe under a full moon...the rules are weird in our realm.

"We spent centuries cataloging and studying the various species. We track down and isolate pathogens, the ones we could contain. Only recently have we truly begun to understand by mapping their unholy genomes. Science is truly the real miracle.

"So when He let loose onto the world this virus, as was prophesied, we knew we had the tools to combat it. Personally I don't think He expected that. Between you and me, I think His Dark Offer was a double-edged sword this whole time. Giving us reign over the earth but killing everyone but those with immunity. A cruel trick.

"But I like this plan we came up with. Instead of us being the only ones left, we could save the world with our own antibodies. The problem is there are only a few of us who can perform the *Bli'lg Caep'nej* ritual to become Shepherds, and not enough of our blood to go around. But thanks to you and the other guests, we can farm you out. You'll go on to our facilities above as virtual factories of the antibodies needed to regain control of this realm."

The old man stared at Spence for a few seconds before standing up and returning his attention to his tablet. "It's a bit different for everyone. According to your chart, you were born in 1998. May twelfth. Since you arrived here, you've been dreaming of being chased by an all-seeing demon. How fun! And you're gay. That's my favorite sin. The sins mankind comes up with always amuse me." He scrolled farther down his tablet. "That puts you in line with the Order of Bael. We're looking at around thirty demon types under Bael, but you're only genetically compatible with... Rhymet himself!" He leaned in wide-eyed. His combed-back hair glowed from the light above, painting his face in a silhouette halo. "The master of sight and prophecy, bringer of sorrowed fortune." He set down his tablet and picked up the surgical scalpel again. "And so, for you, we'll be taking out your right eye. Feel free to scream."

DARREN WAS STANDING in the hallway with Alice and Hannah, watching the news feed from Hannah's phone. Alex and Yuri had theirs out as well, streaming news from their home country. Down below, guests gathered either at the bar, where multiple screens were tuned to emergency broadcasts. Some called and texted their loved ones back home. Others were posting their reactions to social media.

Before, the Ozark virus was only transmissible between people, but now it could be carried by animals. There were confirmed reports of a dog who had bit a man. He was a coroner in Sacramento answering to a report of a resident who had died in their house. The dog bit the coroner; it was assumed to have been protecting its owner. The coroner ended up dying of the virus a few days later. Further tests from animals captured from pest traps confirmed the new variation, which caused a wave of speculation online. Was the virus no longer airborne? Could it also be spread by insects like mosquitos, ticks, and fleas?

Ms. Birch's voice sounded over the PA. Her voice was strained and quick. Both she and the Zenith Pharm app instructed everyone to observe social distancing until they could all be tested again; preferably they'd remain in their rooms unless necessary. No one could go outside, and everyone had to wear a mask outside their rooms. All staff members were recalled to their barracks for testing as well. Only those in protective gear could enter the castle.

It was after the news had broken, after Ms. Birch had made her announcements, after everyone had the chance to text and chat with loved ones, after the castle had locked its doors and gates, that Alice, Darren, Hannah, Alex, and Yuri collected what was left of their complimentary mini-bar vodka and sat in Darren's room.

Everyone shared their experiences at the castle, with no exceptional revelations. No one had seen any of the guests leave, just that they were no longer there. Alice told the others what she told Darren about the luggage she and Vlad had found in the basement. Spence hadn't answered his phone or the door in hours; they suspected he'd been taken as well.

Darren's jaw clenched and hurt his teeth whenever his thoughts returned to the man in the room next door that was no longer there. He took a sip from his glass every time and forced his jaw to relax.

To the benefit of the others, when Alice and Darren told them all they knew, they didn't immediately scoff or dismiss them. Hannah always had follow-up questions. Did they see Harry's luggage in the room? How were people taken from their rooms without anyone noticing? Could they even trust Vlad? Alex sat in patient silence next to her brother, taking in all the information. Yuri, for his part, believed everything they said. He'd nod with an affirmative "wow" or "holy shit."

Then Alice and Darren told them about the nightmares. This got everyone's attention, include Alex.

Hannah got up. "I need more ice for this."

"My nightmares seem to vary, but they get more intense every time. There's always a person in a robe, just a different person. It got so bad I had some kind of anxiety attack," Darren said.

"Did I tell you mine?" Yuri asked.

"What was it again?"

"So," Yuri said, "I have to get to my leg. But I cannot get there in time because I have no leg. My leg is going to be eaten if I cannot get to it. I'm always somewhere different. Mall. Home. Even here. I can see my leg in a big copper bowl just out of reach. And blood is everywhere, jetting from my body. I get to the bowl and it's gone. It's in another bowl, just out of reach."

Darren shuddered. "Jesus. And it's the same every night?"

Yuri nodded. "But I woke myself up last time!" He slapped his legs. "A-okay!"

Hannah returned with more ice for her vodka. "Can we all just agree we're getting creepy dreams and move on? Like, can we even go back to our rooms? How do we know we're not going to get snatched while we sleep?"

Alex agreed. "This place isn't safe; can we all agree? But we can't leave either. We can do the buddy system. Keep an eye on each other." She slapped her brother's hand as he reached for her glass.

"Honestly that's not a bad idea," said Darren, "Have you seen the way everyone on staff has been scrambling to lock down the castle? I'm not sure they were prepared for the new virus variant. We might be fine."

"I'm fine!" Yuri stood up. "Unless either of you two

wants to be bunk bed buddies." He noticed both Alice and Hannah giving clear looks of rejection. "I'm off. 'Night!"

* * *

Zenith Pharm 7:45 p.m.: NOTICE! Important health procedures are now in place at Monostori Castle. Review our post for instructions and guidelines.

Zenith Pharm 7:00 a.m.: Your blood test is scheduled for 8:00 a.m. See you there!

It was raining that morning, the drops pinging against the glass roof above Darren. The giant sliding doors that led to the back patio area were closed for the first time since his arrival. Hotel staff had closed and locked all the doors to the castle late last night after the news had broken that the virus had mutated.

The staff spent the early morning wiping down all surfaces and spraying empty rooms, including Spence's. Darren heard Spence's door open and spotted a hazmat-suited person holding a loud electric fogger that filled with the room with a white cloud that smelled of pungent chemical lemon. Darren's fear was confirmed that Spence was gone.

Looking back on all the conspiracies floating about Zenith Pharm, he didn't think they took the news about the mutation well. Ms. Birch's instructions, despite her trying to bring order, only instilled more panic in the guests. The staff worked in a frantic manner. If they did make this virus, like the tin-foil theorists thought, this mutation had caught them completely off guard. Had their pet beast escaped its leash?

Darren peered into Spence's room. From what he could see in the disinfectant fog, Spence's luggage, phone, and personal items were gone. Alice told him about the room she and Vlad had found. The room with the luggage of everyone who had left. Not left. They were taken. Now the basement housed Spence's luggage. Where did they take him?

"Hey!" Darren yelled at the person in the hazmat suit over the ear-ringing buzz of the fogger. The person either didn't hear him or ignored him. He shouted again and stepped toward the figure. "Hey! You! Where did you take the guy..." They caught his approach and turned. That's when Darren caught the flash of a gun strapped to the hazmat suit's side. Darren stopped.

They paused the machine just long enough to say in a voice that had zero patience for hospitality, "This room is off limits. Get out now" before resuming the spraying of the tiny bathroom.

Darren understood that as a nonnegotiable order and left the room. Yuri was walking from his room in a pair of jeans and a shirt and hoodie. Something nonathletic for once. It was a hoodie with a sports-gear logo on it, of course.

"Can you believe this? This overreaction?" Yuri said, gesturing at the closed doors that led outside.

"What are you talking about? We've got a deadly new strain out in the wild."

"Yeah, in America's California! When that state catches fire, do the other states go on high alert?"

Darren scoffed. "Yeah, they do. Fires travel. States have the same forests and the same hot summer temperatures. Sometimes hotter. They share the same air quality; depending on the weather, other states can get hit bad."

"Okay. Okay! But not across ocean! They haven't found

any sick dogs here. It's like I can't go do my morning runs because some bird might poop virus on me."

"You know they have a gym on the first floor, right?"

"It's locked. I even volunteered to clean it for them."

Alice came out of her room. Her eyes looked deep-set, with dark circles under them. Darren asked, "Another nightmare?"

Alice nodded. "I'm getting coffee. Good luck, by the way. You sure you don't need my help?"

Darren had almost forgotten he'd told her about the USB drive. He was scheduled for another blood test, finally giving him the chance he needed to get to a connected computer.

"I'll let you know if you need to pull a fire alarm," he said.

It was still early, about twenty minutes before 8:00 a.m., but the main hall conference room was already open when Darren arrived to get his blood drawn. He felt a tinge of guilt for having drunk alcohol the night before. If they had an error in his blood work the first time, they were almost assured of getting it again. Not that it mattered to him; he reminded himself that he wasn't here for any of that.

Looking back, Darren thought he must have been naïve when he'd agreed to go on this espionage assignment. Some guy online had convinced him to betray his father and subject himself to blackmail, all for a bit of insider information. GenNTech had no idea just how dire things at the castle had become.

None of that mattered. He needed to find out what Zenith Pharm was doing with the missing guests; more important, with Spence. Hopefully, the servers would tell him the truth.

Two people in hazmat suits stood behind the workstations in the conference hall. The room still displayed all the laptops, desktops, and servers as before. Underneath the wall of screens and mess of cables was a router with eight cables attached to the four laptops and one server rack with four units rack-mounted beside the screens. Nothing was wireless.

Two of the laptops were closed, their workstations unoccupied. The other two were barely handled by the two people who were in charge of all duties. The last time Darren was here, ten people in bright white lab coats worked in tandem with the efficiency of a well-oiled machine. Now two people, who walked with all the grace of astronauts, were too busy to even notice his presence.

Darren coughed. "Hello?"

One of the hazmat-suited technicians jolted up. "Take a seat, would you? It'll be a few minutes."

"I got it," the other one said as he snatched a testing kit from the table.

Darren sat in the chair closest to the man as he shuffled over and opened the kit.

"Name and room number," the man said.

"Darren Montoya, 405." Darren rolled up his sleeve and watched the man roughly apply a sanitizing swab to Darren's arm, then tie the elastic tourniquet to find a vein. It was tighter than last time. Darren looked the man up and down; a set of keys and a key fob were attached to his waist. He didn't see a name badge on him, though. He knew these doors used keycards for access.

Darren winced as he felt a pinch on his arm. He kept his eyes from watching. He let out an exhalation and finally said, "I'm never ready for that."

The man didn't reply.

"I forgot my key fob in the lab," the other technician announced as she left the room toward the staff elevator.

"More good news," the man uttered under his breath.

"Just the two of you this morning? Sounds like you're going through it." Darren tried to strike up some kind of conversation with the man.

"'Going through it' is putting it mildly," the man finally replied. "I've got a full workload on top of everybody else's workload while they all isolate."

"I'm digging the new uniform, a very fashionable bunny suit," Darren said. That made the man chuckle. "You do this normally? I mean, are you subbing for someone else?"

The man replied, "I do systems analysis for DynaImaging." He tapped at a black space at his breast. "Well, if I was wearing my name badge, you'd see 'Tanner Riggs, Senior Systems Analyst.' Yup, there it is on my desk, right where I forgot it." He motioned toward the desk behind him.

Tanner pulled the venipuncture and pressed gauze over the puncture. "Hold this, would you?" Darren put pressure on his arm as Tanner untied the tourniquet and labeled the vial.

"'Senior systems analyst' doesn't sound like a blood-work kind of gig."

"No shit. We're all wearing multiple hats around here today. But when your boss knows you got your background in epidemiology by working with animals, it makes you an expert in collecting blood from people, I suppose. After this, I get to help bring up dry goods from the storage area to the pantry." Tanner looked up to see some of the other guests trickle into the room. "Where is Stevens? Shit! Look, you're good to go. I've got to run this downstairs to imaging before it gets hemolysis."

Darren watched Tanner gather his kit and head toward the elevator down the hall. No staff remained. Darren was free to attach his USB stick into one of the computers. When he looked at the table, however, he saw the technician's name tag and keycard. He wouldn't be able to access the elevator without it. It would be only a moment before he'd return and see Darren messing with the computers. And with other people in the room, he couldn't just plug in the USB stick unseen.

Darren had to think quickly. He pinched the USB stick out of his pocket and made a brisk walk to the table, where the name badge and keycard were sitting next to his laptop. In one hand motion, he stuck in the USB stick into the laptop's port, grabbed the badge clip, and turned to catch up with the technician.

Darren was just out of the door when Tanner returned. He held up the badge. "Tanner! Hey, thought you might need this."

"Oh, my God." Tanner took the badge with his free hand. "Thanks so much. You get two cookies today!"

Darren laughed. "Just trying to help." When he turned to leave, his gaze landed on the laptop. It flashed a blank screen, and the start-up screen came on. It worked! Darren tried to play it cool as he walked back to his room. By the time he was back in his room and connecting to his laptop, that little USB stick would be erased, leaving no trace that anything nefarious ever had happened.

"Watch it again. Here."

Alice watched the video play on Peter's phone. On it, Peter was participating in a question-and-answer interview with a famous online personality, LaterGan. The video, titled, *Here's the Tea on Project Zenith*, had millions of views. LaterGan asked Peter all sorts of questions about the program, including who was there, how far along the program was, and whether it was safe. For every question, Peter had the right answer.

"So tell me, what happens afterward? Does all this go away?" LaterGan asked.

"That's a great question. I think it will! But more than that, the world will change. We will have a better sense of humanity. This vaccine is only possible because of our sacrifice to be here, and we couldn't have been a part of this without the world having our back. That says a lot about humanity if you ask me."

"I didn't say *any* of that!" Peter's arms bend toward the phone with every word. Peter was also a popular online personality. He'd made his name reviewing tech gadgets in video essays. If there was a new phone, computer, or speaker system, he had a review of it.

The rain on the glass-and-metal roof filled the lobby with a loud ambience, making the video hard to hear. Alice handed the phone back to Peter. Hannah, sitting next to her, was scrolling through her phone when she said. "I found one. Here's Harry taking a selfie on the trail. See the time? It says yesterday." She held it up to Alice. The photo was of Harry in sunglasses, a shirt, and a light jacket with a view of the hills of the property behind him. The caption read, "It's not all lab work all the time. #findthecure #savetheworld."

Alice had her notebook out; she'd been writing notes on their findings. She went around and asked everyone if they knew which guests had left and when. When she got their names, she and Hannah looked for them on social media. When they found a post or photo or even video, they noted when it had been posted.

Peter helped her identify his room neighbor Maggie Reisman. Maggie also kept making posts online with the theme of enjoying herself but still taking this very seriously.

"How did you find this video?" Alice was typing on her phone. "When I try to find it, I don't get any search results for it."

Peter showed her the side of his phone. "It's a dual-SIM phone, great range. Expensive data plan, though. I stopped using the castle's Wi-Fi when half my apps didn't work."

"Hannah, you have an EU SIM card too. Can you find this video?" Alice asked.

Hannah entered the title of the video. "I'm not getting anything." She showed them the results screen of closely related videos, but none matched Peter's interview. "I even looked through LaterGan's profile, and it won't load."

Peter wore a look of confusion. "Can I see something?" He held out his hand. "Do you mind?"

Hannah shrugged and handed it over. "Don't look at my pics. Or do, actually."

Peter thumbed his phone's home screen and scrolled through the apps until he found the Zenith Pharm app. He scoffed at it and handed it back to Hannah. "Your phone is jacked." He pointed to the app.

Alice and Hannah looked at each other. They both had installed the app, no doubt at the insistence of Zenith Pharm, in order to complete the application process back when they enrolled.

Peter tapped the table. "That app must have done something keep you from seeing this video."

"You never installed the app?" Alice asked.

Peter scoffed. "Not on this phone. I just got it to do a review. What better way to test the dual-SIM and extended-range features than here? My personal phone is in my room. That phone has the app, but I haven't used it since I left. Just kept it in the charger. I only found the video because I started getting a ton of notifications after it went live."

"If your phone has access to that video and ours doesn't, what else can't we see?" Alice said.

"Are we even on the Internet?" Hannah said. "Half my apps don't work. Some guys were complaining their hook-up apps don't even get past the loading screen."

Yuri and Alex joined them, each carrying bowls of colorful cereal. The only food left to eat for breakfast was dry goods like cereal, granola bars, and make-your-own peanut butter sandwiches.

Alice pointed to Peter's phone. "Look up 'Yuri Petrov.'"

"Huh?" Yuri was in the middle of his first bite of sugary crunch.

"We're seeing what you've been posting," Alice explained.

"I'm not online. It's all propaganda. Also, 'Shoot to Loot' game doesn't run well. The ping is too high to do any good. I keep getting killed in the first minute," Yuri said through his food.

"'*Алекс і Юрій Петров працюють над порятунком світу. Інтерв'ю.*' Did I say that right?"

"No," Alex said.

"It translates to 'Alex and Yuri Petrov working to save the world. Interview.' posted two days ago on the Sport 1 Ukraine channel." Peter showed Yuri his phone.

"What interview? We didn't do interview." Yuri reached over and tapped the link. Alice heard the audio of Alex's and Yuri's notable accents speaking in Ukrainian with whoever was interviewing them. Yuri's eyes widened as he continued eating and watching the phone play back the video. Alex stopped eating completely.

"Uh…" Alex lightly laughed. "We didn't do that. Did I black out and forget?" She pulled his phone out to try and find the video for himself. "Where is it? We didn't make video."

"Look up 'Hannah Bell,'" Alice said.

Peter typed in the name, along with "Zenith Pharm," and clicked on the first link, which took him to a video of Hannah in a commercial. She was dressed in a professional-looking blue dress in the middle of a laboratory with tubes, glass cabinets, microscopes, centrifuges, and a whiteboard covered with molecular diagrams and math equations.

"When I joined Project Zenith," Hannah said in the video, "I knew the importance of the work we'd be doing to find a cure for the Ozark virus and save the world. While I'm proud to be a part of the Zenith Pharm team, at the same time, I'm concerned about the growing worries expressed by so many Americans regarding why other companies are taking so much time developing a vaccine." Hannah walked alongside the lab table as the camera followed. "While Zenith Pharm is making unprecedented breakthroughs in developing a safe, effective vaccine, thanks to the generous funding by our government, some drug manufacturers are treating this like business as usual." A new shot of Hannah close-up. "I'm not okay with that. Are you?" Fade to black, with the large white words "Why the wait?"

Hannah, at the table, gasped. "Wow, I'm a bitch!"

"Did you do this?" Alice asked.

"No! I don't even own that jacket." Hannah peered at the screen. "It's cute, though."

"So, for all we know, Peter's phone here is the only one that can access the real Internet. And the rest of ours are, what, hacked?" Alice held her phone with a look of disgust.

"If that's true," Yuri said, "then what news is real? Fake posts and fave videos. Is it all fake?"

Alice pulled up her browser on her phone and went to a news site. "*The New York Times* reads, 'CDC Urges Schools to Remain Closed While Facing Pressure from the Senate to Reopen.'" She held out her phone to show everyone the headline and a photo of someone in a suit talking to a press podium.

Peter did the same thing. "'A Nation Reacts. Arsonists Target Animal Shelters, Zoos, Farms.'" Gasps came from the table as Peter showed his screen of firefighters putting out a fire at a sheep farm. He scrolled to the next headline: "Riots Break out across Europe as Food Supply Evaporates.

North Korea Targets US, Cites Blame for Virus Outbreak. Brazil's Government Risks Collapse Due to Poor Response to the Virus."

Alice scrolled through the headlines on her phone. "I don't see anything like that."

"What's happening? Why do we have a fake version of the Internet, while our likeness is used to prop their program? It's like they don't want us to know what's happening out in the world. To keep us placated?" Hannah said.

Alice cracked the knuckles in her hands and thought out loud. "This isn't just some research study, is it? It's a PR effort. Get a bunch of celebs, use their likeness to be the face of Zenith Pharm's 'Save the world, find the cure.'" Alice made finger quotes "Meanwhile, make sure we don't know how bad it is out there. Keep us placated so we don't leave."

"You're losing me," Hannah said. "If the world is on fire, why would we leave? Seems to me this is the safest place right now."

Peter chimed in. "These are today's headlines. We don't know how things were going before the mutation occurred."

"Obviously things aren't going as they planned. Nearly their entire staff is in lockdown, leaving us to fend for ourselves. Peter, how long did you know?"

"How long we've been hacked? Only since last night. I assumed everyone knew how bad things were out there. But everyone just kept going on like it was fine, so I thought I was the one overreacting."

Yuri dropped his spoon into his empty bowl. "I think you are all overreacting. We have state-run media do this all the time. You're just not used to propaganda." He stood to return his bowl. "It is fine. Don't use phone, don't get bullshit news. Anyway, I'm going to do some weights. Alex?"

Alex scoffed at him and shook her head, "Gym is closed, *мудак*."

"Maybe a nap instead." Yuri chuckled and walked off.

Alice was still kneading her hands, even though all her knuckles were thoroughly cracked and hurt from the pressure. How much of her phone had been compromised? The social apps that worked had fake posts on them; the ones that didn't must have been blocked from getting data. That must mean not all apps could be compromised. But did that mean every app she used couldn't be trusted? Alice pulled up her videoconference app. She waited as the dialing screen sat with its waiting icon animation for several seconds. Finally her roommate Mandy appears on the screen.

"Mandy!" Alice said, relieved to see that familiar smile in their apartment. Maybe it was the way the morning sun broke through the windows, but Mandy's face beamed with happiness.

"Alice, friend. How are you? Having a good time? 'Saving the world?'" Mandy laughed. Alice held the phone at an angle on the table to get her in its front-facing camera, but everyone around her could also watch. Surely a live connection with Mandy couldn't be faked.

Alice tucked her hair behind her ear. "I'm good. I miss you tons. Tell me what's been going on since I left."

Mandy made a dismissive gesture. "Oh, that. I'm not worried. I'm just waiting things out while you and your friends save the world and find a cure!"

"But the mutation. The virus can now be spread by animals. You must be worried," Alice said.

Mandy rolled her eyes. "Well, it's not like I'm living in a

forest, Alice. I'm just jealous I couldn't come with you to be in that great study. I'm even a bit jealous of all the cool friends you're making."

A cold shiver ran down Alice's spine. Mandy was way too cheerful. Sure, she was upbeat most of the time, optimistic to a fault. But this Mandy was so sweet in her voice it gave Alice a toothache. Alice felt a hand on her shoulder as Alex slid into the view of the camera.

"Oh, hello there!" Mandy said.

"*Привіт, справи?*" Alex replied.

Mandy paused and cocked her head in a small quick motion for a moment so small it could be mistaken for video lag. "*Привіт, друже. Як ти? Добре проводиш час?*"

Alex looked at Alice, whose face turned white. She gave a meek wave and pressed the "end call" button on the screen. "I'm guessing your friend doesn't speak Ukrainian?"

Shaking her head slowly, Alice said, "Are you kidding? She failed Spanish. That couldn't have been Mandy."

"Is she in our time zone too? Because the sun was out."

"You're right! It's got to be midnight in Virginia."

"How would a drug company be able to do this?" Hannah asked. "They make medicine, not deep fakes."

"They're not deep fakes," Peter clarified. "Deep fakes take existing video and put new faces over them. This is pure artificial intelligence. Just like the helper app everyone installed that has a talking avatar of Ms. Birch. It doesn't look great on a phone app because a phone only has so much processing power. But a server farm could do it. They acquired DynaImaging, who made the movie *Drive Until Dawn*. Complete AI. One scan of the actors, and the rest was computer rendered. If they can do something so realistic on the big screen, with all the acting and the emotional range of the performers, they can easily fake a conversation without us being able to tell the difference."

"Like the server farm underneath us," Alex added.

Alice stood up, knocking her chair over. "I can't stay here! This place. It's all some giant secret trick!" She gripped her phone so hard it might crack.

"Trick for what, though?" asked Hannah.

Alice looked at the front desk. There was real-life Ms. Birch wearing a black facemask, typing at the computer. "I don't know. I don't want to know. I'm not participating anymore." Alice turned and marched toward Ms. Birch.

Ms. Birch didn't look up from the computer while she worked. "Whatever it is will have to wait, I'm afraid."

"I need to leave." Alice's voice was deeper than she'd expected.

"Be my guest. There's the door."

Alice didn't let that dismissive tone dissuade her. "I'm checking out. Now. I need you to take me back home. Today."

"Ha! Okay. And who will drive you? Everyone is locked down while they await testing."

"You can do it. I no longer want to be here. You...you can't keep me here captive." Alice forgot there wouldn't be anyone available to drive her back to the airport.

Ms. Birch finally looked up from her screen. Only her eyes could express her emotion, and it was cold. "Ms. Whitmore, do you know what I've been up to today? Last night? Well into the night, no doubt? While all of you get the fortune of restful isolation, some of us still have to run things. I spent hours on conference calls with health experts from the home office to review protocols for this new mutation. I had to verify that we can still use meat if it's cook properly or if we're going vegan for the rest of your stay.

We're not, by the way. Now I have to find a food supplier to replace every perishable item in the kitchen. Restock all the cleaning supplies after we scrubbed this place head to toe during the night. I'm sure, however, I'll find some time during this emergency crisis to get you a taxi."

Alice didn't realize how much Ms. Birch was responsible for, or at least how much had been given to her, with so many staffers gone. But that didn't change the fact that she couldn't stay here and be a part of their experiment.

"I'd call a taxi myself, but my phone doesn't think I should leave for some reason."

"Ms. Whitmore, whatever problems you have with your phone are your responsibility. If you manage to get yourself a taxi, I'll let the guard at the gate know to let them in." Ms. Birch paused. "No. Wait. The guards are in lockdown too. The gates are locked."

Alice's face heated up; she was really stuck here. "You're telling me I can't leave then?"

Ms. Birch set her hands against the countertop with a sturdy slap. "No one can leave, Ms. Whitmore! Not you, not me, no one. Believe me, if I were capable of sending you back where you came from, I'd make it my top priority." She took a measured breath as she recomposed herself. "This isn't like before. We're no longer dealing with a simple matter of maintaining the bubble of security. Viruses do not simply 'change' in this manner. They replicate themselves; sometimes copy errors are made. Tiny ones. Unlike influenza, the Ozark has 'proofreaders' that make it more difficult for variants to occur. But this wasn't a tiny error.

"We have to be very careful for the next few days until we understand what we're up against. Do you understand? Or should I expect to see you on the security cameras attempting to scale the fence on your way out?"

Alice didn't say anything; she couldn't. In the attempt to argue her way to get what she wanted, again Ms. Birch had won. Alice turned and headed back to her room.

Again, Alice was without an argument. When she'd tried to confront Ms. Birch about the other guests no longer at the castle, it was perfectly feasible—and reasonable—for the guests to simply leave. She knew they'd been taken, but she had no proof. She couldn't point out the room with the luggage without implicating Vlad. Now that she'd tried to leave, she couldn't prove she was being held captive. It really was too dangerous to be out where the virus was suddenly much more contagious. Alice should feel foolish, but she knew this place wasn't right despite Ms. Birch misdirecting her concerns.

Alice wanted to push the fact that everyone had hacked phones, but what would that change now? What could Ms. Birch say? *You got it; you caught us. Mwaa! Ha-ha-ha-ha!* No, she'd probably try some gaslighting argument or deny it or...

And then what? What would change? They couldn't leave. But at least, maybe, if everyone had real access to the outside, she could have really talked to her mom and dad. Were they healthy? How were they really managing? Were they even alive? Guests were disappearing; the outside world was on fire; and here she was, caught up in medical/public relations experiments that created more questions than answers.

She needed to find her own answers; staying and doing nothing wasn't an option. Alice returned to her room to get her notepad. It was a roster of every guest she knew and which rooms they stayed in; she circled the ones that used to be occupied but were now empty. When she counted it up, the number astonished her. In all, she calculated only sixty-two percent of all the guests remained. So many people had left so gradually that almost everyone didn't notice how few remained. She knew Darren would want to see her notes. At least he wouldn't dismiss her conspiracy theories. His were wilder than hers.

Alice must have stood up too fast, because she felt a rush of light-headedness. A hissing from the air vents in the ceiling caught her attention. White mist jetted into the room, making the air moist and pungent. She must have inhaled some of it. Her mind raced as she struggled to keep balance. She was being gassed. This must be how people disappeared. She was next.

Alice held her breath and ran to the door, only to find it locked. She couldn't get out of the room as it filled with a toxin that made her weaker by the second. It wouldn't stop until she succumbed completely. She needed to hold her breath as long as possible and get help. She picked up the room phone, but there was no tone. She couldn't bang on the walls. Her neighbors were Harry, who was gone, and Hannah, who was still down in the lobby.

Out of desperation, she shoved her door card under the door. Maybe, by some grace of God, someone would see the card and try it on the door. Maybe? Alice was panicking. She knew she couldn't hold her breath for long. At some point, she'd break and breathe in the misty air. Would she die? Pass out? Either way she would be gone. Just like everyone else in this death trap of a castle, and her friends wouldn't know what happened. Alice imagined Darren, Hannah, Yuri, and Alex discovering another friend gone. Hannah! What did she say about diving and holding a breath?

"So we have the same genes as seals and otters, and our

bodies actually are more efficient at holding our breath underwater"

Hannah was talking about freediving. No scuba gear and being able to hold her breath for several minutes. Would that work? How long would the mist last? If Hannah was right, if Alice even had a chance, she had to get her head underwater. She stumbled to the bathroom and opened the door. She immediately noticed no vents spraying a mist in the bathroom. She shut the door behind her, and there were no hissing sounds. She decided to risk it and take a breath of air if there was any left. She gasped and coughed. The air had that same pungent sweetness but wasn't nearly as bad as it had been in her room; even so, it had an effect on her. She knew she didn't have much time before the air would be too toxic for her.

The bathroom didn't have a bathtub to submerge her face, so she stopped up the sink and turned on the cold water tap. The basin filled up enough to let her submerge her face, and she went in.

If Hannah was right, this would help her hold her breath. Or did she need to be underwater completely? Did she need to be in the shower instead? No. She needed to focus. Slow her heart. *Stop panicking. Think calmly. Just be calm. Please, be calm.* Alice's abdomen jerked.

"But they show me techniques and how to work through the urge to breathe when your body freaks out."

This must be what she meant; Alice's body was freaking out. But Hannah had said she'd worked through it and could hold her breath much longer now. Even so, Hannah had practice and didn't have noxious air in her system either.

Alice didn't know how long she held her breath or if her burning lungs would cause any lasting damage. She didn't know if the toxic air had gotten through under the bathroom door. She didn't have much longer to think about it until her head jerked up and her body convulsed to the floor; she finally gave up and inhaled. The air wasn't as sickly, but nonetheless her head swam more.

Outside the bathroom door, the hissing ebbed. The room was now completely flooded with gas, and it seeped in from under the door, where Alice lay on the floor, trying again to hold her breath. It was the same cycle as before, only shorter. Now it felt like mere seconds passed before her body began convulsing. If she could stand, she would try to submerge her face in water again in hopes that mammalian instinct would kick in.

As she lay on the floor watching the tainted air seep toward her, from the corner of her eye she spotted the wall sliding open. She glanced over to see the wall become a sliding door revealing a foot, then a leg, then a torso, then two torsos. She dared to glance up to see two gas masks. The two masked figures stepped out and flanked her.

"Why is she all wet?"

"She doesn't look injured. Check her pulse."

Two fingers pressed into her neck. "Hard to tell through the gloves, but it feels erratic and a bit fast. We'd better call the gas tech. The mix might have been too high."

"He's in fucking isolation."

"He can wear a clean suit. Her pulse is higher than it should be. You gonna help me pick her up or what?"

They sounded familiar. Alice realized they were the same men from the basement when she and Vlad had hidden behind the luggage. Two hands pulled her legs up, and two more lifted her limp body from under her arms. Her skin pinched from the grip, and the shift in her body made holding her breath all the more difficult. However, she wasn't shaking anymore. She had made it past the involuntary spasming stage Hannah had talked about. Either that or she too drugged to tell the difference.

They lifted her body behind the wall as it slid closed behind them. Alice felt her gravity shift as they descended. She was in a lift. All this time, her bathroom was oddly small because it offset the space for an elevator. It must have connected to every room directly beneath hers.

When the doors finally opened again, they stepped out, and Alice dared to slowly take in air. She wanted so badly to gasp and breathe in as hard as she could. Her lungs begged her to. She had to force herself to hold her breath intermittently, or else the two abductors would find out she was awake. She felt lights pass over her eyelids as they shuffled along. She didn't hear anyone else around them—no other footsteps or conversations.

They hoisted Alice onto a plastic cushioned matt. One of them pulled off his mask.

"Hey, what about the mutation?" the masked one said.

"You know, for a Shepherd, you're a fucking idiot. What demon did you get paired with? The Lord of the Flies?"

"What?"

"Hello? We took the ritual. We have the antibodies already. We can't catch it."

"Oh." The other man pulled his mask off. "But that doesn't mean we can't pass it to others."

"Nope. Everybody else is in lockdown. Just us Shepherds down here."

Alice heard a ding and the sound of more elevator doors opening. She felt the rumble as she was wheeled into the car. The elevator doors closed behind her, and they descended farther.

"By the way, be careful around Dr. McCormick. She's a

one-woman show today. If she tells you to do something, do it."

"Yeah, sure." There was a long pause. "A Nuckelavee."

"A what?"

"Nuckelavee. It's my demon. A water horse demon."

"They have those? Huh."

"They got the name from Orcadian mythology. It's actually a very interesting—"

"I don't care."

"Oh. Who's yours?"

"Oni. Big ol' Japanese ogre demon."

"Nice."

Alice counted the elevator dings as the two talked. She didn't understand what was happening to her. She was almost knocked out by gas in her room, then dragged through a hidden door in her bathroom by two men who thought they were immune from the Ozark virus, and now she was being taken to a doctor.

The elevator made a total of seven dings when it finally stopped and the doors opened. "We're here, McCormick!" one of the men called out.

Far away, a woman called back, "Here, in room eight!"

They pushed Alice along and eventually slowed to turn into room eight. "Set her on that bed there. And check her blood pressure with that monitor next to you. I'm just about done with this one," said the woman. Alice was lifted clumsily then set down on a mattress. Small electronic beeps floated around her. The room smelled of cleaning products and fresh plastic. Someone lifted her right arm and fit a strap around it.

"Uh, which button starts it?" one of the men asked.

Heeled footsteps came toward Alice. "That power

button on at the top, then the green button below it. And while you do that, I'll get a drip started."

With a beep and whirring sound, the strap around her arm tightened. It was measuring her blood pressure. Alice's heart never stopped pounding in her chest; she knew the readout would be far from normal.

"Her heart rate is way up, Doc."

They would know in a few more seconds that she was, in fact, conscious. She was so caught up with being found out, the sharp pinch in her other arm surprised her, and she jerked.

Fuck.

Alice saw the woman next to her dressed in a white smock jump back. She was holding an IV needle, and she and the two men next to her wore surprised expressions. Alice didn't wait for anyone to respond. She flew out toward the woman with her fist landing perfectly on her face. Her other arm, still attached to the machine, pulled it over, crashing into one of the men.

She ripped the arm strap off and took in the room. The woman lay still on the floor with a bloody nose; she was blond with glasses and wore a lab coat. Three other hospital beds were occupied. There, she saw Yuri lying unconscious, hooked up to a drip and monitors. She turned to the two men, who stared at her with dumbstruck faces. One was her size, similar age. The other was older, slightly taller, and heavier, with patchy gray in his hair and on his face.

Alice instantly thought of every self-defense class she'd attended, every training event her dad had made her go to, including when she had disarmed Mr. Reed. She was getting out of here. She was going through them.

The older man, flustered, ran to her, reaching for her arms. He should have been watching her legs. He screamed, and he immediately fell, clutching his groin for protection. He screamed again after Alice put all her weight into a stomp against his knee. He struggled to stand with his good leg but fell down after a swift kick to his face then stopped moving.

Alice wheeled on other man, her face locked on her target. He flinched and stumbled backward, losing his balance against the gurney behind him. She was on top of him instantly. Left. Right. Left. Right. His arms tried to block every blow while he cried out in pain. "Stop! Stop! Please!"

Alice spun around and sat on top of his chest, pushing her knee into his neck. His face was red and bloody. "What the fuck is happening?" she shouted.

The man struggled to talk. "You [cough] you were chosen!"

"Chosen for what? What were you going to do to me? To *them*?"

He gurgled sounds and his face turned purple. Alice eased off his neck a bit. He coughed. "You're in line with them for the cure. You all go down to the operation floor, get assessed, then go to the City for the ritual. You were supposed to be asleep."

"I wasn't tired." Alice stood up and went to Yuri, stepping over the older man. She removed his IV and shook him. "Yuri. Yuri!"

"He's sedated for the surgery," the younger man said as he pulled himself up.

"Yeah, well, surgery is canceled." Alice walked to the other bed. It was Claire Montag. She removed the needle from Claire's arm, walked to the next bed, and did the same to a guy she recognized but never had met.

She turned back toward the young man. "How many more are there?"

"J-just you four. We were going to get more, but we're short-staffed, so..."

"This is what you've been up to? Kidnapping us? Performing surgery? What kind of surgery? What does any of this have to do with making a vaccine?"

"Oh, it doesn't. I-I mean, it does kind of. We had to know if you were compatible with the ritual. That's what the tests were for. To see if your DNA has the right markers. And even then, it's not a sure bet." He reached up to his face and added, "I think you broke my nose."

Alice half listened to him. She pulled the IV drips from the beds to the two people she'd just knocked out. She couldn't wake up Yuri and the others, but she could keep the woman and the older man from waking up. She hoped that when Yuri and the others eventually came around, they could escape.

"You run, I'll get you. I'm way too high on adrenaline to be outrun. Tell me about this ritual like I don't know what the fuck you're talking about because I don't. And don't run," Alice barked while she attempted to attach a needle to the older man's arm. She did her best to find a vein, but it was only a guess. She knew it was unsafe to reuse a needle. It would be more unsafe for her and the others if they woke back up.

The younger man explained, "I'm a Shepherd. You're a Ram, or you might be. I took this ritual in the City, where I accepted the His Dark Offer. And because I—"

"Whose Dark Offer?"

"Why, our Lord Satan. He who has delivered us from harm, avenged our enemies, and imbued us with the gift to rule this realm."

"What the what? How hard did I hit you?"

"Surely you've heard his call. In this place, he reaches into your dreams. He's waiting for you to come to the City." The young man unbuttoned his bloodstained shirt and revealed his chest to her. A large black tattoo of a two-headed goat lay across his chest. A red slick smile broke across the young man's face. "This is the gift for the chosen, to become two beings in one. I am a Shepherd among the Sheep."

Maybe she did "hear his call." Those dreams that had woken her up in a panic were so vivid. They didn't fade like vague memories. She noticed the man start to relax as he talked about his devil worship, as though the talk of Satan brought him comfort. She didn't want him calm; he needed him scared of her, but he was much more forthcoming in this state than he was with a knee pressed into his neck.

"The texts from our prophets told us of the coming plague," he continued. "There were ways to prepare, but the methods are...not acceptable in society. To be a Shepherd like me? The acts we had to do in His honor are truly heinous. But! That's how you get His Gift."

"And that's how you're a Shepherd and immune from the virus?" Alice made her way to the woman and hooked her up to the IV drip.

"That was the only way we thought existed. But, oh, clever Satan gives knowledge and hides it too. There is a shortcut!" He held out his hands to her. "The Rams of our Sheep. A much simpler ritual that let's you offer a small sacrifice to your paired demon."

"Sacrifice, huh?" Alice stood up. Both the man and woman were now attached to an IV drip. "And the operation floor. Down a level?"

The man buttoned up his shirt. "Yes, that's where the selection for sacrifice is made."

"Take me." Alice pulled him by his shirt and led him into the hallway, where she saw for the first time a space that looked like a night shift of a hospital ward. Most of the lights were off, the room doors open and dark. To the right, by a nursing station, she saw the elevators and pushed him along toward them. She pressed the "down" button to call the elevator, but nothing happened. She pressed it a couple more times with no results.

"You need a keycard." The young man slowly reached down and pulled his name tag from his waist. Alice snatched it from him and pressed it against the metal plate next to the button and tried again. This time the "down" button lit up briefly, and with a ding, the doors opened.

"You're really going down there? You're not going to try and get out or something? You must really believe," he said.

Alice shook her head. She looked at the name badge: Tim Baker. "You know what, Tim? I think you and your friends are a bunch of cult-y, murderous pieces of shit. You lied to us, tricked us into coming here, kidnapped us, and now you're sacrificing us to your hell god? No, I'm not going up. I'm...I'm going to stop this."

"You sure you don't want to—" Tim's head smacked into the frame of the elevator and sunk to the floor.

"I don't."

IT WAS Alex who first realized Alice was gone. When she couldn't find her brother Yuri, she tried Alice's room. When Alice didn't answer, she got Darren.

Darren was poring over the data he'd pulled from the servers. By accessing the technician's laptop, he was able to network directly to the server farm beneath the building. About half of them were running predictive content engine AI. The other servers, the ones he was really after, were performing genetic sequencing.

He found Spence's profile first. It was recognizable, but he didn't know from where. The lab results had stats and probabilities he didn't understand. If he asked a geneticist, he still wouldn't. He played back a simulation output file of Spence's DNA. He didn't know what to look for, but he watched as a strand of DNA floated in rotation. It looked like the same examples of DNA he'd seen in biology class: a long chain of base pairs attached to two sugar-phosphate backbones. Then, small black flecks floated into new protein chains, growing their own backbone. The simulation of Spence's DNA altered into a triple helix.

He needed to get all the data to GenNTech. He opened a terminal window and ran a ping to an IP address he had committed to memory. It was sent and was received successfully with zero packet loss. He had a clear connection to GenNTech; they could take all this data and he'd be done.

"Darren?" Alex called with a high pitch and a rapid knock.

Darren double clicked an icon on his desktop. A GenNTech splash screen came up. He put the laptop under the bed, making sure it stayed open to let the app continue operating.

"Oh, thank God!" Alex cried as Darren opened the door. Her face was flushed with panic. "I can't find Yuri or Alice. Look." She pointed down to the courtyard. "They're not with the others, not in their rooms either. Are they gone too?"

Darren's heart dropped. "Have you checked the gym? Or maybe they're raiding the kitchen?" It was a dumb idea, he knew, but he so desperately didn't want to accept the reality that they were getting picked off.

Alex grunted, "I'm done with this." She leaned over the railing and yelled, "Hannah! Come!" She turned back to Darren. "They aren't in the gym or kitchen! They're gone, like everyone, and soon us too. We can't be apart for one second with without someone going missing."

"Okay, what do we do then? Sleep in the hallway?" Darren asked.

Hannah came up from the corridor. "I should be annoyed that you just hollered at me like that. But at least I had a good excuse to leave that boring conversation."

"Alice and Yuri are missing," Darren said.

"What? When?" Hannah walked over to room 403, Alice's room, and spotted the door key on the floor.

"We don't know. Alex here just found out." Darren and Alex followed her to Alice's door.

"She was here just a couple hours ago. Here." Hannah pushed in the card, and the door beeped its approval.

Hannah gasped and jumped back. Darren looked to see what shocked her. Sitting on the bed, in all black staff uniform, was Vlad. He didn't move when they entered. He just sat there, looking at his feet.

Alex jumped at Vlad and grabbed him by the shirt. His head wobbled as she shook him with her fists. "Where is my brother? Tell me!"

Vlad looked up at them with dead eyes. "Down. With the others."

"The others? All of them? Every person who left?" Darren asked.

Vlad nodded.

"Get him back!" Alex shoved him backward as she stood up.

"I only cleaned up the rooms. I didn't know they would take so many."

"They?" Darren scoffed. "You're wearing their uniform. You *are* them."

"It's not like I have a choice! It's this or death. You don't leave the Shepherd family." Vlad's eyes turned to Darren. "Even you."

Hannah and Alex turned toward Darren.

"What did you say?" Darren asked.

Vlad shook his head. "The only reason you haven't been taken below is because of your dad. You and I? We're family members. I was born into this. Grew up here. But you?" Vlad chuckled and shook his head. "Why did you even come here? Your dad is a Shepherd. Your family is covered as long as he has the antibodies. Hasn't he gotten you immunized?"

Hannah took a step away from Darren. "What's he saying? Why does he know about your family?"

"I'm not immune. He hasn't. I don't know what he's talking about. My dad..." Darren tried to explain. "He, he became part of this secret organization called the Shepherds as soon as his company was acquired by Zenith Pharm. He got this crazy tattoo on his chest to go with it."

"A two-headed goat," Vlad said. "It's the symbol of the group, same as the City. My parents have it too. All Shepherds do." Vlad lifted his shirt to reveal a bare chest free of markings. "I'm not a Shepherd. I haven't gone through the initiation."

"I don't care about your skinny chest. Take me to my brother!" Alex demanded.

"Hold on," Hannah interrupted. "Are you part of this, Darren?"

"No! I came here to expose them! Zenith Pharm manipulates its own stock by manufacturing outbreaks. I thought this was the same thing. I thought I could give away the data they used for testing vaccine candidates to prove it. But they're not testing for vaccines are they." Darren turned back to Vlad, who shook his head. "It's our DNA. They're testing to see if they can alter it."

"My brother. They're going to alter him. His DNA?" Alex asked.

"It's more than that." Vlad stood up, his hands up in defense. "I like Alice. I...I was raised to think some things. How the world was. My place in it, by divine right and all that. But I didn't know what it would cost. I want to help."

Darren said. "Do you know where they are? Can we rescue them?"

Nodding, he pulled out his keycard. "Once I use this, they'll know it was me." He stepped into the bathroom and held his card in place against the metal wall in the shower stall. The wall pulled away to reveal an elevator. "This way."

Hannah's jaw dropped. "Does every room have this?"

They piled into the car, and the door closed behind them.

"After they...we flood the room and the person passes out, they're taken below. I didn't know where at first, but when everyone had to isolate, I was able to take a look in the City unnoticed," Vlad explained. "In order to become a Shepherd, you have to do some...things. Very dark things. It's a ritual. It involves the souls of the innocent, pain, desecrations. It's pretty brutal. Shepherds have to do this to join with a demon. They consume the soul of a demon, and their body changes. They can survive in hell that way. It's about power and immortality. It also means they have the natural ability to build antibodies for this virus."

"Why the virus?" Darren asked.

"It's from hell," Vlad said.

"This virus is from hell?" Darren asked.

The elevator doors opened, and Vlad hopped out. "This way."

"Where are we now? Do all these lead up to our rooms?" Hannah stood in a dark concrete hallway lined with elevators.

Vlad nodded. "It goes all the way around with elevators for every room here." Vlad held his hand out flat and moved it with each word. "This is B1. We're going to medical: B5. This way."

"So what happens after we find Alice and Yuri? We

can't just go back to the castle as though everything is cool. And can't exactly leave either," Darren said.

"I'd rather take my chances out there than in here. Plague birds or not, I'm not spending another second in this place," Hannah said.

"Above us are the garage floors with vans," Vlad explained. "When you come back, there will be keys by the front desk. Just take my key card on the way back, and it will get you access to the garage."

"You're not coming with us?" Darren asked.

"No, he's not coming with us. He's one of them!" Yuri said, pointing at the ground.

"You're right. I am one of them. I couldn't leave if I wanted to. As soon as I left here, they could find me." Vlad's expression reminded Darren of a dog being reprimanded. "We find the others, whoever we can. You're going to have to take my card by force, okay? Like, it can't be known I helped."

Vlad led them to a metal freight elevator door, pushed his keycard into the metal plate, and pressed the "down" button. They watched the LED beside the panel read out the car's progress: B6, B5, B4...

"What if someone is there when the door opens?" Darren asked.

"I don't know about you, but anyone who stands between me and my friends is in my way." Hannah tilted her head with a tiny crack from the joints in her neck.

"Almost everyone here is in isolation while they wait to be tested for the virus," Vlad explained. "The only people who should be there are Shepherds. But I don't know how many are working in medical."

The LED read B1, and the elevator dinged. Darren braced for what was on the other side. The doors opened. It was empty. He sighed and stepped into the car with every-one. Vlad pushed B5, and the doors closed.

"What's on B6?" Darren asked.

"It's for...operating on the Ram candidates. The only floor left intact since World War Two. We don't want to go there," Vlad said, almost like he was sharing a secret no one should hear.

"But what if they're not in medical?" Hannah asked.

The elevator door dinged a final time and opened to a darkened linoleum hallway. In front of the doors lay a body with blood dripping from his face. "Check the rooms. Quietly." Vlad bent down to the body, got a pulse, then pulled him to the side of the hallway.

Only one room toward the middle of the hall had light coming from the doorway. Darren skipped the other rooms, stepping as quietly as he could. He found a gurney on its side. A man and woman with mangled bruised faces lay on the floor with IV drips attached. Darren found Yuri sitting straight up, staring back at him.

Behind him, Alex exclaimed, "Yuri!" She crossed the threshold and went straight to her brother with open arms. "You're okay! You are, right? Are you okay? Yuri!"

Yuri shut his eyes tightly. "My head is so loud." Her sister released him and gave him a once-over. "Where am I? Did I get hurt?" he said.

Hannah came up behind Darren, who was still standing in the doorway, taking in the scene before him. "The rest are empty. Oh, my God, what happened here?"

Darren turned to her. "Empty? Alice isn't here? Are you sure?"

Hannah stepped to a bed where a woman was sleeping. "Hey, wake up. Come on." She turned to Darren and tilted her head toward the other hospital bed.

Darren went to the other person and shook his shoulders. "Can you hear me? You gotta get up. We should, uh, find your clothes too."

The man batted away Darren's arms. "Stop it already. Ugh."

"What's going on?" the woman in bed asked, her voice trembling.

"Look at me. You were taken. You were brought here against your will. We've come to get you out of here," Hannah explained. "I'm Hannah. You're Claire, right?"

Darren helped the guy sit up and looked around the room for clothes. The room looked like a crime scene. Knocked-over equipment, two beaten and drugged people on the floor. Whoever did this probably was responsible for the other guy in the hall. Was it Alice? Did she manage to get away?

Darren spotted a shelf with clothes poorly stuffed onto it. One pile had a black and pink blouse. He grabbed its contents and handed them to Claire. The other was shoes and a tracksuit. He gave it to Yuri and the other bag of clothes to the man. "Here you go..."

"Zach." He accepted his clothes. "You're from the castle. I recognize you guys. How did we get here?" Zach said as he shook out his jeans.

"Our rooms are a trap. You must have been drugged and brought down here," Darren said. Zach looked at him suspiciously. "We're directly under the castle."

"Wait, I thought there were labs. This looks like..." Zach said.

"A hospital?" Vlad stepped into the room, pulling along a stumbling man with a bloody nose. He pushed the man to the floor. "It is. It was remodeled to treat patients while they were administered various medications Zenith was proving out." He took a look around and saw the two bodies on the floor. He then turned to the man. "Did Alice do this?"

"We thought she was asleep." The man pinched his nose to hold back the bleeding. "Took them out, drugged them, then went below to the 'butcher' floor."

Vlad's face went white. "She...went down?"

"Okay, let's get her."

Darren started to the door, but Vlad held his hands up to stop him. "You don't want to go there. I don't even want to go there." He swallowed. "If Alice went there, she's already been caught."

Hannah came up to them. "Alice evaded getting kidnapped and trashed these guys. She obviously unplugged our friends too. She might be trying to do the same for the people on the floor below. The 'butcher' floor? Is that what you called it?" Hannah shook her head. "Would you leave her in a place like that?"

Darren shook his head. "What are we getting into, Vlad?"

"It's the operating floor, but that's a joke. They take a piece of you. An organ, a body part. It's an offering for demons. The surgeon...he runs the floor. It's just him, his guards, and the bodies he works on. If Alice went there, she's in terrible danger."

The young man spat blood at Vlad's feet. "You and your family will pay, Vlad. You'll never be a Shepherd. Even the sin of betrayal can't redeem this!"

Darren grabbed his arm. "Help me get him into one of these beds. He can test out their arm straps." Darren and Vlad pulled the kicking and screaming man up and strapped him in place. Yuri, Claire, and Zach were back in their old clothes.

"I'm going down," Darren told them. "You don't have to come. You've been through enough already."

Yuri shook his head. "I was heading there anyway. Besides, where else can we go? Not back to our rooms. Not outside either."

Claire, pulling at her jacket, said, "I just want to go home. But I don't know how that's possible."

"They were going to kill us!" Zach objected. "Nobody has come back. They're all dead. We should get out of here."

"If they survived the ritual, they're still alive," Vlad explained.

"I don't care," Zach said. "Look, by this time tomorrow, the entire staff, the other workers at whatever shithole hospital this is will be back to the business of plucking us off one by one. We need to leave."

The man strapped in the hospital bed strained against the armbands. Eventually someone would return to this floor, free him, and revive the others. Darren plucked the man's keycard from his waist. "Someone could go back with this, get the keys to the vans from the front desk, and get everyone the hell out of here. The vans are kept in the garage?"

Vlad nodded.

"And then where?" asked Claire. "The virus is still floating around, killing everybody. We don't even have a vaccine yet."

"I'll take my chances." Zach accepted the keycard from Darren. "I'll take as many people who'll come with me. It'll be easy to get back to the airport once we're on the road." He looked to Vlad. "I'll be sure to avoid any cult towns on the way."

"You two be safe. Leave a van for us if you can," Darren said.

Zach stepped to the doorway and turned to wait for Claire to follow. "You coming?"

Claire, with her jacket cuffs in her fists, took a deep breath, "You should go. I'll stick with Hannah and the others."

"You're serious?" Zach scoffed.

Claire tried to put on a positive attitude despite her nervous body language. "It only takes one person to pull a fire alarm, you know? Besides, I think there's strength in numbers." She smiled at Hannah as a friendly arm wrapped around her back.

"Whatever." Zach stepped out of view. A few seconds later, they heard him step into the elevator.

Darren and the others rummaged the floor for anything they could use to protect themselves. Hannah found the supply closet with gauze, bandages, oxygen tanks, pharmaceuticals, gloves, tiny scissors, and a big box of sterilized disposable scalpels.

She handed Darren a scalpel. "Things are about to go sideways."

He put it in his back pocket. "Things are already sideways."

"Okay, more so."

"We need to get moving." Darren was already by the elevator. "The longer we wait, the more harm they might be in."

"Right," agreed Hannah. She sidled up next to him, and the others followed. Vlad called the elevator with his card. "And you've never been down there?" she asked.

"I've only seen footage." Vlad said, "It's not like the other floors. Everything from here up was rebuilt in the eighties, plus upgrades for servers and such. The area below is old; it survived the collapse of the tower.

"Everything is still the same since the Nazis occupied the castle. They were obsessed with finding a new power for their superiority. And for a time, we helped them. We worked with them. Uncovered forbidden truths to power. After they left, even after the collapse of the tower, we kept experimenting. One floor below."

"So you helped the Nazis then? You weren't just occupied?" Darren said.

Vlad shrugged. "In the end, they helped us more than we helped them."

Darren and the rest filed in when the elevator doors opened. He was about to go where even Alice's boyfriend, another cult member, wouldn't go. But Spence was down there, so that was where he was heading.

A WAVE of stale warm air came over Darren's face as the elevator doors slid open. He closed his eyes as the smell of sickness and copper filled his nose. Behind him, Claire stifled a gag; ahead of him was a long corridor. Fat electric cables draped along the walls, lit by single-bulb lamps that hung from the curved stone ceiling. The lights were on, but they glowed so low that the details of the walls and floor were barely visible. He stepped out onto the floor's metal grate. His footing made weighted metal sounds as he moved down the hall to the first room.

He peered into the first door's barred window, but it was too dark to see inside. He pulled out his phone and turned on its flashlight. Inside stood a large metal table, one that could be mistaken for one of the autopsy tables he often saw on television. It even had a drain in the center. But autopsy tables didn't have restraints. Red shiny unmistakable fluid glistened against the light. The smell was stronger here. The floor was decorated with lines of black paint and littered with long-burned-out candles, bones, and more of the shiny red.

"Oh, my God," Hannah whispered. "Are they all like this?"

"We shouldn't linger," Vlad whispered back.

Darren steeled himself and checked the room on the other side. It was the same. The room next to it was unused. He stepped into each room, verifying if they were occupied. As he came closer to a crossway in the corridor, with each room used and bloody, or soon to be, he felt the sense of being too late. Each disgusting room had held someone—someone who couldn't escape.

Yuri firmly gripped Darren's arm. "Slow down. You are very loud," he whispered.

Darren turned back and realized he was far ahead of the others, who were doing their best not to make stomping sounds, a precaution he was ignoring. The corridor ahead of them split into three, an intersection of more rooms connected by bad wiring and dismal lighting. Darren peered around the corner of the intersection, which was empty. However, it seemed to lead to more intersections and more corridors.

Hannah and the others caught up with Darren and Yuri. "It doesn't look like anyone is here," she whispered. "But can we not stomp around like we're in a fucking marching band?"

"I'm sorry," Darren replied.

"What's ahead of us?" Hannah asked.

"Looks like more of the same. All the room lights are off."

"Then let's verify that no one is in them and move on. Quietly."

Darren nodded. "We can cover more ground if we split up."

Claire came up immediately, her hands waving for them to stop. "That isn't a good idea."

"Nothing about this is a good idea," Darren countered, "I don't know how big this place is. Do you?"

Claire's eyebrows pushed her forehead into deep wrinkles. "Please."

The others looked back at him as though the decision were his to make. "I'm going this way." Darren pointed to the left and moved before anyone could object.

The path looked as it did before. There was only one room on the right, but it had no barred window to peer in. Darren observed that the gap between the floor and the door was dark. He looked back behind him. Yuri was with him. Going in the opposite direction, Vlad and Claire continued on, Claire staying very close beside Vlad. That must have meant Hannah had gone forward by herself.

Darren carefully gripped the cold metal doorknob and turned it until it stopped. With the gentlest use of force, he nudged the door open and looked inside. The light from outside showed a collection of buckets, mops, a hose, a washbasin, and a jug of bleach. The tension in Darren's shoulders eased as he quietly closed the door.

Darren and Yuri checked the corridors at the next intersection. The one in front of them was a dead end, as was the one to the left. The right-hand corridor continued farther, with another intersection about as far away as the last intersection.

"Let's check these two then move on," Darren whispered.

Yuri nodded. "I'll go straight. It'll be faster."

Claire's idea of not splitting up was lingering in Darren's mind. Now they were splitting up even more.

Darren turned left and assessed the layout. The left side

had more rooms with windows. He stepped into each room and peered in as before. These hadn't been used yet or at least had been cleaned to be used later. Darren made it to the last room and examined the remaining side. The right side had two rooms with normal doors. They had signs on them he recognized right away—BĂRBAŢI and FEMEI: restrooms. Light sneaked out from underneath the door in the men's room. Inside, feet shuffled.

Someone was here with them. Darren couldn't move. He replayed the last moments in his mind, wondering how much noise he'd made and if it had been loud enough to be heard by the person on the other side of that door. He was exposed; anyone stepping out of the restroom would see him immediately. Maybe he could hide in the women's room. Maybe if he just stayed still, he wouldn't be noticed.

Yuri made his way back to the intersection. He spotted Darren and shook his head. He headed toward him, but Darren waved his arms toward the men's room door. Yuri froze in place, his eyes widening as they followed Darren's motion toward the men's room door. His face went paler than a glass of milk.

In the span of seconds, that felt like entire minutes, Darren stood frozen in place while he thought out his next moves. He could try to quietly walk back toward Yuri or maybe he should take his shoes off; both of them should. Shit! *Why didn't we take our shoes off sooner?*

Darren slowly moved to push his shoes off his feet while standing in place, but he kept teetering on losing his balance. He crouched and started unlacing his shoes, but his fingers had forgotten how undo laces. He fumbled at the knots on his feet while Yuri, catching on to his strategy, lifted his legs one by one and slipped off his sneakers.

Darren had managed to undo one shoe when a toilet

flushed. A door opened. Darren saw the black boots first, then the tucked-in dress shirt and black pants, a gun holster and baton hanging from an unbuckled belt, and an open fly being pulled up by white hands in black jacket sleeves. When he finally saw the man's face, the face looked back. A clean-shaven man in his thirties, maybe older, looked Darren up and down with a confused expression.

He was one of the guards Vlad had referred to. The guard didn't yet see Yuri even though he was still in Darren's view. If he kept the guard's attention, Yuri could get away and warn the others.

"You didn't wash your hands," Darren said.

The guard blinked, and then his face resolved to anger. He took a step forward and reached for the gun in his holster. Yuri leapt from behind and pulled down the guard's pants down. The guard and Yuri fell, with Yuri still holding on to the guard's pants. The baton clanged against the floor. Yuri went to reach for it, but the guard was already on his back and kicked him in the head with his boot. Yuri yelped as he fell to the side of the corridor. And then he lay still.

Darren jumped on the guard with his fists flying wherever they could land. He had no idea how to fight in any skilled sense. He managed to get a couple of punches through the guard's arms to his face and ear but lost the upper hand when he was shoved off completely.

The guard was up before Darren could get to his knees when a punch to the head sent Darren on his back next to Yuri, who was still out. The guard pulled his pants up and stood over Darren as he reached for his gun.

The guard huffed with a smug grin. "Doc's gonna love cutting into you two." He looked down at his hand, trying to find where his gun was. His belt had fallen out of some of the belt loops, and the holster was no longer at his side. He looked behind him, where it must have landed.

Darren flinched from a loud bang. He saw part of the guard's face fly away in a red blur. The guard fell back, and Darren scrambled backward as the guard landed on his legs. Darren kicked back to get some distance; small pieces of red were on his face, hands, and clothes.

Through the ringing in his ears, he heard, "I imagine everyone here has heard that." Darren's eyes darted up.

"Alice!"

Her face was flushed, and she was breathing heavily, but she looked happy. Happy to see him? Happy to save him? Alice helped him stand back up, then immediately went to Yuri. She lightly patted his face until he batted her away. "You're finally awake, I see."

Darren asked, "Where did you come from?"

"Give me a hand with him," Alice answered. They pulled Yuri to his feet, making sure he could stand on his own.

"I'm good; I'm good. Oh, shit! He's dead!" Yuri said.

"Alice got a hold of his gun and stopped him. She saved us. How did you get here? The hallway was empty," Darren said.

"I was hiding in the women's bathroom. I was checking the rooms when I heard someone coming. Guess it was this guy."

Darren never had seen a dead person in real life before now. He couldn't stop looking at the aftermath of this guard he'd watched die. Where his face should have been...

"Darren," Alice snapped at him. "We have to go. Get with it."

Alice already had fastened the gun to its holster on her hip, and Yuri was wielding the baton. Darren realized they were waiting for him. They did have to go; others would have noticed the gunshot, including the "Doc" the guard had mentioned and possibly even more guards. It was safe to stay. And they still had to find Spence.

"Okay. It's just..." Darren came up to Alice and hugged her. After a second, she hugged him back. "I'm glad you're okay."

"I'm not okay. I'm angry," she said.

"And you've got a gun now," Yuri added.

Alice pulled away, smiling back at Darren. "Thank you for coming for me."

"And Spence. And Harry and any other people we can find. Hannah, Alex, Vlad, and Claire are here as well. We split up," Darren said.

"Vlad? Is he here?"

"He is. We couldn't have gotten here without him."

Echoes of gunfire caught their attention; the direction was indiscernible. The three headed back down the hall where they had come from. A few minutes later, they reached to the first intersection from the elevator.

"This is where we split up," Yuri said.

"Let's go left," Alice replied.

They quickly made it to the next intersection. They could only go left or right. Darren tried right. At the next intersection, they heard sounds coming from the left. Another guard was crouched by a doorway, looking in. Behind him, Claire lay on the floor. She was crying while holding on to her leg. Blood covered her pants and pooled around her.

Darren moved so Alice could get in front of him. He watched as Alice checked behind her and to the left before she removed her gun from its holster and held it with precise aim. Darren and Yuri covered their ears. She didn't hesitate. A simple squeeze, a loud bang, maybe a couple of seconds passed, and then Alice stood up and holstered her piece. She looked back at Darren and Yuri. "It's clear. There might be more."

Darren turned the corner and saw the guard lying face-down with a cratered hole for a head. He went to Claire, who had a single hole in her leg, likely from the gunfire. He thought maybe Hannah or Vlad were inside the room.

He called out, "Hannah, we're here."

Hannah emerged, quickly stepping past the dead guard. "Bring Claire inside! Come on!"

The room was large but had a low curved ceiling and used the same lighting as the hallways. Along the walls were more hospital beds, like the ones above with monitors and drips attached to people who Darren recognized from the castle. Each of them was unconscious with a breathing mask over their face; none of them were Spence.

Vlad was toward the back of the room. He wielded a fire ax in both trembling hands behind an old man in a black rubber apron who was sitting down. The man seemed amused by all the commotion; his eyes beamed at the sight of Claire as she was carried to an open spot on the floor.

"She's been shot in the leg. Can you fix her?" Hannah directed her question to the old man.

He chuckled. "She's already been claimed, I see." Vlad hit the man's shoulder with the end of the ax handle. "Yes, yes. Quite so." He came over to Claire and eyed her leg. "Someone want to bring me some tools? In the hallway behind this room, there should be a stack of tool-boxes. One of those should have enough equipment for this."

"You expect us to find any more armed guards?" Alex asked.

"Those two are more than enough to service my operation," the old man said.

"*Were*," Alex replied. She and her brother had left the room for the supplies.

Hannah sat down by Claire and applied pressure to her thigh; Claire moaned through her tears.

Alice went straight to Vlad, still wielding his ax, and pushed a finger at his chest. "You. You knew about this place, didn't you? Are you a part of this? Did you know what's happening?"

Vlad briefly closed his eyes but didn't divert his attention to the old man examining Claire. "I was and I did. I can't change that, and I know you don't buy that. But as long as I can help get you out of here, I don't care if you believe me."

"What's wrong with these people?" Darren asked as he went to one of the patients for a closer look.

"That's what we were getting to before we heard gunfire," Hannah said. "We got these two by surprise. We were playing Bad Cop, Worse Cop when we heard gunfire, and that guard over there took the opportunity to...well, Claire here got in the way of him shooting me."

"I don't know what I could possibly tell you that you don't already know." The man turned to Vlad. "Isn't that right, young man?"

"I've never been here," Vlad said.

"Oh, but you know all about it. You were raised in the City. You know the path to His Dark Offer must pass through here. Don't tell me your family teaches you the rights of *Bli'lg Caep'nej* for the Shepherd and *Z'njm Sej'pal* for the Ram. This is where the proverbial sausage is made."

Everyone was looking at Vlad. From the expression on the young man's face, Darren sensed his guilt and shame.

Quick steps from outside the room came fast as Alex and Yuri returned with a toolbox. Yuri carried his baton as well as a couple of handsaws. "In case any more guards or whatever come."

The old man cut away the cloth from Claire's wound and applied a cleaning solution before working to remove the bullet, humming all the while.

Darren turned toward Vlad. "Were you able to check the rest of the rooms?"

"They're all empty. Only these four remain, but they look too weak after their operations to be moved," Vlad said.

"Induced comas," the old man spoke up. "They'll have to be transported to the City. You can't exactly walk with a missing lung, can you?" He returned to his humming.

"You took their lungs?" Vlad said incredulously.

The old man laughed. "If it's in their charts, I take the parts!"

Vlad swallowed. "It's...part of the ritual. When we commit ourselves to be Shepherds, we consume the soul of a demon. One that aligns with our demonology chart. It makes us immortal, but there's a price. It's called, uh..."

"Reclamation!" called out the old man.

"Reclamation, right. Shepherds can die but only from injury. Shepherds risk the demon returning with the power of a human soul. They become a gateway to loose a demon on earth."

Darren had heard some of this already. "That guy upstairs was a Shepherd. He didn't exactly come off as a demon-wielding immortal."

"He's young. Over time he'll grow and become much more formidable. It takes centuries, but he'll get there as long as he doesn't die from injury. Even then, that will be hard to do."

"Centuries? How many of you are there?" Darren asked.

The old man scoffed. "Too many if you ask me. Back in my day, we had to prove our worth. Took years. Now these kids can take an online course, like VCR repair."

"If there are so many of you out there," Alice asked, "why lure us here like this? Why not just recruit the willing?"

Vlad answered. "It's about power. If you had the power of immortality in your blood, would you want to give that away? I'm only immune from the virus because of my parents. But there's another way to grow antibodies without becoming immortals."

"The Rams," Darren answered.

"Rams don't consume the soul of a demon, owning it wholly. They make an offering. A body part, a piece of themselves. If the demon accepts the offering, it joins with the Ram. The body part is restored in its image, and the Ram is now immune from the virus."

"It's a farm," Darren said. "You're making a farm of people to grow antibodies. That's your cure to save the world."

"Save the world! Ha!!" the old man barked. "Save it from what? Itself? No, I don't think so. The people of this world had their time; it's our time now. Your countries, your governments, your gods have assigned no value to a virus. No, my children, this is the Shepherds' time to rule the world of sheep. That is His promise to us. The Rams were our idea."

Nodding, the old man pointed a finger at Darren. "You don't even belong here, young man. Yes, I see you. Your father is a Shepherd, no? Are you just here for your friends? Such a good friend." *Such a good friend.* The words sent a shuddered spiked into Darren's chest. The old man smiled, twisting his face in offensive glee. He tapped his chest. "The mark of the goat. You'll have one soon enough, but what do I know? You and Vlad, peas in a pod. And you." He pointed to Alice. "I can smell His curse from here."

Alice said, "What do you mean?" when Yuri screamed in anguish. A blood-red skull-shaped head with dog ears sank its teeth into Yuri's shoulder.

Alex screamed and fell away, scrambling for safety. The mouth pulled away, and Yuri's shirt filled with red. Crying out, he fell to the floor. Behind him, the red skull with pointy ears sat atop a black jacket with black pants with no belt and an open fly.

Behind him, Darren heard Vlad call out, "Reclamation! The guards were Shepherds!"

Before Darren could piece together what that meant, the guard-bodied skull-dog thing leapt toward Alice with a deafening roar. The beast was knocked aside; Vlad fell against a nearby hospital bed. The creature crashed with Alice against the wall as it tried to lay its jaws into her. Darren ran to the fallen ax amid the chaos. He might not know how to land a punch, but he knew how to swing a bat. He aimed the ax and followed through with a concise hit. The dog skull popped away from the body. Alice screamed as blood jetted from the severed neck. She kicked it away from her as hard as she could muster.

Vlad ran to help her back up. "They're Shepherds! They're fucking Shepherds, and their bodies are open for the Reclamation. That was a demon."

Still stitching Claire's leg, the old mad chuckled to himself. "You interested in being a guard? We're now hiring."

Darren turned toward the doorway. The other guard's

body was writhing, trying to stand back up. From atop his head, green and yellow tentacles writhed down to its neck and back. The beast gripped the doorway for balance. Tiny slithery appendages seeped from the sleeves on its hands.

Darren brought the ax down on top of where a normal person's head should be. Instead of a cracking sound, or the feel of hitting something solid, he felt like he'd hit a Jell-O mold. The tentacles hemorrhaged inky fluid as the body collapsed in a withering seizure of shiny flesh and black liquid.

Darren threw up.

"If you keep moving like that, you'll break the stitches." The old man behind him tutted Claire over her cries. He wrapped her leg in gauze and tape as though nothing else had happened. "You'll want to have someone take another look. Possibly get a prescription for antibiotics as well. This isn't a clean place for this kind of surgery."

Alex looked over Yuri's shoulder. She grabbed some peroxide to clean out the bite marks, but the old man interjected. "Put pressure on his wounds. Let them finish bleeding. He'll be fine."

"Oh, sure!" Alex shot back. "He'll be fine, just flesh wounds from an ordinary hell dog!"

The old man stood up. "I can take a look if you're worried." Alex and Yuri shrank back as the man stepped forward.

Darren stepped between them. "Just tell us how to find Spence and..." He stopped midsentence, dropping the ax involuntarily. His mind couldn't register the amount of pain in his left bicep. He looked down and saw a stainless-steel scalpel deftly held by rubber gloves. His eyes met those of the old man, whose smirk told him the catastrophic misstep

he'd made by getting too close. The man must have pocketed the scalpel from that toolbox.

Darren fell back into Yuri and Alex but not before the
scalpel, which he gripped for protection, traveled farther
down his arm. He tried to keep more distance from the old
man, but his reach was long and fast. The old man pulled
him up by the other arm and tossed him like a wet wash-
cloth. Darren crashed against one of the hospital beds,
knocking over the table next to it.

"I'll do better than just tell you where Spence and the
other Rams are, Darren Montoya. I'll take you there
myself!" the old man said.

Hannah frantically pulled herself and Claire away from
his path. Alex came up behind him with the ax, but the old
man was too fast—his fist was too fast. He knocked Alex
away before she could even bring the ax down. Alice yelled
something while Darren tried to scramble away, only to
make the floor slippery beneath him.

"Yuri Petrov: Star of Kludde, the blue flame of chase
and pain!" The old man towered over Yuri, who tried to
distance himself from the sharp end of the madman's knife.
A shot fired, and the knife and part of the man's hand flew
away. He turned and screamed at Alice, whose gun was
drawn on him. It didn't slow him down, though; he grabbed
Yuri with his good hand and tossed him at her and Vlad like
a toy. The room was turning into a pile of bodies for the old
man's pickings.

"You wound me!" The old man laughed. "This is a gift
I'm offering. Just as I did for your friends. They're on their
way to take His Dark Gift by offering something of theirs in
exchange." He held up his mutilated hand in ponderance.
"It's a small price for such power. See? Better already."

Darren watched in astonishment as the man's hand became whole, as though it were never injured.

Two shots, bright and loud, fired from Alice into the old man's chest. He staggered and wheezed just a couple feet from where Alice and Vlad stood pressed against the stone wall. "Ungrateful! And stupid! Heh. Vlad Alecsandri knows how to pick 'em." A wet cough amid the old man's chuckle escaped his lips as he spat out blood. "Alice Whitmore, from the first ones, you should be more grateful! You're not even supposed to be here. Yet you were called, weren't you?"

Darren found the ax next to Alex. The old man was still giving his spooky talk while standing in place. Darren couldn't use his left bicep without experiencing searing pain. He still had one good arm, though. Swinging an ax like a baseball bat was still possible even with one arm out of the game.

"It's going to be so much better. Don't you see?" The old man's voice was less garbled now. "The power of both realms. The joining will give you new blood. *New* strength! Your new blood will cleanse the world from weakness, sickness, and futility. Earth's inhabitants will know only purpose. And pain!"

Another shot rang out; Hannah grazed the old man's head. He stumbled to the side and landed on one knee. *Do it now, Darren!* With both hands gripped around the ax, Darren darted in two steps toward the old man. His arm felt like it might shatter in pain. Before the old man could react, Darren pulled the ax down in line with where the neck met the shoulders. He felt the impact then the loud clang of the ax head smacking the metal floor.

Darren cried out as in pain and frustration. He must have missed and hit the floor instead. He tried to lift the ax once more, but so much pain shot through his arm that he dropped the ax. When the old man came back toward him, Darren jumped away to avoid his reach.

But the old man didn't reach for him. He didn't reach for anything. He just fell over, without a head.

Darren's eyes darted around the room; Vlad tried to block Alice from reaching him. Claire huddled in tears behind a hospital bed while Hannah stood guard with her gun drawn.

Vlad went to the body and removed the scalpel from its grip. Alice pulled Darren over to the toolbox and fished out a ton of gauze bandages. Yuri wrestled his sister back to consciousness. Hannah stowed her gun and pulled Claire back from the pool of tears.

Darren winced as Yuri tied a tourniquet around his arm. "It's not so bad. Clean cut. But you can't keep bleeding out."

"Is he...is he coming back?" Claire asked. "Like the others?"

Vlad stepped up to the body. "Maybe. We should tie him up or something." Alex clapped her hands and stepped quickly out of the room, likely looking for any excuse to leave the scene. "He's not like the guards. They've only been Shepherds a short time." Kneeling, Vlad pulled the black rubber apron from the corpse and unbuttoned his shirt.

"What are you doing?" Claire asked.

"Every Shepherd has the mark of the order, the two-headed goat. You can check them if you don't believe me." He pointed to the headless guard slumped in the corner.

"My dad has that tattoo," Darren said. "That explains what the old man meant when he said I didn't belong here. Like you, I already have an 'in.'"

His jaw clenched. Vlad stood up after uncovering the

old man's chest. "He's not a Shepherd. He's one of the first." Darren came over and saw the mark of a red double cross. It was the same as the ones he and Spence had noticed in the tomb underneath the cemetery. "A knight Templar," Vlad continued. "I've only ever met a few. They built this place: this castle, the City, this slaughter-house, all of it. They didn't take the rituals we do now; what they did is secret to us. If he ever consumed a demon's soul, it's been centuries since it could do any Reclamation."

"We didn't build this floor," said the old man.

Darren and the others jumped—a few even screamed—at the sound of the old man's voice emanating from the lobbed head. Darren forced himself to turn and look to the source, the disembodied head. The old man's eyes were wild, and his mouth moved with a grin. Darren wouldn't ever want to know what made a monster like that smile.

"The Nazis built this floor, and the ones above, but it was—"

Screaming, Hannah ran to the talking head. She pointed the gun and squeezed the trigger, but only clicking sounds came from it.

"Calm yourself, Hannah Bell. You've won. My guards are dead. Their demons are dead. Good job on that. And I'm a hood ornament now." It laughed.

Darren pulled Hannah back. He tried to get her to ease her grip on the gun, but she shook him off. "Shoot it, Alice! Don't let it come back!" she demanded.

The old man's wide eyes were now beaming; he was enjoying himself. Darren wanted to bring the ax back down on him again, but the thought made his arm ache more.

"Are you?" Darren asked. "Coming back? The Recla-mation your guards got..."

"You killed my guards. Of course, there was a Reclamation. I'm not dead, as you can see," said the head.

"If I bring that ax back down on you, would that work?" Darren said.

Alex came back but without the rope. She was holding her arms, trying to warm herself. "It's my door."

"What do you mean? What door?" Darren asked.

"From my dream. Sometimes it's a door. Other times it's a well or hole in the floor. But it always feels the same."

"A cave going down," Alice said. "You feel you must keep going."

Alex nodded.

"A grave. I can't stop digging," Hannah added.

"A baby crying in woods. I can't find it no matter how close I get," Yuri said.

"A man beckons me. He's standing in doorways, always around a corner," Darren said. "Alice and I thought it was just us, but we're all having nightmares."

"In the city, He calls," the talking head recited.

"*Сука Блять!*" Alex yelped at the sight of the old man's head talking.

Yuri rushed over to his sister. "It's okay! It's okay! He's just a head now. No walking devil tentacle thing." He turned to the others. "Right?"

Darren ignored him. "What about the door?"

Alex was still staring at the old man's head. "It's here. Down the hall. As soon as I saw it, I knew."

The door that had stirred at Darren every night since he'd gotten here. This was the path to it. Come to the castle, hear the door beckon, step through. Step through? To where exactly, though? *In the city, He calls.*

Alice turned to Vlad. "The city you're from. I assumed it was Lupeni, the city we passed on the way to the castle.

But it's not, is it? It's whatever's on the other side of the door."

Vlad took a deep breath. "It's been there for centuries. It's from a discovered cave system stretching miles everywhere. The first ones built the castle on top of it. That's where I'm from. It's where I go when I'm not here. There are other passages throughout the area. I can take you. I'm familiar with most of them, although, like this floor, there are areas I'm forbidden from entering. That's where everyone's been taken. I don't know how to get to their location from here."

Hannah turned to the old man's head. "I bet this monster knows it well enough."

The head made a pout. "Plan on seeing the sites? Going to play Rescue the Princess?"

Hannah snatched the head by its hair. "Yes. And you're our tour guide."

The door was like any other metal door they saw, even down to the barred window. It was what was in the room that shook Darren. The man inside. The man from his dreams, from the tomb in the cemetery, featureless in every sense, now stood in the room for all to see. Behind him a stairway led down to the City. It was well lit, and he could see how far it went down.

"That's the sheep," Alice said breathlessly.

"I don't see anything," Yuri said. "Only hear crying baby."

Alice turned to Darren. "You don't see a sheep, do you? Only that man from before?"

Darren nodded as he watched the man turn toward the steps and fade away, urging him to follow.

SPENCE WAS TOO weak to eat or drink. His fever kept him warm even though he lay naked, chained to the stone floor. His fingers were numb from the cuffs. When he slept, fever-induced dreams replayed, with him trying to hide from the eyes of a man with wings. Spence would hide behind rocks, under furniture, in alleyways, under cars, but the winged figure kept discovering his position.

He thought about controlling his situation and confronting his pursuer, demand to know why he was being chased and who was chasing him, but he knew what would happen. He already knew the answers. It was Rhymet. The flying demon he was told had genetic compatibility, at which point his right eye was cut out.

Spence never got a good look at Rhymet in his dreams. He only ever felt his presence and his taunts. Sometimes he'd catch a glimpse while he was hiding in a cupboard. Rhymet was a monster with hard, red, leathery plating. It walked like a man. In fact it might have been a man at one point or a fallen angel perhaps. But its voice echoed in

Spence's mind every time it came near. "You cannot evade me. You will see me. I am your escape."

When Spence was awake, his thoughts first turned to his eye. It lay in a copper bowl in front of him, just out of reach. His eye socket and the right half of his face ached. His eyelid was swollen shut. Not that he could see from that side any longer.

What he could see as he lay curled on the floor were other naked people also chained to the floor. His remaining vision was too blurry to make out who they were with certainty, but he heard them well enough. Some cried, some pleaded, others coughed and struggled against the chains. He suspected they had been brought here just like him.

Spence couldn't make out the details of where they were either. The floor had chiseled grooves and hieroglyphs that followed up the unending wall behind him, which circled the entire room lit by torches. A set of arched doors lay open but revealed nothing. The room was large; he could fit a makeshift rodeo in the space or maybe a skating rink, two things he'd never see again.

He could tell he and the others were arranged in a circle, chained to the floor. In the center, cultists wearing black robes worked to arrange a massive stack of bones, candles, knives, bowls, and what looked like sand. A small whisper column of smoke floated up from the center. He saw some optical trick of light bending toward the ceiling, like he was looking through wobbly glass.

They were all here for the same reason. The old man had butchered him and acted like it was a routine teeth cleaning. But it was clear what was happening was the odd-sounding name he had referred to. This was where he was going to be "farmed out."

Farmed out for what? Honestly it didn't matter. Not

anymore. It was obvious to Spence that he had the virus. He was in a full onset fever. Feeling his breathing worsen, he resisted the urge to cough. If he started coughing, he wouldn't stop.

Spence looked over to the man to the right of him. It was Mads Porter, who was trying to stifle his sobs. He kept rubbing his hands over the bandages where his legs used to be. His legs instead rest upon a large copper tray, out of reach. To his left, a woman lay intubated to a machine to help her breathe; a mass of unidentifiable red and blue organs was piled in a bowl in front of her.

Spence looked back to his own eye. It had bits of dirt sticking to it. He inhaled sharply, which hurt his chest. He coughed as he saw the horror of a piece of his own body laid out in front of him. It was his no longer; they just took it. They took that man's legs, that woman's organs, his eye. The swollen socket throbbed so hard that his whole head felt like it would crack from the pressure.

"I don't see how you could object, Father Asdomus. This is what you requested." Through the ringing in his ears, a muffled conversation emanated from the doorway and grew louder and more discernable as two men entered the wide chamber.

"More candidates, yes. All at the same time? This will lead to ruin. His gaze is already upon us. Do you want His wrath as well?"

"The wrath is already here. The virus mutated less than a day ago. It's clear to me that He's willing to glass this realm unless we get ahead of it. The only way to do that is to farm out more antibodies. We can't clone them. We can only grow them from these candidates."

"Each time we invoke *Z'njm Sej'pal*, the membrane between earth and hell weakens. It needs time to heal. Each time we reach in, lure an offering, trap a demon for its blood and return it or kill it, we tear at the walls between our realms. You have no idea what kind of destruction a loose demon could cause."

Spence watched two men step around the center of the room. The older man, dressed in filthy robes with tattered edges was almost pleading with his hands as he spoke. The other man Spence recognized from the castle. His gray business suit had smudges of dark red on the sleeves and legs.

"Demons, as I understand it, come through all the time. We have an entire movie franchise about them possessing people and picking fights with Catholics."

"Small! Small demons, Brother Davis! The ones who manage to slip through the cracks and cause trouble like little rodents." He waved his arms around the vast chamber. "This is not for finding mice in tiny cracks. This...this is a place of our most unholy passage." He called to the other robed people in the center of the chamber. "Stop what you're doing! All of you! You can't feel the membrane weakening? You can't see it?"

The other robed people ignored him. Spence saw the air above them quiver and fragment the light.

Brother Davis put his hand on Father Asdomus's shoulder. "I've spoken with the Elders, Father. They didn't appreciate the attempt you made on my life. They also don't seem as...troubled?...with the risks of danger to our realm when we spoke. It seems they weren't made aware of the urgency we face. I assured them I'd make up for the lost time you caused."

"I caused?" Father Asdomus pulled away from Brother Davis's hand and pushed a finger in his face. "That altar is still in place, I'll have you know, Robert. I can end you now. If you don't cease this immediately—"

"You do what you think is best. I have a realm to save and a deadline to meet." Brother Davis turned from Father Asdomus toward the center of the chamber. "Let's get this started, shall we?"

Grunting, Father Asdomus stomped out of the chamber, each foot echoing about.

"Let's start with this one: Mr. Collins." Brother Davis pointed to a man two positions away from his left. Mr. Collins's jaw was heavily bandaged.

Spence watched as robed bodies made a circle just outside the arrangement of bones and sand and fire. One of them placed a bowl in the center and returned to the perimeter.

The people in robes launched into a syncopated chant that filled the chamber. The air cracked, accompanied by the smell of smoke. The center of the room was warped and cracked, and insects swarmed from the openings in the floor. The swarm grew in size and noise, drowning out the chants. They grew so much in number Spence couldn't see past them. Thousands of insects moving together formed shapes recognizable as limbs stretching into the final shapes of legs and arms until only a shiny green iridescent female figure stood towering before them, holding the offered bowl in her hands.

Spence averted his eyes as the woman glanced around the chamber. Robert stood over Mr. Collins. He held out a dagger with a wavy blade in his open palms. "You are of the Thrixus. Accept his offering as compensation for this summoning."

A deep laugh came from the center. "Compensation? I will have your bones for this." The woman exploded into a swarm of insects again. Spence flinched back only to feel his head punish him for the exertion. None of the insects left the boundary of the summoned circle. Their buzzing grew louder, and they climbed all the way to the ceiling and back down again before remerging into the shiny green demon. She screamed so loudly Spence's bones shook.

When she stopped, Robert stepped closer to her, still holding the dagger. "A compensation for summoning you, Thrixus. Take of his body. He will take of your blood."

"When you join us, I will find you. The devouring of your flesh will never cease!" Her skin bristled, and her shiny skin showed insects skittering briefly before she resumed her solid form.

"Take of his body. He will take of your blood. The summoning will end." Robert quickly placed the dagger inside the circle and withdrew his hands before there was an opportunity to grab it.

The demon inhaled sharply. "Ah, I know you now. I can smell your soul." A grin grew across her face, making Spence shudder. "See you soon, Robert." She tipped the bowl to her lips, and its contents slid in her mouth. "I've had worse." She smirked. The dagger clinked against the floor when she lifted it by the handle. She then poked the blade into her arm and let black fluid pour into the bowl. Her endless black eyes stayed fixed on Robert.

That was the robed cultists' cue to begin chanting again. The tall demon set her bowl on the floor as her body transformed back into a swarm. Just as the swarm had entered, they disintegrated back into the ground until they were no more.

One of the cultists took the bowl and knife back to Mr. Collins. "Your offering was accepted. Take of their blood and live. Hold out your arm to accept, Mr. Collins."

Mr. Collins lifted his arm as high as the chains let him. "Keep your arm still." The cultist pushed the tip of the blade into the flesh of his forearm and tipped the bowl to let the inky black fluid pour down the blade. Black venous lines crept up his arm and over his body, giving his skin an iridescent sheen. He muffled a scream of pain as his head jerked back, his body falling away from the blade. He writhed on the floor, flailing his arms and legs against their chains.

Cultists came upon him and pinned him to the ground until he slowed into heavy breathing. Spence stared as they pulled away the bandages. Mr. Collins's face had nothing wrong with it other than the shininess of his skin. He coughed as he unclenched his jaw and let out an achy moan.

Robert clapped his hands, "Welcome, Mr. Collins, to the rest of your life. Okay. One down..." He looked around the room "Nineteen more to go? For now, at least." He snapped and pointed to another robed person in the doorway. "He's ready." The person quickly came over, removed Mr. Collins's chains, and helped him into a set of clean red robes.

As Mr. Collins was taken out, Spence called to him, "What did they do to you?"

"They took my tongue. My fucking tongue!" Mr. Collins called back with perfect clarity as he exited the chamber.

"There you have it, Mr. Dixon. *Z'njm Sej'pal* is an exchange. Part of yourself is given in exchange for theirs. Mr. Collins has a working tongue again. We really should have been doing this in batches. It's so much easier to explain this once."

"But his body. It changed. He looks...like that thing," Spence said.

"He's got her DNA, so to speak. It's all in the dagger. Cursed thing actually mends wounds so well it alters your genes to adapt it to toxic demon blood. That's why Mr. Collins now makes the right kind of white blood cells that produce antibodies. Whatever the Thrixus was immune to, he is now immune to, including the Ozark virus."

The man next to Spence muttered, "Demons are immune to our viruses?"

Robert must have heard that. "Not at all, Mr. Porter. Hell has viruses just like we do. This one is one they killed off centuries ago. And since demons are eternal for the most part, their genetic knowledge is now our knowledge."

It was clear to Spence that his turn would come soon. He would have to accept the dagger if he wanted to get his eye back and be cured of the virus. But his demon was Rhymet, red and leathery. Would Spence become a disfigured creature with leathery red skin?

"Count me out," said Mads. "I can live without legs. Lots of people do. It's not worth getting my legs back if it turns me into some fucking monster!"

"We're infected," said Spence.

"What?"

"They infected us. Can't you feel it? The fever. The trouble breathing?"

A look of panic came across Mads's face. "Oh, God."

"God's not here!" snapped Robert. "Let's keep going. Any volunteers?" The chamber was silent. "Actually, let's do her next. She can't even breathe on her own, much less speak." He pointed to the woman next to Spence.

The ritual was the same as before; only this time a column of water appeared, with a green swarm of tentacles swimming in the center. When the water receded, a hunched-over figure with squid-like tentacles covering its head stood in the center holding a long curved pole arm covered in barnacles. The smell of saltwater filled the room.

"They don't look much like demons," Mads whispered.

Mine does, Spence thought. The one from his dreams was like any grotesque red-skinned monster he'd seen in movies. Maybe that was the only way his mind could understand what a demon was. Maybe, in reality, it was even worse. A transforming swarm of bugs. A sea-walking creature with an octopus for a head. What could possibly be waiting for him?

He watched as the creature accepted the bowl and drained its watery green blood into the bowl before floating away, leaving the bowl and knife behind, surprisingly without the seawater.

Spence could see more clearly how the space above the circle bent and twisted the light. It was the membrane the old robed man had warned of; it was breaking.

Another cultist took the bowl and knife and poured the fluid into the woman's punctured flesh. Her skin didn't change. As the last drop traveled into her body, the cultist pulled back the dagger, leaving no mark.

After a few seconds, the woman's eyes burst open, and she began coughing. She reached for her mouth, but her arms were still chained. The cultist moved to her and removed the tube from her throat. She sat up and coughed a bit.

Spence and the others looked surprised. There wasn't any change to her appearance at all. She seemed perfectly fine, like she'd merely woken up. Another cultist removed her chains and helped her into new red robes. Then Darren saw it. She pulled her hair back through the neck of the robes, and he caught a glimpse of her neck, with two large gills protruding. Within a minute, she was standing on her own and was escorted from the chamber.

"That's the last of the incapacitated. Who's next?" Robert asked.

"I'll go!" Mads said. Spence could see the change in Mads's attitude. The last person to do the ritual hadn't become a sea monster. Merely a couple of gills had been added. Now Mads was ready to get his legs back.

"Wait! I'll do it." came another call.

They all wanted to be healed. Spence was about to call out as well, but Robert already had selected Mads. A cultist took his legs and placed them next to the bowl in the circle. The ritual began again with the chants. This time, the room turned cold and dark. Snow fell from the high above the circle, and Spence heard barks and howls in the distance. Something angry was approaching.

He wondered what demon Mads had been assigned. Spence's mind replayed his dreams of his demon flying toward him in a never-ending chase. It was a chase Spence knew he could keep going if he had to. He was used to running away from whatever he feared.

A large vermillion four-legged creature pounced on Mads's legs and thrashed at them, pulled the meat from the bone with its wide-fanged jaws. Its blood-matted legs tore at the flesh, and its red-quilled back bristled as it consumed Mad's legs. Mads scooted back in horror as he watched his body parts being eviscerated right before him. The legs and feet quickly became mottled bones and blood splatters.

When the beast seemed to reach the end of its dinner and looked for a way to leave, one of the cultists yelled, "Now!" Then another threw chains around the beast's neck. Thrashing against the chains, the beast yelped as the dagger slammed into its rib cage. Steaming blood poured into the bowl. A loud howl reverberated throughout the chamber. The beast ripped itself from the chains and leapt away into nothingness. The snow disappeared, but the glint of distortion Spence kept noticing was rapidly undulating.

The cultist came to Mads with the dagger and bowl. Mads was breathing hard. "No. I...I'm not so sure! What was that thing?"

The cultist only responded, "Your offering was accepted. Take of their blood and live."

Mads looked back at Spence for answers. Spence wanted to tell him he didn't have to do it. He wanted to say, "Don't take the dagger." *They won't let him die; they have antibodies for this. They just told us that!* Spence wanted to say he could live without the use of his legs, but he knew that was hypocritical. Not having both his eyes terrified him, even if he wasn't blind. But the possibility of turning into a monster scared him too. How could that guy whose skin had turned shiny green like oil and the girl with gills ever go back home? Or just go out in public? They'd be rejected. People would be horrified by them.

But this was the only way they could get cured of the virus. The only choice was to live as part demon monster or die as a dismembered human. *Is this worth giving up your soul for?* Spence knew where his soul would end up anyway. He'd known since he'd realized he was gay. In his father's eyes, that kind of person was already a monster. Maybe his father was right.

Mads reluctantly held out his arm and let the dagger pour thick warm blood into his body. He winced at the pain as the cultist did her work. When the dagger was pulled out, he let out a deep sigh. "Now what?" He stared down at his legs. Nothing happened.

Then he twitched. The stubs of his legs began to itch, and he pulled at the tape and bandage. He screamed in pain as new flesh stretched past the wounds, forming new bones, tendons, skin, hair, and toenails. More screams came from his sharp-fanged mouth as his back, shoulders, and legs were covered in dark-red fur. Shiny red quills pushed out of his back. By the time the quills stopped their protrusions, Mads was on his new feet. He broke free of one of the chains and gripped the cultist's throat. "I'll fucking kill you!" and reached for the cultist next with his mouth.

Mads immediately fell to the ground with a tranquilizer dart stuck in his neck. Two cultists behind him gingerly picked him up by the arms and dragged him away, leaving a cultist recovering from a bruised throat.

"Come on. Get up!" Robert said. "You're not getting paid by the hour."

Spence heard the cultist utter something in Romanian under their breath as she stood up.

Spence was up next. Rhymet was coming. The chants began. Robert watched with the satisfaction of a job foreman watching his workers do as they were told. The space within the circle cracked with distortion loud enough to hear.

A small plant pushed through a tiny groove in the floor of the circle. It reached a few inches before whipping around in search of light. A white bud pulled itself open from the stem. It grew several feet with hardened bark and branches that reached out, making thick tangles. Moss and lichens settled into the deep crevices of the tree trunk under its large canopy, which now covered the entire chamber. The thick tree trunk's heartwood had rotted out, leaving a large black hollow.

Spence saw the eyes first. They glinted from the depths of the hollow. Out stepped Rhymet, his demon. It wasn't red and leathery at all. It was pale. Almost transparently so. Where its moss-green fur stopped, its thin light-blue skin bore red and blue veins over the muscles of its torso and arms. Its hooves stepped on the forest floor, it stood up to a staggering height. Its antlers, covered in moss, reached beyond the range of the circle. In one of its four hands, it already cupped the bowl holding Spence's eye. It looked past his surroundings and directly at Spence with shiny black eyes that glowed amber.

"Y-you are Rhymet. Please accept his offering as compensation for this summoning," Robert said, holding the wavy dagger.

Spence couldn't look away. He tried to avert his gaze. The terrifying dreams of being found by this demon finally had come true. Rhymet, however, turned his eyes to Robert.

When Rhymet finally spoke, his voice didn't emanate from his mouth. It was directly in Spence's head. It was the same for Robert, who took a quick step back.

"I am not Rhymet. They will not be answering your summons. Nor are there any other of our kind." It's voice fluttered in Spence's mind like it was reciting poetry.

Robert stammered, "You are summoned. You, uh, are here to accept his offering as compensation."

The bowl, and the eye in it, turned to dirt in his hand, falling through the demon's fingers to the floor. "Lucifer gave you His Dark Gift. Yet you steal from us. Like little mice chewing at our border."

"You're wrong. We have accepted His Dark Gift. We just—"

"Have we not given you everything He promised? I have seen your Elders. They live as immortals. Your 'Shepherds,' which you devised? We were fine with that to a point. But still, you wanted more." The tall antlered, hooved demon stepped out of the circle toward Robert, who stumbled backward, dropping the dagger. "You were supposed to stay here and worship us. Be fruitful, multiply, and do our bidding. Love us. Fear us. But stay here.

"You wanted more. You wanted power. So you stole from our realms. You took things back to this realm and realized we don't breathe the same air. We don't drink the same water. We don't have the same building blocks of life. And then you started getting sick. You started dying. Now all of humanity is awash with sickness from our realms, and you decide the answer is to steal more from us."

"That's not true. The virus was His final plan!" Robert said. "It was to purge the land of all who refused to follow Him. We would inherit the earth in His name."

Dark roots from the tree pushed past the circle and stretched past the cultists. Their spindly fingers grasped at the robes and wrapped around their feet and legs. The chamber rumbled, and pieces of the walls flung away to make room for dark wooden roots pushing through the chiseled rock. Spence was struck in the arm by a piece of debris. Suddenly the ground became dirt. Spence's chains lifted easily when he jerked his arms back to protect his body.

"You would lie to me? Even now in the presence of your final end?" The demon's pale face tilted slightly. "No, I don't think so. You believe what you say is true. Did you not know of the broken pact?"

Giant portions of the walls collapsed. Beyond them, Spence saw amber-lit passageways of steps carved from stone. Giant pillars of bare rock reached up to an unseeable ceiling. From the carved-out doorways, more robed cultists scrambled for safety as bits of stone fell away, crushing anything it landed on.

Several older men and women in tattered robes rush into the chamber. They ran up the creature, fell to their knees, and pushed their faces to the mossy ground at the demon's hooves.

"Please!" one of them pleaded. "Please, ever-watchful Borewit, Lord of the Dark Woods, forgive our children! They are in your service. They are all children of Satan and followers of His wrath. Please release yourself from this realm!" The cracks in the walls started losing rubble, and the tree and the ground expanded around them.

"You have faltered. I am your consequence." Roots latched on to the cowering robed bodies. Their robes were ripped to shreds. Thorns dug into their flesh and flayed them on the damp mossy dirt floor.

"You have torn the boundaries between realms. Your ruin is here."

Robert was standing frozen in fear when a piece of the ceiling fell on him, knocking him to the ground. He scrambled past the chained guests and ran.

In the distance, an explosion of fire erupted out of Spence's line of vision, but the stone walls facing it lit up with its fiery heat. A flock of screaming bat-like things took to the open air above the panicked cultists.

Spence couldn't hear over the screams of everyone either trying to flee the pale demon or escape the carnage they faced from more emerging demons. A hand gripped his shoulder from behind. He flinched from it and spun to avoid whatever monster was on him.

Darren held his hands up to avoid any further scare. Next to him were other people from the castle, but Darren was all he could see. Spence tried to turn away to hide his face, but Darren quickly came up to him and wrapped his arms around him.

"I found you," Darren said. "We're getting out of here."

Spence whispered, "Go where?" but Darren ignored it

and helped Spence get up to leave when Spence fell forward back onto the ground. Flowers blossomed from the vines that grew around his feet.

Darren shouted something. Other people came to them and pulled at the vines pinning him.

Spence finally had kicked his feet free when he heard the pale demon's terrifying voice.

"Would you leave me? Abandon your own offering, small one?" Its song made his whole body shiver. He turned around to see Borewit kneeling before him.

Tears poured down his cheek. "I didn't have a choice," Spence said. "I didn't want this."

Borewit's face was inches from his. His breath smelled like wet leaves rotting. "But you did. You would pluck your own eye to save yourself from sin. No?" The demon looked up at Darren and the others. "Lucifer will never stop trying to destroy this realm. It is unnecessary, I think; you're already doing it for him. Your horrors are small but effective, with new sins to hurt yourselves with."

Borewit leaned in until his face was all Spence could see. He wanted to back up but couldn't move. Both he and Darren were frozen in fear. The pale demon lifted one of his narrow bony hands to his face and removed his own right eye from its socket. Red blood poured onto Spence's body, and licking vines grew up to whisk away their nutrition. The demon's hand was almost burning against Spence's face as it pushed its own eye into Spence's eye socket. The pressure made him cry out as the monster pushed it in place. Another scream erupted as his body jolted about from this foreign other-realm object that had joined with him. Clutching his head, he sobbed and shook. Darren never let go of him.

Finally Spence blinked.

He squinted as new images of his surroundings came to him. It was more than clarity. He looked back up at Borewit; its face, already restored, looked curiously back at him. It vibrated with terrible energy. It wasn't something Spence understood, this way of seeing. If it was a sound, it would have been the radioactive scream of the sun.

Borewit stood back up, its antlers quietly stretching outward with room to move. Behind, the tree pushed out farther as the ceiling knocked down tiny leaves and branches. "The Gift of the Dark Lord is over." The demon's voice rang out all around them. "They will atone for their trespasses." Borewit looked to the other people in chains, unable to flee from their removed body parts. "I will resolve your offerings, and then you will leave while you can."

It was Hannah, who held out the severed head like a lantern and took in the lead when they descended the butcher floor. At the end of each turn, she gave it a shake and told it to give directions. It was unsettling to watch. Words gurgled from the old man's lips as fluids dripped from his cleaved neck. Darren couldn't make out what it was telling Hannah, but she understood well enough to know which way to head.

The path downward wasn't just physical, Darren felt a sinking in his heart. The farther down he went, the more despair clung to him. He was wading into an unknowable fate. Nothing real in his world remained. He didn't know who was still alive, who had turned into Rams. He didn't know what to expect when, or if, he found them.

By the time Hannah led them to the chamber, they were already dashing from falling rocks and swooping winged demons trying to pick at them. The sight of Spence shook him. Spence was crawling backward, away from an immeasurably terrifying yet beautiful creature.

Your ruin is here.

The words punched his heart. His reptile cortex screamed in his mind for him to flee. But Darren didn't. He ran into the crumbling chamber as fast as he could. He held on to Spence and didn't let go. Even as the antlered demon had descended on them, pulled its own eye out, and replaced Spence's. Even as Spence's whole body vibrated violently. Even as they ran for safety.

They had to hide in one of the myriad of dwellings set in rock as monsters and cultists had swarmed the labyrinthine caves. Their original path, which had led them to find Spence, was cut off. A giant horned beast rammed against the cave wall so hard the ceiling collapsed on top of it.

The City was under attack from the unleashed forces of hell. Enormous bats flew down, grabbing people as they ran. Gray faceless ghouls jumped from wall to wall, some with pieces of recent flesh hanging from their mouths. A pack of beasts feasted on a body. Their spiny backs furled when they snapped at one another over who got the next piece.

Against the background of a deeply nested network of small buildings carved in place with walkways, ladders, and stairs that clung to cavernous walls, pedestals and statues of revered demons and long-dead knights stood in front of entrances. The ground beneath them rumbled as a distant cave collapsed. Explosions echoed throughout the caves. Statues toppled and shattered against dark stone on their way down.

Darren looked out into the chaos from a small window while a twelve-foot demon, with horns, hooves, and a tail lumbered down a street. The City must have housed thousands of cultists living here. The floors of the caves were littered with them.

"It's not leaving," whispered Alice as she also kept watch.

The dwelling had crude wooden furniture for sitting, a table where they'd set all their weapons, a fire pit and cauldron, a door to another room with a small bed inside, and a ladder that led into another room Darren hadn't yet examined.

Spence hadn't said anything since they'd found him chained and naked. That thing, that creature with antlers, did something to his face, from what little Darren could see. Spence kept the hood of his robe up to hide his face from view.

"As soon as it's clear, we need to get to that stairway," Hannah whispered. "My handbag here says this place is the farthest from the exit."

Alice turned and whispered, "Why the hell are we going away from the exits?"

"We're not. We're avoiding where the action is."

"I don't think that's avoidable for much longer. At some point, we've got to go where everyone else is heading."

Vlad handed some clothes to Darren. "Found these. They're old, but they might fit." They were a pair of jeans, a pair of sneakers that had worn souls and curled up, and a white T-shirt with a Guess Jeans logo on it. "These demons are probably more interested in Shepherds and Rams. Best not to look like one."

"And would that include you?" Darren hissed.

Vlad looked away. "My parents are here. If the demons make it to the upper caves, I don't know if they'll get out."

"Do you know how to get out from here?" Darren asked.

Vlad shook his head. "This is the deepest I've ever been. My family and I have only ever stayed in the upper caves.

Only the fully vested ever come this far down. We're probably in one of the Elders' living spaces."

Despite the furnishings, Darren couldn't imagine this as a living space. If the wooden door and windows had bars, it would make a better dungeon cell.

He was about to take the clothes to Spence, who was sitting alone on a cot in the next room, but Vlad held him by the elbow and leaned in. "Don't trust that head. The sooner she stops carrying it, the safer we'll be."

Hannah hadn't let go of her grip on the talking head's hair since she'd first picked it up. She seemed rather casual about it actually; it could have easily been a phone in her hand. "He doesn't seem to mind."

"He's an Elder. That means he keeps his soul. His hybrid soul. It doesn't go anywhere he doesn't want it to go. Right now his soul is possessed in that head. What happens when he wants to possess someone else? We were taught to fear and avoid the Elders. They're not human anymore. As soon as I recognize where we are, we have to get rid of him."

Darren looked back at Hannah, who was whispering with Alice and the others. The head's eyes were watching him and Vlad with a grin. Darren shuddered and left the room.

He sat next to Spence with the clothes in his lap. "I don't know if these fit, but it's gotta to be better than a satanic robe. It's putting a target on your back with these demons chasing down their worshipers."

Spence didn't say anything.

Darren put his hands on Spence's knees. "I'm so sorry this happened. But I'm so glad I found you. I didn't think I'd see you again."

Spence let out a deep sigh. "You shouldn't be near me. I have the virus."

"You also have the antibodies, right? That's what was explained about this whole thing. You have the cure." Spence didn't respond, so Darren carried forward. "We're going to get out of this place then find someone who can administer us a dose." He gave Spence a reassuring grip on his knees. "I'm not even worried about that right now. I'm just happy you're safe."

"Safe?" Spence's whisper rose. "I'm not safe! I'm...the opposite of that. I'm something dangerous. I'm one of them now." He pulled back his hood, letting Darren get a look at his right eye for the first time. It was the eye from that giant demon; it was onyx black with a piercing amber-gold iris. His eyelids were missing his blond lashes. Around the eye, Spence's skin was paler than the rest of his face, and secondary eyelids retracted when he blinked.

Darren reached up and cradled Spence's face. Spence's body trembled with heat under his fingers. "This doesn't change who you are to me."

"But I can see things. Energy maybe. It's under the surface of reality. It's forbidden in my mind, but I have to see it anyway. I have thoughts people shouldn't think. I watched the demon Borewit pull a bunch of cultists to the ground and shred their bodies. I was horrified. Now I can feel part of them in me. I can feel how trivial and tiny the cultists' tainted souls were as Borewit absorbed them. I can see my own soul, Darren. I'm not even me anymore, just some abomination made up of it and me. I'm not safe to be around."

"So that guy, Vlad, the one who might be a thing with Alice, he's from here, the City. Raised by devil worshipers. Born to be bad and all that. But he's been a good guy in all this. Imagine growing up raised in an evil doctrine, taught to believe that Satan himself wants to have dominion over humanity. Or he was supposed to become a Shepherd to have control over humanity."

"Sounds like church."

"Yeah, well, cults gonna cult." Darren wasn't sure if referring to Spence's entire childhood as a cult was the most helpful choice of words. Maybe now wasn't the best time to assert his atheistic views on the Church. Was he even an atheist anymore? "I heard him, you know."

"Who?"

"The giant sexy tree person. 'You would pluck your own eye to save yourself from sin.' It was his voice, but I heard it here." Darren tapped his forehead. "You're not a sin, Spence. You're not an abomination. You never were. And you're certainly not evil." He put his hand on Spence's; it was hot, and he let Spence's large fingers grip his. "In fact I think you're quite extraordinary."

Spence's face began to melt; it was an expression Darren could see with or without a demon eye. Spence leaned toward him, which made Darren breathe in, thinking he was about to be kissed. But Spence merely leaned into his shoulder and put his arm around him. This was a hug, and Darren did the same.

Spence's body didn't feel wide and strong like before; rather, he felt heavy and weary. His arms didn't squeeze and pull Darren into him like before; this Spence was just trying to hold on. Hold on to anything.

Spence let out a light sniffle. "Thank you." He swallowed. "I think you're extraordinary too."

Darren lightly kissed Spence's neck. They held each other in the dark room, in the quietness as long as they could. Darren knew it wouldn't last long. He knew the reality of their predicament. But for this moment, he let all his fears of losing Spence wash away. As long as he could, he wouldn't let go.

From the hallway, he heard Alex call Vlad to come to the room. Hannah was talking with Alice about the paths out of the caves. Claire was resting at the wooden table, still in a lot of pain from her wound. Outside, the ambience of raging fires and screams bounced off the cavern walls.

Vlad hopped back in from the ladder with Alex and Yuri. "It's gone. We spotted several people heading for a different way out, which we think is a better path to follow. It's toward the entrance that demon came from."

"I'm going to see what's up. Change into these if you can." Darren handed Spence the clothes from his lap.

Darren stood to leave, but Spence pulled him into him. Spence's lips were strong again, and they knew exactly where to land. Darren kissed him back. It was short but enough to be everything.

"If we stay to the right on the path, there will be stairs that lead through the farm, where all the Rams are housed. It'll have the most accessible exit," Hannah said calmly.

"Is that what the talking head told you?" Darren asked as he stepped through the doorway.

She turned to him with a bored expression.

Alice asked, "How is Spence?"

"He's fine. He's trying out a new look, but he's...okay. He brought up a point we haven't considered. He was infected with the virus. That means everyone in that chamber we pulled him from probably was too."

"And we walked right into it," Alice said. "Anyone turned into Rams would have to be where their blood could be drawn easily for getting antibodies to distribute. That would have to be near some lab equipment so they could process it right away. When they drew blood samples from us, time was critical to the techs. If we can get there, we can get our vaccine, get out, and never look back."

"They'd need an easy path out for transporting the vaccine to the surface," Darren said. "It might work, but we have to be fast. This place is coming down."

They left the enclave and moved quickly, staying close to the walls and shadows, trying to avoid wide-open areas. Darren heard distant screams of people and beasts against the backdrop of the crumbling world around them. He still had his ax with him, but his right arm ached from the slice, and he kept bleeding when he tried to use it.

Occasionally Spence gripped his shoulder when the corners and edges were tight. He looked comical in his dusty oversize clothes. Darren felt as though Spence was in a good mood. Here they were trying to escape for their lives, yet he kept sneaking Darren's hand into his. Not exactly romantic, Darren thought, but he wasn't letting go if he didn't have to.

Hannah led them on without consulting the head she was gripping. Somehow she knew the passageways from earlier instructions. Darren had no idea how much the head had told her. The choices she made; which turns to make, which doors to step through—they were incredibly specific.

After a seemingly endless climbing through the dark labyrinth, Hannah stopped at the gated entrance. "We have to wait."

Darren peered through the gate's iron bars. The area before them flickered with light from nearby fires. It appeared empty, but unlike the other areas they'd passed through, this place was more structured. It wasn't a haphazard collection of carved-out nooks and stalactite structures. The ground was cobblestone and smooth. There was a large courtyard with a circular fire pit where a bronze statue of a knight glowed brightly. Large steps had been set upward around the courtyard, with its Roman-style buildings. It reminded Darren of an old public square where vendors and tourists might gather, but the smoke was thick here. As his lungs struggled for air, he pulled his shirt up over his mouth.

"De Molay Square," Vlad said. He pushed the gate open and stepped through. "I know where we are now. I can take us the rest of the way to where the Rams are kept. There's a large passageway on the other side. This way." They stepped into the square. Vlad turned to the head Hannah held. "You can toss that now. We don't need it."

Hannah didn't move.

"I think she likes me," it said. Hannah didn't respond; her face was unreadable.

Darren's stomach dropped. The head was controlling Hannah. Just how long had it been using her? Vlad had warned them about keeping the head around.

"Since you took away my body, I was in need of a new one," it said.

"Hannah, let go of it!" Darren moved to release her grip on the grinning head, but a scream came from behind him, and he stopped to look over his shoulder.

Yuri's leg was caught in the mouth of a red-quilled beast as tall as all of them. Everyone jumped back from its reach as it growled and shook Yuri in its mouth.

Alice was the first to move, with her gun drawn. Alex shouted, "No!" but she fired and struck the beast in the face. It jerked back as the bullet knocked a chunk away from its head. Yuri's screaming body flew against the steps. Alice fired the rest of her rounds, the beast flinching with every contact.

Alex ran to Yuri. Darren instinctually followed Alice's

lead and forged ahead with his ax. His arm stung again as he raised the weapon. He felt the wind being knocked out of him when the beast easily batted him away, and he dropped the ax with a loud clang.

Darren staggered to his feet for round two but was flanked by several security guards wielding automatic weapons. He felt someone pull him backward, away from their path. Before he could realize it was Spence, Spence had lifted him with the full strength of his arms and put as much distance as he could between them and the guards before they unloaded their bullets into the beast.

The beast howled an ear-splitting roar as it fell to the onslaught of bullets piercing its thick hide. It landed with a thud that shook the ground. Blood traced around the edges of the courtyard's stones.

The firing stopped, and the last of the bullet shells fell to the ground at the security guards' feet. A distant "Clear!" came from the far side of the square. More people in military garb moved throughout the square, checking entryways and corners. These were the same kind of guards they'd encountered on the butcher floor. "Spence, we're not safe. These aren't just guards, they're—"

"I can see them," Spence said. "I can see they're demons." His onyx eye flickered from one guard to the next.

Darren shifted his stance, ready to move. "We've got to run! They work for that mad doctor! They tried to kill us."

"They work for me at the moment, Mr. Montoya." A man stepped from behind the line of the guards, who were preoccupied with reloading their weapons. It was the man they'd seen flee the room where they'd found Spence.

Spence immediately put himself in front of Darren. Darren tried to move to see, but Spence's hand on his arm became an immovable object. Spence spoke in a tone

Darren had never heard before. "Take another step toward us, and I'll put you down." The weight of his voice was so intense, Darren felt intimidated.

"Mr. Dixon, I'm not here to hurt you." The man splayed his arm open. "This is a rescue operation."

IN 1314, after seven years of imprisonment and torture, Jacques De Molay and two other Knights Templar were sentenced to burn to death on a pyre in Île de la Cité. The night before, Lucifer came to Jacques to offer him a gift in exchange for his soul.

The fallen angel offered to save His people. But Jacques refused, knowing he would be with his lord in heaven. Nonetheless the Devil persisted. "How can you go to heaven when the sovereign king himself and the holy church has condemned him? Are they not ordained by God?" The Devil spoke of the fates of Jacques's brother knights. "They would be hunted down and suffer the same fate. This is what God would allow his own righteous servants."

So Jacques De Molay listened to Lucifer's offer. If the Knights Templar agreed to serve Satan, he would lead the knights to a land where they'd be saved from certain death and, in Him, have true everlasting life on earth. Lucifer would exact revenge upon the King Philip IV and Pope Clement V for their misdeeds.

To make a pact with Satan, however, Jacques De Molay had to curse his family forever. They would know no wealth, no happiness, no prestige; all that there was to enjoy in life would be denied them.

Jacques had no family that he knew of. His wealth already had been seized by the king to pay for his useless wars. So Jacques agreed.

After his immolation, kid goats visited every knight who had escaped arrest. The goats led a hundred knights across Europe to an undiscovered cave deep in the forests of Romania. The goats spoke to their wranglers, telling them the caves were there so they could be close to Satan. The goats told them to sacrifice them on an altar and consume their demon souls to become immortal—there they would be immortal.

Thirteen of the knights accepted the offer. Understanding the sacrilege, the rest refused and rebuked the thirteen. But the thirteen knights gained immortality and all the attributes and benefits that come from consuming the soul of a demon. They slaughtered the remaining knights in an offering of thanks to their Dark Lord.

The knights built their temples in the deep caves of Romania. They worshiped the Devil with prayer and sacrifices, hoping for more gifts. But no other gifts came. For generations they tried to please Satan for more gifts. Still none came. So they listened to their consumed souls. They made their souls tell them secrets, hidden things in the world, unknowable truths.

The knights realized this was the true gift of Satan. They now possessed true knowledge and true power by learning all the secrets of the realms.

* * *

Alice hadn't yet released her grip on the handgun, even after the beast had fallen. The magazine was empty, but she couldn't let go while she stood in front of a row of ten armed guards pointing guns in her direction.

"A rescue? From these meddling kids, I hope," said the head dangling in Hannah's hand.

"Elder LeBlanc!" Robert rushed toward Hannah. "We've got to get you to the temple while there's time." He turned to Alice, "Take her and the others."

"I'm not going anywhere with you," Alice replied. "We're getting out of here."

"What's wrong with Hannah?" Claire stood behind Hannah, wanting to reach out to her, but Vlad pulled her back.

It was the first time Alice had noticed Hannah's blank stare. The constant threat of demons and falling rocks kept her more focused on her surroundings than on what her friends were going through.

Robert grabbed Hannah's the shoulders away and moved her away from the scene. Not resisting, Hannah calmly stepped with him as they headed toward one of the buildings at the head of the square. The guards flanked Alice and the others, weapons drawn, and herded them to the same building.

Alice walked with Vlad through the square. "What is this temple?"

"It's the final resting place of Jacques De Molay," Vlad said. "It was his curse that led them to have their immortality. The Elders use it to reincarnate themselves when they're too injured. If Hannah is possessed by the Elder, if they complete the ritual, he's going to become her."

A sharp bump to Alice's back pushed her forward.

"Keep walking." Alice turned to see the bartender from the castle leering at her.

"How's your nose?" she asked.

The bartender smirked as pulled down is face shield. His nose was fine. "I heal quickly. Do you?"

"You want to find out?" Alice said over her shoulder.

The temple's arches reached the top of the cave's ceiling. Chiseled serpents roped about pillars that held up a backlit stained-glass depiction of knights engulfed in flames. The guards pushed them along the aisle past the pews. The floor inside was polished stone with chiseled scales and a large round table at the back displaying a crystal urn.

"What's the status? Are we losing this one?" asked the head.

"The lower section is gone. We're holding the line, but I can't be sure. The other warrens are fine. People are heading to the one in Arizona now," Robert said.

"We'll need to move the urn. Can't have our glorious leader getting knocked over now," said the head.

"First things first," replied Robert. He went to Alice and pulled a dagger from his inside coat pocket.

The head quietly laughed. "The bastard returns. Oh, Brother Robert, you are a clever man. Maybe I should take *your* soul instead."

"What are you talking about?" said Alice. "I'm not a bastard of anything." Alice pulled back from Robert's grip, but she recognized the point of a guard's gun when it jabbed her in the back.

Robert pulled her to the table and removed the urn's lid. "Your great-great great-grandfather was. You come from a long line of men cursed with being the direct descendent of Jacques De Molay. We recovered his ashes after he was burned for crimes never committed."

"When you share a soul with a demon," said the head, "you learn things. They start as whispers. Whispers become insight. Insight becomes a greater truth. That truth will bring back the Grand Master. 'May his father's revenge never end.'"

Robert moved to position Alice's hand over the urn. She tried to resist, but the guard behind her compelled her. "You see, after a few centuries of chipping away at the veil, we learned how to do things on our own. We no longer need more deals with the Devil. Take this knife, for example." Robert pushed the knife into Alice's palm. She screamed at the pain of its bitter steel, which set the nerves of her flesh on fire. Blood poured over the knife and fell into the ashes inside the urn. A small puff of ash escaped into the air. Alice's arm shook from the pain, and she tried to pull back. Again a guard stepped in and held her in place.

Her friends watched from gunpoint as blood freely poured from her hand over the dagger's wavy blade into the urn. Her blood turned a rose color over the ash. Alice's cries and the sadistic laughter of the head echoed throughout the giant hall.

Robert pulled out the knife and let go of her arm. Alice instinctually pulled her hand close to her body. She looked down to see the horror of her injury, but her palm was fine; in fact, her hand didn't even hurt. Her eyes widened as she flexed her grip and felt her formerly injured hand with her other hand for where there must surely be a gushing wound.

"The mending blade of Horus." Robert held out the blade. "It heals whatever it passes through." He took the dagger and placed it, blade down, into the urn then uttered a quiet chant. "*Hwurla tadaeitsia dsijla 'afihs. Hwurla tadaeitsia dsijla 'afihs.*"

The head chanted the same words. The guards joined in too.

"*Hwurla tadaeitsia dsijla 'afihs. Hwurla tadaeitsia dsijla 'afihs.*"

Alice's head flinched; she felt like a mosquito had tried to land on her. Then she saw it too close to her face for her to focus, and she batted it away. A louder buzz went past her. This creature was bigger, like a fly. It landed on the table briefly, then took off again. The chanting continued while the occasional buzz transformed into a constant noise as more insects gathered in the air.

Alice recalled her dream of the sheep in the cave. It had blurted a scream so loud and terrifying and filled with flies that it had woken her up. This wasn't like that; this was more annoying. The kind of constant threat she'd feel from too many insects ruining her picnic.

"*Hwurla tadaeitsia dsijla 'afihs. Hwurla tadaeitsia dsijla 'afihs.*"

Across the table, she saw Spence, who was taller than everyone else in the room, move past the others to get farther away from the table. The guards were more focused on making their spell work than keeping track of Alice's friends. When she angled back from the table, her guard ignored and moved closer to the table, reciting the incantation.

Hannah stood to the side, still firmly gripping the head's hair. If Alice could get to Hannah, she could get her to release the head; that might release its grip on her body. The chanting continued as more and more insects raced around in the air above them. The chants and buzzing were total noise. Alice moved unnoticed behind the guards and stood directly behind Hannah.

She grabbed Hanna by the wrist and vigorously shook

her arm. Although her grip didn't loosen, the head yelped. This caught the eye of a nearby guard, who moved toward her. Alice buckled Hannah's knees from behind and pulled her to the ground. She then slammed the head against the ground over and over. The constant buzzing muted the cracking sounds of the skull. The guard ran over to save the head, but it was already loose, and with a final bounce it rolled under a pew.

Hannah screamed and shook out the remaining tufts of white hair from between her fingers. Alice pulled her away from the table as the guard dove to recover the head. Alice and Hannah scrambled to the others, who were huddled behind the thick pillars.

"Their chant isn't working! That's not their guy! Don't let it see you!" Spence yelled over the deafening pitch.

The insects filled the temple; there was no hiding from them. The light from the torches was outmatched by the density of the swarm. Alice covered her face, as did the others, fearing one might fly into her mouth or nose.

The roar of the swarm climaxed into one solid banshee scream. It shattered the glass above the doorway, an orchestra of glittered fragments raining down on the floor.

"Thrixus," Spence whispered.

Alice uncovered her face. A giant naked woman with oily green skin and ripples of tiny shiny insects with shimmering exoskeletons, stood at the table.

"I told you I'd find you." The woman let out a single peal of laughter. "I heard about your ridiculous attempt at a resurrection from my realm and just had to see it for myself." She walked up to the urn and pulled out the dagger. "The dagger thing never would have worked. You can't mend a pile of ash. A family curse, however..."

With all eyes on the naked lady, Alice crept toward the exit. Hannah, permanently attached to her arm, followed.

"No, no," said the Thrixus, looking over its shoulder. "I haven't excused you." A wall of black formed a barrier at the exit. The tall creature held up the dagger and examined it. "You play with scraps you find in our gutters, and you think you have power. You're like an ant that crawls on a person's leg and thinks it's found a new world. What does it know about hands or teeth or the things a person can see? What do you think happens to the ant when it bites the leg? Does it think it invoked the wrath of a great power, or just annoyed a person who immediately forgets about that ant?" It walked around the table while Robert and the guards—and the one now holding the head, with its bald spot—froze in place.

"You were given one gift! One time! In exchange, Jacques De Molay, God's most righteous soul, is stretched across the mantel in Lucifer's lair. He's quite fond of that one. Since you're so determined to be with him again, let me help!" The Thrixus burst into a thick raging storm of insects as it whipped around the table. Robert and the others flailed their arms and screamed at the beast. The table and walls around them were sprayed with red blood, and they all fell to the floor. The swarm followed them, violently covering their bodies until it finally reformed back into the woman sitting on the table, legs crossed, her feet easily resting on the ground. Only bones, dust, and shredded clothes gathered at her feet.

The Thrixus lifted its chin and smelled the air. "You must be the lucky girl." Alice's stomach dropped as its eyes met with hers; it knew who she was. The eyes of a supremely powerful being had noticed her, and it was addressing her. "The daughter of a man of a man of man and so on, carrying the curse of your ancestors all because the Lord of Hell has a never-ending score to settle." Its hand twirled around in the air. "I never cared for this realm. Heaven has tossed off long ago. Only hell seems interested in this realm for purpose of destroying it."

The beast walked toward Alice then bent down and examined her more closely. Alice froze still, averting her eyes. "Just between you and me, I'm not from hell. I am, however, from a place adjacent enough to answer to them, but not so much that I think the innocent should suffer. Punishment is for the guilty; I see no guilt here. But we will raze this place to the ground."

The Thrixus descended the steps until it was out of sight and gone.

Out in the square, a gate flew away from its hinges, revealing a gaunt, pale figure sitting atop a large skittering arachnid-esque beast, accompanied by several hunched humanoid gray figures. More giant bats flew in and filled the air with their screams. They spread out across the square, growing in numbers and reaching toward the temple's entrance.

"Vlad, how do we get out of here?" Asked Alice.

He gestured around him. "Most of these buildings are interconnected. We can still get to where the Rams are being held."

"Is there a quicker way out?" Alice asked. "We should take whatever path gets us out of here the fastest."

"Hold up," Alex said, helping her brother stand on one leg. "We're infected still, yeah? If we leave without the vaccine, we're as good as dead. And what about the people at the Farm? We can't leave them."

Alice shook her head. "We'll be lucky to get out of here alive as it is. You think that mob out there is only interested in the 'guilty'? That thing that attacked Yuri wasn't."

"No. It's not right." Alex stood with her chest out, not budging from this. "If we can get there, we have to try." She turned to Vlad. "Can we reach it?"

He nodded.

"It's too late for them! Don't you get it? We got Spence and Yuri back. These cultists have been shut down. If we stay here any longer, we'll die," Alice pleaded. Why didn't they understand this? The window for escape was closing; instead, she saw her friends look at her in judgment.

"Alice," Spence said, "if it was one of us in that farm, you wouldn't hesitate. People like me are being held there—abducted, tortured, mutilated. If they're there, we have to help them."

"Harry's there," Hannah added.

Alice wanted to kick the nearby pew but thought better of it, remembering it was made of stone, just like everything else in this place. "Fuck. Okay."

They were right, of course. After all, she had come this far for them. She had fought her way down here not even knowing the dangers ahead. The choice had seemed much simpler when she didn't know just how terrible the consequences were.

She looked back at the piles of bones and shredded clothes left behind. She walked over, reached into the rubble, and found what she'd hoped to find. "Slightly scratched, but..." It was one of the Vector submachine guns the guards had held. She popped out the rifle's magazine, found it fully loaded, then popped it back in place. "These should be useful. Let's stock up first."

The others joined her, retrieving more rifles and ammunition. Darren found a discarded keycard belonging to

Robert Davis. Spence and Claire recovered a couple of wallets with cards and money.

Locked and loaded, Vlad led them through side doors between buildings as well as rooms filled with cluttered desks, tall bookshelves filled with thick brown grimoires, storage racks of artifacts, and walls decorated with paintings and unholy icons. They stepped behind doorways to privies, hallways between offices, narrow gaps between the large carved structures, all the while evading hell's army, which occupied the square outside.

The metal gate to the passageway remained shut, but their detour already had led them inside without detection. From there, it was a long repetitive sequence of stairs and corners. The stairway was stone, like before, with a light bulb attached to a single metal pipe lighting their way upward. Every few turns, a rounded metal door presented itself. With each turn they made, Alice's unease lifted a bit more. They were getting closer to the top.

No one spoke while they kept going upward. Alice's legs ached from the travel. Both Claire and Yuri had sustained serious injuries, but neither complained nor slowed down.

Vlad finally stopped at one of the doors, nearly out of breath even though he tried to act like he was fine. He leaned against the wall next to it. "This is the access floor below the residential floors. The City as I knew it was largely here." He took a deep breath. "The Farm is near the labs and the infirmary."

Alice thought back to their first night in isolation when the man next to her had gotten sick and was taken away. Scott Wilson. He must have been brought to the infirmary. The isolation building had an elevator at the end of the hallway. If that's how he had been. Moved here, they must be near the exit.

The thought of giving up on the Farm and bolting for the elevator was tempting, but Alice thought better of it. First, the Farm. Help those trapped inside, get the vaccines, then make their escape.

They followed Vlad into the underside of the residential floors. He pulled out his phone and turned on his flashlight app with the others. They were in a modern construction of concrete columns and steel supports with insulated pipes and conduits installed along the ceiling carrying electricity, water, and air to the floors above. Spence closed the door behind them. The ground still rumbled, the screams and roars going unheard.

Vlad gripped a metal pipe bolted into a ladder that was bolted to a concrete column and climbed into the darkness. Alice followed him. They stepped over a gap onto the top of a metal roof. Alice saw light shining up from vents. She helped Vlad work an access hatch; he peered inside briefly before whispering, "It's empty. Come on."

The hallway was dimly lit with only floor lights to guide them. Alice mimicked Vlad's crouched, slow walk toward whatever path he was taking until he stopped at another door. He tried to turn the handle, but it wouldn't move. Without prompt, Darren pushed the keycard against the panel next to the door, and it made a happy chirp and a single green LED light blinked.

On the other side of the door was a warehouse the size of a football field. Evenly spaced throughout were empty cages with heavy metal bars and tall enough to stand in.

"Where's the Farm?" Alice whispered.

"If the Rams were taken anywhere, it's here," Vlad said.

Alice walked lightly but quickly between the cages. Her

eyes scanned for anyone who might be stuck inside, but she saw no one. The place was empty. No vaccines, no missing people. Just a vacant lot of empty cages.

Spence moved purposefully past her. Darren followed. Alice heard him speak in the distance. "Hey. Can you hear me?"

She found the two of them talking to a man curled on the floor of a cage with only a blanket. His arms and chest were covered in matted red fur, and his back had protruding red quills like the beast they had encountered earlier.

Spence hit the cage's bars. "Hey! Mads! Wake up. Are you okay? Do you know how we can get you out?"

Mads looked up slowly, blinked, then lunged at the bars. "You! You were there! Tell them I'm sorry. Tell them I didn't know what I was doing. I didn't mean to try to bite them. I was scared."

Spence put his hand on one of Mads's hands. "You didn't do anything wrong. We're going to find a way to get you out. Do you know where everyone went?"

"Hey! You can't be here. You should be with the others on evac," a man yelled from the far end of the warehouse. His feet clicked against the floor as he moved toward them. Alice gripped the shoulder strap of her rifle. The man wore a lab coat and carried a tranquilizer gun.

As he got closer, his stride slowed slightly. "Wait a minute. Hannah? Is that you?"

Hannah squinted. "Harry? Harry Brown?" Harry's face lightened with a smile. Hannah began to move to him but stopped. "You're okay? You're not..." She pointed to Mads.

Harry's walk was slow now. "A Ram? No! Of course not. I'm a Shepherd. I joined earlier last year. Father wanted me to"—he made air quotes—"be among the flock, as it were. They were about to cut me open. Could you imagine? Good thing this tattoo is impossible to miss."

"Where are the others?" Alice asked. "The others who were taken from the castle. This is the Farm, right? Where is everyone?"

Harry took a step toward them. "The Farm? That's not here. You think we'd keep beasts like this in the City? This is just a holding area. They're on their way to Arizona. Much more sun." He took another step toward Hannah. "I was just on my way back with some sleepy juice for Mads here." He held up a gun with a tranq dart already loaded. "Buuuuut maybe he could use some friends?"

Hannah gripped her gun defensively. "You knew this whole time. You were a part of it?"

Alice ignored her. "The vaccine. You must have some nearby, right? And some lab equipment for your staff."

Harry sighed. "Yes, it's for the staff. Are you staff?" He looked at Vlad. "What are you doing here anyway, Vlad?"

Vlad opened his mouth to speak, and the sound of a high whine, melodic and loud, rang out. He closed his mouth. The whine came again and rose in pitch until the metal ceiling above them tore open.

Harry didn't look up in time to see the maw of teeth and eyes lined along an unending stretch of red-scaled hide fall upon him and crash through the floor. The warehouse split in two, and the cages slid away.

Alice landed in a pocket of three cages with Spence and Darren, with Mads on the other side. She looked for the others. She looked over the cage door and noticed the electronic lock. "Try your key card!" she yelled to Darren. "Hurry."

Darren ran the card over the lock, and it beeped and emitted a green light. He pulled the door open, and Spence pulled Mads out. Another loud whine and crash of torn metal erupted at the front of the warehouse. Cages flew up against the ceiling and bounced around like loose dice while the red serpent punched through and disappeared into the ceiling, causing sparks to rain down from the busted lights.

"Here!" Vlad was a few cages over with Claire. Her leg was bleeding again. They were on top of the cages, making their way toward Alice. "The exits are blocked!" Cages at both ends of the warehouse piled up against the doors.

Alice pulled herself on top of the cages. Spence and Darren as well. Mads practically hopped up. "Where are Alex and Yuri?" she asked. No one could see them among the cages. Another loud whining noise came from outside. The warehouse shook from a nearby crash.

"Over here!" Alex appeared from a hole in the wall. She made it to an attached hallway along with Yuri and Hannah. Yuri slumped against his sister as she waved to them. They traversed over the cages one by one to the hallway. Mads, Darren, and Spence were the first to make it. Alice helped Vlad lead Claire from one cage to the next. The last ten cages to the hole in the wall lay flat, allowing them to walk easily.

Another whine came from above them; a few seconds later, the tearing of the ceiling jumbled the cages again. Alice was on all fours as she made her way across the last few cages; Alex caught her hand and pulled her in. Vlad went back to reach Claire. She had fallen backward and landed between two cages and couldn't move.

Alice went to go help them, but Hannah pulled her back. "You can't go back out there. That thing is coming back!" Another whine came from the floor beneath Vlad and Clair. Alice teared up. "No." Vlad only had a second to respond before the floor buckled. He jumped from the cage under him as it fell away. Claire fell away with cages crashing into her.

Vlad hopped across the cages and leapt to the hallway slightly short, but Spence and Mads caught him midair and pulled him in. They ran down the hallway to the nearest exit.

They raced into a wide-open cavern filled with multi-story housing, electric lampposts, and paved walking areas. It looked very livable aside from the flying red serpents that sang deadly whines and crashed into buildings with predatory grace. The area was empty of people. Whoever lived this far up had had time to escape.

After Vlad got Alice's attention, she followed him to a nearby set of double doors. The room was cluttered with metal benches and shelves filled with lab instruments. Although the lights were flickering, Alice recognized where they were.

"Check that fridge! Quickly!" Vlad commanded as he ran to another fridge and frantically pillaged its contents. "If there are any vaccines left, grab what you can. We can find syringes later." He rummaged some more, cursed to himself, then moved to another fridge.

Alice ran to the fridge but found nothing. The others joined her, but the lab was empty. Mads pulled a lab coat from a hanger and put it on to cover himself up. Another whine filled the room. The lab rumbled; equipment fell from the shelves and crashed to the floor.

Alice slammed the door to the last fridge. "It's been emptied out."

The lab shook again. Vlad looked outside and came back panicked. "The buildings are collapsing. We have to go. Now."

They exited the lab and followed Vlad to a locked door.

Behind them, more buildings collapsed from the onslaught of the whining serpents. Then the lights illuminating the cave powered off briefly before the sound of power generators revved up and the lights came back on. Darren pushed the keycard against the panel, but it didn't work. It beeped and flickered its red LED.

"The infirmary will lead us out, but this is the only way in." Vlad threw himself against the door to no avail.

"Okay, okay. What's another way?" Alice fumbled with her phone while looking for the flashlight app.

"They're over through all that. We'd have to get through the resident housing." Vlad tried to knock the door open. "Fuck!" He rolled away from the pain.

"Stop doing that. It won't open," Alice said.

"He's not wrong, though." Darren held his phone to the top of the door. "If this is magnetically locked, we should be able to open it."

"It's obviously not!" Hannah snapped. "What's another way in there? A window or a vent? Maybe like the warehouse, we can get below where—"

The roof of the cave above where the dorms had once stood collapsed, bringing down more buildings above it. A wave of dust overtook them. Alice coughed against the ruined air and buried her face under her shirt. She couldn't see beyond a few feet.

Darren coughed as he yelled. "The generators are keeping the doors locked—unless we have a crowbar or something. We need to turn off the power to this place."

"How can you be sure?" Alice replied.

"No. He's right," Vlad answered. "The doors are supposed to unlock during an evacuation. Even Satanists have fire drills. I'll go turn them off. As soon as the lights go out, head for the elevators. The stairs next to it will let you out."

"No, wait!" Alice protested, but Vlad took off into the cloud.

Crumbling rocks and the whines of flying monsters echoed around the cave. Yuri rested on the ground to take weight off his leg. His shoulder was already red and swollen from the attack of the demonic guard earlier. Occasionally a new sound came from the dust—the sound of sparks, metal bending, a distant earthquake, even the roar of some monster they hoped was too far away for them to worry about.

Alice had to convince herself Vlad knew what he was doing. He had to know where the generators were located; he could turn them off and find his way back in the darkness. Or maybe he was planning on staying here. Maybe he didn't want to leave his home. Maybe he was doing all this out of guilt.

"Hey, did you hear that?" Hannah elbowed Alice to get her attention. Her phone's flashlight beam pointed toward the cloud of ash.

"Hear what?"

"Shh!" Alex stepped toward them. The others stopped talking and moving and listened.

There, in the ambience of the world crumbling around them, came another whine. Shorter this time and pitching upward like a question. Alice pointed her phone and tucked her rifle into her arm. Again. A simple, short whine like a tender question. A puppy asking for attention. Then she heard tiny footfalls. Another short whine. Closer this time. A shape emerged from the ash, barely visible. It was about knee-high and shiny, with bright pink skin and shaped like a salamander with no eyes. Its whine came again, and it cocked its head, listening to the sound of its own echo.

Its head curled back like a flower full of hundreds of sharp tiny teeth as it leapt onto Hannah's chest. She screamed and flew backward. It whined while trying to latch onto her body, tearing at her clothes and arms as she tried to defend herself.

Alice reached for the creature's tail, but it slapped and flicked around too fast for her to grasp. She reached again but was knocked aside by a giant blur. Mads roared as he moved in front of Alice and smashed the pink lizard thing to a pulp against the ground. His quills poked out of the back of the lab coat as he tore the little monster to pieces.

He turned to Hannah, breathing quickly, his face splattered with blood. "Are you hurt?"

Hannah stood up and felt her chest. The lizard's claws had managed to land against her collarbone, but aside from that she wasn't injured. She tried to slow her breathing. "I'll be fine."

More whines cut through the dust. Mads stepped behind Hannah and Alice and stood guard over Yuri. "You might want to get your guns ready. More are coming." More whines came, but they didn't sound like questions anymore; they sounded pouty.

Darren joined Spence and the others. "How do I fire this?" he asked.

Alice took a look at his gun and switched a toggle, then checked the other guns. "This is set for a single shot per trigger. You've got twenty rounds." She felt like she was back at the ranch, giving lessons to the other militia kids. A job she'd always resented—but now might save her friends' lives. "Try to only fire on ones closest to you. Don't go crazy."

"Define 'crazy,'" Darren said.

When the first lizard demon was visible, Alice called it and fired a round directly into its head. It split apart and flew away from the impact. "These guns have a downward recoil, so keep a grip."

The next one came walking with its mouth splayed wide open toward Darren. He called it and fired but only nicked its upper mouth. It screamed and ran toward him. He got in another round that hit in the center, and it fell.

Two more came, but three bullets put them down. Another ran and fell. Then another. Another. More. They didn't stop coming. Mads yelped from behind Alice. A lizard had come around and jumped on him. He quickly threw it down and stomped on it, but he was no longer next to Yuri. One landed on Yuri's back, making full contact. Mads kicked it off and hurled it as hard as he could. Yuri howled when its teeth pulled the flesh and muscle off his back.

The lights shut off completely; Vlad apparently had managed to turn off the generator. "Mads! The door!" Alice yelled. She was the only one holding both her gun and her phone to see the oncoming heard of lizards. The door flung open with the solid thud of Mad's body. She glanced over her shoulder for a second to see him help Yuri in the doorway.

Hannah's gun clicked empty. Alice pulled a magazine tucked in her waistband. "Reload inside!" Hannah fell away. "You three fall back. I'll cover you." She stepped back to the doorway after them. She found Hannah in the doorway already reloaded. "We have to wait for Vlad!"

"Is this the last magazine?" Hannah asked to no answer. "How the fuck do I reload this things?"

Ahead of them, shots rang out, and they could see

flashes of light come toward them. Alice spotted two more lizards running to her. She stopped them. She didn't see the third come around the corner. Before it reached her, its mouth flew apart.

"Alice!" Vlad yelled. He ran up to her and Hannah. Blood covered his face and clothes. "They're everywhere." Vlad coughed. Blood landed on Alice's shirt as he stumbled to his knees. "They came up from below."

Alice pulled him inside the room and closed the door. The others pushed furniture against the door. It shook against the pile with a choir of whiny demons pushing to get in.

"Alex," Spence said, holding his phone over Yuri's back. Alex came over and clasped her hands over her mouth. "Noooo, no, no, no," she cried. Yuri lay on his side on the floor. His upper right back revealed a large chunk of ribs that had broken when the creature had come off him. His breathing was short and wet.

"*Мій дорогий брате*," whispered Yuri.

"Alice," Vlad said, "I'm not doing so good. I..." He coughed up more blood. Alice pulled his hand away from his chest and lifted his shirt to reveal a large puncture. The creature must have punched into his lung, which was filling with blood. Behind her, Alex sobbed over her brother, speaking softly to him in their language.

Alice sniffled. "Okay, here's what we'll do. We have bandages and medical equipment here, right? I'll grab what we can, and we'll get you out of here. We'll carry you, and it'll be fine, and there will be a hospital nearby..."

Vlad put his hand on hers. "Give me your guns. I can cover your escape."

Alice shook her head, "You said that the fire escape is over there."

"This place is going to collapse at any moment. These doors won't hold." As Vlad wheezed in a breath, Alice heard the sound of air bubbles in his chest. "A fire escape won't save you if you have to carry me out of here. You...go now."

Alice wiped the tears from her face. "Why couldn't you have been a Shepherd? You would have been able to heal."

Vlad smiled. "I couldn't live with myself if I were."

The furniture against the door screeched back an inch. Mads and Hannah pushed it back in place.

Darren approached Alice. "I'm sorry, Alice. I'm sorry too, Vlad."

Vlad nodded. "Help me up."

They moved Vlad to a nearby chair; he winced as they lowered him in place. He positioned his phone in his lap, its flashlight aimed at the doorway.

"I'm going to stay here too." Mads stood by Vlad. "I don't belong up there anymore. Not looking like this."

"You don't really want that," Spence said.

"Not really. But what choice do I have? I'll help hold them off."

Spence stepped up to Mads and looked him up and down. Spence's onyx eye glowed with an amber center.

"You have one normal eye," Mads said. "You can wear an eyepatch."

"My eyes can see many things. I do not see a monster," Spence said.

Mads looked up back at him. His face softened, and his shoulders slumped. "I feel like one. Don't you? I mean, with what they did to us?"

"I did. But eventually I realized they don't define me. Only my actions can do that. You're a good person, Mads. Come with us. Please."

Mads slowly nodded. He gave Vlad one last look and walked toward the back of the infirmary.

Hannah set her gun by Vlad. "It's got about ten rounds left."

Vlad nodded and continued to silently look forward. Alice couldn't see his face clearly in the dark, but his tears touched her lips as she kissed him.

Alex wiped the tears from her face and rose from her brother. "He can't move. I gave him this for the pain. From the drug cabinet." She set a bottle of morphine on the counter and headed to the back.

The fire escape was pitch-black. Even with their phones, the group stumbled as they ascended another seemingly endless stairway. Alice heard shots from below. Vlad had twenty rounds at most. Alice tried to keep track but lost count almost immediately. When she could no longer hear the firing, she didn't know if it was because Vlad had run out, he was overrun by demons, or they were too far away to hear the shots.

Alice brought up the rear while Mads and Spence led the way. Alex had the most trouble with the stairs. For all her Olympic training, she was too fatigued by recent events; they all were. She kept listening for more whines, but they didn't come. Nothing came. She wished for the sounds of Vlad's footsteps, but there was nothing.

In the distance ahead of her, Mads roared, "We made it!"

Light eased into Alice's vision with an almost unnatural blue. Its hue was warm even. Her pace quickened as much as her legs would allow. The final step outside hit her with a jolt. They were outside, behind the isolation bunker. She dropped to her knees and wept.

Alex cried into Hannah's arms.

ALICE WALKED along the small road toward the nearest town, which was eight kilometers from the castle. In the light of day, she stood out as dirty, bloody, and disheveled. She was in good company. Spence's borrowed shoes were about to fall off, and Mads had no shoes at all. Aside from the lab coat, he was naked with fur and quills.

They could still see smoke rise from the direction of the castle. They wondered how many guests had gotten out in time. Did they get the keys to the vans and leave? What had happened to the ones who had been with Spence and Mads?

Hanna uninstalled Zenith Pharm's app on her phone and managed to reconnect to the Internet. "I sent some texts to some of the guests, but I haven't heard anything back."

"You're the only one with a working cell plan among us," Alice said. "They might not be able to respond."

Alex was sniffling while flipping through photos on her phone. "It just not fair. This was the closest I ever felt to Yuri. He'd never been happier in all the years since the

Olympics were canceled. He would have stayed there running around the castle hills as long as he could."

Alice patted her back. "I really liked him. I'm so sorry."

"I'm glad to be alive. I'm glad we all made it. It's just a lot," said Alex.

It was late afternoon when they reached the outskirts of Lupeni, the first town they'd encountered on the highway. Houses were scattered along the road between small shops and laundromats. Traffic was sparse, and only a trickle of people ventured into the shops.

They were hungry, tired, and Mads needed to cover up. Hannah searched the Internet and found a secondhand clothing store, but it was closed due to the pandemic. They found a clothing drop box behind the shop full of clothes that hadn't yet been processed. Mads pulled off the lock. It seemed almost everyone needed something. Hannah found a hoodie to cover up her torn, bloody blouse. Alice's shoes were caked in blood too, but she didn't find anything that fit. Alex found a sealed pack of disposable facemasks. Darren didn't care if anyone saw his dirty clothes as long as everyone else found what they needed. Spence fashioned an eye covering from a T-shirt. Mads settled for a trench coat and sweatpants but couldn't find any shoes.

The next goal was finding food; Hannah located a small grocery store a few more kilometers farther in. They had enough money from the wallets they'd retrieved from the guards' remains—a few thousand Romania leu and three credit cards if it came down to it.

Alice's stomach growled with every cafe, cafenea, and restaurant they walked past. She wasn't alone. Mads's stomach grumbled so loud everyone heard it.

Most of the buildings they passed were closed for business. Some even had their windows boarded up. Alice couldn't read the signs, but it was obvious that even this tiny town had been affected by the pandemic. They were a couple of kilometers from the heart of the city when Hannah gasped. "Wait right here." She ran ahead of them and ducked inside a shop with plastic tables and chairs left stranded on the sidewalk.

A couple of minutes later, Hannah, Alice, and Darren came out holding six paper plates of gigantic pizza slices and six cups of cola.

"So much! Yes!" Alex exclaimed.

Everyone eagerly took a plate and cup and began their feast. No one spoke, but several "mmms" were passed around.

This was their first meal together, a chance to sit down and pause the world around them. It was a bittersweet solace and the promise of a return to normalcy, whatever form that took. Several happy, greasy, sugary minutes had passed when Mads spoke. "I wonder if I'm still lactose intolerant," he said while cleaning the spicy sauce from his fingers.

"It's been a minute since I had pizza, but this is good, right?" Darren asked.

"I don't even care," Spence replied. "Right now this is the best fucking pizza."

Alice felt full and a little bloated but rested. She felt her body making the best use of everything she'd just gobbled down. She watched the others finish their last bites while the sun cast an orange glow along the town's main road. Spence and Darren quietly chatted, almost seriously, to each other over their meal. Spence picked off his pepperoni and put it on Darren's plate. Hannah removed a crumb from Mads fur. Alex was mostly quiet and ate in peace.

"You know, real-time CG is a thing now," Hannah told

Mads. "Half of the people I play against stream with fake avatars. There's no reason you couldn't resume your live-stream show."

"You think that's possible?" he asked.

Hannah nodded. "Definitely."

Spence reflected on his new vision. "I know now what I see. It's like energy in a dimension I can't yet interpret. Maybe I'm color blind to it, but there's this sense I get from demons, which is different from what I get from the insect lady and the Thrixus, and then there's..."

"Giant sexy tree person?" Darren asked.

Spence gave him a light shove. "Yes, that's the official title. Much better than 'Borewit, Lord of the Dark Tree.'"

"Ooh, I like that," Darren said.

"What about me? What energy do I give?" Mads asked.

Spence looked back at Mads and smiled. "You're just ugly."

"I will kick your ass."

"So..." Spence said, detecting that everyone had finished their slices. "I know we need to figure out food and trans-portation, maybe even a place to stay. But we should talk about the bigger problem." He paused to get their attention. "Mads and I need to find a way to get our antibodies to you all. So far, Darren is asymptomatic, and I haven't heard any of you complain of symptoms yet either. But we should assume you've been exposed to the virus. It only takes a day from the first signs of sickness for the Ozark virus to become deadly."

"You think they have it?" Mads asked.

"Everyone in that room with the portal was infected as an incentive to make sure we went through with the ritual. We were shedding particles of the virus everywhere. I was practically hyperventilating."

"Me too." Mads looked down. "But I don't know the first thing about getting what's in here"—he pointed at his heart—"to you all."

"Is there a hospital nearby? Maybe we could talk to someone," Darren said.

"It's more than that," Alice said. "We'd have to convince someone—a doctor or scientist—that we've got the cure to the virus. What would we say? 'These two guys have been cured of the virus. Could we have their blood broken down and antibody cells collected for our use?'"

"That won't matter," said Darren "If we tell a doctor that Mads and Spence have working antibodies, why wouldn't they want that?" Darren didn't notice much enthusiasm from the group. "No? What are our other options? We could do it ourselves? Hannah, search for do-it-yourself how-to videos for getting antibodies."

"I don't have the answers either, Darren." Hannah snapped.

"We do the hospital thing." Alex finally said. "We shouldn't have to run around for answers. We have nothing to hide. We show them the truth. There's no shame in that. We'll just tell them what happened."

"I agree." Mads stood up after a pause. "There's nothing to hide. Like you said, I'm not the monster here."

They replaced their facemasks and went inside. Alice thanked the boys working the counter for lending them their chargers. They smiled brightly and told them all to take care in their best English. Her phone had a partial charge, even though it still couldn't connect to a network. They would have to stop by a store and buy some SIM cards with data plans.

"Check this out." Alex pointed to the mounted screen by the counter. Alice didn't understand the audio, but the video was clear. Aerial footage from a helicopter showed live views of a forest and a clearing. In the center of the clearing was the rubble of what once had been Castle Monostori.

They left the shop and headed for the hospital Hannah found half a kilometer from them. The small town of Lupeni was a dim pink as the sun fell behind the hills. Streetlamps automatically came on to lead them to the hospital. Alice braced herself for the upcoming conversation: "Hi. We have the cure. Can you please help us get some of it?"

They reached one of the few intersections of the town. A single sign bore the red cross symbol for a hospital. Alice could see the building from the intersection. It was a modest, four-story structure with a large circular driveway and a lobby entrance. Somewhere in there was a doctor they hoped spoke enough English to help them—more importantly, *believe* them.

They were heading down the street toward the building when Ms. Birch stepped out from a parked van in the alleyway. She stood in front of the van in a tightly cinched trench coat. Her hair was, for the first time, not in its immaculately pulled-back knot. It was barely held in place by a pencil and hung around her exhausted face.

"Holy shit!" Alice exclaimed.

"Ms. Whitmore, when I said you were free to leave, I had no idea how seriously you'd take my suggestion," Ms. Birch said. "I knew some of you would get out alive eventually, but I didn't know it would be you."

For once, Alice didn't let Ms. Birch interfere with her. "Man, get the fuck away from me." Alice moved to push her to the side when Ms. Birch pulled a pistol from her pocket. Alice's mind went to the steps in disarming someone, but she was fatigued and didn't think she could do it without the gun potentially going off. Although Ms. Birch was petite, she was fit. This made Alice doubt her ability to protect her friends.

"Seems like you six were on your way for a check-in. Hmm? Maybe a little blood work while making off with some of Zenith Pharm's property?" Ms. Birch nodded to Mads and Spence.

"Ms. Birch, this is over," Alice said. "We're going to the hospital and speaking to the first person who'll listen to us."

"And what? They'll help you tell the truth? Is that your plan? Who do you think funds the hospitals in Romania? Zenith Pharm owns six of the biggest hospitals in the country and has lobbied the government to the point that they operate here with impunity. That building is your ticket back to the Shepherds like cattle stock."

"I'm not their property," Spence called over Alice's shoulder.

"No, Mr. Dixon, you're not. Not yet. In any case..." Ms. Birch coughed into her sleeve, making sure her gun held its position. Alice recognized the cough and stepped backward. Facemask or not, she wasn't taking chances. Ms. Birch gathered her composure and continued. "In any case, it seems you have something I need."

Ms. Birch gun waved them behind the alley into the back door of a small white plaster building. They found themselves in a kitchen, beyond the counter, the chairs sitting upside down on top of the tables.

"Over here," Ms. Birch instructed while directing Spence with a gun-pointing motion to a prep station. Alice turned to see a collection of vials, syringes, and what she assumed was a centrifuge. Ms. Birch leaned against the counter. "Grab a chair—all of you. You too, Mr..."

"Porter," growled Mads.

Alice came up to the group with a chair; Ms. Birch brandished her gun. Alice paused but didn't set down the chair. "Everyone is getting their antibodies," Ms. Birch said.

Alice looked over the lab equipment. "You know how to work all this?"

Ms. Birch stared at her for a moment before putting her gun in her pocket. "I've seen it done enough times. Heh. The scientists even let me assist them in the labs."

Once again, two of the guests of Castle Monostori submitted themselves for blood work. Darren and Alice followed Ms. Birch's instructions step by step. It was familiar to them, but Alice never had committed the steps to memory much less administer the antibodies herself. She wouldn't have remembered how to tighten a tourniquet band and wouldn't have been able to find a vein. She followed Ms. Birch's instructions at gunpoint. Quickly she took the bags of blood, sealed five vials with the right amount and set them in the centrifuge, then let it separate the red blood cells from the plasma.

Hannah brought Ms. Birch a glass of water, which she begrudgingly accepted.

Alice watched the centrifuge power on and spin the vials. She turned to Ms. Birch. "Why aren't you vaccinated? I assumed you were one of the people in charge."

"Oh, I am. Or was. All I ever tried to be was worthy of their membership. How much do you know? Well, it doesn't matter. You've seen everything already. Shepherds are the most powerful entities in our civilization. To be one of them is to know only wealth and success. I was on track to join them. And then I was still on track to join them. And I kept staying on track while my counterparts bumbled their way in. They just showed up! All they had to do was get their penises verified, and then they went on their merry way. Meanwhile I kept getting told what a good job I was doing and my time would come." She coughed, and flecks of blood landed on her glass. "This project, this vaccine...it was going to send me..." Her eyes met Alice's, and her lips pursed. "I guess it doesn't matter now."

The centrifuge kept whirling in silence. There wasn't much Alice or anyone could say. Alice wanted to call out Ms. Birch for participating in the deaths of innocent people, but what guilt could she inflict? For that matter, what guilt could it change? She watched Ms. Birch sit in silence as she continued to struggle to breathe.

The whirring slowed to a stop; the five vials had separated. Spence pulled a handful of sterile syringes from a box and prepped them with the antibodies from each of the vials. He administered the first one to Ms. Birch. It wasn't clear if it would make any difference given her condition. Alice, Darren, Alex, and Hannah received the remaining shots.

An awkward silence settled upon the room as everyone nursed their arms. Ms. Birch finally spoke, pulling her fallen locks away from her face. "Well, now. We're all doped up, it seems. I think you can see yourselves out. I'm going to sit for a bit and catch my breath." By her tone, Alice knew that was a lie.

Quietly they stepped back out into the alleyway. Alice remained behind, watching Ms. Birch push to retain her composure, but didn't make eye contact.

"What is it?" Ms. Birch was visibly annoyed by Alice's stare.

Ms. Birch was dying. She was abandoned. She could have walked into that hospital and been back in the arms of her employer. Alice really wanted to ask her if it had been worth it. She wanted to know just how much sacrifice Ms. Birch had given just to be in a club. Did she regret any of it?

Eventually Alice said, "Nothing. Sorry."

"'Nothing. Sorry.' That about sums me up." She coughed again. "Ms. Whitmore, do yourself and your friends the biggest of favors and hide." Ms. Birch reached into her pocket and tossed Alice a set of keys. "The van is parked in the alleyway. The guests took all the others but not that one. Take it, go home, remove yourself from the Internet—from any records you can get your hands on—change your name if you have to, and stay out of sight from the Shepherds. They won't forget this. If they find out you're alive, you'll lose everything."

Alice contemplated the keys in her hand. It felt true. Ms. Birch's warning was real. They knew everything about her. They knew how to mimic her roommate. They knew about her ancestry, something she hadn't even known about. Any interaction online would be traced, and any medication she took would be cataloged.

"Is that possible? Can they do that?" Alice asked.

Ms. Birch struggled to hold out her arms. "We'll see!"

* * *

It was a four-hour drive to the airport, which was their next destination. Hannah had gotten through to her mom in Monte Carlo and explained the danger they were in. Her mother told her to get to the airport, where she would coordinate their flight back.

Alex drove along the dark road while Hannah gave updates from the passenger seat with her phone plugged into the cigarette lighter adapter. Hannah's mother had found a jet they could catch. Hannah got directions to the service gate where someone was expecting them.

"Looks like you're all coming to stay with me. Just when we couldn't get enough of each other," Hannah said.

"I don't know of anyone else I really want to be around," Alice replied.

"I do," Alex said.

"Yeah, I do too," Alice said, thinking of the final stair climb away from Vlad and Yuri.

Hannah tried to change the tone of the conversation. "You don't have to stay with me, but I really want you to. Mom can get you back home on other flights. You don't have to worry about your passports."

"What does your family do?" Alice asked.

"Imports."

"I'm not sure I'm ready to go home," Mads admitted. He was playing with the last red quill in his hand. "I mean, I just learned these things can come out, which helps, but I still don't look a thing like I did before."

"I'm not sure I'm ready to return to Virginia. I...can't just go back and act like everything is over," Alice said.

"I'll be going back home," Alex said. "I want my country to know my brother died a hero. I want my people to know what really happened."

"Will they believe you?" Alice asked.

"Enough will believe. The truth will be known."

Darren and Spence were talking to each other quietly enough that Alice couldn't hear them.

"Hey, Mads," Darren said. "You can come with us. No one knows you in Boston, yeah? I'm going to get a space there while Spence figures out what he wants to do."

"Yeah, law school seems less of a priority for me at the moment," Spence replied.

"And with my parents being satanic cult members, I'm steering clear of them. Like, living on the opposite coast clear."

Mads slowly nodded. "I'll think about it. How much is the rent?"

It was nearly midnight when Alex turned into the Bucharest airport. Hannah guided her from her dad's instructions to a road that diverged from the one that would have led to long-term parking. A security guard was waiting for them by a chain link gate covered in a green tarp. She signaled for Alex to roll down the window.

She yelled through her mask over the noise of airport traffic, "Follow this road to last building. Then leave the van and go inside." She didn't wait for an acknowledgment. before pushing the gate open.

They pulled up to the last building, got out, and stepped into a large hangar, its door wide open, with a single jet waiting for them. Beside the open door to the plane, a man wearing a pilot hat and facemask called out, "*Ta mère est impatiente de te voir!*"

Hannah turned to her friends. "He says my family is waiting for us!" she said, then hurried up the steps and into the cabin.

Alice and the others followed, took their seats, and buckled in. The captain was closed the plane's cabin door. He looked up at his passengers, who were all ready to go. "You're obviously eager as well."

The engines whirred to life, and the plane lurched forward onto the tarmac. Alice saw the pilot and copilot in the cockpit, chatting over the radio. Everyone looked on as the plane made its way to the runway.

Mads sat across from Alice and rested his hairy hand on the armrest. She finally noticed just how large he was. She reached over, took his hand in hers, and gave him a warm smile.

"So many times I thought I was going to die," he said with watery eyes. "First they cut off my leg...and then they turned me into this. We saw people die. We left people behind."

Alice squeezed his hand. "I'm sorry this happened to you."

"Every time I thought it couldn't get worse, it managed to get worse. You all were the only good thing that happened since."

Hannah was in the front seat across from Alex. She turned around. "I don't think we're ever going to get over this."

"Oh, no. I'll be in therapy forever," Mads said.

Alice noticed that the plane was no longer moving. They were idle on the runway, and the captain was still talking to the radio. From her window, she saw that the runway was clear. If it was a traffic issue, she didn't see it. The longer they stayed in Romania, the more she felt she'd never leave. Why wasn't the plane moving? Were they stalling?

They won't forget this. If they find out you're alive, you'll lose everything.

The copilot unbuckled from his chair, went to the back, and disappeared. Alice looked at Hannah, but she didn't seem to react to this. The copilot returned with a cup of coffee and retook his seat.

The engines sped up again, and they were moving forward once more. Alice's stomach shook. She was letting her anxiety overcome her. Everything was fine. Everything was fine.

The engines got even louder, and she felt the thrust of

the plane push her back into the seat as it sped down the runway and lift into the night. Higher it climbed, farther and farther away from this unending nightmare.

Hannah was the first to pop out of her seat after they reached cruising altitude. She rustled in the back of the cabin with the sound of glass and ice shaking. She reappeared with a tray of drinks.

"I'm taking the edge off. I highly recommend you do as well." She handed Alice an old fashioned. Every one took one.

"Should we toast?" Mads asked.

They collectively said, "No" and drank in smooth silence.

Alice might have been embarrassed by finishing her drink first, but by then she didn't care that she had made herself a second round while Mads was still letting his ice melt.

The pilot informed them that it would take them six hours before they reached Monte Carlo. He turned on the television, which played the day's news. It was in French, and Alice couldn't understand it, so she just nursed her brandy while imagining what was happening within the country's government. The video showed scientists popping bottles of champagne. According to the chyron, someone from GenNTech was speaking. He spoke in English, but the news covered his voice with French audio. The Eiffel Tower was lit with fireworks. Politicians stood in front of microphones, with flashing bulbs all around. It was all pointless to her.

Ignoring the television, Hannah texted on her phone as it charged from the chair's port. Mads watched over her shoulder, asking what she was writing. Hannah was happy to translate what her friends back home were up to. Alex was curled in a ball against the side of the cabin with her arms folded under a blanket. Darren was trying to sleep on Spence's shoulder as he looked out the window.

Alice let the weight of the brandy wash the day away. The pressure behind her ears, which she didn't know existed, lifted, and the strain in her eyes eased. Her mind shifted for a moment. She was alive, and they knew she was. That was what Ms. Birch had said. Or did she tell her to go offline? It didn't matter. She would have enough time to figure that out. Maybe Hannah could help her. And Darren was good with computers.

Alice's mind drifted to the hotel in Monte Carlo Hannah had described. No retrofitted castles there. Just casinos and sports cars and beaches and French news that played in her thoughts as she drifted toward sleep with only pleasant dreams.

The television feed switched to an American news report, where people had taken to the streets. They were celebrating. From Paris at night to Times Square in the morning, where barricades were toppled over by citizens. At the San Francisco pier, it was just dawn, and fog blanketed the city. A crowded dance party was well underway. She saw live footage of people celebrating. They gathered in massive crowds, hugged, kissed, and cried without masks.

GenNTech CEO and Chairman Hal Pritchard recited his statement over the helicopter footage of the SF Bay. "We have overcome the strongest of darknesses: fear. The worst fear is that of the unknown. When will we recover? Can we recover? What lies beyond?" Above the crowds beyond the Golden Gate Bridge, a barely visible shadow moved almost imperceptibly due to its sheer size.

"It is not madness to gain knowledge to overcome the limits of our minds," he went on. "This is the only way we can move forward. To accept the infinite and those who reside there." The shadow couldn't cut enough through the fog to be perceptible. The camera footage on television pulled back as far as it could to take in a wingspan that blocked the sun from warming the foggy city.

"The realm of man will not fall today," Pritchard said. "Though we may succumb to the temptation of madness for our progress, know that we are not alone. Thanks to our research, we've unlocked the cosmic horror and made contact with the eldest of beings from the stars, and now they are with us. And with them we are saved."

THE END

ACKNOWLEDGMENTS

I'm so incredibly thankful for the encouragement and support of my husband and our dear friends JJ Wynne and Sean Jackson. You kept me going. I'm extremely grateful for my editor, Angela Brown, whose expertise in the craft is unsurpassable. Special thanks to Scott Elfstrom, Michael Erickson, Joshua Hunt, David Lybarger, and Matthew Martin.

ABOUT THE AUTHOR

Chris Williams is an emerging author of horror fiction. He grew up in Oregon and moved to Dallas, Texas and lives with his husband and their pack of rescue dogs. This is Chris' first book.

- facebook.com/amboyoo
- twitter.com/amboyoo
- instagram.com/amboyoo